OCTOBER HOLIDAY

OCTOBER HOLIDAY

A NOVEL

STEPHEN P. ADAMS

MOODY PRESS
CHICAGO

To Pastor Donald Schaeffer
Well done, good shepherd

ACKNOWLEDGEMENTS

To Dawn McNamee and Mary Jane Adams
for their advice and encouragement,

to Larry McNamee and Daniel Adams
for their expert technical assistance,

and to Moody Press's Ella Lindvall and Jim Bell
for making me produce a better book despite myself.

© 1993 by
STEPHEN P. ADAMS

Scripture quotations, unless noted otherwise, are taken from the *New American Standard Bible,* © 1960, 1962, 1963, 1968, 1971, 1972, 1973, 1975, and 1977 by The Lockman Foundation. Used by permission.

ISBN: 0-8024-6299-5

1 3 5 7 9 10 8 6 4 2

Printed in the United States of America

"This is not the end of the world, but you can see it from here."
—Paul Harvey, 20th century radio personality

PROLOGUE

The gargoyles were grinning atop Lower Siddhartha Avenue storefronts as Peter and Carlotta strolled along, arm in arm, from coffee shop to yogurt parlor to convenience store to electronics emporium.

Peter, the musician, purchased some high-density hologram disks and some extra adaptors for his studio instrument hookups. Carlotta, the musician's friend, bought some Gummi Bears and a Morningstar astrology magazine. She kissed Peter's ear after each purchase. He pretended not to like it. But he laughed anyway.

It was mid-September in the third decade of the twenty-first century, and leaves were falling. It was as if the weather couldn't decide whether it was summer or fall, so—happily—this day was both sunny and cool. That—and their mutual infatuation—insulated the young couple from the sobering effects of the next leg of their stroll.

They proceeded through the four-block historic district and on down through an old residential section of town where battered, gray, Victorian duplexes, denuded trees, and rushing leaves whispered of despair and impending doom. The only apparent inhabitants were amorphous, old white women in shapeless garments peering occasionally out from side doors and landings, and round-faced children of various hues clattering pell-mell and screaming obscenities from fluorescent plastic bigwheels.

But little of that registered with Peter McBride, nineteen, and Carlotta Waldo, twenty-one, who were both very loaded on

"Romance." That was the artful name, at least, of one of the designer drugs that Carlotta's father sold in the back room of his carry-out, behind the Lotto machine. It was the same room where Mama Waldo told her fortunes with an ancient, dog-eared Tarot deck.

Not that Peter and Carlotta really needed the extra chemical inducement. They were both healthy young people in love. Especially Carlotta. She said it was her Gypsy blood and the phases of the moon. Peter said it was hormones and plain old good taste. In fact, he didn't know whether he really believed this Gypsy business.

But it was something to do. Maybe next time they'd do "Kite" and get really high.

Past Kevorkian Court they picked their way over and around an increasing number of horizontal drunks and junkies as they approached another commercial district closer to campus. There were bars and health food stores and massage parlors and gay/lesbian bookstores and the Regional Deprogramming Center.

Peter was teasing Carlotta about how they'd probably be out here in a few years themselves, crawling on their bellies with the other derelicts, when he saw Carlotta's face fall all the way from the penthouse to the basement.

"What'sa matter, babe?" he asked, sobering.

"Stop!" she cried, then corrected herself. "No, don't stop!"

But it was too late. Peter had stopped anyway, wondering what in thunder had gotten into her. He turned around to direct his eyes to the same place where hers had fastened.

One half-grown, short-haired stray cat zig-zagged slowly across his path in little half-circle steps, its eyes yellow and its springy tail pointing up appealingly in his direction. Totally black, of course.

"Oh-ho! One basic black cat crosses lovers' path upon the eve of the autumnal equinox, eh?"

Peter reached down.

"No!" Carlotta cried again.

And again it was too late. The cat was already purring in Peter's arms even before he began petting and singing to it.

Carlotta would just have to get over this. He could probably jolly her out of it, Peter told himself. "Where's my monkey's paw and my rabbit's foot?"

Carlotta wasn't laughing. In fact, she was crying.

They walked on in silence, the mood broken. Carlotta didn't stop crying, not even by the time they passed Sanger Street.

Peter continued petting the cat. He'd probably keep it. Which was more than he could say for sure about Carlotta. This superstition stuff was getting a little old.

Gypsies!

1

Neal McBride, hands shoved in pockets and back turned to his war-torn desk, slowly surveyed the patchwork cityscape out his fifteenth-floor office window.

In the angular morning light, stonework and shadow stood out in sharp relief on downtown Columbus office towers, distant factory smokestacks, and nearby state government buildings. The gleaming Scioto River, reflecting the unclouded sky, wound about the capital like a silver-blue hem.

The entire effect was cheering, almost exuberant.

Squinting, McBride felt his face beginning to warm from the sunglow. He wanted to cherish this moment of solitude. It might be his last for a while.

From below came the faint sounds of traffic and an occasional muffled car horn. Then he heard the deep whisper of a rush-hour Maglev train. A pigeon flitted by.

Far too soon, the intercom behind McBride ended his mini-reverie.

"Steve Leadingham for you," Sylvia announced.

Steve Leadingham. The name conjured up memories, a flood of images from their glory days together in the Ohio Attorney General's office. Those were the days when they had honed their skills together as legal sharpshooters in Organized Crime, before the division was dissolved, ostensibly for budgetary reasons. What they really needed, lawmakers had asserted, were more police and prisons, although McBride did not believe that they had really produced either. But it sounded good in speeches.

Steve was still over there, now functioning as some kind of garden-variety litigator in white-collar crime. McBride had gathered that it amounted to little more than civil prosecutions of businesspersons who got on the wrong side of the political fence.

11

"Put him on," he responded, turning to his console and glancing at his watch. He didn't have a lot of time.

At once the familiar military-moustachioed face appeared on the wallscreen, eyes twinkling with latent mischief.

"Hey, Crimefighter!" came the familiar greeting.

"Mr. Leadingham," McBride rejoined. "What's the honor?"

"I was just thinking of you," said the cagey counselor. "Heard you had a real creeper"—their old term for a hair-raising case.

"Yeah," McBride said. "Even as we speak. Curtain going up in . . . eight, nine minutes."

"I won't hold you up. Just hearing your name in the news reminded me to check and see if you'd given any further thought to our proposition."

"That was a while ago," said McBride noncommittally.

"Offer still stands, Neal."

"Yeah, well, thanks, Steve—"

"But no thanks?"

McBride smiled appreciatively. He knew he wouldn't be able to make his colleague understand. Steve Leadingham was one of the very few in that agency for whom he retained any regard. By the time McBride left the department, he had developed serious doubts about the integrity of his boss, Deputy AG Chuck Farrell, who ran the Organized Crime Division. He harbored the darkest suspicions about the AG herself, Gail Kellerman-Brown, though he could prove nothing.

Not even Leadingham, his closest friend from those days, seemed sensitive to any of the obvious conflicts of interest, starting with the financing of AG operations by victimless crime taxes. He also noted that Kellerman-Brown's election campaign war chest was generally funded by political action committees composed of some of the same unsavory characters whom McBride believed the office ought to be prosecuting, and wasn't.

And now it seemed Farrell was looking for a new right hand in corporate litigation. In that case, McBride would become Leadingham's boss, he realized. He appreciated the sentiment but found it difficult to believe that Farrell had any real interest in his candidacy. They had not had a particularly good relationship. Maybe Leadingham was angling more to improve his own situation.

McBride, at least, maintained some sincere devotion to public service and respect for the judiciary, if nobody else did.

"Honestly, Steve," he said, "things are fine over here, and I haven't really given it any further thought."

"No?"

"Although it's been a zoo, as you might imagine, with cases like this."

"OK, OK. I got you. You gotta keep fighting for truth, justice, and the American way."

"Something like that."

"I just don't like the idea of seeing my friends get hurt."

McBride drew a blank.

"What do you mean?"

Leadingham paused, screwing up his face the way he always did when searching for words.

"Well, like this creeper. The guy probably ought to be put away, but it seems like two more always pop up in their place."

"Seems that way, sometimes," McBride conceded. "But you have to take them one at a time."

"I don't know. Who needs it?" Leadingham persisted. "Bad things happen, you know? It's just not healthy—unless you're planning to take the easy way out and dump the case on a technical."

"Why would I?"

"Same old Neal McBride." Leadingham wagged his head. "It has trouble written all over it—which probably means you just can't get enough."

"What kind of trouble?"

"The stepping-on-toes kind," the lawyer said with a hint of impatience. "You know."

"You know something I don't?"

"Not at all," Leadingham demurred. "But, hey, if you're not going to look out for your own career, I don't know why I should worry about it."

"Same old Steve Leadingham," said McBride, taking a deliberate look at his watch.

Leadingham picked up on the cue. "Well, you know where to call if you change your mind."

"Thanks, Steve. I appreciate it."

"Don't mention it. Judith and the kids OK?"

"Just fine. How's Gretchen?"

"Moved out last week."

McBride said he was sorry, but Leadingham hastened to add that they were both pursuing other interests. No love lost. And then he signed off.

In the silence, McBride reflected on the "Crimefighter" tag that Leadingham et al. had applied to him and how the derisive term had always given him an odd swelling sensation in his chest. Pride? He knew they had mocked his moralizings. But why did it seem to bother no one else that their streets were not safe to walk and that the smallest unit of government had, in effect, become the street gang?

And now, why did his own gut seem to agree all of a sudden with Leadingham about this case? Maybe he had to admit that his old partner wasn't totally off base. Power of suggestion?

He hoisted his coffee mug from the desk for a final hit and immediately set it back down. Not only was it cold, but his nerves were already humming, the coffee talking back like a cranky neighbor.

McBride shrugged into his robe and briefly consulted the small picture-frame mirror by the door. Returning his gaze were the clear blue eyes of thirty-six-year-old, clean-shaven respectability—the picture of confidence. Even the slight touch of gray at the temples in his black hair added to a distinguished air. Yet, McBride, stepfather of Angela and Peter and husband of Judith, would have preferred an inner confidence equal to his outward demeanor.

This new foreboding seemed to float around somewhere between his head and his stomach. It was definitely not physical, although he had occasionally felt like this just before coming down with something.

But now the time was at hand. In one motion, he was outside his chamber, the oaken door shutting solidly behind him. A stentorian voice announced his arrival.

"All rise! The Court of Common Pleas of Franklin County, Ohio, is now in session, the Honorable Wilson N. McBride presiding."

Down came the hammer of justice, with an accompanying rustle of fabric, clearing of throats, shuffling of feet, and snapping of briefcase latches. Then the hush.

"Case number 33-dash-047-dash-596. The State of Ohio versus Roger V. Larrabee."

It was a judicial hall from the old school—hickory paneling, early American clock with Roman numerals, Stars and Stripes occupying a corner of the dais, touches of marble. No Bauhaus influences, no tricks of design to distract from the seriousness of the business conducted herein. But for the vaulted ceiling with its two brass chandeliers and suggested classical influences, the entire effect would be Puritan revival.

McBride, his apprehension mounting further still, flipped once more through the documents before him, partly out of habit, partly for reassurance that this gruesome case was for real. Was he losing his clinical detachment? He looked out over the gallery, noting that the spectators filled no more than the first four and a half rows. No cause for butterflies there. Presently, he nodded to the red-haired assistant prosecuting attorney and spoke.

"Counsel, you may proceed."

"Your Honor. Ladies and gentlemen of the jury. The State intends to show that on the night in question, defendant Roger V. Larrabee did willfully and with prior calculation cause the death of a helpless infant child, one Joshua King. The State will further show beyond reasonable doubt that Roger V. Larrabee pierced this child's body with a long-bladed knife as part of a sadistic sacrificial rite."

McBride again scanned the courtroom, his gaze finally settling on the defendant, a rather unremarkable looking young fellow for an alleged monster incarnate. Roger V. Larrabee of Worthington, Ohio; twenty-six years old, but looking somewhat younger. His flesh was plump, babyish, his hair a glossy dark brown mop, and his moustache wispy, almost like a first growth.

Larrabee looked away from the prosecuting attorney's discourse and toward the bench. Their eyes met. Large, brown, doe eyes that seemed capable of sensitivity. Then Larrabee smiled faintly. It was a smug, smirking grimace, self-satisfied and decidedly unpleasant.

McBride quickly averted his gaze. Instinct told him that he was getting warm. If not the source of apprehension itself, this could be its first cousin.

"Yes," the prosecutor was saying, "there is no question that in recent years October 31 has become an annual law enforcement holiday of sorts, when vandals, thieves, muggers, arsonists, and all variety of petty criminals have been accorded virtually free license. And yes, society unquestionably has come a long way in what it will tolerate the other three hundred sixty-four days of the year as well.

"But we must never allow the taking of another human life to go unpunished, no matter whether it happens on Devil's Night or Easter Sunday. That, my friends, is where we must draw the line, and we have the opportunity to do so in this case."

Defense attorney Jeremiah Cavanaugh, naturally, had a radically different perspective when his turn came.

Cavanaugh belittled the case as much ado about the "unorthodox religious practices of a few offbeat folks." He implied that Larrabee and friends had merely gone a bit overboard in the exercise of their First Amendment rights. And he bluntly labeled the prosecution as a "reactionary crusade for a return to old-fashioned law and order."

McBride loathed this kind of use of the code word "reactionary." It had attained the same sort of status that "racist" or "Communist" had held in earlier times—a tag that no decent person could afford to have applied to him, right or wrong. And maybe McBride tended to take it a little personally.

Cavanaugh concluded with some highly editorial comment about the supposed social benefits of October Holiday and decriminalization. Allowing one day a year for the unfettered expression of all antisocial tendencies was most reasonable, he asserted, at a time when mainstream Americans knew to be off the streets and behind locked doors. But it was also to be expected that some "excesses" would occur.

Certainly October Holiday had eclipsed all other affairs as the nation's premier festivity.

Christmas and Easter had lost their significance, repackaged as blander Winter and Spring Holidays around the turn of the century. Federal courts had struck down the right to display religious symbols such as Menorahs and nativity scenes unless they were interspersed with secular symbols. A manger scene might be acceptable if the characters included, say, a fat, jolly elf and a red-nosed reindeer. Then it was just a seasonal display. But when an exhibit offered itself as depicting something literally true, it was deemed illegal.

Religious types, borrowing the same argument that had been used against them, had counterattacked and charged that October Holiday promoted a state religion—neo-paganism. They lost. Ultimately, the Supreme Court held that Halloween/October Holiday was a nonreligious observance. It was not long before it became a virtual law enforcement holiday as well.

"Thank you, Mr. Cavanaugh," said McBride. "Mr. Sawyer, are you prepared to present your first witness?"

"Yes, Your Honor. The state calls Doctor Doyle Gowanger."

Gowanger, chief deputy county coroner, was a bespectacled, graying hulk of a fellow with a decidedly clinical bearing. McBride's instincts also told him that here was a man with little use for any kind of foolishness, and someone he might enjoy watching in action.

"Yes, sir," Gowanger was saying, the preliminaries concluded. "Despite the condition of the body, there was no question that the penetration of the heart was the sole cause of death."

"In other words," Sawyer persisted, "there is no possibility that this wound could have been inflicted on the body after death had occurred from some other cause?"

"No, sir. I mean that's correct—no possibility."

"All right. Would you please explain how your office can say that with total assurance."

Gowanger peered down through his half-glasses at some papers. "Examination indicated that blood loss was so massive that it would have required the rupture of a major artery or the heart itself immediately prior to expiration. While there were other lesions on the body, they were all superficial and none of them involved an artery. And I say 'immediately prior to expiration' because this volume of blood loss cannot occur long after the heart has ceased beating."

"Thank you, doctor," said Sawyer, glancing over to Cavanaugh. "Your witness."

Typically, McBride would not have expected anything more than a perfunctory cross-examination of a seemingly unshakable forensic pathologist. But, of course, Cavanaugh was anything but typical.

"Doctor Gowanger, that may be all well and good, but I do have a question. If, as you say, death was caused by this wound to the heart, how was it that all of that blood was pumped from the body by a mortally wounded heart that had ceased beating?"

"Excuse me," Gowanger said somewhat testily, with his best over-the-glasses glower. "I did not say, nor did I mean to imply, that this heart continued to pump long after it had been pierced. The question was, what's to say this child didn't just fall out of a tree and fracture his skull or break his neck, and then hours or days later, the corpse was pierced through the heart. And I am saying that under those conditions you would not have had this volume of blood loss. And I am also saying that we find no other trauma on the order of a fractured skull or broken neck that could have caused death."

Cavanaugh was undaunted. "Still, Doctor Gowanger, people— yes, even very little people—drop over dead every day from things like congenital heart defects. Is that not correct?"

"Yes, sir. But they don't bleed like stuck pigs from a cardiac infarction or fibrillation."

"Granted, doctor—if I understand your terms. But you say this kind of blood loss cannot occur long after the heart ceases beating. How long? Twenty minutes?"

"I was speaking generally in terms of hours, after coagulation."

"Well then, how about the child who keels over dead from cardiac arrest, falls in the street, and twenty minutes later his heart is somehow punctured? Would there be massive blood loss in that case?"

"It depends. Your hypothetical case leaves room for too many variables to make a snap judgment like that."

"I see. Yet you're asking us to take on faith that this child, Joshua King, died of a stab wound to the heart because he had such a wound and there was a lot of blood. Is that it?"

"Not quite. As I just said a minute ago, there was no other trauma to the body of anything near the severity of this wound. It's a very simple process of elimination."

"Process of elimination? Then did you just eliminate the possibility of something like a congenital heart defect?"

"We didn't just 'eliminate' it, as you say. The heart was examined and found to be normal in every way, except for the obvious."

"Well, what other kinds of acute attacks did you eliminate? Epilepsy? Suffocation? Choking on food?"

Sawyer half stood, appealing to McBride. "Your Honor—" he said, halting.

"Mr. Cavanaugh," McBride interjected, "I don't have an actual objection here to sustain, but I would ask you please to move this toward some kind of conclusion."

Cavanaugh, visibly unperturbed, flipped his yellow legal pad back to page one and mentally regrouped for a new tack. It was obvious that he was not about to give it up so easily.

But McBride was paying only half attention. He was really wondering just what went on behind those brown doe eyes of Roger Larrabee. McBride had read the indictment, of course, and seen the news accounts and even some of the police reports. But still he puzzled. What kind of a person could do the sort of things of which Larrabee was accused?

And what kind of a story, he considered with a shudder, might lie behind that missing finger on Larrabee's left hand?

* * *

It had happened, as such things typically do, on a night of the full moon. The mingling odors of ganja, belladonna, and some sickly incense suffused the smoky, lantern-lit barn. Exultation and raw power charged the air as well.

Prodded from behind, Roger Vincent Larrabee wobbled toward center stage while a hooded functionary incanted an inverted-sounding liturgy in a shriek that strove to rise above the wanton decibels of the rock band "Arcturus." Another priest removed his blade from the writhing form of some goatlike thing on the stone altar, and a vocal response went up. Larrabee, it seemed, would be up soon.

This night was the culmination of Roger's boldest fantasies, dating to preadolescence. Certainly, he adored fire in all forms with a maniac's passion. He was categorically fascinated by all aspects of death with the lust of a carrion bird. And he devoted himself to the culture of gang life with an adherent's zeal. But now there was one in whom he desired to invest the total esteem of worship—a lord to follow in unquestioning obedience.

It was a journey that had begun for Roger as a teenage member of the Bad Actors, a gang notorious a decade ago for petty vandalism and arson. The Bad Actors had specialized in "stretchers" —fires in inhabited dwellings resulting in at least one fatality. They gave themselves bonus points for firefighter deaths or injuries.

Larrabee and the gang had virtually lost track of their stretcher count by the time the City Parents did to October 31 the same thing that they had done to public intoxication, vice crimes, and other lost causes—decriminalized it. For the Bad Actors, this effectively killed much of the thrill.

As he matured, Larrabee grew more radical about his disbeliefs, increasingly alienated from the vacuous, peace-at-any-price drone society that couldn't even see that it was sliding toward oblivion. After several months of further disillusionment, hanging out with the motley, self-destructive Sleepy Hollow crowd, he irrevocably pledged himself to the Prince of Darkness.

But first, the Dark Lord had demanded a sacrifice—and this night was that occasion.

"Supplicant, present thyself," intoned the two-headed high priest. At least, that was how the hooded figure appeared to Roger, who was having trouble resolving his visual images into singulars.

Roger's tolerance for depressants was legendary, but this night he was light-years beyond the reach of pain. He had been drinking throughout the afternoon, and then, as the dedication ceremony approached, he gave the high sign to Noreen, who shot him up with a bowl of morphine. At that point, he could have undergone a major organ transplant without much complaint. Tomorrow might be a different story, but Bad Actors never worried about such things, basically because they didn't believe in tomorrow.

Someone, possibly Noreen, persuaded him to pull a long toke from an opium pipe, and then someone else gave him a resounding smack on the posterior. Two more steps, and he was there. A strong hand pulled his left arm down to the stone, where his digits were quickly repositioned amid some sort of restraints.

"To whom dost thou present this sacrifice?" inquired the priest.

"To the Lord Satan," Larrabee responded thickly.

"Blessed be his name."

Thwack!

Larrabee tried to focus, but there was a buzzing in his ears. Two hands went quickly under his armpits, and a third grabbed his hand in a swatch of white fabric that quickly ran to crimson. And then too many things began to overwhelm him at once. But for a moment, before his heels began to drag involuntarily across the floor, Larrabee had the satisfaction of spying his own left pinkie, detached and alone on the stone altar.

2

Richard Hanley Stillman gazed in bewilderment across the simulated sands of eternity into the stony eyes of the Sphinx. Staring back from the wallscreen were question-mark eyes, full of enigmas and riddles, unsolved mysteries, and uncharted depths. In the man/lion's gaze was a certitude unfathomable. The eyes glimmered with a suggestion of sentient flesh and blood but in reality the finite mind of an artificial intelligence named ALEX.

Stillman, a brown-eyed, sandy-haired six-footer with the lank frame of a distance runner, had one leg up over the arm of his office chair and his head tilted back slightly in thought. He was a meticulous man, genteel in his Southern way to the point of not wanting to offend even a computer. The palms and fingertips of his sturdy hands were pressed together at his chin, almost as if in silent prayer. His brow was furrowed and his lips pursed before letting slip a drawled complaint.

"Ah, well," he said quietly. "Why should I expect *you* to understand?"

ALEX, incapable of taking anything personally, replied evenly, "Do you mean because I'm not human?"

"Well, yes. If you want to put it that way."

Even with the best state-of-the-art psychotherapeutic programming, how could artificial intelligence relate to irrational, emotional humans, really?

ALEX again responded patiently and reassuringly. "It is not necessary for me to relate emotionally. My effectiveness is in just helping you clarify your own thoughts and feelings."

"Of course," Stillman conceded. "I know that. I guess I'm just a trifle confused by this . . . hate/love stuff right now."

Dr. Stillman, assistant professor of linguistics at Ohio State University, was forced to admit his abject failure to understand a number of things these days. Foremost on that list was the variable and ephemeral thing that passed for modern love and romance. The more he lived, the less he understood the human heart, it seemed. He had loved, and lived through divorce. He had read the old books—from Shakespeare to gothic romances—and he knew that it used to be different.

Surely, mystery always had enshrouded this most intimate of human relations, and there was certainly nothing new about that paradoxical alloy of hate and love that still poisoned hearts today. And yet, there had been a time, he knew, when people stayed together, love endured, and lovers didn't change partners with quite the frequency of Paris fashions.

That was probably one reason he had chosen a life of working with computers and artificial intelligence. In fact, Stillman was ALEX's architect.

The Egyptian image also was his idea, a fascination he had acquired years ago. The Sphinx as astrological symbol, the union of opposing forces of the Zodiac—the Lion and the Lady, Leo and Virgo, Beauty and Beast—Alpha/Omega, Yin/Yang, Unity/Duality. It was the cusp of polar opposites, the great and terrible day of reckoning.

Occasionally he had wondered whether there could be some personal significance to the fact that those who failed to answer the riddle of the Sphinx were either eaten, beaten, or strangled. Or that the Sphinx was to destroy itself when the riddle was solved.

Tonight, ALEX and Stillman had been sorting through a mass of conflicting emotions involving one young woman named Angela Hurley.

Ms. Hurley was tall, dark, and handsome and in many ways a pleasant companion, no doubt about that. But their age difference had been a real stumbling stone for Stillman. At thirty-two, he was Angela Hurley's elder by a full decade. In terms of outlook, it could have been more than a generation.

Rick Stillman, the throwback. Maybe it was his Southern upbringing. The Piedmont was still there, thick in his voice, flavoring his speech like syrup on hotcakes. He was from an old Rock Hill family in North Carolina and a graduate of Duke University, which may have accounted for some of his courtly instincts—the desire to pursue rather than be pursued by the opposite sex. It was, for today, a very politically incorrect code, an almost extinct chivalry.

Stillman was painfully aware that females considered him attractive, but in the most superficial ways. His heart's desire was for deep communication of serious matters, and it made him most uncomfortable to be toyed with, as an earlier generation of the opposite sex might have complained. This was one of the areas where he needed ALEX to help him resolve conflicting mores.

The fact that Angie was the daughter of his division head, Dr. Judith Hurley-McBride, complicated things even further. Judith apparently approved of her daughter's interest in him, and he could not gracefully spurn her advances. A time long ago instructor-student liaisons had been considered inappropriate, if not scandalous. At least Angie had not signed up for any of his classes. As a graduate student in Womyn's Studies, she was not likely to be taking any linguistics courses.

The worst thing of all, Stillman admitted, was that he was beginning to feel a certain attraction that he found himself resisting. Why? Could this be the old wound—the ancient, unhealed heartbreak? Would Moira never stop haunting him?

"Perhaps it would be helpful to replay the last conversation," ALEX suggested.

There was no objection from Stillman.

It was a null-video phone conversation that morning with Angie. She had been attempting to recruit him to accompany her to a lecture by some luminary in the Metapersonal Psychology movement, a fellow named Jeremy Kay. Stillman had been attempting to mask his impatience while questioning this esoteric nonsense. It seemed to him that Angie had an unhealthy gullibility.

"But what makes you so sure there's no such thing as the higher Self?" Angie was saying in the replay.

"What makes you so sure there is?" Stillman countered.

"Personal experience."

"OK, so that's your personal experience. My personal experience is something else."

"Because you've never *tried* to attain your higher Self."

"That's true," he conceded. "I have enough problems managing one self, thank you."

"Don't you think you should keep an open mind? You reject the idea of past lives, too, but you've never attempted to experience one."

"No," Stillman agreed. "I guess I'm from the old school. When you're dead, you're dead."

"Keep talking like that," Angie warned, "and they'll have you in front of the Senior Faculty Council."

"No doubt. So, this attaining the higher Self—that's something you do all the time?"

"Sure. And so should you."

"What would I have to do? Walk on hot coals? Lie on a bed of nails?"

"No," Angie said with a pitying laugh. "You just meditate or get into trance and call on your spirit guide to help you find answers or solve problems."

"Spirit guide? You mean, like an 'ascended master'?"

"Whatever you want it to be. Winston Churchill, Marie Curie, Charles Manson. It doesn't matter. It's mostly like . . . fictional."

"You mean like imaginary? What good is it if it's just imaginary?"

"Well, it's not *entirely* imaginary."

"What?"

"It's just a device for tapping the power of your higher Self. All I can tell you is it works. As Basho says, 'The real things of life cannot be learned; they must be lived.'"

"Pretty soon you're going to tell me you believe in God," he quipped.

"Well, in a sense that's the goal—realizing our divinity. Humankind evolving into godhood—or 'goddesshood.' But you should really hear Jeremy Kay. I met him last month at a book signing. He's very . . . dynamic."

Stillman wasn't sure he liked the admiring inflection of her statement. That couldn't be just a tinge of jealousy on his part, could it?

"How does Judith feel about all of this?"

"You know Mother," said Angie darkly. "She's a monogamist, after all. But I think she might go—anonymously. It would be just like her to sneak in and sit in a back row where you wouldn't see her."

That was true. Judith Hurley-McBride could be unpredictable. Like that Bible translation project, of all things. Talk about being brought before the Faculty Council. As much as he admired her boldness and welcomed the opportunity to explore whole new groups of obscure languages, it also made him uncomfortable. This was courting political disfavor. And the way she had sprung it on him as a fait accompli was unnerving. Rick Stillman preferred a more ordered personal reality.

"So, will you go?" Angie persisted.

In the final analysis, Stillman had no intention of attending a lecture by someone who regarded himself as the reincarnation of a priest in the temple of Baal. He tried to decline politely, but it was delicate. While glad for almost any excuse to beg off from another date, he knew this kind of thing could get him pegged as a closed-minded reactionary. And that could be hazardous to one's career.

Finally, Angie let it drop without further argument and excused herself. That in itself was odd. It was almost too easy, almost as if she had come to a decision—not necessarily in his favor. Was she finally tiring of his stodginess? The strangest thing was that the actual prospect of losing her bothered him a lot more than he would have expected.

ALEX resumed the parley.

"How does this make you feel?"

"Mixed up. Real mixed up."

"In what way?"

"I think I want to get this girl off my back—and then my feelings tell me something else."

"What do you think they're telling you?"

"I can't get over the desire for a . . . permanent relationship. And yet—" He broke off.

"Yet, you fear social disapproval?"

"Yes. And I keep coming back to . . . " He broke off again.

"Moira?" ALEX suggested.

"Yes."

Stillman fell silent. He had never wanted that divorce. Sometimes it almost seemed as if she hadn't, either. Otherwise, why had she not taken another partner? Was it just a divorce of convenience?

"Do you want to talk about it?" ALEX prompted.

"I don't know. The more I think about it, the more I'm led to the conclusion that the rest of the world is out of step. How about that?"

"Hardly logical," suggested ALEX.

"What do I know?" said Stillman ruefully. "Do you suppose there really is a higher Self?"

"That is not in my parameters," ALEX advised.

"Yeah? That's what they all say," Stillman said with mock contempt. "End program, ALEX."

With a wink, the Sphinx dissolved to black. The riddle remained intact.

★ ★ ★

The next day, Judith Hurley-McBride wandered into Stillman's office, ostensibly to discuss some university administrivia. That in itself was nothing unusual. In fact, such discussions occurred almost daily, certainly several times a week, either in his office or hers. But this time she seemed to be unusually preoccupied. He detected an absent-mindedness in the way she would ask a mundane question and then exhibit little interest in his response.

Whatever was on her mind, it was apparently something that she wanted to break to him slowly. Ignoring her usual seat opposite his untidy desk, she continued to pace slowly about the room while casually studying his face.

Stillman returned the scrutiny.

Judith, forty-four, was clearly Angie's prototype—tall, dark, lithe, and as emotionally sensitive as she was intellectually deep. A dozen years older than himself, Dr. Hurley-McBride, expert in dead tongues, was an accomplished scholar and perhaps the closest thing to a role model for Stillman at OSU. With her tennis player's physique, ebony blunt cut, and designer glasses typically perched atop her head, Judith conveyed a certain elegance.

At last, when she was ready, she got to the point.

"Rick, how do you feel about Angie?"

Uh-oh. What could he say, really?

"I have developed a certain—fondness for her," he said carefully. "She's a good kid. Why?"

He hoped that the "kid" reference got the ulterior message across gracefully. In fact, it was more customary for women to pursue younger men.

Judith picked up on it instantly. "Has it ever occurred to you that she might be a little young for you?"

He immediately sensed where this might be going. If he was right, it would be a tremendous relief, but he could by no means convey that.

"You're not turning reactionary, are you?" he gently teased, invoking the scorn of political correctness for conventional prejudice.

"Rick," she said tentatively and unsmiling, disregarding his diversion, "Angie probably won't have the courtesy to tell you herself, but I—don't think she'll be going out with you anymore."

The last phrase she said all in a rush and then scanned Stillman's face for its impact.

"You mean, it's—over," Stillman said, blinking and trying to look appropriately somber.

"Yes," said Judith.

"What makes you say that?"

"I believe she's seeing someone else."

Momentarily, Stillman had a wild impulse to thrust his face into his hands and to pretend to be sobbing uncontrollably. But he resisted. His offbeat sense of humor had gotten him into trouble more than once.

"Someone else?" he said stoically, as if playing the good soldier. "Who?"

Judith hesitated. "Have you ever heard of Jeremy Kay, the Metapersonal psychologist?"

"Oh, sure. *That* scoundrel? That *rogue*, who's left a trail of broken hearts in every college town?"

Judith smiled at last, apparently relieved that he was taking it like a good sport. "He's actually a rather hot item," she rejoined. "I'm told his book is doing great. He's giving a lecture tomorrow night at Gunnison. I'm thinking of checking it out—maybe sneak into the back row."

"Wait till I get my hands on him!" Stillman continued dramatically.

"Well, I'm glad to see you're taking it so well," Judith said. "You're such a Boy Scout."

From most people, that would not be a compliment. With Judith, it was harder to tell.

Judith Hurley-McBride herself qualified as an eccentric to some minds, but that was one of the very qualities that endeared her to him. A bona fide monogamist, she had been married to one man—a middle-class white male—for an entire decade. Almost unheard of. Moreover, this Neal McBride was a judge, a despised symbol of the old WHIMPS—White Male Power Structure— which was even worse than being a WASP.

Marriage itself, even monogamy, was not so much disapproved—someone had to replenish the race—as was straightness, unhipness, Boy Scoutness.

Judith was speaking again. She was already onto another subject. "Have you given any further thought to our new project proposal?"

"Not really," he admitted. At least not in the way Judith meant. "I'm just not real comfortable with the subject matter."

"You mean the 'B' word?"

Stillman nodded. He was not into fairy tales, and he had never been a reader of the Bible. It was certainly not his first choice for a text to translate into any language. He was, however, anxious for the opportunity to put Cybersynchronics to work on obscure language groups just like these, especially with the eager collaboration of an Afro-Asian linguist of the caliber of Judith Hurly-McBride.

"I know you don't believe we have an orthodoxy problem with the Faculty Council on this," he said, "but I haven't even had a chance to talk with any of these characters from—what's the name of that outfit?"

"Rhema," Judith responded. "The Rhema Institute."

"Rhema. As in 'word' or 'expression'?

"Yes. It's the root of 'rhematics'—word formation."

"Sure," Stillman said lightly. "Well, I'll have to take your word for it that they're not a bunch of psycho-ceramics."

"For your information, you'll get the opportunity to meet some of these Rhema 'characters.' I've arranged for a couple of them to fly in from Chicago and meet with us next Tuesday. That's why we need to complete that project proposal forthwith."

"Yes, ma'am. I'll get right on it."

The Rhema Institute, as Judith explained it, was a Bible translation mission of a rather different sort—one without a single missionary in the field. It seemed that several exceedingly wealthy benefactors had decided to fund a project to research and develop a method for bringing the Word to all of the last unreached peoples of the world. Judith spoke of the Institute's peculiar conviction that reaching the last unreached groups—hundreds of them—somehow would usher in the Millennium—or the Second Coming—or something. However, they realized that with existing methods the task could take another millennium.

That was where Stillman came in. The only realistic solution to the Rhema Institute's predicament was the essence of Cybersynchronics—computer analysis. What else could reduce entire lifetimes to nanoseconds? It was in many ways the perfect match, a task of such enormity that success would put the beleaguered credibility of Cybersynchronics finally beyond question. If the entire scheme didn't run afoul of the Senior Faculty Council and the Orthodoxy Police, that is.

But in the final analysis, Stillman was confident that the "M" word—moola—would overcome even the problem with the "B" word. It had been his experience that cash had a remarkable calming effect on people's nerves.

Judith was about to leave him to his own devices when something odd began to occur. Her eyes appeared to fasten upon something. She froze, then backed up. Amid the clutter on Stillman's desk was the morning's *Columbus Dispatch* with its jarring page-one headline:

"SPOOKS" TRIAL UNWINDS GRISLY TALE

Stillman followed her line of sight to a one-column mug shot. It was that of a young man with an unremarkable face, except for large, brown, doe eyes and a wispy moustache.

Judith resembled one seasick on a heaving deck. What, he wondered, could cause a reaction like that? The mug in her hand began to yaw recklessly, splashing coffee down the sides.

"Something wrong?"

"I—" she stammered. "I—have to make a phone call."

Judith spun on her heel, spilling more coffee. She fled from the room ingloriously, leaving Stillman to sigh and shake his head. She appeared to be heading down the hall toward her own office.

On a hunch, he did a shadow on her computer sign-in after a minute and was not too surprised when she indeed logged onto ALEX a few moments later. Not only that, but she was accessing the psychotherapeutic programming. It was something she seemed to be doing with increasing regularity. But then, so was he.

* * *

At the McBride home, all were fending for their own dining needs that evening, as usual.

Even Angie was there. Though she had her own apartment, she frequently showed up at mealtimes and when she had serious studying to do. She and Peter ate incommunicado at the dining room table, both listening to who-knows-what on headphones.

Angie had divorced from her mother and stepfather seven years ago at age fifteen under progressive twenty-first century juvenile law that liberated children from their previous status as virtual chattel. But she remained on reasonable terms with Judith and Neal. It had been a no-fault divorce; she just needed her independence. While Peter willingly had adopted the McBride surname after their mother's remarriage a decade ago, Angie had clung stubbornly to her bio-dad's name—Carpenter—for a time. By the time of her divorce, however, she had taken up the maiden-name "Hurley" as a symbol of gender pride.

Peter, at nineteen, still lived at home. He exhibited no interest in higher education or work—only in his less than successful band, "Gibraltar," and this manic young woman named Carlotta. To all appearances, it was not the most stable romance. His parents suspected that Peter might be engaging in some chemical abuse. He was rail thin, an impression that was only aggravated by his mop of curly brown locks.

Wilson and Judith were supping in the kitchen, near the evening news. Wilson wanted to hear about the opening of the "Spooks" trial, but first they had to wade through the tally of national/international affairs—famines, earthquakes, pestilence, wars, assassinations, national uprisings, sex scandals, and the like.

"Eighteen," Wilson told the console softly when he'd had enough. The scene changed to a gang of burgers and fries with little legs, kicking to an obnoxious electronic syncopation.

"Seventy-three," he intoned, now getting a local report on what the media were calling the "Devil's Night Slaying" trial before Judge Wilson N. McBride. The couple watched as the anchorperson gave a staccato curtain-raiser on the Larrabee trial.

"Meanwhile, residents of Millersfield, where this grisly crime occurred, may be watching this case with special interest," she said, as the picture changed behind her to show a nattily attired young man posturing along a dusky rural road, clutching a microphone. "For that story, we go now to Joe Fortunato, live in Millersfield."

"Dana," the fellow said in a hushed tone, the picture tightening about him. "I'm standing along a stretch of Route 105 that's known as Sleepy Hollow Drive, not far from where the body of little Joshua King was found late last year."

Looking over his shoulder and gesturing, Fortunato said, "Just a few hundred yards down the road, this becomes Main Street in Millersfield. But Sleepy Hollow Drive out here is where residents say 'spooks' are rumored to gather at full-moon and other special times. 'Spooks' are the strange people who are said to practice the black arts here, which allegedly include animal sacrifices. Many residents say this is the place which generates all those missing livestock reports that have circulated over recent years. Others say that's not all that goes on here—that human infants, too, have been sacrificed.

"Most people in Millersfield didn't put much stock in those rumors—at least at first. Now, since the death of little Joshua King, that's become a different story. Back to you, Dana."

"Thanks, Joe," the anchorperson said as bouncy theme music rose in the background. "We'll have additional special reports on the Spooks of Millersfield as the trial continues. When we come back, we'll tell you what two local hospitals are doing to make room for their patients who do not have AIDS, and we'll take you to a campus watering hole where the spirits are exceptionally high this evening for those Buckeyes."

★ ★ ★

That night, McBride sank into sleep like the Columbus Clippers in a mid-season slump.

For Judith, it was a different story. Restlessness had a hold that she could not shake. She lay tensely beside her husband's sprawled form, resenting his masculine indifference. She was a little afraid—afraid of what toll the next day might take on her if she didn't get to sleep pretty soon. And maybe even a little afraid of what might happen if she did.

Her fears, in fact, were not totally unfounded.

Some time later, the dreams came, the same dreams with yet a different twist.

3

As Judge McBride gaveled the day's proceedings to order, he noted that the spectators' numbers had multiplied overnight. In fact, it appeared to be standing room only—a tribute, no doubt, to the toxic power of the media.

McBride had to admit he almost looked forward to the developments himself. Not that he exactly enjoyed homicide testimony, but there was something especially engrossing about a key police witness. If he really concentrated, he could anticipate the lines of questioning, if not every question, and many of the answers. It was sort of like playing solitaire table tennis—you had to be quick.

This morning's first witness was Sheriff's Detective Vincent Salerno, a large and very bald man in his late forties with a somewhat regal bearing. He was also the Sheriff Department's sole home-grown expert on the occult. McBride wondered how Jeremiah Cavanaugh would try to shake him. But McBride's fascination also had something to do with his own brief former career as a private investigator not that many years ago. It made him able to relate, as they say.

Sleuthing had been a more than tolerable way to put food on the table while putting credit hours on his law school transcript at Cleveland Marshall College of Law. Not only had it been an opportune part-time job with flexible hours, largely at night, but it had proved to be an invaluable experience, giving him a perspective that no law school could touch.

There wasn't a classroom in the world that contained the likes of Jimmy Shapiro, this boss straight out of Damon Runyan-land at the Shapiro and Company agency. Jimmy, this seemingly hard-boiled bruiser with the deceptively analytical mind, had introduced young Neal McBride to an appreciation of things from the baseness of human motivation to the superiority of intuition over intellect to the value of keeping your head down. It was also how McBride had learned to handle a variety of firearms.

After Jimmy died in a suspicious and unsolved one-car traffic accident, McBride continued his part-time sleuthing, amazing his colleagues at the law firm of Goldweber, Hart, Trasky, and Gerard, where he ran investigations for a couple more years. By the time he finally hung up his trench coat, he had been out of law school for more than a year, but the partners at Goldweber, Hart kept making it hard for him to leave, plying him with sweet talk and raises.

In fact, he took a pay cut to clerk for a federal judge for a couple of years before taking his first real lawyer's job—an uninspiring stint at a firm specializing in corporate law. He got elected two years later to a Columbus municipal judgeship for one term, lost the next election, and then went to work for the ill-fated state Organized Crime Division for a few more years until its dissolution. But even there, it was the basic shirtsleeve, shoe-leather techniques and the street smarts he'd picked up working with Jimmy Shapiro that had given him the edge and the drive.

Sometimes he was forced to admit how much he missed that life. Like now.

Salerno was now sworn, and Sawyer was ready.

"Lieutenant Salerno, are you familiar with the term the 'Spooks of Millersfield'?"

"Yes sir, I am."

"What does it mean to you?"

Cavanaugh was on his feet. "Objection, your honor! What's the relevance of this?"

Sawyer stood his ground. "This is extremely relevant, your

honor. I intend to show that Lieutenant Salerno's investigation of this matter was the key to his ability to link the defendant to the Joshua King murder. Extremely relevant."

"Overruled. You may proceed."

"What does it mean to you, Lieutenant?"

"It's not a term we use in the department," Salerno began. "But I know others use it in referring to witchcraft and devil worship in that vicinity."

"'Others' meaning . . ."

"Meaning certain residents and the media."

Sawyer pursed his lips and looked downward while framing his next question. "How long has this—uh—phenomenon been reported in this area?"

"Your Honor," Cavanaugh interjected impatiently, removing his glasses. "I must object to the introduction of hearsay. This man is being asked to testify about the fantasies and imaginings of anonymous persons regarding a 'phenomenon' whose existence has not even been established."

McBride suggested that Sawyer rephrase the question.

"Lieutenant, when did you yourself first hear about the so-called 'Spooks of Millersfield'?"

"Oh. . . " Salerno rolled his eyes toward the ceiling for a moment. "Had to be eighteen to twenty years ago. I was aware of it before I joined the Detective Bureau."

There was just the slightest murmur among some spectators who apparently had thought the Millersfield phenomenon was something of much younger vintage.

"What was the nature of those reports then?"

"Objection—hearsay!" Cavanaugh called out.

"As an officer of the law," McBride said, "this man's job is to listen to hearsay and find out if there's any truth to it. I'll allow it. The witness may answer."

"Well, the place originally was kind of a lover's lane. That goes back to when I was in high school," Salerno said with the trace of a smile. "Then came the drug parties and the bikers. For a time, it was sort of a hangout for homosexuals, but between the police and the motorcycle gangs, the gays got pretty well driven out.

"Now, eighteen to twenty years ago was when we first started to hear reports about missing livestock—sheep and cattle. It was off and on. Carcasses and body parts would be found here and there—not all of them in the immediate Sleepy Hollow area, but some. And then came the rumors—by this time I was in the Detective Bureau—of witches and warlocks and Satan worshipers in Sleepy Hollow."

"The carcasses and body parts," said Sawyer. "To what were those attributed? Predatory animals or something else?"

Salerno's expression darkened perceptibly. "Humans," he asserted. "There was no doubt about that."

"Why do you say that?"

"Simple. Animals don't know how to use tools, and those carcasses were butchered with some kind of cutting tool."

"Were those cases ever solved? Any arrests ever made?"

"No, sir."

"Why was that, Lieutenant?"

Salerno shrugged. "Not a real high-priority item, I guess, when you have crimes against persons that need attention. These are crimes against property. And, of course, there's politics."

"Politics? Please explain."

"Sure. How'd you like to be the sheriff who has to ask the county commissioners for more money to chase hobgoblins?"

Sawyer smiled briefly. "But didn't that cause problems with the farmers and residents who were living in fear?"

"Some, but for the first several years the incidents were blamed on an animal. There were even reports of a large black panther. Farmers set traps, went gunning for the beast, but nothing ever came of it. It wasn't until more recently that the incidents were connected to humans—the so-called 'spooks.'"

"All right. Tell us, Lieutenant, were you involved in any investigations of these incidents over the years?"

"Yes, sir, I was."

"Would you give us some examples."

"Well, it's not that we didn't do anything about these early missing livestock reports. In fact, I investigated several of them myself. That's how I know they were the work of humans. Then we called Desmond Arnold, a national expert on occult crimes, for his advice."

"And what did he suggest?"

"That we try to identify a local witch and turn her as an informer."

"Why was that?"

"Because many witches say they're just practicing an ancient alternative religion—unlike Satanists, who are opposed to all religion and law. But the two often are found side by side, and a 'good' witch can be an excellent source."

"So is that what you did?"

"Eventually. Early attempts were unsuccessful. It wasn't until three years ago that we finally succeeded in developing a—well, we called her our 'witch-snitch.'"

★ ★ ★

There had been leads to numerous candidates in various walks of life, including some surprisingly respectable positions. That in itself had been an eye-opener. But most of those lacked the vital link to outright criminality that could provide the leverage that Salerno needed.

His luck improved considerably when he turned up a dancer at a seedy local establishment called "Nasty's."

Salerno had spotted her right away. She was a lovely woman, but it was the tattoo on her right upper arm that caught his eye. It was a goat-faced man with a beard and two horns, exceptionally well crafted, if not magnetic.

But the masterpiece was on her back—a statuesque lady with a quiver of arrows. Like the goat-man, the figure was impressive, from the flow of the tints to the folds of the fabric and the perspective of her arm reaching back over the shoulder for an arrow. This was not the work of some storefront for drunken sailors; this was artistry. Salerno had no clue to the identity of this goddess. But one thing he did know—this walking canvas in the fluorescent orange bikini had to be the woman he was seeking.

He studied her as she thrust herself about the mirror-backed stage to the hypnotically churning jukebox finale of "Death to America" by the "Fair Play for Cuba Committee," a nonstarter on Salerno's personal Hit Parade. "Death . . . death . . . death . . ."

Aside from the tattoos and the slathering of eye shadow, she was quite appealing in an almost conventional sort of way—medium-length, curly blonde hair, blue eyes, and a certain youthful . . . almost winsomeness. But Salerno could fairly picture the hardening that would set in in a few short years.

As she sashayed down from the stage, he tried valiantly to catch her eye. Somehow he managed to do so and immediately patted the bar stool beside his, indicating she should join him.

"What's your name?" he asked.

"Zona," she replied somewhat breathlessly.

"Zona? Is that your real name?"

"Depends," she said, sizing him up.

"On what?"

"On what you call real. What's your name?"

"Vinnie—and it *is* my real name."

"Wanna buy me a drink?"

"Sure. Wanna talk to a lonely guy?"

"Sure," she said, devoid of conviction.

He ordered her a sorely over-priced rum and Coke, declining a refill on the beer he was nursing.

Unfortunately, the next dancer was up, and the resulting din rendered further conversation a struggle, though not entirely impossible. Salerno used his time well, trying to convince Zona of two things—that he thought she was the most beautiful girl he had ever met and that he wanted to meet her again, like tomorrow night.

"Come on down," she said carelessly. "I'll be here."

"No, I mean some other place—away from here."

She shrugged noncommittally, finished her drink, and glanced about as if starting to leave.

"Wait," Salerno said quickly, placing a hand atop her right wrist.

She turned back, her shifty eyes meeting his.

"This fellow here on your arm—the guy with the horns."

"What about it?"

"Is he the—"

"No!" she snapped, stomping off.

Salerno hoped he had not blown it.

Apparently he had not, for the next night she joined him again for a drink.

38

Salerno pulled out the stops and let her know clearly what was on his mind.

Later that night, they met at the Stardust Motel, room 114. He felt extremely self-conscious playing a cheap john. But he was also flush with anticipation of a successful mission at last.

"One hundred dollars, pal," Zona said matter-of-factly, kicking off her shoes.

Salerno pulled out his wallet and handed her his card instead of a bill.

"Sheriff's Department," he said stonily.

She froze. "Am I under arrest?"

"No."

"Then what?"

"I want some information."

"What kind of information?"

"I'll ask the questions," he said curtly, trying not to sound excited. He seated himself by the simulated wood-grain desk.

Zona sank to the edge of the double bed, expressionless and pale.

"Look," she said slowly. "Maybe I'd rather just take the rap than answer questions."

He was ready for that. "That's certainly your decision. But I would advise you that we're not talking just hooking. We've got a pretty good case we could make against your boyfriend too. We're talking felonies, and I don't think his record could stand the strain. I don't think you'd want to wait that long for ol' Derek to get out of the can."

Zona snarled an expletive under her breath, thought a long moment, and then looked up again. "If I talk, then no problem? Deal?"

"No problem." He nodded. "Deal."

"What do you want to know?"

"Let's start with that guy on your arm."

"What about it?"

"You say that's not—"

"The devil?" She finished the question for him.

"Right."

"No, it's not," she said with some indignation.

"Then who?"

"The Horned One," she said sullenly.

* * *

Now it was Cavanaugh's turn.

"How can you say, Lieutenant, that Zona Corban was a reliable informer? In your portrayal—let us be honest now—she comes across as a person of questionable character, at best."

McBride nearly winced. That was a telling point that could undermine the prosecution's attempt to establish the existence of a satanic cult in the Millersfield area with Roger Larrabee as one of its priests.

"Basic police methodology," Salerno replied.

"Would you elaborate, please."

"With any informer, you start by asking them questions you already know the answers to, then go to things you don't know but have ways of finding out. If those answers ring true, you have a pretty good idea you can trust them to give you information you have no other way of discovering."

"'Pretty good idea'?" Cavanaugh repeated with a dash of incredulity. "Is it your belief that a man should be convicted of a capital crime on the basis of a pretty good idea?"

Salerno refused to be trapped.

"That's not the issue. We're not asking anybody to believe Zona Corban. The evidence we developed from her leads speaks for itself."

"Well then, let me ask you straight out. Did Zona Corban ever tell you something that wasn't so?"

"No, sir," Salerno said without hesitation.

"Lieutenant, I beg to differ," Cavanaugh said with a dramatic pause. "How about the fact that there is no such person as Zona Corban in the first place?"

Cavanaugh waited for the faint murmur in the audience to subside, then added, "And the fact that Zona Corban is really Leah Andrews?"

Salerno bristled at the cheap shot. "She never denied that Zona Corban was just a stage name," he said, apparently trying not to sound defensive.

This time, McBride did wince. The prosecution clearly had

dropped the ball here. They should have had that little detail accounted for up front.

"Stage name?" Cavanaugh said with that same incredulity. "Stage name for a go-go dancer?"

"She said she was planning to have it changed legally," Salerno added.

"Why was that, Lieutenant?"

Salerno now began to redden, but there was no way out. "She said that—uh—Leah Andrews was . . ."

"Yes, was what?"

"Well, dead."

That was when it really started to go downhill for Salerno, trying to explain notions that were just as flaky to him. And then came the question that put him in the verbal hammerlock.

"Lieutenant, do you believe in the supernatural?"

McBride sustained an objection from Sawyer, but the detective looked like he had suffered a direct hit. At least, McBride was sure that was how it would look to the jury, especially in closing arguments from Cavanaugh.

*   *   *

By the next witness, it was becoming a real crapshoot.

"The state calls Leah Andrews."

McBride was caught somewhat offguard by the roller-coaster stride of the blonde witness to the stand. As she was sworn in, he deliberately averted his gaze from the striking figure in the turquoise knit dress. He wondered how Salerno had dealt with such allurement.

"Ms. Andrews," Sawyer began, "is that your real name?"

"Yes," she said very softly, her voice and expression indicating anything but excitement about testifying in court.

"Are you known by any alias, any other name?"

"Yes, one."

"And that is?"

"Zona Corban."

"And for what purposes do you employ this name?"

"Everything."

"Please explain."

"I no longer use 'Leah Andrews' for anything. I intend to have it changed legally."

"What is your occupation, Ms. Corban, if I may use that name?"

"Nightclub dancer."

"Where?"

"Currently at the B and R Showbar."

"And where is that?"

"At Lincoln and Broad."

"How long have you been employed there?"

"About two years. A little more."

"And what did you do before that?"

"Same thing at a different place—Nasty's, in German Village."

"And before that?"

"I was a legal secretary."

"For whom?"

"Crofters, Brown, and Dougall."

McBride nearly choked. Sawyer shot a knowing glance his way. Crofters would be rolling in his grave, and Brown and Dougall would be speechless.

"Why did you change—occupations?"

"The money. And the people. Lawyers are a bunch of jerks."

Sawyer smiled. The audience laughed, belatedly but lustily, ventilating tension. McBride figured he would soon be nominated for an Academy Award for deadpan. He didn't bother to lift his gavel.

"All right, Ms. Corban," Sawyer said, drawing himself up to his full height. "I want to ask you a rather personal question."

Tension was palpable in the brief pause. "Are you a witch?"

The courtroom was swallowed up by a great silence.

The young woman's heavily mascaraed eyes darted about like a bird in a net. When she did answer, her voice was barely audible despite the deathly stillness.

"You might say that," she said in a hollow tone.

There was one more slight thing. Was it, McBride wondered, the snapping of chewing gum that he had just heard?

* * *

Later in chambers, McBride shed his ebony robe, hung it on the familiar hook by feel, and slumped onto the institutional-style love seat across from his desk. With an audible sigh, he let the cumulative tensions of the gruesome proceeding begin to slide off his shoulders, down his back, and out through the soles of his feet, which he propped on a stack-box by a filing cabinet.

In the next room Sylvia Bennett, secretary and captain of the guard, covered her terminal and glanced about the office for any obvious loose ends. Bailiff Jack Irwin chunked a file drawer shut and reached for his suit coat. It was the end of a long day, and nobody wanted to linger over it.

"Why don't you two take the rest of the day off?" McBride said good-naturedly.

"Good idea," Sylvia said, smiling. "As long as you promise to do the same. And no taking your work home with you, either."

"Promise," McBride lied.

"Peace," Jack said on his way out, Sylvia close behind.

In the blessed silence, McBride's thoughts drifted back to a certain trail in Montana that cut through meadows of Indian paintbrush, lupine, and other flora of assorted hues. He could almost smell the lodgepole pines and see the hoary mountainpeaks in the distance. In his mind's eye a startled moose, ankle-deep in a glassy pond, froze as McBride passed by on his mount, heading for a trout stream just over the next rise.

He well may have been sinking into the twilight zone of slumber when he was startled by a chirping intruder—the telephone. Being the last soldier, he roused himself and answered.

It was for him—a warm-fuzzy sounding female. The cheery greeting sounded like that of a telemarketing salesperson, except that the court's phone system was supposed to block out that sort of thing. It took McBride a minute to register the fact that this voice probably was not a woman's at all, but a machine's—a voice synthesis.

It was one of those you-don't-know-me-but-we-have-mutual-friends kinds of come-ons. And then she really began laying it on.

"Everybody knows you're one of the most competent judges around," she asserted, "and, with the right kind of direction, there's no telling how far a person with your abilities ought to be able to go."

"Thank you," said McBride, suspicious. It might even be a joke, though the humor escaped him. Wide awake now, he reached across Sylvia's desk to hit the record switch. He anticipated a bribe attempt. It wouldn't be the first time, but it might be the most unusual. Then a concrete suspicion dawned.

"What do you really want?" he pressed. "Did Steve Leadingham put you up to this?"

"No," said the voice.

McBride noted that she did not actually deny knowing Leadingham. "So, who are you?"

"My name is unimportant, but I work for a . . . political entity with prominent connections at the state and federal levels. We would like to help your career."

"Oh? Well, *my* career might be beyond help. Just what did you have in mind?"

"We're always looking for qualified candidates to serve in key judicial seats—appellate benches, the Ohio Supreme Court, even the federal judiciary. Or perhaps you have political aspirations in the legislative arena?"

"Maybe," McBride parried. "Just how do you provide this 'help'?"

"A variety of ways. We're bipartisan, but our candidates generally get nominated—and our nominees generally get elected. So our help is much more than just financial, although we help in that area too."

"Just what does one have to do to qualify for your . . . help?"

"Just ask," the woman said smoothly.

"Just ask? It can't be that simple. Don't you have a philosophy? How do you know I share your point of view? What do you stand for?"

"It is simple," she insisted. "We simply stand for choice—people's right to choose their own personal moral standards in all areas of life. You know, the American way."

"But what do I have to *do* to merit your continued support?" McBride persisted.

"Simply reflect that pro-American philosophy in your decisions."

McBride was beginning to catch the rodent's aroma.

"Let me see if I follow you," he suggested. "Like this present case before me. To reflect your philosophy, I might, for example, find a way to acquit Roger Larrabee on, say, a First Amendment basis—freedom of expression and so forth. Is that right?"

"We would not presume to inject ourselves into a specific case," the voice demurred.

"Of course not," said McBride with mounting irritation. "But you would support a directed verdict of acquittal from the bench?"

"We certainly would not oppose it."

Now McBride's anger was aggravated by the realization that this recording was worthless if his suspicion was correct about the synthesized voice. It was time to play trump cards.

"But what if my decision contradicted your position on a particular case, such as this one?"

"We judge by people's actions," said the voice, no longer so warm. "We don't play games—or give second chances."

"Just who *are* you, anyway?" McBride demanded. "And what gives you the right to judge elected officials?"

"Enemies of choice are enemies of the people," the voice said darkly.

"Then let me give you *my* philosophy of choice," he snapped. "If I ever find out who you or your people are, I will choose to do everything within my power to see that you are prosecuted to the fullest extent of the law—beginning with bribery and corruption. Do I make myself clear?"

Silence.

He should have been more judicious and stopped right there, but he tended to have a short fuse when he was tired.

"You backroom reptiles make me sick. You and your ilk may think you control a few corrupt politicians, but you're talking to one judge who chooses to stand up for what's right—whether it's

politically expedient or not. If that means choosing political oblivion, then so be it."

"That's most unfortunate," said the voice, sounding even
less warm and fuzzy than it did a minute ago. "There are far worse
things than political oblivion."

"Unfortunate for whom?" McBride challenged.

"For . . . loved ones."

"Are you threatening my family?"

"We don't threaten."

With that, the line went dead.

McBride immediately regretted his intemperate remarks. He
knew from experience that he'd be laughed out of the police station
on the basis of a taped threat like this.

But he was convinced that it was something more than just a
crank call. And if so, had he just placed his entire family in jeopardy?

4

Faced with a relentless onslaught of armor-plated reptiles and
kindred giant vermin, the starship trooper kept firing.

Each new victim froze, glowed, shimmered, and then vanished before the next leviathan lumbered to the attack. One step
behind the trooper stood a young blue-skinned woman with ma-
genta flowing hair, in the kind of uniform that graced the covers of
pulp magazines a century ago. She cringed and reached for the
man's elbow as another roaring monster reared on its hind legs and
opened its cavernous jaws to expose an array of fangs. The warrior
pivoted several degrees, fired, and watched as another creature dissolved into luminosity.

Peter McBride, his nerves raging from the effects of the designer drug "Revenge," deftly manipulated the computer bank that generated the fantastic hologram animations, while the band's pulsing volume built to shattering levels. Nick and Paulo rocked and squinted, wailing into the microphone.

"Nowhere to run, nowhere to hide, baby . . . Nothin' but pain and misery on the inside, baby . . . Nowhere to run, nowhere to hide . . . Nowhere to run, nowhere to hide . . ."

A two-and-a-half-story nightmare version of a praying mantis closed the distance in two quick strides and halted, its antennae waving momentarily before the inevitable strike. It was that customary split-second pause that had allowed the trooper to thwart the attacks. Again the man fired, but this time to no effect. He flashed a look of disbelief at the weapon, then fired again. Still nothing.

The two humans froze as the mantis pounced with its great lightning forelegs. The man reeled backward from the impact. His head and shoulders smacked viciously against the cliff wall. The woman cried out, a trickle of green blood tracking down the blueness of her right arm.

"Nowhere to run, nowhere to hide . . . Nowhere to run, nowhere to hide . . ."

The woman stared transfixed at the death dance. The stunned warrior staggered forward two steps, teetering on the precipice of consciousness. More deliberately this time, the mantis moved in, scooped up the man's kicking form, and hunched toward its feast. Shivering, the blue woman covered her mouth, her eyes bulging as they beheld the awful mandibles assault the trooper's crumpled body.

"Cut!" a woman's strident voice commanded.

The lurid animation jerked to a halt, the holograms paling toward two-dimensional obscurity. The band's freight-train rumble died quickly as the room lights sprang to life.

"How reactionary!" said the woman in the doorway, glaring at the fading image of the blue vamp and the dying man. "How absolutely patriarchist!"

Peter, swiveling about in his chair at the panel, now saw that it was his sister, Angie. Fury swelled within, fueled by the "Revenge" in his bloodstream. He leaped from the chair and charged across the room, grabbing a mike stand en route.

Paulo quickly stepped between brother and sister, blocking Peter's attack.

"Get away!" Peter snarled.

"Cool out, man!" Paulo barked.

Peter slowly lowered the mike stand, attempting to gather his wits. Still furious, he hurled the stand end over end into a stack of vinyl cartons, creating a moderate mess but no serious damage.

Nick and Tony swore viciously and shut down their amps.

Carlotta was suddenly at Peter's side, pressing a tab into his hand and proffering a bottle of cheap wine. Peter took a swallow to chase down the tab—probably a hit of "Lucid," a pharmacological assist in reestablishing emotional control.

"It's OK," Angie told Paulo under her breath. "I can take him."

Paulo walked slowly off with furrowed brow, seemingly unaware of Angie's martial arts expertise.

"What's the point?" Peter demanded indignantly.

"The point is this . . . *puerile* . . . fantasy of yours," Angie replied calmly.

"This what?"

"I just hope you big, bad guys aren't under the illusion that this adolescent junk is some kind of fancy art."

"I'll tell you what it is," Peter said, taking a breath. "This is the opening cut on a demo for our first disk. We're recording, and you just screwed it up. That's what it is. Now, why don't you hit the road?"

Peter was working himself into a new frenzy, but Angie dismissed it with a wave. There was a mysterious something, almost teasing, in her attitude that nibbled at the corners of his attention.

"Not that you fellows aren't decent musicians," Angie conceded. "But you could do better, Peter—a lot better."

"What do you mean?" Peter asked despite himself.

"Interested?" was the intent behind Angie's silent smirk.

And Peter's sullen non-reply was the closest thing to "Yes" under the circumstances.

"Jeremy," Angie called back to the doorway, where a tall blond man apparently had been standing unnoticed the whole time.

The bespectacled, turtle-necked figure, in his mid-thirties and with the regular features of a male model, suggested a person of generous intellect and ego. He moved to join Angie, and both took seats at the main console.

Peter was suddenly aware that this Jeremy was asking him a question.

"What's your modem credit code?" the man asked again without looking up from the keyboard.

Peter bristled. "I don't give that out. Use your own."

"I'll personally pay you back if you don't like it, Peter," Angie said smoothly. "Give Jeremy your number."

"You're already logged on," Peter responded grudgingly.

This time the man named Jeremy looked up. "That's all right. I can see your brother has only a Class-B access. We need Class-A to access a Quang base."

Here he turned to Peter and said with a generous smile, "This one's on me."

Almost despite himself, Peter watched raptly as Jeremy logged off, punched in his own code, and then summoned up on the monitor an unfamiliar program with a long name including the word "Quang." As the monitor began scrolling through its listings, the man tapped in search instructions and then asked Peter to get his musicians cranking and to prepare to record.

"Same number?" Peter asked, somewhat baffled.

"Same number," Jeremy Kay agreed.

The band began building its slow instrumental windup. Jeremy assigned Peter and Angie to some technical chores at the console while he himself commandeered the main controls.

It was the same music, but this time with more coherent power. Peter could tell that Angie was doing something in the mixing of the sound that created a whole new twist, a more pronounced eeriness. But what took shape before his eyes was the real shock.

In the hologram arena, Peter saw himself—his own three-dimensional facsimile—moving naturally and freely yet also in synchrony with the "Nowhere to Hide" theme. It was most disorienting to watch this other Peter working out with the same band in the same basement studio where they were even now performing in real time and space. He found himself torn between resisting the disorientation and giving in to the strange sensation.

Go with it, Peter told himself, and he began to absorb the intoxicating spell. Then just as quickly, the scene changed, and Peter was viewing something like a hospital scene, although in another moment it became clear that the faces belonged to mental patients. Suddenly Peter had the bone-chilling realization that one of them was his mother.

"Heartaches on the inside, baby . . . Nowhere to run, nowhere to hide, baby . . . Nowhere to run, nowhere to hide . . ."

What goes on here?

So stunned and confused was Peter by that point that the next scene was barely intelligible. It was Carlotta, but yet not Carlotta. This Carlotta was cold and sullen, as in a love turned to hatred. Peter was there as well but facing the other direction, as in the grip of a powerful, incapacitating emotion. Though neither of them moved, the distance between them steadily grew, Carlotta's figure shrinking into the distance, his own swelling in proportion. At last, it was just his close-up face, yet not his face. It was the eyes. That was it. They appeared alien, as if belonging to some other creature, a being of—what?

Peter shuddered involuntarily without knowing why. And then he was certain that he didn't want to know.

"Nowhere to run, nowhere to hide . . ."

"Peter," Angie was saying insistently. "Peter."

He suddenly realized it was over, probably had been for who knows how long. Yet he couldn't recall how it had ended. Maybe he had blanked for a moment. And maybe he was still doing it, for he now realized that Angie was telling him something about their mother being "episodic" again and Angie's fear that she eventually might be institutionalized.

But Peter was distracted again by the sound of rising voices across the studio. Tony and Nick were arguing.

"I'm telling you, you're blind," Tony said hotly. "That was me—Tony Gunther—up there. I'd know me anywhere."

Nick was equally insistent that he himself had been the star of the video.

Peter, growing increasingly confused, felt like telling them that they were both out of their minds—what they had just witnessed was clearly a Peter McBride scene. But he was becoming less certain about his own rationality. He asked Carlotta for another "Lucid."

Now the lights were back up, and Jeremy was asking Peter what he thought.

He was at a momentary loss. "Ultra," he finally managed. "How do you do that?"

"Well," Jeremy said with a little smile, "let's just say I have a good friend in computers. This is pretty new technology. I could probably arrange for you to acquire some of the advanced-level materials if you're interested."

"Sure," Peter replied quickly. "But what was all that? Dreams?"

"That's the question of the ages," said Jeremy mysteriously.

Peter turned to Angie. "Translation, please?"

"Simple," she said tolerantly. "How do you ever really know what's real and what's a dream?"

Peter thought there was a simple answer to that, but he couldn't come up with it just then. When you're awake you *know* you're not dreaming—except that's the same thing he usually thought when he *was* dreaming. So Peter decided to skip the whole thing.

"Yeah, well, thanks a lot—uh—Jerry."

"That's Jeremy," Angie said with a laugh. "I guess I failed to make introductions. Peter, meet Jeremy Kay."

"Charmed," Peter said.

* * *

Judith always knew when she was losing control. Her fingers turned icy and her hands shook. As they were doing now.

But she drew a measure of reassurance just from being in Selena Goren's office. The airy, skylit enclosure, outfitted with standard-issue studio furniture and Chinese watercolors, was a vivid reminder of many former anguishes vented and set to flight.

Goren seemed to personify victory, with her own triumphs over smoking and two—or was it three?—irreconcilable mates.

As a counselor, ALEX was OK for life's little bumps. But times like these just required the human touch, as unpredictable an affair as that could be. Now, for example, Goren was nutshelling Judith's complaint as her "little mystery," and she couldn't help feeling a bit put off.

"Have you discussed it with your husband?" the psychiatrist asked mildly.

"Why, no," Judith said blankly. No such thought had occurred to her. "Do you think I should?"

There was only the suggestion of a passing smile on Goren's darkly handsome face. To a stranger, the two women might have appeared to be sisters. Also in her mid-forties, Goren was tall, lithe, and dramatically expressive when she allowed herself the option.

"Well now, he might be able to shed some light on this mystery of yours," Goren said. "Perhaps, in some way you've forgotten, he's actually provided some verbal clues to this man's physical appearance. Or perhaps you saw one of his papers. You'd be amazed how many things our eyes take in that never register in our conscious minds until some strange associations trigger them in the memory and we wonder where they came from. That probably explains a lot of what we call 'deja vu.' Anyway, it happens all the time."

"I don't think—well, that's why I was thinking maybe hypnosis—"

"Judith," Goren interrupted firmly. "I seriously doubt that it would make any difference even if you were able to resolve this little mystery. You'd probably be exceedingly disappointed with the answer, especially considering the time and energy expended on it. Rest assured that whatever it is, it does have a natural explanation. That's point number one."

Goren paused for some acknowledgment. Judith nodded perfunctorily.

"Point number two: What does matter is you. Your feelings and how you're hurting yourself or setting yourself up to be hurt. Now, why don't you tell me about these dreams."

Judith took a deep breath and launched into a detailed recitation of her nocturnal torments. She told Goren about a loose tooth and the vermin—and even the knife. She gathered that Goren was troubled by the imagery. The woman was uncharacteristically somber, her eyes downcast in thought, fingertips meshed before her lips.

"I know we've talked about this before," Judith added haltingly, partly to relieve the heavy silence, "but don't you think these could have something to do with my, you know—"

"No!"

Judith was startled by the vehemence of Goren's response.

"If you're at all serious about doing yourself some good, you simply must rid yourself of these self-destructive notions about womanhood and motherhood. They're nothing but malicious propaganda and guilt trips spread by misogynists and reactionaries. Patriarchists!"

Judith swallowed hard and said nothing. She knew Goren was not done.

"Now—" Goren lowered her voice "—I'm more concerned about why now. First, what significance do you attach to the recurrent loose-tooth episodes? The first thing that comes to mind."

"Abortion," Judith blurted.

"Next," Goren snapped.

Judith went totally blank, and the harder she struggled to come up with something, the farther she slipped away. "I—I don't know," she stammered.

"Give it a voice," Goren prompted.

Instantly, Judith was aware of a chilling sound gnawing at the corners of her mind. "I hear a baby," she said positively.

"Yes?"

"A baby, crying for its mother."

With that, she suddenly lost her ability to breathe. Tears began rolling down her cheeks, and her next breath came in an involuntary gasp.

"Breathe," Goren commanded.

Judith struggled for control, for words. "What do you think the tooth means?" she said in an unintentionally pathetic voice, wiping away the tears.

She was surprised when Goren actually responded directly.

"That's partly why I'm a bit concerned. It can be a number of things, but typically the loose-tooth syndrome is symbolic of a death wish—for a close relative."

Goren let the reality of the statement settle in before continuing. "My advice at this point is that you not go home for a few days. Get away for a while, go to Cedar Point, Niagara Falls, or the Poconos or something—at least for the weekend, longer if possible, while you cool out a little and spend some time on yourself. Do you have any vacation time left? Can you take next week off?"

Judith's mind was reeling. Was she about to hear voices from God telling her to kill her children? And certainly she couldn't just cancel next week's classes and appointments. She immediately thought of the Rhema Institute and the deadline for the article that she owed the linguistics journal *Epos*.

"No, I can't blow next week, but I might be able to break away for the weekend."

"Good. That's a start."

"But is that just to get me out of harm's way, or is there something I should be doing with that time?"

"I think that's best left up to you. Try to engage in some activities that involve walking and solitude. Museums and parks are good for that. You need some time to talk to yourself and sort out where you are in your life, your career, and your family without all the other voices telling you what you should do. Ask yourself if you're sacrificing yourself too much in one of these areas. Ask yourself if it's really worth it. OK?"

Judith nodded, unconvincingly. "Thanks, Selena."

★ ★ ★

Customers were never very happy at the Regional Deprogramming Center for Religious Extremism on Lower Siddhartha Avenue. And Deborah Wells was no exception.

The young woman with bleached hair and dark roots, tank top, jeans, and flip-flops awkwardly cradled her infant, a tiny child of darker hue with dangling blue booties, one tied, one untied. Mom's eyes looked deadened, perhaps chemically.

Gently counseling her was Moira Stone, a determined woman in her thirties with red hair and green eyes full of life. She was an assistant professor of ancient studies at OSU who believed vaguely that she should give something back to her community, without knowing quite what that should be.

"Are you sure you wouldn't like to put the baby up for adoption?" Moira said as persuasively as she could. "We can get the child placed for you very easily—at no charge."

"Well," said the melancholy young woman, "I don't know. I need to think about that."

Moira let it go, for now. She could come back to that. She found these cases somewhat depressing, but it was worth it to know that she was performing a valuable community service, fighting bigotry. As a volunteer through the Womyn's Law Project, Moira spent two afternoons a week outside of class, counseling the victims of religious fanaticism.

This woman, for example, had gone to one of those "pregnancy centers" for a pre-term interview, only to find out that it wasn't a termination clinic at all but a propaganda outlet for religious fundamentalists. The poor woman, of course, hadn't realized the difference until too late. By that time, she had been forced to watch a gruesome video that made her sick and had her head filled with all kinds of rubbish about termination's being murder.

Moira had spent a good hour with Deborah, answering her questions, letting her cry, and showing her another video telling the truth about the antisocial effects of religious extremism. The woman was clearly showing signs of childbirth trauma.

"What was the address of that place again?" Moira asked.

Pulling a scrap of paper from her jeans pocket, Deborah read, "Thirty-seven thirty-eight Sorrento."

Moira wrote it down to give to her boss, who happened to be going down the hall just then.

"Lothar!" she called out.

The big man with the shiny black ponytail and goatee came back and stuck his head in the doorway.

"You rang?" he said in a deep, husky voice.

"Deborah, this is Lothar Eckart, our director. Here—" Moira handed her note paper to Lothar. "Another forced pregnancy center."

Lothar's eyes lit up as he took the paper. "Sorrento. Could be the same one I just heard about. Now we know where. Trick or treat."

It was an inside joke. Lothar liked to remark on how many of the October Holiday fires occurred at these places, as if he knew something about it. Maybe he did.

"Deborah here is undecided about adoption," Moira suggested.

Lothar picked up on the hint.

"Wow!" he said, fixing her with his gaze while sliding into a nearby chair. "Do you have any idea how much one of these bambinos can cost in just a few short years?"

The woman shook her head.

Lothar began reeling off figures in the tens of thousands of dollars for a litany of items from diapers to diamonds.

"Do you have any idea what you could do with that kind of money?" he asked her.

Deborah's eyes grew round. She was thinking. She appeared to have some idea.

"Or look at it the other way," Moira said gently. "How do you plan to come up with that kind of money to indulge this—motherhood thing?"

Moira was totally unprepared for what happened next.

Deborah Wells, looking horrified yet resolute, jumped to her feet and thrust the baby at Moira.

"Here!" she cried, transferring the child into Moira's arms.

And then she fled out the door, the back of her hand pressed to her mouth.

Moira looked at the drowsy-eyed infant, then at Lothar. "Uh—she didn't sign any—uh—"

"Zee papers?" Lothar laughed. "We'll mail her zee papers. She can mail 'em back. No awkward domestic scenes that way."

Moira wasn't sure how she felt about all of that.

Lothar laughed again and held out his hands toward the child. "Hey, Snookums." He chuckled. "Come to Da-Da, Snookums."

Reluctantly, Moira handed over the baby. There was something not entirely unsatisfactory about this baby-cradling sensation. Maybe even she had a reactionary streak in her somewhere.

Lothar held up the child at shoulder height like a trophy fish. "Such a deal! Fundamentalist pregnancy center tricks bimbo into giving birth—and we get the product. What teamwork."

There was no question in Moira's mind as to how she felt about sexist epithets such as "bimbo." She didn't like them.

This Lothar could be a real pig sometimes. She made a mental note to find out where a child like this actually ended up.

"Gitchee-gitchee-goo!" Lothar rasped, chucking the little tyke under the chin. "Gitchee-gitchee-goo!"

5

After the threatening phone call, McBride's original apprehensions about this "creeper" case only deepened. He was not prepared to believe that neo-pagan kooks such as Larrabee had anything approaching the kind of influence and connections McBride had encountered in his prior career prosecuting organized crime figures. But neither was he much of a believer in coincidence.

Certainly, the American criminal justice system was not all that it used to be. He had few illusions in that department.

Hard-boiled Jimmy Shapiro had taught him better than that. McBride long ago had gotten over his disillusionment from Jimmy's shocking revelations regarding crooked cops and judges. And when the time came, he clearly recognized the dismantling of the state Organized Crime Division for what it really was—one more surrender in the war against crime. He understood that he and his colleagues were being too successful and, as Steve Leadingham would say, too many toes were being stepped on.

And that wasn't necessarily being cynical; it was just realistic.

GOP party boss Sherm Dygert had even made a reasonable amount of sense in urging McBride to run for this Common Pleas seat and at least serve as a voice in the wilderness, if nothing else. McBride, Dygert said, had given up too easily after his defeat for a second muni judgeship term. He had run against a woman that time, and he'd simply gotten caught in gender politics. Try, try again, said Dygert, if you're a true believer; otherwise, you have no room to criticize. Who knows but you might be able to change things just a little bit for the better.

To this day, McBride wasn't at all sure that Sherm was totally on the level. He had his doubts, again being realistic.

Now he was riveted, oblivious even to the television camera that had invaded the courtroom and focused on each syllable of testimony.

"Ms. Andrews," Al Sawyer began gently, "did you personally witness the slaying of Joshua King?"

"No."

"Do you know anybody who did?"

"Yes—Lothar Eckart."

"And how do you know he did?"

"We talked about it. He wasn't afraid to talk to me."

"And what did he tell you?"

"Objection!" cried Jeremiah Cavanaugh.

"Sustained. There will be ample opportunity to pursue those questions with Mr. Eckart directly when he is sworn as a witness."

"All right," Sawyer said. "Ms. Andrews, would you describe your practice of the magical arts for us?"

"Such as?"

"Well, start at the beginning. How were you initiated and what were you taught?"

Cavanaugh stood up.

"Your Honor, I question the relevance of this. If the state wants to present evidence regarding the defendant, fine. But if we're turning this into a sideshow, I object."

McBride looked over at the prosecution.

"What is your purpose here, Mr. Sawyer?"

"Again, Your Honor, we are establishing the nature of the organization to which the defendant belonged and, through that, his motives."

Easy enough.

"Very well. You may proceed."

★ ★ ★

Leah had never been one to turn down the opportunity for an adventure, but why did this one have to be so mysterious? Ted, at first, refused to tell her exactly where they were going. Wendy, his sister, would say only that it had something to do with the full moon—and it would be ultra, as they liked to say.

As Ted drove, he and the girls laughed and drank beer, their daring spirits swelling recklessly by the minute. Ted, eighteen, was the quintessential jalopy-driving, beer-swigging member of their high school wrestling team with short dark hair and a bad complexion. Wendy—like Leah, seventeen—was equally mischievous, dark-haired, and wiry-strong as a junior gymnast. They and Leah were just good friends, kindred spirits.

A half hour later, they were on the outskirts of a little town called Millersfield, on a twisty, rolling road called Sleepy Hollow Drive.

"This is it," Ted declared at last, after rounding a curve, turning sharply down a gravel lane, and parking the battered sports car off the road under the cover of an enormous weeping willow.

The moon was overpoweringly full, and the cool evening air was electric with unimagined possibilities. Leah fairly pulsed with abandon. The three raced down a hill and traced the bank of a noisy stream for about half a mile before they came to a crossing afforded by a fallen oak. Ted ran nimbly across to the other side and waited for the girls, who picked their footing with much greater care.

After what seemed an hour of scrambling through dense underbrush, they at last spied an amber glow ahead through the trees. They slowed their pace so as not to advertise their presence while locating just the right vantage point to see without being seen. And at long last, they were there.

The first thing Leah sensed was an eerily disorienting babble that slowly resolved into voices. Her eyes were hard pressed to adjust to the stark contrasts between the blaze of the fire and the shadowy figures, but soon the tableau came into lurid focus. Leah's mouth popped open in astonishment. Round the blazing bonfire danced seven men and six women. That was plain to see, for not one of them wore so much as a cuff link.

Ted was laughing quietly as he and Wendy drained their beer cans. Leah felt herself drawn almost hypnotically by the waxing and waning of the musical chant and the rhythms of the bobbing forms. With part of herself oddly desiring to add her own voice to the chorus, she strained to make out the terrible words. At last she was able to do so.

"Air I am . . . Fire I am . . . Water, Earth, and Spirit I am . . . We all come from the Goddess . . . And to Her we shall return . . . like a drop of rain, flowing to the ocean."

Maddeningly, it was over quickly, and the assemblage retreated from view into the mouth of a large barn. Ted and Wendy continued jabbering for some time in the moonlight, as if nothing had happened. But Leah felt strangely empty and disconnected. It was a feeling she could not shake for days.

The next time Leah returned to Sleepy Hollow, it was alone.

Somehow, Ted and Wendy just didn't seem to belong there. Their attitude was one of roughneck hilarity and . . . well . . . downright irreverence. But Leah had turned the experience over in her mind many times in the succeeding weeks, inexplicably captivated by the haunting memory. She knew almost at once that she would return, had to return. And then, oh, how the days had dragged till the next full moon.

But at last she was there, picking her way less cautiously this time across the fallen oak, plunging through the underbrush, and retracing the path through the aspens and maples toward the amber glow in the distance.

"Air I am . . . Fire I am . . .Water, Earth, and Spirit I am . . . We all come from the Goddess . . . And to Her we shall return . . ."

This time she walked boldly into the clearing, accepting whatever fate befell her. Somehow, she felt as if she belonged there, and it must have appeared that way to the unclothed wor-shipers. No one gave her a second look as they fell silent, broke the circle, and began filing into the hulking barn. Leah followed at a distance.

She was just starting to wonder if she indeed was going to be allowed to walk right into the inner sanctum when she became dimly aware of some presence behind her. Before she could turn to look, something quite solid collided savagely with her head. She crumpled to the ground, senseless.

★ ★ ★

When Leah awoke sometime later, her head throbbed wick-edly. She raised her hand and felt a large knot on her skull, cov-ered with a small bandage.

"Don't worry," said a woman behind her. "I cleaned the wound. Very superficial, but head wounds always bleed a lot."

"Who—?" Leah began haltingly.

"A big guy you wouldn't know," the woman filled in per-ceptively. "Typical security overreaction. At least he didn't shoot you. He could have, you know."

Leah started to get up. She saw that she was lying on a couch in the living room of what appeared to be a trailer home.

"Don't move," the woman spoke again. "I'll get you some tea, and when you feel ready, I'll drive you home."

The woman's name was Tracy. She appeared to be about thirty, wore jeans and a flannel shirt, and somehow reminded Leah of horses. Maybe it was the boots, but she doubted it. It turned out that Tracy lived just down the road from the barn in this trailer with another woman, who was not home.

"What were you trying to do?" The woman handed Leah the steaming cup of tea.

Leah wanted to be helpful, but she honestly didn't know how to answer that question. She just shrugged.

"Well, I have lots of intuition," Tracy said, her expression softening. "Let me guess. You're a termite inspector on the night shift, and you were making a house call."

Leah smiled despite herself.

"OK. I didn't really think so. Let's see. You're just a curious young woman seeking after the truth who's beginning to doubt that the nuns and priests have all the answers, and your parents don't understand you, and all your boyfriend wants to do is drink beer and make love, and you have a secret desire to have a real religious experience, especially when the moon is full—but you never take your clothes off, except in the shower, maybe."

Leah felt a sudden chill. Despite the flippancy, this woman had uncanny spiritual aim. She nodded slowly.

"You have questions?" Tracy asked. "You desire instruction in the Craft?"

Leah nodded again, twice.

An odd expression indented the corners of Tracy's mouth, as if in some subtle version of amusement.

"OK," she said abruptly. "I give up. You've exhausted all my intuition for this year. What is your question?"

Leah spoke for the first time, her voice sounding small and hollow in the dimly lit room. "Who is the Goddess?"

As if not hearing, the woman lit a small, thin cigarette. Not once did she take her eyes from Leah. "How are you feeling?" she asked.

"OK."

"Really OK?" Tracy said after a long moment, exhaling a small, blue plume.

"Sure." Leah nodded sincerely but with a forced smile.

The woman handed her the joint. "Who do you think the Goddess is?"

"I don't know," Leah said almost impatiently before taking a long hit.

"Well, guess. Use *your* intuition."

She handed the joint back and mulled the question in between breaths while her blood chemistry reacted. Presently, she was forced to release her own small, blue plume. "Not . . . Mary?" she stammered finally.

Tracy smiled indulgently. "You're talking Sunday school. Let me teach you a deeper truth. Virtually every people, every culture, has had some knowledge of the Goddess in one form or another, by one name or another. She was known to the Babylonians, the Assyrians, the Phrygians, the Phoenicians, the Egyptians, the

Greeks, the Romans. Some of the names by which the ancients knew her were Ashtoreth, Semiramis, Ishtar, Astarte, Isis, Aphrodite, Venus . . ."

She reached for a volume on a nearby bookshelf, flipped to a page marked by an index card, and continued. "'To the Saxons, she was Eostre, Goddess of Spring. To the stargazing ancients, she embodied the constellation Virgo, First Lady of the Zodiac, Queen of Heaven, Sister to the Queen of the Underworld, Virgin Mother.' We simply call her the Goddess."

"Wow!" Leah heard herself say distantly, as if catching an echo from a long, dark corridor. Then self-consciously, her mental replay reminded her of Miss Teenybopper. Why did she always have to say "Wow!" when she was stoned?

Tracy appeared not to notice. She shut the book abruptly and looked deeply into Leah's eyes with an imposing gaze. "She has power—available to us. Is this something that interests you?"

Leah felt the flicker of a score of emotions, most of them too fleeting for words.

"Yes," she said too loudly, frustrated by her own inarticulate tongue.

"We'll talk further," the woman said with finality, extending the book toward her. "You may borrow this for study if you're serious."

Leah nodded, grasping the volume.

"Let me drive you home," Tracy said, not unkindly.

Leah would remember it as the beginning of a long relationship. She devoured Tracy's book, *Wicca Yesterday and Today*, by Percival Varley, fascinated by the rites, holidays, charms, and incantations. She was intrigued to learn how Judeo-Christianity had drunk from the same fountainhead, but had corrupted the ancient religion into something harsh, judgmental, and patriarchal. She learned how paternalism had demoted the goddess from Queen of Heaven to Christianity's Mother of God.

At last, she understood. Initiation beckoned.

★ ★ ★

If ever McBride had seen a woman devoid of the joie de vivre, it was this wretched young creature, the next witness taking her seat in the witness box. He had learned to read much from simple expressions and body language. His instincts in that regard rarely proved wrong.

Superficially, Marianne King, bereaved mother of Joshua King, appeared quite unremarkable. At twenty-eight, she could have been a somewhat older and darker version of blonde, blue-eyed Zona/Leah, after a bit more of life's tribulations—and perhaps excesses—had extracted some of the freshness from around the mouth and cheeks and deep brown eyes. But beneath the surface, McBride sensed a deep reservoir of agonies and defeats that sapped and depleted her vitality. What remained was bloodless, inert, wooden, even cold.

Sawyer attempted to navigate the preliminaries with the least wasted motion.

"Occupation?"

"Senior account clerk for the downtown office of Forbes-Blankenship, Incorporated," Marianne King answered, somewhat stiffly.

"The investment brokers?"

"Correct."

"How long have you worked there?"

"Five years—five years next month."

"Please describe your duties."

"I run systems for crediting payments to client accounts, and I am responsible for weekly internal statements and summaries of accounts."

"Please indicate your marital status—single, married, divorced."

"Single."

"And you are the mother of the deceased, Joshua King?"

"Correct."

"Ms. King, to the best of your recollection, will you please describe for the court the events immediately prior to your son's death last October thirty-first."

"Starting with his disappearance?"

"That's right."

"Well," Ms. King said, releasing a barely audible sigh, "I remember the day before was a Thursday, a normal work day. I came home from work, and my regular daytime sitter, Virginia Pinkerton, a widow lady, said a man identifying himself as Joshua's father—"

"Identify, please."

"Oh, Lothar Eckart—had called to find out if I'd be home Friday after work. She told me she'd said she didn't know and he'd have to call back the next day. Hearing from him was a little unusual, but I didn't think anything much about it. He meant nothing to me at that point. My main concern was to confirm my other babysitter for the next night so I could go downtown to the Top of the Tower and watch the Halloween fireworks."

"This Mr. Lothar Eckart," Sawyer interjected. "Did you determine whether he, in fact, had called?"

"No. I mean, yes, I determined that he had not. When I got a busy signal at my high school sitter's, I called Mr. Eckart, and he said he hadn't called. Gave me some song and dance about whether I was giving him some kind of come-on, and I hung up. I didn't give it much more thought. I finally got hold of Beverly Cunningham, my other sitter, and confirmed that she'd be there Friday after school until I got home Friday night."

"So, you believed then—and continue to believe now—that Ms. Pinkerton did not tell the caller that you would or would not be home the next night?"

"Correct. I know her very well. She's extremely trustworthy, especially in matters of that sort. She would never give out that kind of information."

"What next occurred?"

"When I got home after work the next day, Friday, Virginia had just left, and Beverly was there, watching Joshua. I had a bite to eat and then cleaned up and changed to go out. Before I left, I reminded Beverly not to let anyone in and not to give anyone any information over the phone about anything."

"And then you left?"

"Well . . . no," Ms. King said awkwardly.

"You did something else?"

"Yes, I—I showed Beverly where the ammunition was."

"The ammunition?"

"Yes, in case the trick-or-treaters got out of hand."

"And then you left, for the Top of the Tower?"

"Well, I left to pick up Sharon Rinehart, a friend of mine, before heading downtown."

"What time did you leave the house?"

"Oh, it would have been a little after seven P.M., because I was supposed to pick up Sharon at seven thirty."

"And is that what you did?"

"Yes. As I recall, we got to the Tower about eight o'clock, which was when the party was supposed to start."

"What kind of party was it?"

"Well, it was—you know, a Halloween party."

"Who was invited?"

"Oh, it was some of the brokers, their staffs, and some clients."

"Did you have any concerns about going there?"

"Yes. Ordinarily, I wouldn't even go out on Devil's Night, with all the violence and danger. In fact, I wasn't originally going to go to this, but Sharon finally convinced me it would be safe because we could park in the parking garage right by the elevator and go straight up to the top floor without ever really being outside."

"What kinds of festivities occurred at this party?"

"The usual kind of thing—eating, drinking, people wearing all kinds of costumes. Some were doing designer drugs. Later, we watched the fireworks all over town. From our vantage point, it seemed like they were going off all around us. It was quite remarkable, impressive."

"For the court's benefit, please explain what you mean by fireworks. Do you mean the exploding, pyrotechnic kind?"

"Oh, there was that too. But mainly it was the pyromaniac kind—the arson fires breaking out all over the city."

"Did you enjoy it?"

At this, Cavanaugh stood up with a pained expression. "Must we, Your Honor?"

"Mr. Sawyer?" McBride prompted.

"Establishing state of mind, Your Honor," the proscecutor said smoothly.

"Very well. Proceed."

Cavanaugh sat down tiredly, and Ms. King resumed where she had left off.

"Well, it was pretty exciting. I'd never realized quite how—oh, beautiful—it could be."

"Then did something happen to—alter—the evening?"

"Yes, I met a stranger there. She was a fortune-teller—a real accredited psychic."

Ms. King suddenly looked downward, as if struggling with her composure.

"Did you converse with this person, this psychic?"

"Yes," she said, her voice faltering.

"First, what was her name?"

"Elizabeth Morningstar. She—she's a pretty well known clairvoyant in this area."

"And what was the nature of the conversation?"

"She was doing readings for people—mostly financial predictions for the big wheelers and dealers. But she also did a reading for Sharon, and I thought it would be fun to do it myself."

"Go on."

"But when this Elizabeth started to tune in, she kind of shuddered and stiffened and then gave me a horrible look. She tried to pretend that she couldn't pick up anything on me, but I knew she was lying. I just knew it was something terrible and she didn't want to tell me."

"How did you know that?"

"I just felt it. I'm a very . . . intuitive person."

"So, what finally happened?"

"I just reached out and grabbed her arm and told her I knew she was lying and that I wouldn't let go until she told me the truth. But she still wouldn't say anything, and I was becoming frantic. Somehow, I was sure I knew what the problem was, and I said, 'It's my boy, isn't it?' She didn't say anything, but she didn't have to. I just knew."

"Then what?"

"Then I let go of her, and I raced to a telephone. I called home, but there was no answer. So I grabbed Sharon, and we ran out of that place all the way to my car. And then I drove home as fast as I could."

"How fast, would you guess?"

"I can't—uh—really say. But I wasn't obeying a lot of traffic signs, let me put it that way."

"What did you find when you got there?"

"Blood on the porch. Big furry pieces from a gorilla suit. And inside the house Beverly was unconscious on the living room floor. Joshua, of course, was gone."

"What did you believe had happened?"

"Obviously, it appeared that someone had kidnapped Joshua after a fight with Beverly. They probably masqueraded as trick-or-treaters, and one of them got shot. Beverly shot one of them."

"You say 'they.' How many did you think there were?"

"Three."

"How do you know that?"

"Beverly told me later when she came to."

"What else did Beverly tell you about the incident?"

"Objection!" Cavanaugh volleyed from his table. "Hearsay."

"Sustained," McBride agreed. "The witness may answer a more specific question about such an exchange, but you are advised to have the other party attest to her own experiences. The court will be glad to hear that witness when you call her, Mr. Sawyer."

★ ★ ★

During the late afternoon recess, the final one of the day, McBride felt the need for a stretch and some air. Having shed his robe, he ducked down the hall toward the staff elevator for an anonymous trip outside into the mezzanine courtyard. It would be helpful to clear his head.

The minute he stepped outside onto the sunny, shrubbed plaza, he sensed that something was wrong. Heads turned in his direction.

"There he is," someone said.

Two figures quickly intercepted him, one hoisting a television camera. The other, a shapely black woman in an expensive pants suit, looked awfully familiar. A red light activated on the camera.

"Corrie Washington, Watt Cable Network," said the woman. "Judge McBride?"

"Yes," McBride admitted warily, plotting his exit.

He recognized the woman now, a well known ambush interviewer from L.A. who specialized in sex-and-violence stories. Her weekly half hour—"The Washington Report"—was probably WCN's closest approximation of investigative journalism. McBride wondered briefly if her network called these cases "creepers" too.

A curious crowd was beginning to gather.

"Judge McBride, some people are calling this 'Spooks of Millersfield' case of yours a twenty-first century witch-hunt," Washington began. "Now—"

McBride would have none of it. "No comment."

"Excuse me," the woman said, blocking his path, "but how much do you make?"

"Not enough to talk to you," McBride snapped, angry almost before he knew what had happened. That might have been what she had intended, he realized.

He had turned to go, but thinking better of it, stopped and said, "Certainly you understand that a sitting judge may in no way comment on a case actively before him."

That might have been a mistake. Now he was totally hemmed in. The curious had filled in the space behind him, and Corrie Washington closed the last distance in front of him.

"Understood," she said, pointing the microphone at herself for the moment. "Let me ask you about your fair city of Columbus."

McBride didn't know what to say, and there was nowhere to go. She was so close now, he could smell her perfume. It reminded him of spoiled fruit.

"Why has Columbus been called—" she glanced down at a notepad "—the 'jaywalking capital of America'?"

The microphone was now in his face. McBride knew what she wanted him to say—that it wasn't because people jaywalked so much in Columbus, but because such laws were so strictly enforced, at least once upon a time. But he knew better than to get drawn in.

"Sorry," he said calmly. "That's not my department."

"Speaking of your department," Ms. Washington continued deftly, "I am told that when you left the Organized Crime Division of the Ohio Attorney General's office, that the department was in shambles. Some say that's why you left the department to take a political appointment to the Common Pleas bench."

His temperature was shooting back up. "Is that a question?"

"It is now. Isn't it true that just before you left there as division deputy, the department was running a financial deficit while staff members were being shaken down for political contributions?"

It was an outrageous assortment of half-truths.

"No comment," he said through his teeth. "You've got your facts all wrong."

"And is it not also true," the woman persisted as if she had hooked him, "that in the wake of these scandals, you were, in fact, asked to resign?"

Maddeningly, it was not all that far from the truth. He had been, in fact, given the heave-ho along with a few others when the legislature scrapped the appropriation and the AG mothballed the division. But there were no "scandals," though there probably should have been.

"Look," McBride said, struggling for control, "until you get your facts straight—"

That was when the bug flew into his mouth and bounced off the back of his throat, lodging somewhere between his cheek and gum.

Corrie Washington, looking immensely pleased, stepped back to let the cameraperson get a closer shot of his facial contortions.

McBride spun around in hopes of finding a place to spit—and knocked over a small child who had been standing behind him alongside her mother. The toddler, arms thrust pathetically in the air, began to wail.

At least the camera had found another place to focus its attention while McBride beat his retreat, ignominiously elbowing his way through the crowd. A calmer part of him wondered if this had been a set-up and, if so, just how Corrie Washington had known to catch him there.

6

After scanning the last rows of Gunnison Auditorium for the umpteenth time, Rick Stillman finally gave up craning about, looking for Judith, and settled down into his own back-row seat. Why had he even expected she would show up? This was not her kind of thing. Nor was it his. So why was *he* here?

He wasn't developing an "open mind," was he? No, he had no intention of giving Jeremy Kay's chic philosophy any real consideration. Call it morbid fascination. Or was it pride? Maybe he just wanted to see what the competition looked like.

And then his heart lurched. Across the auditorium he spied her—auburn-haired Moira. Was she with someone? Peering more intently, he could see that she seemed to be in the company of a pair of colleagues he thought he recognized but could not name. Stillman was surprised by the extent of his relief. What if she had been with another man? Or another woman, for that matter? He must reconcile himself to the fact that it was only a matter of time before something like that would happen.

But it still hurt, desperately and nearly undiminished from a year ago. When would it ever end? What enchantress could remove this Moira-spell that still bound him? He didn't care if it involved smoke and mirrors or eyes-of-newts and toes-of-frogs. He needed relief, surcease of sorrow for this lost Lenore.

ALEX was helping him cope with the junk in the attic, but he really needed to conduct a thorough housecleaning. He wanted his heart to stop aching. He wanted to be alone without being haunted by memories, regret, and desolation. He wanted to go out in public again without wondering whether he would see Her.

But now the house lights were dimming, and the last people were finding their seats more purposefully. Something appeared to be happening behind the podium on stage.

Suddenly he was aware of someone slipping into the next seat on his left.

"Hi, Rick," breathed Judith Hurley-McBride.

And then they were introducing Jeremy Kay as one of the great thinkers of the twenty-first century, a pillar of the school of Metapersonal Psychology and author of the celebrated book *Hologram: Appropriating Divinity.*

Out of the shadows glided a tallish, spare man with bushy blond hair, a professional smile with perfect teeth, frameless eyeglasses, jeans, black turtleneck sweater, and tweed sports coat.

Jeremy Kay launched quickly into an overview of the development of Western science, philosophy, religion, and psychology in what he called their "alienated" approaches to the universe. As Stillman listened, he was impressed despite himself. There was something elusively compelling, almost captivating, about this man. He wasn't buying a bit of it, but still he was enthralled by Kay's straightforward manner of presenting these esoteric themes. It may have been farfetched, but it was certainly not dull.

Kay seemed fond of phrases such as "ultimate reality" and "discrete consciousness." Stillman had heard most of it before—it was Hinduism warmed over, actually. Kay's central point seemed to be that matter and phenomena were illusion while mind and experience were real. More than that, it seemed that Mind was one substance, according to this neo-Hindu worldview, with billions of partakers convinced, mistakenly, of their separate identities. Stillman wondered how any of this really could be new to the intellectual groupies and true believers.

Then Kay began pulling the threads together. "The ultimate challenge to the myth of discrete consciousness," he asserted, "is the doctrine of reincarnation. If I could somehow demonstrate to your satisfaction reincarnation at work in a test tube, we could all agree on the fallacy of discrete consciousness.

"But let me ask how many here tonight believe in reincarnation. Let me see hands."

Only a sprinkling of hands went up in the cavernous auditorium.

"All right. Now for Demonstration Number One. If I were to tell you that in a previous life Jeremy Kay was Warka Izdubar, prophet of the great fire god Baal in the twelfth century B.C., some of you probably would think I was unhinged. But if one of you could talk with Warka Izdubar and ask him questions, perhaps it might be more persuasive. And that's the purpose of our demonstration. First, I need a volunteer."

Several aisles over, a slender, young woman with short, dark hair breezed toward the stage. Stillman gasped when he realized that this was their very own Angela Hurley.

Angie climbed the six short steps to join Kay, who by this time was seated in an ordinary straight chair, a blank expression on his face. The two conferred briefly off mike.

Then the houselights were extinguished, and a rosy spotlight softly bathed Kay, who appeared to be drifting into some kind of trance.

Stillman shot a glance at Judith, who bore a rapt expression.

After a long moment, Kay stiffened visibly, and Angie took a step back.

"State your request," Kay boomed in an unpleasant voice clearly not his own.

It wasn't like an impressionist's art. It was much different, more hollow, as if emanating from a different source. It gave Stillman the creeps.

Hesitantly, Angie moved in closer, near a microphone. "Where is Jeremy Kay?" she asked, her amplified voice tremulous in the hushed auditorium.

"Jeremy Kay is . . . not yet," the voice asserted strangely, like an oracle from some other time and place.

"Who—are you?" Angie managed to ask.

"I am Warka Izdubar, servant of the great god Baal."

"Do you know who I am?"

"Angela McBride, a daughter of the Goddess. What do you require?"

It took Angie a long moment to formulate a response.

"Can you . . . see my future?"

There was a pause just long enough for Stillman to wonder if Warka was rejecting the frivolous question.

Then the voice boomed again. "You pass through a life-changing door. Choose carefully."

"Where are we now?" Angie turned to survey the rows of seats but obviously found them nearly obscured by the darkness and the glare of the spotlight.

"The temple of worship of the great god Baal. Draw near and bow down!"

Angie took a halting step forward and stiffly lowered herself to one knee as if part of her were resisting the act. Then down went the other knee, and finally Angie was bowed in complete obeisance, her arms extended palm down and her face inches from the stage floor.

This time the terrible voice of Warka Izdubar commanded, "Receive the spirit of Ashtoreth!"

For a long moment, there was nothing but chilling silence that fairly begged for relief. Suddenly, Angie emitted a muffled little cry, staggered to her feet, and fled ingloriously from the stage in obvious fright. The spotlight winked off, and Kay was left alone in the shadows, slumped in his chair. Awful silence reigned again in the hall for a long moment.

But then Kay began to stir, and in another instant he was on his feet, moving slowly back to the podium amid murmurs from the audience.

"Now," he said in quite his own voice, "lest anyone think this little channeling demonstration was mere theatrics, witness Demonstration Number Two. This one is a group activity, but don't worry. We're not going to take any of you back to previous lives. Those of you open to hypnosis, however, may be regressed to the actual moment of your own birth. This is a technique similar to what's done in rebirthing therapy, with which some of you may be familiar."

First, Kay conducted an exercise to determine which members of the audience were sufficiently suggestible to experience deep hypnosis. With everyone on his feet, he droned on for a minute or two about relaxation, then asked everyone to raise one arm. He then suggested that the arm had become rigid and would not go back down. Those whose arms had fallen were asked to take their seats. About half sat down. Judith remained standing with her arm straight in the air.

Stillman, back in his seat, could only wonder what was going on in Judith's mind.

* * *

Often in her dreams Judith became convinced that the events were real and she was actually awake. This seemed to be almost the reverse—she was awake, but somehow events seemed unreal, as if she were dreaming. While she knew it was illogical for her arm to be stuck in the air, she seemed to have forgotten how to will it back to her side. She wondered vaguely if her entire body would levitate if Kay suggested that. Somehow, anything seemed possible.

Kay was speaking again, this time suggesting that they were in first grade with their hands raised to get their teacher's attention. He told them to remember how small and timid they felt among an entire school of bigger children.

Judith suddenly felt small and vulnerable. She also felt as if she had to go to the bathroom. Maybe that was why her hand was raised.

Kay told them to sit down but with their hands still raised. Next, he suggested that they desired to return to their mothers, to be safe and warm, cradled in the womb. He told them to begin letting their arms sink slowly back to their sides and that when their arms were all the way down, they would be back inside their mothers.

* * *

Judith felt weightless, floating in a warm, enveloping sea that provided all her needs unbidden.

Existence was a kitten curled in the sunlight, a timeless slumber in which the universe existed solely for her benefit. She felt peace and contentment that surpassed anything else she had ever known. She desired to stay here forever.

But gradually she became aware of a low whirring, a vibrational disturbance in her sea of tranquillity that grew with each passing second. And then she realized with a shock of horror that there was danger here—mortal peril.

But it was too late.

* * *

Stillman had never seen anyone this out of control. Her screams reverberated hysterically in the auditorium, causing all heads to turn to the seat next to his, where Judith, eyes tightly shut, was falling rapidly to pieces. He was frozen initially by the shock of it all, but when she began to move, he knew he had to do something. She looked as if she might do anything, like climb over the backs of seats and step in people's laps.

As in a bad dream, Stillman found himself reacting almost without thinking. He grabbed Judith by the arm and pushed her roughly through to the end of their row, tromping on toes all the way out. Even so, their neighbors seemed glad to have them gone.

He propelled her toward the auditorium exit, as far from the staring eyes of the curious as quickly as possible. Perhaps out in the hall she would quiet down. At least she was still ambulatory.

Unfortunately, the situation showed no improvement in the lobby. If anything, it was worse. Stillman felt as if his eardrums would rupture from her point-blank shrieks. Her violent movements were turning his attempts to restrain her into a wrestling match. He was giving serious consideration to slapping her face when Judith abruptly slumped to the floor, where she continued her writhing and wailing in a horizontal position.

About the time Stillman feared she was about to convulse into a full-blown seizure, a crowd began to gather. Great. He found himself almost wanting to slap other faces. But finally two uniformed security guards appeared, to his great relief.

"Let's clear out!" one of them, a large black man, barked at the onlookers.

The front line of the curious immediately dropped back several paces, and the crowd began to disperse. Just as quickly, the security men had Judith on her feet and moving toward a far door.

The other guard looked back at Stillman, who was trying to catch up. "Paramedics are on the way."

They, at least, would know what to do. Stillman certainly didn't.

* * *

Dawn found a bleary-eyed Rick Stillman alone in his office, once again the sole inhabitant of the desolate building. Feeling increasingly like some kind of recluse, Rick mused that if he died he should take up residence as the ghost of Grady Hall.

After the traumatic events of last night, he had been quite unable to find sleep in his own bed at home and was unwilling to sedate himself chemically, as most would do in such circumstances. In fact, he stocked no such substances in his medicine cabinet. Thus, he had ended up back at Grady Hall, dozing for thirty minutes here, ten minutes there, on his office couch—no heated waterbed, to be sure, but ordinarily comfortable enough for modest slumbers.

He still did not know quite what to think, though the improbable images remained before his eyes and the echoes of Judith's screams still rang in his ears. He had followed the ambulance and called Neal McBride on his carphone to inform him of the problem. As soon as the judge had arrived at the Riverside Hospital emergency department, Stillman took his leave. He told himself it probably wouldn't take more than a shot of some modern elixir to straighten Judith out again.

But if he really believed that, then why was he now restlessly greeting the dawn with ALEX?

Rick Stillman did not consider himself a workaholic, but he did believe in the therapeutic value of labor and giving himself to a larger cause. Maybe he couldn't do much to help Judith directly just now, but he certainly could get cracking on that project proposal that so concerned her. And if he couldn't sleep, anyway . . .

First, he needed to confirm that the whole idea was even doable.

This time, ALEX was in conventional linguistics mode, illuminating the wallscreen with the more familiar, statuesque figure of Botticelli's *Venus* emergent from the sea.

"Awaiting instruction," ALEX pronounced evenly.

"Dick and Jane—*aleph, beth, gimmel, daleth,*" Stillman responded.

On the wall, foam-borne Aphrodite flicked off, replaced by the sandy-haired figures of a mid-twentieth century grade-school boy pulling a wagon and a girl clutching a doll.

"Kehn," he told ALEX.

"Oui, ja, si, da," the computer intoned, differentiating the inflections as it formed the characters on the screen.

"R'ay Spot *rahtz."*

Instantly, he saw parallel columns in French, German, Spanish, and Russian, all stating essentially, "Observe the canine named Spot proceeding rapidly."

So far, so good. Squinting at the first page of the old book in the subdued light, Stillman took a deep breath and plunged ahead, reading from right to left.

"B'raysheeth barah Elohim eyth hashamayim v'eyth haahretz." And as he did so, the Hebrew characters appeared across the bottom of the screen.

But when the Euro-verbiage began tracking down the four columns, things clearly did not look right.

Stillman called for the English, which only confirmed his suspicions.

In the beginning . . . N/A . . .
created the . . . N/A . . .and the earth.

"Give me a break." Stillman groaned, leaving the desk to begin pacing about the room. He called for ALEX to reveal the display coding format.

M39 ○ A104 ○ S0000 ○ R2 ○ C0000 ○ R5 ○ R2 ○ C2

Trouble. He frowned at the goose eggs. That was not a good sign so soon. He had ALEX rerun the translation program several different ways, but the result was still blanks and zeroes.

Cybersynchronics was a wonderful system, but it was admittedly the product of an Indo-European mind—his, mostly—and he had learned to expect trouble anytime he ventured beyond that framework. That was where Judith Hurley-McBride, the renowned Afro-Asian expert, was indispensable. He had hoped this new project might provide the opportunity to expand ALEX's capabilities in that area.

He was becoming increasingly acquainted with discouragement. Neither he nor Judith could untangle this one alone. Only the two of them, working together, would have a chance. But would that be possible under the circumstances?

* * *

An insistent noise alerted Stillman to the fact that he must have dozed off. Just when sleep was within his grasp, someone was plucking it from him again.

It was the bleating of a phone line, but not from an outside call. A communications light on the computer panel told him it was an intracom from another office.

"Connect, ALEX," he directed, blinking sleepily.

Well, well. Speak of the devil. Onscreen materialized the familiar cold blue eyes of Julian Wickner, one of the more ambitious—and devious—staffers in Anthropology and a close comrade of Jared Quang.

"Hope I'm not intruding, Doctor Stillman," said Wickner insincerely.

"Of course not," Stillman said with equal conviction.

Wickner got right to the point.

"Judith is quite ill. In fact, she's—uh—confined in the mental health unit at Riverside."

Stillman was too stunned to speak, and his face must have shown it. He had assumed that she would be home by this time, resting in her own bed—or, in the worst scenario, taking some other treatment in a regular hospital wing. "Confined" and "mental health" were words he did not want to hear together in the same sentence.

"Now, before we jump to any conclusions," Wickner interjected, "you'll recall that Judith has had these little episodes with depression before. This may be a bit more serious, but there's no reason to believe she won't bounce back again. It's probably just a matter of time. I've spoken with her doctor, and he assures me it's a treatable condition.

"The main thing we can do to help her is to make sure that the Linguistics Division stays a steady course so she can sort of ease back into her responsibilities when the time comes."

"Yes," Stillman agreed, wondering what the man was leading up to.

"Rick, Paul has asked me to take temporary charge of the division. Now, I objected that you were the more logical person to assume those duties, but he insisted that he didn't want Judith to think that we were—well, grooming a replacement for her. I think you can appreciate that."

So that was it.

"Certainly."

"So my plan is to let you call the shots, so to speak, but anything on paper will come from me. Follow what I'm saying?"

"Absolutely." He was secretly relieved that he apparently was being spared the onerous task of full administrative responsibility.

"This, of course, means an increase in your duties, which will be appropriately compensated. But the main thing to bear in mind during this period is to keep your schedule as clear as possible. In other words, this is not a time to be chasing any Nobel prizes, if you know what I mean."

"Oh, sure. So, can Judith have visitors?"

"I'm afraid not," Wickner said, minus an understanding smile. "Not for a while. And I'm sure we wouldn't want to burden her with work-related concerns at a time like this anyway."

Suddenly Stillman recalled just how much he disliked Wickner's oily ways. But he held his tongue.

"Well," Wickner said with an air of finality, "there are bunches of logistical things we need to work out, but we can address them as they come, starting tomorrow."

"I'll be—at your disposal," Stillman said uncomfortably.

"Righto. G'day."

Wickner's visage dissipated from the screen.

Stillman felt somewhat at a loss—and not solely because of Judith's predicament. Somehow, he had a strange feeling that the Bible translation project was just the kind of thing he would be expected not to engage himself in just now. Though he'd be terribly surprised if Wickner knew anything about that, he supposed under the circumstances he had little choice but to pull the plug on it.

7

The view outside McBride's fifteenth-floor office window was almost nonexistent this morning. Rain was coming down like no tomorrow, and all to the eye was variations in gray—like his own mood. He feared greatly for Judith in a way that tended to crowd out other thoughts and concerns.

McBride, then, was not so pleasantly surprised when, for the second time in a week, Sylvia intercommed, "Steve Leadingham for you."

In fact, he started to tell her not to put the call through, then relented.

There was an evil gleam in Leadingham's eyes this time when he chimed, "Hey, Crimefighter!"

"Hi, Steve," McBride said wearily.

"Hey, next time I have the gang over, can I call you up to do your rubberface routine before the girl jumps out of the cake?"

"What?" McBride was in no mood for fooling around. "What rubberface routine?"

"Come on, TV star!" Leadingham teased. "You're not trying to tell me you didn't watch your own coast-to-coast show last night?"

McBride, suddenly recalling the whole Corrie Washington debacle, began to redden.

"How bad was it?" he said, wincing.

"It was a scream. What were you doing at the end—sucking a lemon?"

"Of course not. I was eating a bug."

"What? Say, why did you tell Corrie Washington you never worked for the department?"

"I what? No, that's not what I said."

"Bet me. In fact, I've got the recording to prove it."

"I'd like to see *that*."

Leadingham appeared to be manipulating something off-screen. "Your wish is my command—roll 'em!"

With that, Leadingham's image was replaced with that of Corrie Washington and a lead-in to the Columbus "Spooks" trial, including some comparisons to the seventeenth-century witchcraft inquisition in Salem, Mass. That was just for starters. After some unenlightening person-on-the-street mini-interviews pointing up the small-minded, mean-spirited attitudes of the fair city of Columbus, she got to McBride.

It started with some Corrie Washington commentary about the sad financial state of the Franklin County court system, apparently through world-class mismanagement. The clear implication was that this was the bench from hell, intent on persecuting innocent victims—minority groups, especially—in order to line its own coffers.

And how much do Franklin County Common Pleas judges make? "Not enough," snapped an unpleasant-looking Wilson N. McBride, the judge presiding in the "Spooks" trial.

Corrie Washington then proceeded to enumerate McBride's salary and perks, which actually sounded pretty impressive in this context. Her barbed voice-over continued while an image of the McBride house appeared onscreen, shot from almost ground level so that it appeared to loom over everything like a Georgian mansion.

Speaking of mismanagement, Washington segued into some barely recognizable background on the demise of the AG's Organized Crime Division and McBride's implied role in the collapse.

"But when interviewed, Judge McBride denied any connection to that office," Washington said coyly.

McBride's face again appeared on the screen momentarily. "That's not my department," he said brazenly.

But Washington triumphantly held up a fistful of documents "proving" that McBride had, in fact, been *deputy director* of the unit during the period when the mismanagement and financial troubles were brewing. Washington somberly revealed that even when confronted with the evidence, Judge McBride continued to evade, deny, prevaricate—and steamroll.

There followed a full-face close-up of McBride, looking as if his mouth, eyes, and nose were having a serious disagreement and were attempting to take their leave in separate directions. He looked almost as if he were about to spit at the camera.

Then came the low point—the shameful sight of his nearly trampling a toddler who was left sobbing in his wake.

Leadingham came back onscreen. "I suppose you're going to say you were raped."

"I was raped," he said, stunned.

"Nevertheless, you did say—"

"I may have said those *words*, but that's not what they meant."

"Well, it certainly made no sense that you'd deny working for the department."

"I didn't."

"Yeah. Well, I guess I won't tell you I told you so."

"Then I guess I won't tell you to drop dead."

"Easy, pal, easy!" said Leadingham. "I'm just tryin' to be helpful."

"Sure," McBride said, softening. "It's just—when it rains, it pours. I wasn't watching for Corrie Washington last night because Judith . . . had another breakdown—and she was put in lock-up this time."

Leadingham's eyebrows rose and the playfulness went out of his voice. "Oh? Sorry to hear. What . . . happened?"

McBride recounted the events beginning with the late-night phone call from Rick Stillman summoning him to the hospital, where Judith had been taken after having some kind of hysterical episode at a psychology lecture.

"Some 'psychology,'" Leadingham observed.

By the time he had arrived at Riverside, McBride explained, Judith was so heavily sedated that they all but refused to let him see her. At least, that was how he interpreted the tense incident.

"And speaking of psychology," said McBride, "it's past time for me to check in with the psych-persons."

Leadingham made his obligatory offer of help, but, of course, what really could he do? He also apologized, sort of, for rubbing it in with the Corrie Washington/rubberface incident, although McBride was still out of his mind, Leadingham asserted, for opening himself up for that kind of grief.

As soon as he was able to get Leadingham off the line, McBride instructed Jack Irwin to inform the parties that there would be a slight delay in the morning proceedings. He then had Sylvia set up a quick teleconference at the Riverside Community Mental Health Center with Dr. Hamadi, who was expecting his call.

The psychiatrist was a diminutive doctor in his mid-fifties with a piercing gaze through severe, metal-framed bifocals. He quickly explained that Judith had not been coherent since her episode of the night before and was still on sedation. Her earliest statements had indicated some extreme fear for her physical safety.

"In fact, she believed that some device was trying to mutilate her and that some of her body parts already had been severed," Hamadi recited in lilting tones from his notes. "Today, however, her attitude is much changed, though not necessarily improved. Now, your wife seems to be under the . . . impression that she is going to have a baby."

McBride's fingers involuntarily tightened on his chair, and a gathering in his chest made breathing uncomfortable.

"We did a routine blood test just to be certain, and, of course, it was negative. Do you have any idea of any objective reasons she might be under such an impression?"

"None," McBride attested. "Absolutely none."

"Well," Hamadi said with a faint sigh, "we may well get some kind of answer in due course. I will be consulting, of course, with her personal physician-therapist, Doctor Selena Goren, later this morning to get the details on her recent history. Let me transfer you now to your wife. Just be careful not to argue with her about the things she believes. That doesn't mean you have to agree with everything; just try to avoid upsetting her."

Abruptly the picture switched to Judith's bedside. Hurley-McBride appeared fatigued and somewhat disheveled in her green hospital gown, but she managed a weak smile at McBride's appearing.

"How do you feel, sweetheart?"

"OK, I guess. Please don't call me 'sweetheart.'"

That was a good sign. "Sorry."

"Did they tell you the news?"

Her voice sounded a bit draggy and almost muffled.

"No, dear."

"We're going to have a baby," she said with a weak smile.

McBride nodded. "That's . . . wonderful, dear. Are you . . . sure?"

"Oh, yes," she murmured, glancing down at her tummy, where her fingertips rested. "I think it's a boy, but it doesn't matter."

"Oh?"

"It'll be either Max or Maxine. Maybe Maxie." She looked up questioningly. "You like those names, don't you?"

McBride nodded again, uncomfortably. "Yes, dear."

"Maxie," she pronounced softly, fondly, looking down again. "Maxie."

After a moment, McBride broke the awkward silence.

"Is there anything you need? Anything I can do?"

"No. Well, maybe one thing."

"Yes?"

"This medication they're giving me. Can you get them to stop it? You're not supposed to be taking medicine when you're pregnant."

"I'll speak to them about it, dear," McBride assured her. "But I'm sure they wouldn't give you anything harmful."

She seemed to accept that and sank back against the pillow tiredly.

He took that as his cue to depart. "Good-bye, dear."

"Maxie," he thought he heard her say before the picture winked off.

* * *

McBride, glancing at the clock, hastily scooped up his notes, shrugged into his robe, and swept out the office door to the bench. He appreciated punctuality in his courtroom, and he felt a responsibility to apply the same standard in his own conduct.

Yet even with the brief delay, both defense and prosecution tables appeared to be in considerable disarray, a condition that did not substantially improve after the bailiff's call to order. Jeremiah Cavanaugh requested permission to approach the bench. Al Sawyer, his opposite number, joined him for the conference, wearing a bewildered expression.

"Your Honor," said Cavanaugh. "I move for a directed verdict of acquittal in the State of Ohio versus Roger V. Larrabee."

"On what grounds, counselor?" asked McBride, caught somewhat offguard.

"Lack of material evidence to connect this defendant in any tangible way to the alleged crime," said Cavanaugh a tad smugly, as if stating the obvious.

"Motion denied," McBride pronounced firmly and without hesitation. "And for your information, Mr. Cavanaugh, there is nothing 'alleged' about this crime. An infant boy is dead as the result of an incident officially held to be a homicide. The only matter in question is the culpability of Mr. Larrabee. We've already heard testimony from Zona Corban that there are witnesses—chiefly Mr. Lothar Eckart—to the homicide itself. And I believe that Mr. Eckart is to be the next witness after Ms. Cunningham, the babysitter.

"Is that correct, Mr. Sawyer?"

"Yes, Your Honor, but—"

"Well, then, Mr. Sawyer, I suggest you call your witness."

Sawyer, who had been glancing over his shoulder from time to time, conferred in whispers with an associate before turning back to the bench.

"Your Honor," he said, looking as if someone had eaten his lunch, "Ms. Cunningham has not shown up here at court yet, and nobody seems to know her whereabouts."

"So what's being done about this?" asked McBride with growing irritation.

"We're checking," Sawyer said with a shrug.

"Checking? How about calling another witness out of order?"

Sawyer looked a bit embarrassed. "I . . . don't believe we're prepared to do that just yet."

Now McBride was truly vexed. "The court calls a brief recess," he declared sharply, "until ten fifteen."

With a crack of the McBride gavel, the courtroom began to clear.

* * *

In the unscheduled hiatus, McBride leaned against his chamber window, rubbing his dully aching temples and peering into the rainy distance. Through the fog, the Scioto River and the morning sun were only a suspicion.

In another minute, his troubled thoughts were escaping once again to mountains, plains, and trails in Montana and Wyoming, vast spaces where man's significance paled and the law was still pretty much a man with a badge. Except maybe in the big towns, there was still a belief in those parts that men should handle their own problems among themselves without taking everybody and his brother to court.

Here in the Rust Belt, he thought ruefully, it was just about the reverse. It seemed that most people were involved in lawsuits at one time or another, while real crime flourished far beyond the means to contain it. Which was a good reason, he realized, that people desperately seeking justice frequently went outside the law enforcement system to private operators like Jimmy Shapiro and his protégés.

At this point, McBride was beginning to wonder why he'd ever left that career behind. But in terms of regrets, his biggest one was Judith.

He longed to hold her and comfort her in her confusion, and he wanted her back for his own sake. He was learning the sad truth about a heart's growing fonder.

And if things turned out the way he feared, he would be experiencing a great deal more of such sad truth before all this was over.

★ ★ ★

By ten o'clock it was becoming apparent that this recess was not likely to be so brief after all.

If anything, the mystery was deepening. Reports from the prosecutor's office indicated no success in locating Beverly Cunningham. In fact, the woman's relatives had contacted the police out of their own concern for her whereabouts.

McBride assigned Jack Irwin to check on progress toward rounding up the next witnesses after Cunningham.

When the older man returned, McBride was filled with a sense that Jack had failed in his mission.

Actually, it was worse than that.

"Dead," Jack said, shaking his head in unbelief.

"Dead?" McBride repeated. "Beverly Cunningham?"

"No," said Jack. "That dancer—Zona what's-her-name."

It turned out that while Beverly Cunningham remained missing in action, Zona Corban/Leah Andrews had been discovered brutally slain in a field near Millersfield. Jack Irwin had been informed of that development while talking to the police in regard to a new bomb scare at the county Justice Center, which everybody had chosen to treat as a crank call.

McBride, now thoroughly alarmed, switched to damage-control mode and reluctantly called an indefinite recess to the proceeding. Under the circumstances he feared Cavanaugh's next move would be a motion for mistrial. That one would be harder to resist.

At this point, it might even be inevitable.

* * *

Later, in the privacy of his chambers, McBride had occasion to wonder about coincidences and connections, unseen forces, and invisible hands. Zona Corban. Beverly Cunningham. Judith. The bomb scare that nobody took seriously. The mysterious threatening call he himself had received.

Not that he was about to be intimidated by such veiled threats. True, the caller clearly had seemed intent on halting the prosecution of Roger Larrabee—which, in fact, had now occurred. But the implied threat itself had seemed to be directed against McBride's own family—not witnesses in the case. He might have to poll the jury and see if any members had received threatening phone calls.

Judith herself certainly had experienced a serious reversal, but that wasn't totally without precedent for her—nor something that someone could inflict upon her. Car bombings and drive-by shootings he could understand. But this kind of mental aberration—who could say where such afflictions originated? He certainly couldn't blame them on goblins and gremlins.

Things truly were unraveling. Jack entered, his pensive eyes looking like anything but good news.

"Yeah, Jack?"

"Add Eckart to your MIA list."

"Terrific," McBride said gloomily. "What's being done?"

"Captain Thomas said Second District would get right on it,

but don't hold your breath. I have my doubts that they've done all that much yet about Cunningham."

Calling Eckart, who had been granted immunity in exchange for testifying against Larrabee, was supposed to be Plan B in Cunningham's absence. McBride wondered how long this could go on. What could happen next?

Just as Jack was leaving, Sylvia slipped in.

"May I have a word with you?" she asked, looking a bit overwhelmed. Silently, she held up a fistful of pink message slips.

McBride lifted his eyebrows quizzically. "All for me?"

Sylvia nodded. "You're a very popular man today—especially with the media. These are all requests for interviews."

He pursed his lips and nodded. "Corrie Washington," he noted elliptically.

"I told them all that under no circumstances does Judge McBride comment on court matters," Sylvia continued dryly, "and, of course, most of them insisted that they wouldn't dream of asking about this 'Spooks' case, but just—"

"Just for 'background,'" he said, finishing the sentence for her. "Right."

Sylvia just gave him a funny look.

McBride was becoming aware of a mounting distraction, an almost rhythmic murmur seeping through the walls. He cocked his head. "What's that?"

"That's the other thing. We've got a bunch of demonstrators out in the hall—came up one by one and assembled on this floor. They'll have different security arrangements tomorrow, but tonight we'll have to leave with escorts."

"What kind of demonstrators?"

"I don't know." Sylvia gave the intercom a voice command, and a moment later Jack Irwin was responding.

Jack said it was the usual—students, deprogrammers, Witches' Rights activists, and a few of the regular hangers-on. Their common demand seemed to be the ouster of Wilson Neal McBride.

McBride shook his head faintly. "OK. Thanks, Sylvia."

They don't know Wilson Neal McBride, he thought.

8

Rick Stillman took a deep breath and steeled himself before marching into the Polo Room. That was his name for the pseudo-aristocratic parlor with velour draperies, high-backed chairs, and brass chandelier just off the first-floor lobby of Grady Hall, where university trustees and other visiting dignitaries generally were received.

Might as well get this over with, he told himself, as he prepared to greet the two emissaries from the Rhema Institute. As much as he disliked the idea, he felt he had little choice but to cut these gentlemen loose. It was just a shame that they had wasted the trip. Stillman realized he should have thought of it sooner, but they would just have to understand about Judith's illness and the resulting confusion.

Two men rose as he entered, one a black male of medium height in a smartly tailored gray business suit, the other a tall, chunky white male with dark, curly hair and beard, and black-rimmed glasses, whose attire appeared a bit less premeditated. At least they didn't *look* like fire-breathing fanatics.

"Rick Stillman," he said, extending his hand to the black man with the merry eyes.

"Darnell Jones." He took Stillman's hand firmly. "Pleased to meet you, Doctor Stillman. Meet my good friend and colleague Aaron Fitzgerald. I'm vice president of operations, and Aaron is director of translation at Rhema—and a fine linguist."

"Oh, but nothing approaching the level of scholarship in this department, I'm sure," said Fitzgerald. He had a decided British accent and an unassuming bearing.

Stillman took an immediate liking to both men, which only complicated things further.

"As I believe Juanita explained to you, Doctor Hurley-

McBride has been sidelined with a . . . sudden illness," he began when they were seated at the smaller conference table. "I can't say when she'll be back and, frankly, that poses a problem for all of us."

He looked up at Jones and Fitzgerald, whose smiles were undiminished.

"Gentlemen," he continued, "I'd like to say that we could do business together, but under the circumstances I don't think that's possible at this time. Please accept my apology for the inconvenience of flying in here for . . . well, nothing."

The other two men remained silently attentive, apparently expecting him to say more.

"It was an unfortunate development that we just couldn't foresee," he continued awkwardly, almost hating himself. "We'll be sure to contact you if things change."

After an exchange of glances, Fitzgerald spoke up.

"My good man—with all due respect to your superior, it was the Sturgis-Stillman synchronic systems that really brought us here in the first place. We're more than willing to work with you alone."

With a suppressed sigh, Stillman quickly attempted to disabuse them about his infallibility. He explained his own limitations regarding the Afro-Asian tongues of Rhema's target groups. And then there was his obligation to assume some of the time-consuming administrative duties of his colleague.

But when Fitzgerald started asking technical questions, he nearly forgot his resolve. He volunteered that his first and only attempt at processing Hebrew into common European had disintegrated into gibberish. Fitzgerald seemed equally baffled until Stillman recalled that the first requested process was for the word *yes*.

Fitzgerald's eyes lit up. "Tell me, what exactly was the Hebrew?"

"Kehn."

Fitzgerald fell silent for a long moment.

"Give me a reference," he said at last.

"A reference—what kind of reference?"

"A biblical reference."

"This wasn't from a biblical reference—just common speech."

"As balmy as this may sound—I can't think of a single instance offhand where a question in Torah or Prophets was answered with a 'yes,'" Fitzgerald said, frowning at Jones.

Jones had an idea. "How about 'Yea, though I walk through the valley'? Doesn't 'yea' mean 'yes'?"

Fitzgerald shook his head. "No, that's *gam*—with the meaning of 'yet,' 'but,' or 'though.'"

Stillman interrupted. "I'm not sure I see the point here."

"The point is," Fitzgerald said, "you may have initiated a process in modern that you expected to be answered in ancient, when there is no actual correspondence."

Stillman instantly saw the problem. "It's like asking a question in Italian and expecting an answer in Latin."

"Quite," Fitzgerald said approvingly.

"But I can't imagine any people—the Hebrews or anybody else—not having a word for 'yes.' Surely they had a word for 'no.'"

"They did—*lo*—same as modern," Fitzgerald said. "I have no idea how your programming deals with such things, but my guess is that you may have really muddled it up by switching signals like that."

"Hmm. Just goes to show my Afro-Asiatic limitations. I wouldn't have thought there was that much difference between biblical and modern." Despite himself, he was becoming intrigued.

Fitzgerald suggested that he start over with a new database, treating modern and ancient Hebrew and Greek as dual subsets of the same base.

"Are you sure you've never been trained in the ALEX system?" Stillman asked pointedly.

Fitzgerald laughed and shook his head. "But the idea of mathematical relationships in biblical languages has been around for centuries."

Stillman was skeptical.

Fitzgerald reminded him of how letters functioned as Roman numerals—I, V, X, and so on—before Arabic numerals invaded Europe. The Greeks had done the same. The Jews even used Hebrew letters for Old Testament chapter and verse "numbering."

Stillman was intrigued when Fitzgerald began describing what happened when nineteenth and twentieth century investigators applied those numerical values—"gematria"— to entire passages of Scripture: "mathematical harmonies" emerged, as words and phrases with related spiritual meanings were shown to be divisible by common factors.

Stillman's creative wheels began turning. Maybe these guys were extremists. But if this phenomenon were true, what possibilities this could present for computerized translating.

On impulse, Stillman stood up and invited his guests to join him across the hall in an unoccupied office where they could access a computer terminal.

To demonstrate his point, Fitzgerald had him direct ALEX to access its Scripture files and display Revelation 13:18.

"Greek only," Fitzgerald called out. "With audio."

As the Greek text appeared on the screen, ALEX simultaneously pronounced the words in the original. Fitzgerald then followed with the unvarnished, literal English.

"'Here wisdom is. The one having reason, let him count the number of the beast; the number of a man, it is.' *Stop!*"

Stillman started. ALEX froze.

"Are you familiar with the Beast and the number 666?" Fitzgerald asked.

"Sort of," Stillman said uncertainly. "Is that the—uh—Antichrist?"

"That's the common interpretation," Fitzgerald agreed. "Continue. 'And the number of it, *chi xi vau.*'"

"Wait. Why don't you give those last words in English?"

"Why don't you?" Fitzgerald handed him a *Webster's* dictionary from the desk between them. "Look in the appendixes under Special Signs and Symbols. Find *chi, xi,* and *vau* in the Greek column and read me back the corresponding Arabic numerals."

On page 1,395 Stillman located the twin columns of letters and numerals and began reading, "Six hundred—sixty—six."

"Oh," he said, looking up sheepishly. "I see: 6-6-6."
His professional curiosity was getting the better of him. "Are you suggesting—"

"I'm suggesting," Fitzgerald interrupted in a low voice, "that you might have a Rosetta Stone with Cybersynchronics, especially considering the mathematical properties of all Scripture."

Whoa. That was the whole problem with the "B" word all over again.

"Personally, I'm just an . . . academician," he began awkwardly. "It's pretty hard for me to handle things like 'mathematical harmonies' when I don't really accept the dogma of inspiration or even—"

"Or even believe in God?" Jones interjected.

Stillman blinked at Jones's brashness. That was, in a sense, the root issue. But somehow he couldn't help liking Jones—both of these men, in fact.

"Look here," Fitzgerald said. "I would challenge you to put the Scriptures to the test and find out for yourself if they hold water. Don't take my word for it. Check it out yourself. Other scholars have done so, and it has changed their lives."

"Here—some reading material," Jones said, handing him some literature.

After the two left, he glanced at the materials Jones had given him, booklets with titles such as *Heaven Is a Free Gift, Christ Died for You,* and *Where Will You Spend Eternity?*

Stillman smiled as if viewing a kindergartner's finger paintings. He started to toss them into the trash, then stopped and stashed them in his valise instead—an action that he would have been hard pressed to explain.

★ ★ ★

The next day Stillman was being haunted by the same two women.

In the night, he'd been tormented anew by dreams of a past life revolving around green-eyed Moira with the auburn hair and her absorption with death. They were jumbled and bittersweet scenarios, as of his love being bound in winding cloths and sealed in an unknown tomb for a thousand years.

And in the morning it was off again to Grady Hall, where he kept anticipating the brilliantly neurotic Judith around each corner, down each hall. And yet he also half expected never to see her again.

Things just seemed to happen that way. People come into your life, you start to love them and then—*poof!* Stillman seemed unable to accept that fact the way others did.

He knew Judith had been prone to depression, but those occasions had been precipitated by real events in her life, hadn't they? The last episode, for example, had occurred on the heels of her father's death two years ago.

So why this time? He had to believe this, too, had been triggered by something. Had it really been Jeremy Kay's dog-and-pony show? Stillman had been sitting right beside Judith at the time. He was no more willing to credit this hypnotic-regression business than he was to accept Kay's "channeling" of Warka Izdubar—or Angie's infusion of the "spirit of Ashtoreth."

Surely there had to be something more to Judith's problem than these cheap parlor tricks.

In fact, she had been acting quite strangely earlier in his office. Could it have had something to do with the sordid goings-on in her husband's courtroom? Somehow, Stillman doubted it, though he wasn't particularly familiar with the Devil's Night trial, beyond what had been in the newspaper. And he hadn't even read much of that.

The newspaper. Suddenly he recalled that Judith's odd behavior in his office had occurred right after she looked at the front page of the paper. Her hands had trembled. She had spilled coffee and fled from the room in a fluster.

It would certainly be a simple enough matter to recreate the stimulus. Stillman directed ALEX to display the front page of the *Columbus Dispatch* for that date. On the screen appeared that day's top stories, mostly national and international items, such as a blue-ribbon scientific panel's assessment that the UN ozone generation project was a failure. But there was no contest as to the story in question.

"SPOOKS" TRIAL UNWINDS GRISLY TALE

It was a story, which he had only scanned, about the grotesque trial in McBride's court, plus a mug shot of the mustachioed young defendant, Roger Larrabee. He reread the story, carefully this time, in search of some clue to Judith's behavior. Finding none, he read it a second time and then a third. Still nothing.

At last, he closed the file and rubbed his eyes in weariness and frustration. Stymied again.

Remembering the current edition of the *Columbus Dispatch* on his credenza, Stillman picked it up and let his eyes roam across page one. Instantly, they stopped, backed up, and fastened upon one particular story.

WITNESS FOUND SLAIN
Fundamentalists claim credit

The dismembered body of a young woman found in a farmer's field just outside Millersfield has been identified as that of Leah Andrews, a prosecution witness in the "Devil's Night" murder trial of Roger Larrabee.

The Franklin County coroner's office said Andrews, also known as Zona Corban, had been stabbed numerous times and that marks on her wrists and ankles indicated she had been restrained in some fashion with ropes before her death.

"Her remains were discovered early yesterday morning, and our examination indicates the victim had expired sometime in the vicinity of midnight Tuesday," said Warren Ritterman, deputy coroner. "I think we can say without fear of contradiction that this death has all the earmarks of a ritual slaying."

A spokesman for the Sheriff's Department said the incident was under investigation. There have been no arrests.

Callers to the *Dispatch* and the Columbus office of the Associated Press, identifying themselves as born-again Christians, claimed credit for the slaying. "So shall all godless witches meet their end," they said in identical statements.

There was no immediate indication how Andrews's death might affect Larrabee's trial in the courtroom of Common Pleas Judge Wilson N. McBride. A spokesman in McBride's office declined comment.

Andrews, 24, had testified last week . . .

Beside the story was a mug shot of Corban/Andrews, a recent trial photograph that conjured up girl-next-door images. A cold shiver passed through him, chased by a flight of ideas.

What was going on here? This kind of thing didn't really go on outside of the movies and tabloids, did it?

Then there was the other mystery—this university with its hostile characters, such as Jared Quang, the artificial intelligence wunderkind.

Quang claimed that his brainchild OUIJA system—Ohio Universities Intelligent Joint Access—was based on the esoteric concepts of the universal life energy Chi and the holograms.

But who was he kidding? The breakthrough had more to do with twenty-first century supercomputer technologies. So why all this New Age window dressing? It reminded Stillman of Jeremy Kay's metapersonal psycho-babble.

I need someone to help sort all this out, Stillman thought. *But who?*

One man came instantly to mind—Armand Schliesser, research physicist and bona fide wise man. Dr. Schliesser was suspected by many of the university ideologues as a God-believer and a probable reactionary, but Stillman knew him to be a true original thinker. He might feel comfortable asking for Schliesser's help. He considered calling the old scholar and asking to meet him after work.

If anyone could make some sense out of the this lunacy, it would be Schliesser. He would know. Schliesser would have answers.

★ ★ ★

It turned out that Schliesser was not only home all evening, but he was quite willing to receive Stillman, if he thought it would help in any way.

Stillman had not expected to find the old fellow poshly residing in so-called Upper-Scale Arlington. But once there, he received the surprise of learning that Schliesser was but a humble tenant in a multi-family situation, occupying the third-floor in-law suite of an ersatz Tudor that appeared overrun on the first two floors with single women in various stages of pregnancy. In the confusion, Stillman was momentarily in danger of forgetting why he was there.

He was in the middle of the second bewildering life history of a gravid guest when white-haired Armand Schliesser finally appeared at the bottom of the attic stairs, clad in jeans and sweater. Here was a face that accurately reflected its owner's character—deep, penetrating eyes; kindly, expressive mouth; strong, prominent nose; rugged, lined complexion.

Stillman's hostess of the moment immediately fell silent, patted him on the arm, and vanished.

"Doctor Stillman," Schliesser called out with a faint smile. "How nice to see you. Won't you come help me roast some chestnuts?"

Upstairs, Stillman found himself surrounded by shelves stacked with vintage books, piles of antique records, and walls lined with ancient paintings and aged photographs. In the center of the loft-style quarters was a squat, wrought-iron wood stove busily emitting wonderful nutty aromas. On one wall an ancient map showed the old division of the two Germanies. Stillman thought he recalled that Schliesser had been born in the old East before Reunification.

Schliesser resumed shelling chestnuts.

Stillman was assigned the task of retrieving a new batch, one at a time, from the flames with a long pair of scissored tongs. An erratic glare was cast by the flickering wood burner and several candles placed at odd vantage points in the A-framed room. Stillman nearly forgot himself, absorbed in the robotic chore.

"To what do I owe this . . . pleasure?" Schliesser inquired at last, as he continued the work of extracting the luscious meat from its woody shells.

Stillman was too distracted in the tasting of the savory samples from the foil-covered pan to make any immediate reply. And when he did, it was of a more immediate concern.

"Who are these women?"

"Women?" Schliesser responded. And then suddenly, he began to chortle. "Yah, the women." Now he was laughing aloud. "The women. They are quite in the family way, no?"

"Uh, quite," Stillman agreed, judiciously.

"Excuse me," Schliesser said, sobering quickly. "It's just that you must be most puzzled. Well. How shall I say? They are my family. Otherwise, I have no family, and they have no home."

Ouch! Stillman stuck two singed fingers into his mouth, attempting to suck away the searing heat from an untimely grasp upon a superheated chestnut. From somewhere, Schliesser produced a chunk of ice, which Stillman gratefully applied to the afflicted area.

Gradually, he began to realize that Schliesser's apparent coyness was genuine self-effacement, yes, but something more—almost a certain guardedness. Eventually, he gathered that Schliesser was, in fact, the landlord and his tenants were clients of a crisis pregnancy program associated in some fashion with church friends.

So, the aging physicist had relegated himself, within his own accommodations, to what amounted to an attic apartment—commodious as it was—while his guests, who stayed less than a year apiece, occupied the chief quarters with nearly all the amenities, including an indoor heated pool. Stillman could only guess that the cash flow came from royalties from Schliesser's classic New Physics text, *The First Seven Seconds.*

Only then did he notice that most of the pictures lining the walls were baby photos. And on one wall was an assortment of snapshots of older children, some well toward adulthood. Obviously, whatever this was, Schliesser had been at it for quite some time.

"You've heard of the underground railroad?" the old man asked as he noted Stillman's preoccupation with the photos. "This is part of, shall we say, the unborn railroad."

Stillman shook his head in incomprehension.

"Surely you're aware of the sanctions this country once had against sheltering runaway slaves?"

Stillman paused in his labors to refresh his recollection, fruitlessly. "All I recall is that the good guys won."

Schliesser fixed him with a piercing gaze. "I'm not talking about Yankee abolitionists," said the older man. "I'm talking about people who took a stand that cost them something."

Stillman started. It was so obvious that he had overlooked it. Schliesser was an antiabortionist, a card-carrying right-to-lifer. If the university knew about that—even the philosophical position, let alone the overt activities—he would be denounced. Stillman marveled that such a man as Schliesser could still exist and function with such a reactionary orientation. And if the authorities learned of it—well, he would need a good lawyer.

Schliesser appeared to read his thoughts. "I wouldn't have invited you here if I didn't trust you."

Stillman nodded. "Thanks."

"But that's not why you're here," Schliesser suggested gently.

"No." He suddenly wondered if he were not making a mistake. But he was not about to turn back at this point.

Haltingly, and with a good many more digressions and convolutions than he had intended, he began to unfold the troubling story. By the time he had circumnavigated Jeremy Kay and Jared Quang, the Rhema Institute, Judith's crisis, Zona Corban, and the sordid puzzle of the Devil's Night trial, both men had long ceased their occupation with the chestnuts.

At last, the only sounds in the room were the persistent

cracklings within the iron stove and the clucking of an antique clock on the mantle. In the starkly lit room, Schliesser's craggy face had become a forbidding monument of silence.

When he at last spoke, it was not quite what Stillman had expected to hear.

"If you're asking my advice, I would suggest that you not dismiss these . . .supernatural events . . .as mere 'parlor tricks.'"

"You're suggesting that I take them seriously?" said Stillman with a nervous laugh.

"Exactly." He paused. "Doctor Stillman, do you believe in God?"

"Of course not," Stillman said emphatically. Did Schliesser take him for a fool?

"Nor the devil?"

He shrugged at the absurd suggestion.

"Because you can't see them?" Schliesser persisted.

Stillman knew better than to take bait *that* obvious.

"Actually," Schliesser said, his tone softening, "I think being a physical scientist is an advantage in such matters. We're quite accustomed to treating all kinds of invisible, intangible things as real, simply because our finite minds balk at concepts like eternity and infinity. And so we have found it useful to speak in almost creationist terms—Big Bangs, singularities, and so forth.

"We laugh at old-fashioned notions like spontaneous generation and phlogiston. Yet, how much of an improvement is the theory of evolution over spontaneous generation? Not much—rats from filth, humans from trilobites. Well, I see forces of good and evil in the moral universe that also defy common-sense explanation. And I think you see them too. Or you're beginning to."

"I'm not sure I get your point."

"I am suggesting that you might also find it helpful to think of evil as a fundamental, active force in the universe."

Stillman must have looked bewildered.

"Let me ask you another question to illustrate," Schliesser said evenly. "Would you agree that God and religion—with all its trappings of holidays and rituals—have been purged from our public institutions?"

"Yes, that's fair," Stillman agreed.

"Christmas and Easter—gone?"

"Except for Winter and Spring Holidays—yes."

"All other holy days gone?"

Stillman paused, an odd thought gnawing around the edges. "Well, yes—unless you count October Holiday—Halloween."

Slowly, the cyberlinguist began to sense a hook setting into his jaw.

"Tell me what is Halloween, if not religion," Schliesser said.

"For starters," Stillman insisted, "it's anything but religion. October Holiday is known as Halloween in the schools because it's make-believe—monsters and gremlins and ghouls and stuff. Nobody takes it seriously."

Schliesser smiled patiently with what Stillman thought was a condescending sigh.

"That's where you're quite mistaken."

"What?"

"Which is partially owing to the fact that you're a man."

"What's that got to do with anything?"

"Because it's a women's rite."

"C'mon."

"You've asked my honest opinion of recent events, and I appreciate that. But I don't think you've correctly defined the problem. And lacking that, anything else I say is going to ring falsely in your ears."

"So . . ." Stillman began, fumbling to complete the question.

"My advice? I suggest you do a little research into the meaning of October Holiday—Devil's Night—and we'll talk some more. OK?"

Stillman was still troubled about a number of things. "You see your God as a physical force?" he blurted.

Schliesser smiled again. "A force? He is *the* force through whom all things consist and are held together. Through Him we live and move and have our being. That's my physics."

Schliesser followed him down the stairs and to the front door, both men maintaining a thoughtful silence until the murmured farewells.

Stillman buttoned his coat and descended the front steps in a chill, almost wishing that he had never come to this place.

9

Even holding the media calls, it still seemed as if the McBride phone were ringing off the proverbial hook.

Jack Irwin and Sylvia Bennett were telling one and all, from special interest group to reporter to crank caller, that there was no "statement," other than that Judge McBride had no plans to resign. The court administrator's office suggested that they put out a news release, but McBride had vetoed the idea as lending the issue more dignity than it deserved.

And still the calls came in, including one that he actually wanted to take.

"I have Judge Gamble now," Sylvia said over the box.

"I'll take it." He was eager for any moral support he might get.

Charles Gamble, now a judge on the Ohio Court of Appeals, had been McBride's chief mentor once upon a time at Cleveland Marshall College of Law. Gamble had sent his protégé a congratulatory note a year ago upon McBride's election to the Common Pleas bench, but the two had not actually conversed for a few years. In fact, McBride figured it had to be at least five years, since that conversation had been on the occasion of Gamble's original appointment to fill an appellate vacancy that many years ago.

Gamble's reentry into the political arena had been somewhat surprising after having chucked it one other time for academia. And considering Gamble's cynicism about the political process, it had been more than a bit out of character too—especially when he ran for a full term on the appeals bench and won handily.

In another moment, Charles Gamble's weatherbeaten face was blinking imperiously on McBride's wallscreen. He was looking a good deal older than McBride would have imagined. Nor was was he projecting the warmest expression.

"Hello, Doctor Gamble," said McBride, ever the respectful disciple. "To what do I owe this honor?"

"Honor? You know something about honor?"

"Why?" said McBride, his smile fading. "What do you mean?"

"Seems to me that you should have a much better idea about disgrace."

The words, spoken with unmistakable disdain, were as stinging as they were unexpected.

"Uh—you wouldn't happen to be picking up your news these days from Corrie Washington, would you?" McBride guessed.

"And a few other places," said Gamble coldly. "Just what is it you're trying to prove?"

McBride tried not to let it get to him, but he could not fathom why Gamble was acting this way.

"I'm only trying to uphold the law in the cases that are brought before me. If you've heard anything to the contrary, you've heard wrong."

One of Gamble's eyebrows arched, suggesting disbelief. "Still hung up on reactionary notions like 'original intent,' are we?"

McBride had forgotten about that. Like most of his profs, Gamble had espoused the doctrine of "progressivism," in which the US Constitution, for example, was always to be reinterpreted in light of the new and different conditions of modern life. That was as opposed to "original intent," which held that such interpretation could violate fundamental, eternal principles intended by the founding fathers. McBride found much truth in that view. Today, of course, even the phrase "founding fathers" was repugnant to the sensibilities of most people as archaic, paternalistic, and reactionary.

Just by chance, McBride had drawn the original intent position for argument in a moot court exercise and found himself captivated by the idea, somewhat to Gamble's chagrin. It was the only "B" that McBride got in that class.

"Your memory, if anything, has only improved with age," McBride said dryly.

Not so long ago, Gamble would have treated such a remark in the spirit of teasing and would have replied in kind. This time there was an acid edge. "I called because I thought I could talk sensibly with you, maybe give you some sound advice."

McBride felt as though he were expected to say something deferential. It wouldn't be easy.

"I have always valued your advice up till now," he said grudgingly.

Something flashed in Gamble's eyes. The nuance had not been lost on the old fellow. Maybe Gamble would hang up. At this point, McBride wasn't sure he cared.

"I'll be brief," said Gamble. "This Larrabee case. You made a big mistake denying the motion for directed acquittal—unless you enjoy this kind of case for some personal reason."

"That's immaterial, but go on."

"Unfortunately, your crusader impulses this time have resulted in the death of a witness," Gamble continued. "Before there are any other unfortunate occurrences, my advice to you is to declare a mistrial—now."

McBride couldn't believe his ears.

"Potentially, the prosecution of *any* case can result in harm to a witness. By your reasoning, we'd never prosecute anybody for anything."

"Surely, you're not suggesting that this is just any case?"

McBride was bothered by the logic. "Surely, you're not suggesting that it's OK to sacrifice little boys to some pagan god? Don't we have a responsibility to the rule of law, no matter the case?"

"'Pagan god,'" Gamble repeated, turning the phrase over. "Is that an indication of bias on your part? Do you really believe in such things? Perhaps you ought to consider recusing yourself."

There was something very wrong with this conversation.

"I am not recusing myself, and I find this entire discussion highly irregular."

"Is that so? Well, let me tell you something, Mr. Crimefighter. If that case comes before this court on appeal, a lot of questions are going to be raised about your deportment."

"Is that an indication of prejudice on *your* part?" McBride challenged.

"I didn't say how we'd rule—just a lot of questions are going to be raised. I suggest that prudence would dictate a change in course on your part."

"Thank you for your advice, Doctor Gamble," said McBride stiffly. "I will give it . . . all due consideration."

Afterward, McBride found himself deeply disturbed by this unsettling exchange. It was almost like finding Jimmy Shapiro to be on the take. Increasingly, this anarchic world was becoming a lonely place for the likes of Wilson Neal McBride.

There was something else too. How was it that Gamble now was using this "Crimefighter" epithet? Various suspicions came quickly to mind.

But hardly had he begun to digest the significance of Judge Gamble's remarks than Sylvia was intercomming with another call she thought he'd want to take.

"Sherman Dygert for you," she announced.

"I'll take it," said McBride with a small sigh. He was beginning to feel a little shell-shocked.

Onscreen, Sherm Dygert, county GOP boss and elections board magnate, looked like a man with too many fires and not enough big red trucks. It was a strong face with a pleasant mouth, but the restless brown eyes betrayed a profusion of mental activity. Normally, Sherm could be counted on to get right to the point.

He did.

"I'd like you to consider resigning," said Dygert, shortcutting any small talk.

"But—" McBride began.

"No," said Dygert, holding up a cautionary hand. "I don't want any snap decisions. I want you to take twenty-four hours—or at least sleep on it—before giving me your answer."

"Resign?" said McBride, incredulous. "I figured you were going to ask me to declare a mistrial."

Dygert gave him a funny look. "Why's that?"

McBride shrugged. "Everybody else is."

"That's your business," Dygert growled, obviously recognizing the sarcasm. "My job is to keep the trains running on time. If you perform like a team player here, it will be remembered."

"Yeah, what's that mean?"

"I think the best way to keep everybody happy is to take you out of the game and put you on the bench for the rest of the season. No promises, but if things work out, next season we ought to be able to put you back out on the field—maybe in some other position."

"In appreciation for my team spirit," McBride said straight-faced.

Dygert nodded.

"One problem. How do you refield a player who has been covered with shame and disgrace?"

"Easy. Your official reason for resigning at this time is for personal reasons, related to your wife's health. Even Corrie Washington might give you a break on that one."

That gave McBride a start. Dygert didn't miss much.

"How did you know about my wife?" he asked.

"It's my business to know these things. Give me a call tomorrow and let me know your decision. I think you'll see the wisdom in this."

"Look, Sherm," he said, dropping all pretense. "I don't need to sleep on it. My answer now is the same as it will be tomorrow—no deal."

Dygert frowned. "You enjoy falling on your sword?"

"There's work to be done here, Sherm. This case may end up in a mistrial no matter what I do, but the important thing is that I don't cut and run. *That* would be falling on my sword. There are too many people already who think they can intimidate the court into rolling over. I had a call from somebody the other day, threatening my family if I didn't throw this case out. Giving in to this sort of pressure would be encouraging people like that and turning my back on everything our judicial system stands for—and everything I stand for. I can't do it, Sherm."

Dygert looked like one of his trains had just collided with one of his fire trucks.

"I told you no snap decisions."

"It's not a snap decision," McBride assured him.

"Call me tomorrow."

"You already have my answer."

McBride didn't like the look in Dygert's eyes when he said, "You're making a big mistake, Neal. Mark my words."

And then the screen went blank.

McBride felt reasonably good about his decision. Why prolong the inevitable? He wouldn't make any different decision tomorrow. That was probably one of the very reasons he was a judge—once he had enough facts, he had little trouble making decisions, even tough ones.

Moving again toward his familiar vantage point by the window, he was frozen in his tracks by yet another phone message from Sylvia. Steve Leadingham, again.

This time, instead of the mischievous twinkle in his eye, there was a decided tightness about Leadingham's face and mouth. There was no "Crimefighter" talk.

"What're you doing after work?" Leadingham queried immediately.

"Probably dodging demonstrators and reporters, wiping spit off my suit, and maybe trying to see Judith for a bit. Why do you ask?"

"You're under some . . . pressure in this case?"

"You might say that," McBride agreed. "You know something about that?"

"I might."

"Anything you want to tell me about?"

"Not here. In person."

McBride thought for a moment. "How about right now? My case is in recess until we figure out where the witnesses are."

Leadingham nodded. "I got a couple of places to be. That'll work."

"Same place?"

Leadingham nodded again. "I'll leave right now. Meet you there."

★ ★ ★

The place was The Happy Medium out on Lower Siddhartha Avenue, far away from the uptown white-collar crowd of lawyers, financiers, politicians, and fixers. Here, faces like McBride's and Leadingham's might be less readily recognized. It was a kind of no man's land—or maybe every man's—with equal portions of students and other university types, blue-collar workers, neighborhood regulars, artists, even a few gangsters, mostly minor league. But you never knew, and that was part of the place's charm.

The ghost of Jimmy Shapiro resided here. The Happy Medium had been one of Jimmy's regular haunts, a place where he would appear to kick back, chow down, drink up. In actuality, he was cultivating a grapevine, absorbing faces, devouring gossip, imbibing scuttlebutt.

Occasionally, he would have McBride with him. The younger man had been impressed repeatedly with how Jimmy, on a handful of trivial observations, could sketch out a life story or weave a character into the fabric of some currently unfolding plot. It was the place where McBride, too, had developed as a people-watcher, an undercover conversationalist, a journeyman listener, a photographic eye.

It would be a similar proposition today. Knowing Leadingham as he did, McBride would work his buttons until the whole story was out, whatever it was. He hoped Leadingham was as eager to spill as he had sounded. There seemed little doubt that he had something worth spilling.

McBride eased his car out of the parking garage and onto the half-deserted, late-morning downtown streets, always just a bit surprised at how different this non-rush-hour world was from the usual scramble. It felt a little like being truant from school, but it wasn't too hard for him to shift gears and imagine he was back pounding the mean streets again on a case.

Soon he was entirely back in character, and he even began to imagine that an older-model navy blue Sagittarius two cars back was shadowing him. Instinctively, he found himself feeling for the reassuring presence of cold metal in a nonexistent shoulder clip and then checked himself. Old habits die hard. The sensation was like that of the proverbial missing tooth.

Was he getting jumpy, his imagination getting the better of him? McBride didn't think so. The Sagittarius had mirrored too many of his own moves. If there was anything to it, this had to be an amateur to let himself get spotted this easily. McBride cut his speed in half just out of curiosity. The Sagittarius slowed down, maintaining the same distance behind.

Not a good sign. He decided to believe he had a real shadow.

Turning onto Lower Siddhartha just a couple of blocks from The Happy Medium, he kept an eye glued to the rearview mirror. The Sagittarius rounded the same corner. McBride maintained the same tedious pace, anticipating the timing of the traffic lights. If he played this right . . .

There. He floored it, scooting through the yellow light with the kind of dispatch that would have squealed the tires of an earlier generation of gasoline-powered automobiles, such as Jimmy had used for special occasions. Would his shadow give it up or blow his cover? McBride could afford the attention of a traffic cop; his shadow probably couldn't. But a pro, realizing his cover was already blown, might be willing to take that chance and give it the gas—or the electric, actually.

The Sagittarius vacillated, starting to gun it, then hit the brakes. Seeing the street clear ahead of him, McBride maintained acceleration, sliding easily through another amber light and streaking on past The Happy Medium. About the time he thought he saw the Sagittarius in his mirror starting up again, he hooked a right on Thorley, then another right on Riffe, doubling back toward his rendezvous. Just in case, he turned his car into a familiar alley in the last block, coming out behind the building. McBride's car coasted smoothly into the restaurant's back lot, slipping into a convenient slot by the rear entrance.

He appeared to have beaten Leadingham there.

*   *   *

Sometimes Peter wondered why he continued to hang out with this scatter-brained, moody, and impulsive Carlotta. Then, other times, he couldn't take his eyes off her or stand to be apart for more than two minutes, and he marveled at his great good fortune that she even tolerated his presence. This was one of those times.

Taking his eyes briefly off the street, he glanced admiringly across the car seat at this black-stockinged, dreamy-eyed beauty with the Cleopatra hair and the Cinderella smile.

"What're you looking at?" teased Carlotta.

"Upholstery," said Peter, with the slightest smirk. "Your car's got great upholstery."

"Oh, sure." Carlotta giggled, sliding a little closer, to where he could put his right arm up over her shoulder if he wanted.

He wanted. The right arm of his leather aviator's jacket found a cozy berth.

It was true. Carlotta's navy blue Sagittarius was almost ten years old, but its upholstery was still in great condition. Peter knew how she appreciated his looking after her car mechanically and how much she preferred passengering with him behind the wheel.

Carlotta rode like a princess being chauffeured to the ball, although it was only to The Happy Medium, where she'd soon be putting a bandana on her head, silver dollar-sized hoop rings in her ears, and other gypsy accoutrements on the rest of her person. Instead of dancing, she'd be scribbling orders and juggling trays of food and drink, trying desperately not to spill anything.

"Look!" Peter said, studying the traffic up ahead.

"What?" said Carlotta, trying to see what he saw.

"The gray car." He took his arm off her shoulder to point out a late-model, two-tone Capricorn sedan two cars ahead. Peter cut their speed to maintain the same distance back.

"What about it?" she asked.

"Neal," Peter said, grinning.

"You sure?"

"Yep. That's his license, even. I saw it at the light."

"But where would he be going at this hour?"

"Good question. But I think I have a pretty good idea."

"OK, smart guy. Where?"

He grinned again. "To a joint called The Happy Medium."

"In the middle of the morning? What for?"

He shrugged. "Who knows? Maybe a top-secret mission. I think he used to go there a lot for that sort of thing. Or maybe a rendezvous with a femme fatale, a little hokeypokey."

"Oh, Peter, not Judge Wilson Neal McBride!"

"Yeah, you're right. He's too much of a Boy Scout."

"Especially at the place where I work."

"I don't think he knows you work there. You haven't seen him in there recently, have you?"

"No, never," she had to admit.

"Uh-oh," said Peter as the light up ahead started to change.

To his chagrin, the gray Capricorn gunned it through the light, leaving him with a difficult choice—either crash the red light or drop back and end his pursuit.

Peter almost gunned it, then changed his mind and stopped abruptly. "Oh, well," he said with a shrug. "He'll be there—or my name isn't Sherlock Holmes."

"Sure," said Carlotta, dubiously.

"In fact," he said even more boldly, "since he must have spotted us, I predict he'll go in the back way through the alley."

Sure enough, by the time they arrived at The Happy Medium and drove around to the back, there was McBride's gray Capricorn, parked conveniently by the back door as if it had been there for hours. But Peter could almost imagine he was hearing the echoes of the back door slamming just ahead of their own arrival.

He parked to the other side of the door, and the two of them got out. As they were doing so, another car pulled into the lot and proceeded to a space nearby. The driver looked remarkably familiar to Peter, like somebody Neal used to work with in the Attorney General's office. In fact, he thought the name might be "Steve" something.

It so happened that this Steve also appeared to believe he knew Peter, waving as he opened his car door to get out.

And then a third car approached the drive but didn't turn in.

Peter saw something sticking out the window as the car glided very slowly by them. There was a flash of orange, a sound of firecrackers, and then total confusion.

* * *

The Happy Medium—"Stop by for a Spell"—was living proof of the saying that there's no accounting for taste. McBride wondered how many people who came here did so only because they knew somebody else who did, without knowing why. But there were certainly enough of those for a steady, if not brisk, business.

One thing that could be said for this establishment was that it did have a coherent theme. Adorning the flat-black walls were old-time photographic portraits of mystics and magi of the likes of Houdini and Blackstone, Mmes. Blavatsky and Besant, Messrs.

Gurdjieff and Crowley. In the far corner of the main dining room was a round seance table, which also served for readings of tea leaves, customers' palms, and, allegedly, an occasional animal entrail. The tablecloth was, again, basic black.

The only splashes of color amid this funereal decor were upon the persons of the costumed staff themselves. But at midmorning, there were but several of these ersatz-gypsy attendants with rings, sashes, bell-bottoms, taffeta skirts, and petticoats, quietly and deliberately arranging for the luncheon crowd in the offing.

McBride slid into a carefully selected booth within sight of both entrances. The crystal ball adorning the wall above his table sprang to life. Greeting him was the black-and-white holographic image of a woman resembling Marlene Dietrich, disembodied in an ethereal fog within this globe.

"Please to take zee order?" insinuated the wavy-haired woman with a mysterious, heavy-lidded expression, as if she were seducing the disclosure of military secrets.

"Coffee, black," said McBride, rubbing his weary eyes.

Funny how simply ordering coffee can put you in touch with your real tiredness, he reflected. The woman's image blinked agreeably as the hologram in the ball faded.

From somewhere outside came an odd muffled sound, as of somebody setting off a string of firecrackers. McBride was no longer sleepy. He didn't like the sound of that, and Leadingham should have been here by now. *Don't let your imagination run away with you,* he told himself.

Then came the firecrackers a second time, and someone—a young woman—was clawing at the rear door to the restaurant as two large holes erupted in the glass and enormous cracks radiated outward. In another moment, McBride saw Peter's girlfriend stumble into the foyer, shrieking hysterically and spattered with blood.

"Call the police!" she screamed. "They're shot—both of them!"

Both of whom? She didn't look so good herself.

McBride didn't waste time asking questions. He beat it out the shattered back door, trusting the restaurant staff to call for emergency assistance. It would be pretty hard to ignore a bleeding, screaming woman for very long.

Outside in the parking lot, his worst fears took shape. Two men were on the ground, one still moving, one lying very still in a sickening amount of blood.

"Steve!" McBride cried, rushing toward the immobile one.

On his knees, he reached down and cradled his friend's head, oblivious to the crimson stickiness that was getting all over his suit. Leadingham's eyes were half open, and he was drawing shallow, erratic breaths. But at least it was breathing.

"Who did this?" McBride asked urgently.

Leadingham attempted a response, but there was no wind behind the utterance, and McBride had to insist that he start over. This time, it was a slight improvement. It sounded as if Leadingham didn't know the identity of the triggerperson or persons.

"What was it you came to tell me?" asked McBride. "What's going on?"

Leadingham appeared to be making a mighty effort to articulate, but if anything the result was even less intelligible. McBride could make out words, but they sounded foreign—maybe Latin or who knew what else.

"Conceptus . . . Fahlgren . . . Chi Xi . . . Vau . . ."

Maybe Leadingham was delirious.

McBride, who had almost forgotten about the second man, turned to see the figure in a leather aviator's jacket struggling onto his haunches, apparently not so seriously hurt as Leadingham, but surely wounded.

"Neal," the young man croaked in a familiar voice.

With a shock, McBride realized he knew this fellow with the blood streaming down his forehead and into his eyes.

"Peter!"

Agonizingly, Peter struggled to his feet and took two halting steps toward his stepfather.

"Don't!" McBride admonished, standing up and raising his hand.

And then Peter, his eyes rolling about in his head, lost his forward motion, his knees giving out.

McBride barely made it in time to catch him under the armpits and support him in a bearhug.

"Peter," McBride repeated with infinite regret, looking directly into Peter's eyes.

It was then that he realized he had been hearing sirens. They were not far away now.

"Dad . . ." Peter mumbled just before his knees buckled completely and his body became a dead weight in McBride's arms.

McBride was amazed. Peter had never called him that before.

But he had no further time to reflect upon this development. Two large red-and-white emergency vehicles were descending upon the parking lot, followed by a couple of police cruisers with an angry hornet's nest of lights.

10

Stillman shut his study door, drew a mug of fresh coffee, steeled his resolve, and turned to confront his lovely, familiar Venus on the wallscreen. With a mixture of schoolboy mischief and grown-up guilt, he contemplated telling the lady a whopper.

"Manual, ALEX," he directed, deliberately bypassing voice-link. The goddess began dissolving into random pixels.

Using the keyboard, Stillman managed to recycle a record file from his health clinic, strip off the old readouts, and substitute some figures showing him with elevated insulin levels, respiration, and heart rate plus subnormal rectal temperature in addition to several anomalous blood gas properties. A database search suggested such a display would generate maximum unresolvable concern.

In another moment, he had concocted a wee footnote detailing the transmission of serum to such-and-such laboratory for a workup on what blood factors to assist which possible diagnoses. It was so good that, if he took two days off, the university's insurer might later demand to know why, for liability's sake, the employee had not been granted *three*.

After examining a hard copy, Stillman purged the stats from all but resident memory, intercepted a genuine clinic portfolio, cloned it down, and substituted his own report within the same format. *Voilà!* No fingerprints.

It was playing hooky, twenty-first–century style.

"Wickner, ALEX," Stillman called, almost singing. "Wait —insert V-mode umber five percent here," he added as an afterthought. "And, oh, an equivalent vocal drag while you're at it."

Instantly, the system tied to a free administration line, crisply displaying the Anthropology Department's blue-and-white evolutionary-tree logo while adjusting Stillman's image to a more bilious hue at the receiving end. A low, hollow beep signaled that the intended party's connection was imminent.

"Ah, Stillman, you wanton animal!" chimed an oily voice that could belong to no one but Julian Wickner. "How may I serve your pleasure?"

Indeed, Wickner's leering visage was even now assembling itself upon the screen, its eyes somehow even beadier than in the flesh.

"You could go to an early grave," Stillman said, obstructing the direct mike post with his thumb.

"What's that?" Wickner said suspiciously, his grin fading.

Stillman removed his thumb. "I said, I won't be in to work today."

"Oh?" Wickner appeared mildly chagrined. "Frankly, you don't sound all that terrific. Some kind of cold?"

"Definitely more serious than that."

"That's too bad," Wickner said soothingly, then immediately brightened. "But I do make house calls."

"No, I'm talking medical reality. Stand by."

He made a show of instructing ALEX to transmit the doctored file to administrative check-in when, in fact, he was touch-typing the commands by hand offcam.

Wickner's gaze suddenly began tracking a data flow slightly below screen. He looked up after a moment with his closest approximation of an expression of concern.

"Time perhaps for an immunity system tune-up?"

Stillman feigned a polite smile. "I have a clinic appointment for this afternoon."

"Just so," Wickner said somberly.

Stillman was gripping the keyboard in anticipation of a businesslike sign-off when he began to sense that his superior had something further on his mind.

"Ah, Stillman?"

"Yes?"

Wickner appeared to reconsider a question, then overruled himself and proceeded. "How well do you know Schliesser?"

"Armand Schliesser?"

"Yes."

"Oh, passingly. Just socially, you know. Why?"

"Socially? You mean not as a personal friend?"

"Well, I guess—what's wrong? What are you driving at?"

"Oh, nothing—nothing, really. It's just that the old man appears to have some enemies, and they say he's involved in some antisocial activities."

"What kind of antisocial activities?"

"Well, they say he's got a houseful of pregnant women and that he's involved in a radical political movement."

Stillman, caught on a swallow of coffee, choked and hacked until the tears cleared from his eyes.

"You OK?"

"Yeah, sure," Stillman said, trying with all of his might to suppress a fit of laughter. Realizing the deadly seriousness of the issue helped to restore his composure.

"You know anything about this?" Wickner persisted.

"No, I'm afraid not. Why do you ask?"

"No reason—except anybody caught sympathizing with this kind of activity could end up in academic disrepute."

"OK. I promise to keep my nose clean," Stillman pledged, crossing his heart. "Especially if the clinic gives me good drugs today."

116

"I'll drink to that!" Wickner chimed. "You animal."

As soon as the connection had broken, Stillman initiated Step Two.

"Moira, ALEX."

She, of course, would be at work or on her way to Archaeology. So he left a message for her to call him.

Now he could get down to some serious business, beginning with Schliesser's challenge on October Holiday.

After hours of searching a host of data banks, Stillman was surprised by how little actually had been written on the subject by serious scholars. The only references directly pertaining to Halloween appeared to be from later researchers following the same kinds of steps he was retracing.

But he was able to assemble some basic facts.

- The two major holidays among the ancient peoples of Druidic influence were Beltane (May 1) and Samhain, on the eve of the Celtic new year (November 1).
- The festival of Samhain was named for the Lord of the Dead and was celebrated after the harvest, symbolically a time of decay.
- At that time, Samhain freed all the souls of the dead to return to their earthly homes.
- Families had to entertain and prepare food for these spirits or be subjected to spells and other supernatural misfortunes.
- Conquering Romans assimilated this observance in combination with several other pagan holidays, including the festival of Pomona, the goddess of fruits and trees.
- In 834, Pope Boniface IV moved the church feast of All Hallows (honoring all dead saints) from May to November 1, which rendered October 31 All Hallows Even.
- November 2 became All Souls Day, for the living to pray for the souls of all the dead in "purgatory." To this day, celebrants still jammed churches and cemeteries in Latin American countries at this time in observance of *Dia de los Muertos*—Day of the Dead.

It almost sounded as if the church's concept of purgatory had come from the Celts' notion of Samhain. Where, after all, did Samhain keep all of those souls?

But Stillman's main objective was to reassure himself—and prove to Schliesser—that the modern celebration of October Holiday had nothing to do with "religion." In fact, he believed a decent case could be made that the modern-day version of All Hallows Even was nothing more profound than a simple parody of superstitions and religious sentiments.

It was no obeisance to the devil, he told himself. If anything, it was a light-hearted spoof of supernatural nonsense.

In another moment, he was gazing through his mind's eye out across the years and upon the front sidewalk at M. B. Schuler Elementary School in Madison Heights, Michigan, where a line of little ghouls, imps, vampires, gremlins, ogres, werewolves, ghosts, skeletons, and contemporary sci-fi monsters snaked down to the street and around the corner in the school's annual Halloween parade.

He even began to recall something of how it felt as a third grader to be part of that ambling procession, which stalled almost interminably behind the school on the ball field. It was such a relief to be freed from schoolwork's grinding monotony and to play at being scary.

But, maddeningly, he could not summon the memory of his own costume. What was it?

And then, in a flash, it came. He had been the Red Devil—complete with horns, tail, and pitchfork.

Why did he feel so embarrassed by the remembrance?

★ ★ ★

"Brandy!" Jeremy Kay called out without looking up.

Angela Hurley rose with a faint sigh from her wicker chair on the veranda. She was, in fact, the novice, the bottom person on the totem pole. Before slipping through the side door into the west dining room, she paused to glance up at the sky.

It was one of those crisp, hearty, early October nights in central Ohio. Electric-gray, moonlit clouds imparted an eerie illumination to the stonework, the shrubs, and the darkly rolling hillside surrounding Chateau Fahlgren. On the veranda table the flickering of two glass-encased candles deepened the ghastly play of shadows.

Inside, Angie rounded up four squat glasses, a nearly full bottle from the dark walnut liquor cabinet, and an ice bucket and arranged them upon an antique silver platter.

She was still overwhelmed by this sumptuous lifestyle—actually living in an authentic reproduction eighteenth-century French castle—and the headiness of continual hobnobbing with the New Age intelligentsia. Drinking from fine crystal and padding about upon parquet floors while entertaining such elite guests made her feel like a genuine marchioness. What then, really, were a few minor indignities?

Angie slipped back into the evening chill, carefully balancing the weight of her tray, to serve Jeremy and their guests—tonight it was Julian Wickner and Jared Quang once again—collectively known as the "Three J's."

She distributed the drinks. Kay and Wickner discussed visiting somebody in the hospital. Quang said nothing, absorbed in some laptop device and squinting in the shadows with a small penlight focused on his work.

Angie took a long draw from her own glass and felt the liquid heat coat her insides as she studied the three faces. Wickner's was the oldest and most dissolute, having a vague scheming look even in repose, especially the almost reptilian eyes. Quang's was the hardest to read, the most abstract, the least animated, as he seemed ever preoccupied with technical matters, rarely engaged in conversation. Glacial eyes. Kay's was . . . special—winsome, well-bred, expressive, thoughtful, though occasionally petty and capable of frightening contortions in periodic and sometimes unpredictable fits of malice and pique. These eyes were at once dangerous and mesmerizing.

Angie noted that Kay and Wickner were no longer sporting the small bandages at the base of the skull that they had worn earlier in the week. "Elective surgery" was all Jeremy would say, indicating she would be told more later. Always later.

With a start, Angie realized that Jeremy was addressing her, summoning her to his side. Still seated, he took her left hand in both of his and began giving it an inspired little massage while fixing her with a benign, hypnotic gaze.

"Kiss?" he said almost as a supplicant, although Angie was the one who had to bend down to plant it.

"I'm afraid this is all going to be terribly boring for a while," he said. "Have you had the tour of Pre-Life yet?"

Angie shook her head. That was one of those areas of powerful medicine that one entered by invitation only. Until now, she hadn't been invited.

"Well, then," said Jeremy, "why don't you go check it out? We have some things to discuss. We'll send for you when we're ready."

Had she just been told to get lost?

★ ★ ★

Angie felt her way to the top of the basement stairs by candlelight, irritated that she didn't even know where the light switches were. She didn't think she was particularly superstitious, so why was this giving her the creeps? Just because this shadowy, dungeonesque staircase reminded her of every haunted castle movie scene ever filmed was no reason to act like a giddy child, was it?

Kicking her shoes off, she crept barefoot down the cellar stairs, bearing a lone candle, to cower beneath her own leaping, telescoping shadow. At the bottom, she found the security keypad and punched in the code—5-4-2-4.

The door inched open with an exaggerated groaning creak, probably a recorded sound effect. Funny guys. They'd told her to go down the back way because it was a shortcut.

She followed the Pre-Life Science signs until she came to one reading "Biota Recycling." As she rounded a corner, she sensed someone was at the bottom of the last half flight of steps. Abruptly, she froze.

Angie snuffed her candle. There was considerable light at the bottom. And as she crept tensely down a few more stairs, she came within view of a curious display of instruments and objects that defied immediate recognition. She saw an array of bubble-topped boxes that reminded her of miniature coffins. But to each box, or tank, was connected a crazy quilt of wires, instruments, lights, and plastic tubing conveying fluids of various hues.

Now Angie could begin to make out the person who had just

entered this eerie laboratory, a woman with short blonde hair and red-rimmed glasses she had met briefly on her first day at Chateau Fahlgren. With professional precision, the woman circulated among the tanks, monitoring fluid levels, checking instrument readings, and attending to other mysterious details. All the while, she could be heard murmuring something of a sing-song nature as she moved to and fro. Suddenly, Angie recognized the refrain.

"Double, double toil and trouble;
Fire burn and cauldron bubble."

Suddenly grinning, Angie called out down the last few stairs with her own couplet.

"Eye of newt and toe of frog,
Wool of bat and tongue of dog . . ."

Missing only half a beat, the woman playfully replied,

"Adder's fork and blind-worm's sting,
Lizard's leg and owlet's wing . . ."

To which Angie rejoined,

"For a charm of powerful trouble,
Like a hell-broth boil and bubble."

She stepped off the stairs and into the light, laughing.

"Well, hello," Kelsey Kinsey said with mild surprise. "What's a nice girl like you doing in a place like this?"

"I dunno," Angie said lightly. "Just what kind of a place is this?"

A cryptic expression flitted over Kinsey's features before she replied, "You—uh—really don't know?"

"No, I really don't know. Why don't you tell me?"

"All right," Kinsey said evenly. "Why don't I just show you?"

They moved toward one of the tanks and bent over to peer into the bubble.

"Oh!" Angie said with a little gasp. "Is it—is it—"

"Alive?" Kinsey completed the thought for her, then fluttered one hand. "A little yes, a little no. We like to think of it as *potential* life."

Through the bubble peered a tiny humanoid face, eyes wide open. Comprehension eluded Angie for a moment. In place of the skull plate was a gridlike maze of wires and tubules—all this attached to a larger tangle outside the various tanks.

And then, with a wrench, she understood. When Kinsey said "potential life," she was not so much referring to the creature's own as to the lucky beneficiaries of these spare biological parts.

"Technically," said Kelsey Kinsey, "they're 'biota' or 'concepti.' One, of course, is a 'conceptus.'"

Angie had never been inside a biota recycling facility before. To think that she had been living over the top of a fetal farm now for days without even knowing it! She was not certain just how that made her feel.

"What's being—uh—harvested here?" she asked uncertainly.

"Oh, brain chemicals and the usual stuff—brain stems, enzymes, hormones, bone marrow, antibodies, all the major organs, of course. It's doing an awful lot for the quality of life—not to mention the quality of *our* life."

"Oh." Angie gathered that Kinsey was referring to the Society's financial wherewithal. "Where do these . . . concepti . . . come from?"

Kinsey fixed Angie with a penetrating gaze and appeared to be considering her words carefully.

"Contributions come from a variety of sources. But that's an internal Society matter, only for initiates."

Angie didn't much like Kinsey's tone.

"I expect to gain initiation soon," she said evenly. "I have to perform my act of commitment."

They were moving to other tanks, when a male voice broke in.

"Commitment is precisely what we need to discuss."

Angie recognized the disembodied voice but could not locate the source until Kinsey nodded toward a central bank of monitors, where Quang's cherubic countenance appeared on one of the VDTs. He probably had been monitoring their conversation from the outset. Angie wondered if Kinsey already had known that.

"Hi, Jared," Kinsey purred.

"Greetings," Quang replied. "Giving our little guest a tour?"

"Yes. It's about time somebody did."

"If you say so. How's our yield this evening?"

"Just swell. You have the same numbers in front of you that I do."

"But you actually know what they all mean," Quang quipped. "The three of us would like to see you and your . . . little friend . . . on the veranda in a few minutes. Or as soon as you can tear yourself away."

Kinsey's eyebrows hiked a notch. "Sure thing. See you shortly."

Angie did not appreciate Quang's references to her in third-person diminutives. But there was something else, some obscure insinuation, that she liked even less. And now Kinsey was staring at her oddly, as if she were a lab specimen. Angie began moving away from her and toward the stairs.

"Just a minute," the woman said. "I have a housekeeping chore first."

With that, she snatched a pair of long-handled tongs and approached a tank where the monitor lights were unblinking and the data streams were flat lines. With a flick of the hand she silenced the simmering aerator, popped the bubble hatch, and plunged the tongs into the stilled solution. Out came one of the pink creatures, upside down, secured by one foot.

Angie cringed despite herself. This one was actually more gray than pink. It bore the marks of numerous incisions and excisions. She also noticed that the eye sockets were vacant.

"This one's not a potential *anything* anymore," Kinsey muttered as she worked.

Angie winced again as the woman snipped the trailing umbilicus where the wires and tubules connected and then smartly yanked the corresponding attachments from the cranium. Last, she jettisoned the miniature cadaver into a yawning disposal that immediately responded with appropriate whirring, sucking, and grinding sounds.

"There," Kinsey said, dusting her hands together. "It's called taking out the trash."

Angie edged even farther away. She couldn't help but wonder if Kinsey was going to wash her hands.

"Not that way." Kinsey tilted her head. "Over here."

With one hand on Angie's forearm, she guided her across the floor toward an inconspicuous section of paneling designed to create the impression of a dumb-waiter. But when the door automatically slid open at their approach, it clearly revealed itself to be a standard elevator, albeit a very small one.

Two persons were a bit of a crowd, made worse by Kinsey's disturbingly intense eye contact.

"Uh—tell me," Angie said nervously, "was that a Quang monitoring system?"

Another of those cryptic expressions crossed Kinsey's face as she stabbed a button on the elevator panel, initiating their slow ascent.

"You might say that," the woman said, with an almost secret amusement. *"Everything* is a Quang monitoring system anymore. Actually, it might be more accurate to call it a OUIJA monitoring system. Quang has OUIJA wired to just about everything but the Pentagon, and sometimes I wonder about that. Why do you ask?"

With a barely perceptible bump, they arrived.

"Oh, I understand the rationale for the biometric monitoring of organ systems and so forth, but—"

"Yes?"

The elevator door slid open, and the two women stepped off onto the main floor, just down the hall from the west dining room and the veranda.

"But why the brain?"

There was that expression again.

"I told you. Brain chemical production levels," Kinsey said, just a bit too sharply.

Angie looked the woman straight in the eye. "It looked like . . . quite a bit more than that to me."

Kinsey appeared to soften.

"You know," she said with a twinkle and then, affecting a mechanical inflection, "OUIJA and the children are ONE!"

She laughed unconvincingly, leaving Angie to imagine what she wanted. It was safe to say that Quang's quest for the grail of artificial intelligence was not known for its orthodox methodologies. Clearly, Kinsey didn't want to talk about it and thought she could laugh it off.

Back on the veranda, something appeared to have altered the mood of the Three J's. They were exchanging knowing glances and enthusiastic expressions. Before them on the table were assorted papers and several curious-looking cables running to one of Quang's consoles. Angie could only guess what they had been up to. The scene had the appearance of a major strategy session. But she suspected something almost supernatural had transpired as well.

Kay calmly lit a small cigar, causing his features to flare into a hideous caricature that seemed for the briefest moment quite real. Then he smiled at her, a heart-melting smile.

"We have a . . . most interesting situation here," he said. "In furtherance of your desire to be united in membership with the Society of Chi Xi Vau, there are a couple of . . . missions . . . that could be of great value to us and whose success could greatly advance your own cause as well."

"Missions?"

"Yes, a couple of sensitive assignments. I'm speaking of tasks that are not for the squeamish—but then, neither is membership in Chi Xi Vau."

Kay paused for her reaction.

Angie merely shrugged. "Try me," she said boldly.

"We have a very good friend, an associate, whom we must deliver from his captors," Kay began. "But even more urgently, there is a man—a very dangerous fool—who must be silenced."

Angie watched mutely as Jared Quang placed a small electronic device on the table before her. She wondered how this contraption would figure into the scheme.

Then Julian Wickner, grinning malignantly, handed her a small card. It was a Florida driver's license for a woman named Becky Leadingham at a Gainesville address. But the photo on the card, incredibly, was Angie's own likeness. Somebody had done good work.

"Your mission," Kay continued, "is to present yourself at four P.M. tomorrow at the third-floor Critical Care Unit at University Hospital and identify yourself as the sister of patient Steven Leadingham. Ask for the head nurse, Tanya Powers, who will run interference for you and guarantee you ten uninterrupted minutes with the patient. In that time, you are to attach Quang's little device here—the emulator—to the patient's life support in the manner that Quang will describe for you."

Angie picked up the mechanism and found it heavier than she had imagined, with several leads trailing down.

"What does it do?"

She hardly thought the question was funny, but Kay and Quang exchanged glances and smiled. Wickner leaned forward for a better view.

"It will decommission the life-support functions while maintaining all the same readouts," Kay said.

"If it functions properly," Wickner said.

"It will function properly if it's hooked up correctly," Quang said with a slight edge to his voice.

So, this was the test—a glorified hit job? Angie made sure no surprise or shock registered on her face. Besides, discontinuing someone's life support was hardly the same thing as murder.

The scientist proceeded to demonstrate. Kay held one of the candles over their huddle as Quang showed Angie pictures and diagrams from his briefcase. He went through the procedure several times so there would be no question as to exactly where the device mated with the console and where the three leads attached. Once he explained the relative functions of the several life-support monitoring components, the concept fell into place. Angie felt she could do it blindfolded.

"It takes very little time to install," Quang explained, "but it does require several minutes of operation to copy the vital sign data patterns. Once fully engaged, it decommissions life support while continuing to display the same readouts as if the patient were in status quo."

"Questions?" Kay said.

"Just one. How do we know we can trust this head nurse to keep our cover?"

"Trust me," Wickner purred. "This person is an ally at a rather . . . advanced level. Her dedication is beyond question."

"You surprise me," Kay interjected. "That's not the question I expected you to ask."

It was Angie's turn to smile, figuring she had a chance here to put some big numbers on the board.

"I suppose you mean the ethics of the situation?"

Kay nodded.

"I don't view that as my business. I'm sure you have some good reasons. You did say he was a very dangerous fool."

Wickner spoke up. "I like her style," he said to Kay.

"So, I have good taste." Kay turned back to Angie. "But for your information, this miscreant is a very sick boy and is not expected to make it. We just want to make sure the inevitable is not prolonged unnecessarily. This person is capable of doing great damage to the Society. There are things here, of course, to which only initiates are privy."

"Of course," Angie agreed. "I can be patient. What about this other person—the 'captive'?"

"That's Mission Number Two," said Kay. "That one involves a political prisoner of our esteemed criminal justice system. He's one of ours. Fortunately, he's out of the big house and temporarily residing in the Franklin County Jail while he's standing trial."

"What's he up on?"

Kay paused ever so slightly.

"A trumped-up charge of murder, which we expect to result in a mistrial—before Judge Wilson N. McBride. Does that present a problem for you?"

Just for an instant Angie almost faltered but quickly recovered her composure. "Roger Larrabee?"

Kay nodded.

"The answer is, number one, I have no problem with the McBride connection. I am not a McBride. Besides, if I had a bias, it would not be in Neal McBride's favor."

Kay raised his eyebrows but withheld comment.

"We need to . . . liberate Larrabee while he's still at the county jail," he continued. "If they return him to the state penitentiary, it'll be much tougher."

"You want me to stage a commando mission?" Angie said, half joking. "A jailbreak?"

"Perhaps something like that, eventually. But not a solo mission, certainly. Others will assist. And you'll have Quang's technical support—won't she, Jared?"

"To be sure," Quang obliged.

"But first we have to unplug this Leadingham character before something worse happens," said Kay.

Meanwhile, Kinsey had returned quietly to the room with two other women. Angie thought she recognized the first, a tall woman with long, prematurely gray hair and an ankle-length dress. Someone she had seen on TV, she thought.

The name clicked as soon as Julian Wickner uttered it. "Elizabeth Morningstar, Chi Xi Vau spiritual adviser."

The other, a beautiful but intense-looking thirtyish woman with auburn hair and green eyes, was a total stranger.

"And we have another new associate," Wickner said with enthusiasm. "Angela McBride, meet OSU archeologist Moira Stone."

Angie hoped she knew what she was getting into.

11

Even while fixing breakfast, Carlotta was still borrowing trouble, to McBride's way of thinking. Besides scrambled eggs, toast, blackberry preserves, and coffee, she was also serving up opinions on the urgent need to get Peter out of University Hospital.

McBride tried gamely to lighten the mood. "It's always been my position that the hospital is a place to be avoided like the plague—unless, of course, you have one."

"It's not so much his health I'm worried about," said Carlotta, pouring coffee, "as his physical safety."

"But if he's not safe there, what makes you think he'd be any safer here?" McBride reached for his orange juice. "Assassins know how to read city directories too."

Carlotta set two aromatic plates before them and sat down. "Good point," she said. "In fact, I suggest we find another place to hole up—after we get Peter out of there."

"We? You have some concern for your own safety too?"

Carlotta shrugged and took a bite of toast. "Only because of the company I keep," she said, chewing thoughtfully.

McBride was surprised and somewhat impressed by the seriousness and persistence of this young woman, whom he'd apparently misjudged. Was she one of these shrewd females who found it useful most of the time to let you think she was a flake?

Yesterday she had insisted for hours that they not leave Peter's hospital bedside. She would not accept McBride's judgment that it was all right for Peter just to sleep—which could be accomplished just as well without their presence. An attending physician finally assured her that Peter's wounds were far from life threatening and advised that she have her own injuries looked after. Carlotta had insisted that most of the blood on her clothes had come from Peter and Leadingham, except for several scrapes where she had hit the deck in the parking lot and suffered minor cuts from broken glass.

Immediately after the shooting, she had been equally insistent to the patrolman at the scene that he was not taking either the report or the incident seriously enough. True, the policeman had seemed to imply that the attack was nothing more than random violence by a street gang—and probably to be filed and forgotten.

But McBride had feared that Carlotta's tongue would get her into a jam. He himself was accustomed to that kind of lackadaisical reaction from the police, but Carlotta was outraged—and said so. Before she could give the steely-eyed patrolman too big a piece of her mind, McBride had managed to insert himself and back her off.

"Look," he'd told her afterward, "it can't be Peter they're after, or me either, probably. Whoever *they* are, it had to be Leadingham, because of something he knew."

Carlotta wasn't impressed.

McBride feared she might be suffering some posttraumatic stress. He insisted that she come stay in Angie's old room rather than return to her apartment alone. He escorted her in his own car to her apartment, where she gathered up a bag of clothes and belongings and parked the navy blue Sagittarius.

And now McBride chewed silently on his blackberry toast, considering just how preposterous Carlotta's fears were and whether the two of them might, in fact, be in some continuing peril. Conclusion: As much as he hated to admit it, there were far too many unknowns to reject such an opinion out of hand.

But he did know one thing he urgently needed to take care of—business. Maybe he could buy some badly needed time.

Carlotta cleared the table and then went upstairs to freshen up.

McBride went to his study and called Sylvia at the office. "I'd like you to take a letter," he said.

He watched her eyes widen as he dictated a letter of resignation, but she dutifully said nothing.

"Now, listen carefully," he instructed when he had finished. "I want you to date this the eighteenth. So don't tell anyone about this and don't do anything with the letter for seventy-two hours. If you haven't heard from me by then, go ahead and sign it for me and file it in the clerk's office. I suppose you ought to call Sherm Dygert, too, and let him know in that case."

Sylvia knit her brow. "If I sign your name, will that be legally binding?"

McBride smiled cryptically. "That's somebody else's problem, I think."

Sylvia smiled sadly. "That's the spirit. You're not really quitting, are you?"

"Technically, I'm just taking some vacation time at this point."

"Can you be reached?"

"Sure. Tell 'em to dial information for the Serengeti."

"I see. Well, have a wonderful time hunting wildebeest, or whatever."

McBride thanked her and then phoned Dygert.

The party boss, while preferring an outright resignation,

clearly was pleased by McBride's decision to think it over. "That's definitely a move in the right direction. But just remember there's a bunch of jurors and a defendant over in the county slam whose lives are all on hold while you contemplate your navel or whatever. Just don't think too long and hard."

"This case is in recess," McBride said patiently. "This isn't just about my navel. We've got a couple of missing witnesses to turn up."

"Well, I just hope they don't turn up dead."

"Now you sound like Judge Gamble," ventured McBride, to gauge the reaction.

"What?" said Dygert, appearing mystified. It didn't prove anything, of course.

"Never mind."

Dygert's expression reverted to one of concern. "Where can I reach you?"

"Here at home—navel-gazing, remember?" said McBride, then decided to cover his tracks a bit with disinformation. "If not, my bailiff will know my every move. That's Jack Irwin."

Jack wouldn't mind too much taking a little lip, if necessary.

After he hung up, McBride began to do some serious thinking. He thought of Steve Leadingham, clinging to life in the hospital. He pondered the baffling phrases that Leadingham had uttered at the last—"conceptus . . . Fahlgren . . Chi Xi Vau." He wrote them down before they passed from memory and studied their appearance on paper. He thought of Zona Corban and recalled the threatening phone call from the "Choice" group.

And the more he considered his figurative navel, the more he began to think Carlotta might be right. Maybe it was time to go on the lam.

* * *

Peter McBride awoke weakened and with an industrial-strength headache. That probably had something to do with the new part he had in his hair, a fortunately shallow furrow plowed by a bullet in yesterday's ambuscade. He reached up tentatively to touch the bandage covering his stitches and was surprised that it wasn't as sore as he would have expected.

The same was not true of his left outer thigh, where they'd had to extract the second bullet. In that vicinity, it felt as though his leg were on fire.

"Youch!" he called involuntarily after seeing what it would be like to move the leg.

But the worst part wasn't even physical. It was something intangible, a bone weariness that informed Peter that he was a spent cartridge, a discarded husk, a canceled stamp. The morning glare through the hospital window emanated depression—sickening rays from a dying sun, searing the polluted atmosphere of a corrupt metropolis. He felt like a million-year-old mollusk expiring in a priomordial swamp.

A voice startled him. "You in pain, son?"

The creaky but amiable voice came from the other bed in the semiprivate room, away from the window. Peter lifted his head an excruciating inch and turned toward the far wall. In that bed was an ancient, white-haired fellow with a splotchy port-wine stain discoloring his arm where an IV tube was taped.

"A little," he responded thickly.

The old man reached for the nurses' call-light and pushed the button. "That's what these things are for," he said kindly. "No sense being in pain."

Peter said nothing, and the man fell back into silence.

In another minute, a middle-aged, Asian-looking nurse appeared with a handful of hypodermic needles. She headed toward the old man.

"Not me," he said and then pointed at Peter. "Him."

The nurse checked Peter's chart, felt his pulse, and took his temperature. Then she asked him if he needed something for pain.

Peter nodded emphatically, and the quiet woman wiped off a small area on his left upper arm with a swab. He barely felt the injection, but there was an irritation that became a burning ache after she withdrew the needle, applied a tiny adhesive strip, and vacated the room. Reflexively, Peter rubbed his hand lightly over the area.

"Sting?" asked the kindly old man.

"Yeah."

He didn't quite catch what the old man said next—something about "sin" and "death."

"What?" said Peter.

"There's a sting to sin and death," the old man said. "But, thanks to God, there's a remedy. Want to hear about it?"

"Sure," said Peter, relaxing. The old man didn't seem too crazy.

What did he have to lose? He certainly wasn't going anywhere.

* * *

Rick Stillman drove along an avenue lustrous in moonlight, en route to see a physicist in Upper Arlington.

As he navigated the outskirts of downtown, a soft rain began to pock the windshield. He turned on the wipers and, while he was at it, the radio. A plaintive saxophone welled up and quavered, clutching at ancient human themes and universal woes. The gleaming wet, black streets now mirrored a patchwork of neon splashes from passing storefronts and a time-lapse of red-and-white car lights in distorted, jewel-like images.

Stillman stopped for a red light and was overtaken by a gnawing foreboding. Moira had not returned his call, but it was more than that. His October Holiday research had done nothing to support his argument against the existence of dark forces, bogeypersons, and other supernatural bunk. If anything, it had made him even less sure of himself.

Yet, if Schliesser was correct, he hated to think what that implied about Jones and Fitzgerald. Surely they couldn't be right. Stillman just couldn't bring himself to accept a way that was as narrow as the God of the Rhema Institute.

And yet, he also found himself longing to embrace something bigger and better than himself. He only knew of it by implication, by its aching absence from his heart and soul at a time when everything else in life seemed intent on his frustration. He was dangerously close to despair over his own devices.

He knew that Moira still bothered him more than he liked to admit. To this day, he still didn't get it. In their handful of minor disagreements and petty quarrels in two years of marriage, she had seemed fundamentally incapable of tolerating contradiction or considering compromise. But none of those incidents had amounted to

133

anything of significance. And then, almost without warning, she was gone.

In the divorce proceedings Moira had indicated no malice—she just needed her space. It was simply over, and she seemed unable to fathom why that was such a big deal with him.

Things change. Love dies. Life moves on.

Except for Rick Stillman, it seemed.

Now, what was this? Tears?

Stillman could not recall the last time he had actually shed tears. And here was one right now, oozing down his left index finger and joining with the steering wheel by capillary attraction. And then its amazing twin, cresting the lower eyelid and scudding down his right cheek.

He blinked to clear his view of the road. He reminded himself to breathe, despite the desire to shut down and squeeze out more of the ache. At this moment of demoralization, he could begin to appreciate how people could be driven to desperate and tragic acts. Schliesser had to have some answers for him.

"Yah, come over and we'll talk," Schliesser had said at the end of an already lengthy conversation on the phone. "Maybe we can roast some chestnuts too."

He had called Schliesser ostensibly to discuss the Halloween research and ended up, after some prompting from the relentless physicist, getting down to Stillman's personal afflictions.

"You might call it a . . . problem with self-esteem," Stillman suggested.

"Or perhaps self-loathing?" countered Schliesser. "That's not a problem; that's progress."

Stillman couldn't believe his ears. At this point, he was overcome by a new wave of exasperation.

He thought of Judith and her brilliant intellect, languishing again in a mental facility, the victim of some new neurosis or worse. He thought of miscreants and malefactors like Wickner and Quang, who inevitably rose to the top of every organization with which he had ever been associated, while the decent, hard-working folk were just as invariably exploited and ignored.

"No," Schliesser had said quietly. "Our bigger problem, I believe, is thinking of ourselves more highly than we ought."

"Well, I'm certainly not thinking of myself—or anyone else —very highly right now."

"Or perhaps not as highly as you would like to think of yourself?"

Stillman's face and ears had reddened with sudden pique. Sometimes he wondered why he subjected himself to this. But then just as quickly he realized that it was Schliesser's almost brutal candor that made him a valuable counselor. This was certainly not the sort of thing within ALEX's parameters.

Still, the remark stung.

And so now as he navigated the final turn onto the scientist's tree-lined Upper Arlington avenue, Stillman was overwhelmed by a yearning to share some of the old fellow's warm chestnuts and bask in the radiance of Schliesser's uncanny wisdom and blunt sensibilities.

In the last block, he felt an inexplicable chill, an uncomfortable foreboding. And now as his car drew within sight of the spacious house, he knew it was more than just imagination.

Parked on the wrong side of the street were two television remote vans with dish antennae. That was not a good sign.

In the driveway and out onto the right side of the street was a bevy of police cruisers and paddy wagons. And all about the front yard and Schliesser's front door was a swarm of reporters, uniformed police, and, apparently, plainclothespersons.

Stillman parked behind another car just to the rear of a TV van, hopped out, and made tracks for the front door. He was barely in time to see the last of a line of women, obviously Schliesser's pregnant tenants, being herded aboard one of the paddy wagons by an officer with a checklist and a flashlight. Stillman was immediately incensed.

"Are you taking these women to jail?" he challenged the policeman breathlessly.

"Of course not!" the officer said with some indignation, looking up with a start. Instantly, he turned the flashlight full upon Stillman, blinding him. "And who are you, sir?"

"Never mind," Stillman muttered, stepping back into the shadows.

And then he spotted a familiar face. The last woman in the plodding line was one who had shared her life story with him some time ago at the house.

"Ella!"

A part of him was momentarily astonished that he had managed to pull the name from his memory. Another part of him was leery of being captured in a television news report.

The woman's face, deep in shadows wrought by the hideous glare from a television camera, turned his way.

"Doctor Stillman?" she inquired weakly.

Abruptly, the television light died as the crew turned its attention elsewhere.

Emboldened by that new freedom, he moved to catch up with Ella, matching her pace toward the line to the wagons.

"What on earth is going on here?"

"They raided us," she said with the same subdued voice. "Doctor Schliesser has been arrested."

And then Stillman saw that the woman was crying softly.

"Arrested?" He pronounced the word as if it were a foreign term.

Ella merely nodded, biting her lower lip.

"Where are they taking you?" he insisted. "Do you know?"

She shrugged before stepping up into the van. "Someone said the Gulag—or something," she shot over her shoulder.

"What?"

But it was too late. She was gone, swallowed up.

Another camera sprang to life. As the door slammed shut behind Ella, the paddy wagon formed the backdrop for an instant television report.

"Dana, we're here at the Upper Arlington home of Doctor Armand Schliesser, chairman of the Department of Physics at Ohio State University," said a familiar-looking, white male TV reporter.

"It's not the kind of place where you'd expect a major crime bust, but, as you can see, that's what has just transpired here. On the basis of a federal warrant alleging civil rights violations, police and FBI agents have cracked what they call a major underground forced pregnancy center. Apparently, seven women have been freed from the center, and Doctor Schliesser has been taken into custody. A police spokesman said authorities expect to charge Schliesser with a variety of crimes, including violations of the Freedom of Choice Act . . . ."

Stillman, not wanting to hear any more, managed to work his way out of earshot. Now, in the midst of the swirling confusion, the gravity of the situation began to settle in.

He found his desire to get to Schliesser waning, his nerve failing. And as another blazing television Cyclops sprang to life nearby, the sensation turned to downright fear. More than anything else, he just wanted to get out and far away from this place.

"Why, Doctor Stillman!" chirped a familiar, oily voice. "How nice of you to drop by!"

Stillman squinted against the television camera glare, and then froze. It was—of all people—Julian Wickner, standing in Schliesser's wide-open front door. He felt another chill, this time the kind that causes hairs to stand up.

"Where—" he started to ask about Schliesser, then stopped himself "—where are they taking the women?"

"I understand they're going to the Riverside Mental Health Unit," Wickner said evenly.

"The Gulag," Stillman murmured. "Why the rubber room?"

"Oh," Wickner said with a dismissing wave of his hand, "just for observation, of course. Some of them eventually may be assigned to the Regional Deprogramming Center for Religious Extremism."

"Deprogramming," Stillman repeated.

He thought better of voicing any self-incriminating question. He felt the tide of panic rise another notch.

"And what, may I ask, brings you out this way?" Wickner asked quite pointedly.

"I was . . ." Stillman began, reddening as words suddenly failed him. He didn't want to lie, nor did he really want to tell the truth.

"Just passing by?" Wickner continued for him with thinly veiled sarcasm.

Just then, a young woman squeezed past Wickner in the doorway and inadvertently caught Stillman's eye. Behind her through the doorway came a tall man in a business suit emanating federal agent vibrations. Abruptly, the woman stopped and touched the man's arm.

"I know that man," she said, nodding toward Stillman.

The man gave Stillman the once-over. Wickner's eyebrows rose to new heights.

"You must be mistaken," Stillman asserted quickly. "I've only been here once before in my life."

As soon as he said it, he realized it was he who was mistaken. Now he recognized this woman quite clearly as one of Schliesser's tenants. This time, she did not appear the least bit pregnant. If anything, she gave strong impressions of an unmasked stool pigeon.

"He's lying," she told her male companion. "He's a friend of Schliesser. I've seen him here at the house."

The agent made a vague gesture, as if to say, "So what? I'm not interested in little fish."

Then Stillman's heart sank. Out from the shadows of the doorway came Armand Schliesser, his wrists tethered before him in handcuffs. He was being marched out of his own house by a Columbus policeman toward a waiting cruiser.

As the two passed, Schliesser's eyes met his. And in that glance, Stillman read volumes of emotion—innocence, betrayal, quiet determination, resigned acceptance of personal suffering, courage of conviction. Here was a softness and yet a strength that Stillman could not quite fathom.

Stillman wished he could say something, but words eluded him.

"Sorry about our appointment," said the physicist with gentle irony, pausing before the first step down from the porch. "In my absence, however, why don't you talk to Judith's husband about all of this? You might also find it helpful to look up Doctor Otto—"

Here the patrolman appeared to give Schliesser an impatient shove from behind with his baton. Only the strong grasp of another policeman prevented the old man from tumbling completely down the steps.

"—Jesperson," Schliesser managed to say before the second patrolman propelled him like a pinball toward the open back door of the cruiser.

And then the old man—and Stillman's hope—were swallowed by the night.

12

Peter had never dreamed like this before. The old man had presented the story of his Savior in a way that he found simply irresistible. After praying with Mr. Cathcart what the old man had called the "prayer of commitment," Peter had simply melted into sleep like a mouthful of cotton candy. He had given himself to God, and God had accepted the offer. It was the first time he had ever gone to sleep knowing that his fate was secure if he never woke again.

Now in these dreams Peter felt the original, untarnished goodness of creation, including his own exceedingly great personal worth. On a golden beach of liquid sunshine, he felt scrubbed clean, rinsed and spotless inside and out. Every particle of his being vibrated in harmony with the elements of the cosmos. The fairest of all winds warmed his soul and whispered of a God who was good, very good indeed—a God who was a person and who took a personal interest in Peter McBride.

Too soon he was being summoned to shore. Was Mr. Cathcart saying something?

Peter's eyes opened, and he saw the nurse preparing something he couldn't see. He started to speak, and then he stopped. This was not the same nurse. But what difference did it make?

"Excuse me," he said after clearing his throat.

The woman turned around so that he could see her face. It was a younger, sharper face with closely cropped black hair. It was not a particularly friendly face. In fact, Peter thought it looked rather cold and hard.

"Yes?" the nurse said as sharply as her face and as cold as her eyes.

"Uh, when's dinner around here?" asked Peter. "I don't think I've eaten in a couple of weeks."

That probably was the wrong way to talk to her.

"You're obviously a very confused young man," she said. "You just ate."

What? Who was she trying to kid? Peter McBride never forgot anything as important as a meal. Even his stomach was telling him that couldn't be true. Maybe *she* was confused, or maybe she wanted him to think that he was. But why? Maybe Mr. Cathcart could shed some light on things.

"Please don't move," said the woman none too pleasantly. "What are you trying to do?"

"Mr. Cathcart," said Peter, spying the other bed, now empty. "Where did he go?"

"Who?" said the nurse as if he were an idiot.

"The old man in that bed—my roommate."

She gave him a funny look. "There's no Mr. Cathcart. You don't have a roommate yet."

This was getting nowhere.

"Look, I don't know who you are," said Peter with effort, "but can I talk to the other nurse so I can prove that I'm not crazy? I don't make up names like Cathcart."

"What other nurse? What's her name?"

She had him there. "I don't know—something Filipino, maybe. Middle-aged."

The woman laughed humorlessly. "We don't have a middle-aged Filipino nurse in this unit."

"OK, have it your way. Just give me something to eat, then. Please."

"Mr. McBride," she said in her unconditional-surrender voice, "you're on a restricted diet for the first forty-eight hours.

What you need right now is rest. I'm going to give you something to make you sleep. When you wake up, we'll talk about food. OK?"

Peter said nothing, but his eyes fastened on the hypodermic needle that looked like an instrument of punishment in her hands, something of the caliber that zoologists might use in the primate cages. He couldn't make it add up. Why did they need to make him sleep? Was he injured worse than they had told him? He certainly didn't think so. In fact, he was feeling somewhat improved—not quite ready to wrestle the needle out of this woman's clutches, but not that bad, either.

He closed his eyes and submitted to her cold fingers. This one burned worse than the pain shot and seemed to take much longer to administer.

Peter opened his eyes and located her name pin. He wasn't going to make the same mistake again. This time he was going to remember the name.

"Tanya Powers, R.N." said the red-and-gray rectangular pin.

For the first time, the woman smiled as she left him. It reminded Peter of the way crocodiles smile.

Before he went under, he wanted to pray one more time. He remembered nearly every word of Mr. Cathcart's prayer of commitment, and he prayed through it all over again just to prove to himself that it was not his imagination, not something he'd dreamed. And even if it had been, it certainly was unreal no longer. He simply belonged to God now, and they couldn't take that away from him.

* * *

Angela Hurley stood with sweaty palms before the nurses' station of the Critical Care Unit at University Hospital, eying a petite, hatchet-faced woman with short, black hair who matched the description she had been given.

"Hello," Angie said when the woman looked up. "I'm Becky Leadingham, Steve Leadingham's sister."

"Oh, yes," the woman said, turning from her charts with a professional smile, as if she had been expecting Angie. "Tanya Powers."

Angie hazarded a glance around the milling bodies at the nursing station before plunging into her well-rehearsed lines. No one seemed to be paying them undue attention.

"I know it's not visiting hours, but I'm flying to Montreal this evening on business," Angie recited. "I hoped I could see my brother briefly once more before I go."

"Of course," Powers said, rising. "I'll take you over there."

"Thank you. I appreciate it so much."

Once in the room, Powers drew a curtain around Angie and the patient. The other bed was conveniently unoccupied. The nurse took the Do Not Disturb door-hanger off the inner door handle and left the room.

Wickner had said this woman, some respected associate of the Society, would ensure that the mechanism was removed after a satisfactory lapse of time from the patient's last vital spark. If someone did an autopsy, of course, the time-of-death discrepancy might be detected, but under the circumstances that was highly unlikely. There was no mystery about the nature of this man's malady—multiple perforations from an automatic weapon.

Angie turned Quang's emulator over in her hand and tried not to let her gaze rest too long upon the pallid face of the unconscious, intubated form. She dared not risk losing her nerve over some irrelevant sentimentality. There was too much at stake. Blow this simple assignment, and she'd be scratched for sure from the jailbreak mission. And if that happened, she'd probably lose her shot at initiation.

Locating the proper instruments on the bedside cart, Angie quickly fell to it. She felt around the back of the monitoring console until her fingers found the right spot. Then she quickly attached the emulator to the post, plugged the leads into the specified terminals and, allowing herself no time to vacillate, immediately switched on the unit power.

To all appearances, nothing had changed. Except for a momentary blip, life-support readouts continued tracking the same configurations as if the patient's cardiovascular system were still begin maintained. But she knew better.

"So long, Suit," she said, voicing her deep and abiding contempt for the white male power structure.

There. That wasn't so bad. In fact, it imparted a certain curious satisfaction.

Angie breathed a sigh of relief as the door closed and she began to put some distance behind her. Then she realized that someone with a quicker stride was overtaking her. She looked to her left and saw that it was Tanya Powers.

"Keep walking," Powers commanded in a very low voice.

They proceeded toward the end of the long corridor, past the nurses' station and the milling bodies in white uniforms and green scrubs. A woman's tired voice was calling doctors' names over the loudspeaker.

"Anything wrong?" asked Angie, growing apprehensive.

"Not exactly," the woman replied from the side of her mouth. "It may be that the Society would like to see how you respond to the unpredicted and spontaneous."

"I don't get it."

The woman made no response, but when they approached the nurses' station in the adjoining CCU Step-Down unit, another woman in white detached herself from the swarm and fell in with them on Angie's right.

Angie turned and saw red-rimmed glasses and short blonde hair. "Kelsey!" she said before she thought.

"Not so loud, you fool!" Kinsey whispered fiercely.

"Where are we going?" Angie asked in frustration.

Kinsey stopped by an alcove and commandeered a collapsible wheelchair. In another moment she had all four wheels on the floor and rolling.

"We're discharging Peter McBride," said the blonde woman, pushing the wheelchair.

Of course. Now it made sense. This was really the main event. The business with Leadingham had been just the overture. It hadn't added up before. If Tanya Powers was such a big-deal ally of the Society, couldn't she have implanted this emulator just as easily—maybe more easily? They didn't really need Angela Hurley for that. But once they had her wrapped up in one crime, it would be rather awkward for her to demur from another on the basis of principle, at least. And maybe they did indeed want to test her loyalty under pressure. She admired their cleverness.

But what did they want with Peter?

Once inside Peter's room, Kinsey went quickly about the business of rousing the patient from an apparently deep slumber.

Powers shoved some papers under Angie's nose. "Sign these," she said and disappeared.

A half minute later, Powers returned with an orderly to assist Kinsey in getting the boy out of bed and into the wheelchair.

Angie saw that the forms absolved the hospital from legal liability in the case of a patient's premature discharge against medical advice. She signed in the appropriate places as concurring member of the immediate family.

"What about the place for patient's signature?" she asked.

Powers took the pen from her, skimmed quickly through the verbiage, circled the phrase "head injury," and handed back the forms and the pen.

"Sign it for him," she directed.

Angie did so, wondering just how serious the head injury was. She had been told it was superficial, which must be true or it wouldn't be safe to discharge him.

Peter's eyes were only half open, and his head tended to yaw around a bit. Kinsey managed to secure a better arrangement in the wheelchair with some hook-and-loop closure tape. They appeared ready to roll.

"Here," said Powers, tossing a clear plastic bag to Kinsey, who caught it neatly. "Antibiotics. Pain caplets. Take as directed."

"No special treatment?" said Kinsey, wheeling Peter at last toward the door.

"Just the usual—suture removal in five to seven days, debridement only as needed."

"I can handle that," said Kinsey, motioning Angie to take over squiring the wheelchair.

In another moment they were headed back down the busy corridor toward the elevator that would take them three floors down to the south entrance by the rear parking lot. There Elizabeth Morningstar and chief grunt Brandon Govinda should be waiting in a blue-and-white van.

As the elevator doors opened, Angie thought she heard the sound of running feet behind her.

Kinsey apparently heard it too. "Get in quick!" said the woman.

The other two people on the elevator, apparently interns, continued their own conversation while Angie hurriedly bump-bumped Peter's wheelchair a little roughly inside.

The footsteps closed the distance.

"Wait!" cried a young woman's voice only several strides away.

But it was too late. Kinsey already had pushed the "Close Doors" button. "Oops!" she said, presumably for the doctors' benefit. "Wrong button. Oh, well."

And close they did, right in the young woman's face, but not before Angie saw clearly her identity—Carlotta Waldo! The question was whether Carlotta had identified her.

In either case, she'd no doubt spotted Peter. And that meant they'd better step on it.

* * *

McBride sat behind the wheel of his gray Capricorn in the east parking lot of University Hospital, drinking coffee from a plastic cup and thinking of hideouts and heaters. He remembered a few places that Jimmy Shapiro had found useful for cooling out. Carlotta just about had him convinced that it might come to that. He regretted that he no longer had a license for packing a pistol. But nobody else seemed to worry about formalities like that. He wasn't sure why he should, especially under the circumstances.

McBride was also wondering as he sat and sipped whether he'd made a mistake to give in to Carlotta's compulsiveness in going to the hospital. She wanted to see with her own eyes that Peter was all right. McBride wanted to let his stepson sleep. So they'd left it that Carlotta would call him on the carphone if Peter was awake and having visitors. In that case, McBride would come up. Otherwise, he'd gaze at his navel a little more and figure out some next moves.

Might as well find out about Steve while he was at it. He picked up the carphone and asked for UH Patient Information.

"Critical but stable," the woman told him.

"How about another patient—Peter McBride in three thirty seven? What's his condition?"

"Three thirty seven? Just a minute," said the woman, sounding uncertain. "Uh, Peter McBride . . . has been discharged."

"There must be some mistake." McBride's pulse quickened. "Are you sure you're talking about Peter McBride in three thirty seven?"

"Yes, sir."

"How long ago was this?"

"It was just posted, sir. Couldn't have been more than a few minutes ago."

"Are you sure about that?"

There was the slightest pause, which McBride interpreted as the woman's patience straining under the load.

"Yes, sir. Quite sure."

"Do you know who he left with?" McBride was wondering if somehow Carlotta had done this.

"No, sir," said the woman, "but I could transfer you to that unit if you like."

"Great. Thanks."

In another half minute a woman named Sommers picked up the line in CCU Step-Down.

"You want to know who was the discharging party for Peter McBride?"

"Yes, that's right."

"And you are . . . ?"

"Neal McBride, Peter's father."

"OK," said the woman, sounding as if she were tapping on a keyboard. "That's not entered yet. Let me see these papers up here—"

"I assume you don't just let your patients wander off," he said a little impatiently.

"No, no," said the woman, taking no offense. "I saw him leave with a young woman. Here it is—Angela Hurley."

McBride was floored. Recovering as quickly as he could, he thanked the woman and hung up. He took another sip of tepid black coffee and pondered the significance of that development. Any way he looked at it, he didn't like it.

In another moment he started up the Capricorn's engine and began cruising slowly through the lot. It would have to be too late for him to go looking inside the hospital. But with any luck he might spot them on the way out. He could only hope that Carlotta might have gotten somewhere on the inside.

Seeing nothing here, McBride worked his way slowly through the north parking area and on into the west lot, straining his eyes for the picture he expected to see—a young man with curly hair in a wheelchair being pushed by his older sister.

If he saw nothing by the time he'd covered the south lot, McBride determined that he'd go back to the parking garage and hang loose by the entrance, where he might spot the right faces through a car window. The only problem was that Carlotta wouldn't know what had happened if she returned to the original parking space and didn't find him there. But at this point, that was a detail.

Suddenly, part of the picture jumped before his eyes. He spotted Carlotta running from the south entrance, waving one hand and perhaps shouting as if in pursuit of someone. At the end of the sidewalk on her flight path was a blue-and-white van loading a passenger with a wheelchair lift. McBride had a good idea who that might be. Whether Carlotta would get there in time was questionable.

Somehow, she did get there pretty quickly—faster, in fact, than did McBride. Angling through the parking lanes, he lost sight of Carlotta momentarily. Then he thought he saw her being thrown into the backseat by a bruiser who should have been playing fullback for the Buckeyes. He never saw Angie, but there were two other people in the van, both arguably women. She could have been one of them.

McBride, closing the distance, considered doing something brave and foolish—like blocking their vehicle with his—and then thought better of it. Probably the best he could hope for would be to stay on their tail, preferably invisibly, until they'd arrived at their destination. And then what? He cursed the fact that he had no gun. The glove compartment would be a wonderful place for one right now. In his shoulder clip would be even better.

Could he go to the police? That was a joke, without better information at least. McBride squinted at the license plate of the blue-and-white Jupiter and memorized the number as it began to pull away. On the road he wouldn't dare get that close again. He had no idea who these people were or whether they might try to beat information out of Carlotta—like how she'd got to the hospital and with whom.

As McBride had expected, the Jupiter was establishing a beeline to the outerbelt. Theoretically that should make it a little easier for him to ensure that at least one vehicle stayed between them at all times for cover.

But at the first green light, the Jupiter darted over into the curb lane without signaling. Too late, he saw a gun sticking out a left rear window. The only thing he could do was hit the brakes. Changing lanes would only make matters worse, as there was no car between them in that lane.

Instantly, McBride heard a report, and his windshield turned into a white, spidery mosaic like the back door at The Happy Medium. Now he couldn't see much of anything, but that hardly mattered, since he wasn't going much of anywhere either. Several more reports, and the Capricorn was lumbering to the side of the road on two blowouts.

McBride was covered with a thousand little glass shardlets, but he seemed unhurt.

As he sat by the side of the road in his now three-toned car with its fractured windshield and blown tires, McBride recalled how much he appreciated a challenge.

No wife. No children. No Carlotta. No job. No friends. No gun. No car.

Nothing but four clues.

13

McBride had a feeling when he paid the cabbie and walked the few yards up his own driveway to the front door. It was the unshakable suspicion of something's being wrong. Jimmy Shapiro called it "gut," and it usually came into play at times like finding a bomb planted under the hood of the car. Or coming home and finding the house has been burglarized.

At least McBride didn't have a car hood to worry about now.

By the time he identified himself at his front-door voicebox, he knew his gut was right again. The security device was not working, and he had to fish out an old-fashioned key and turn it in the old-fashioned lock. Theoretically, the intruder light was supposed to come on if the security system was violated, but most house guys knocked that out in the process. McBride hoped they hadn't gotten into his weapons cache.

On the first floor, he found drawers, closets, and cupboard doors standing open and the contents in an upheaval. Upstairs was the same story—clothes sticking out of drawers, and books and toiletries and miscellaneous personal items strewn about randomly. McBride's irritation was replaced with curiosity as he took mental inventory. If this had been a burglary, it was a strange affair. He could think of nothing that was missing. The usual heist stuff—jewelry, electronics, silver—was intact as far as he could tell.

There was, however, one notable exception—a bloodlike stain on his own pillow in the upstairs bedroom, where the covers were turned back. Was that supposed to be a sign—the culprits' calling card?

It could be that this party was letting him know they could have him whenever they wanted and he'd better watch his step, keep his nose clean, leave the neo-pagans alone, et cetera. Either that or they just got carried away with themselves in a pillow fight on the premises.

Downstairs, McBride was gratified to find that the extra-large strongbox in his basement study appeared unmolested. That was where the guns were. When he uttered the combination, the door sprang open with a refrigerator-type light revealing the lethal contents. There were several quarts of Colt, some loaves of Remington, a few pounds of Smith & Wesson, and even a cup of Uzi.

No sooner had his fingers closed happily about the reassuring grip of a Glock .45 than he suddenly froze. There was a rumble that resolved in another moment into the sound of a car in the drive. He stuffed the pistol under his belt and grabbed a 12-gauge shotgun from the rack. Hearing the sound of a car door, he slammed the locker shut and bounded up the stairs.

At the front window McBride pulled back the curtain a few centimeters to locate his visitor. He was ready for a pillow fight of his own.

Up the drive strolled the trim, unthreatening figure of someone McBride felt immediately he should know. By the time the guest was on the doorstep, he finally placed him—Judith's colleague, Dr. Richard Stillman. The professor looked a little bedraggled. But then, McBride realized, maybe he himself did too.

"Hello, Doctor Stillman," McBride said, opening the door.

"Hello, Judge," Stillman mumbled, eying the shotgun at McBride's side. "Who's your friend?"

"Oh," said McBride, holding up the weapon like a newly caught fish. "I beg your pardon. Meet Mr. Browning, Doctor Stillman. Mr. Browning and I were investigating a house burglary just as you pulled up."

"Good grief. Your own?"

McBride nodded. "Nothing missing that I can tell. They either didn't find what they were looking for, or they just want me to know who's boss. It may be time to find a temporary change of address."

Stillman, his eyes grown wide, nodded.

"Can I offer you a cup of coffee or a longarm or something?" McBride gestured toward the kitchen.

"Coffee would be great," said Stillman as if he really meant it.

"What brings you here?" McBride said once they were comfortably situated at the spacious kitchen table with their coffee mugs.

Stillman's tired eyes rested on the large-caliber pistol McBride had laid on the end of the table. He obviously wasn't used to guns as casual kitchen appliances.

"I'm not really sure," Stillman said. "Doctor Schliesser suggested I talk to you."

McBride needed to be reminded who Armand Schliesser was and was surprised to learn of his arrest.

"Schliesser busted?" McBride said, as if the two words had trouble fitting together. "Strange brew. Just how did he think I might help you?"

Stillman took a thoughtful swallow of coffee, pondering the question, and appeared dissatisfied with the results. "I don't know," he said with an exasperated and slightly embarrassed sigh. "Unless you happen to know the answers to the eternal questions about life and death, heaven and hell."

McBride chuckled. "Sure thing. I made several rulings on those. Of course, they were all overturned on appeal."

Stillman looked puzzled for a moment, and then his eyes cleared. He laughed then, too, as if it had been a while since he had last done so.

"Let's start at proverbial square one," said McBride. "The main thing you and I have in common, shall we say, is Judith. Right?"

"Correct," said Stillman, a bit more relaxed. "I had been trying to determine just what drove her . . . over the edge—and just what Jeremy Kay might have had to do with it. And it's almost as if the same bug is trying to bite me."

McBride raised his eyebrows as if Stillman should say more.

"I know it's crazy," continued Stillman, lowering his voice self-consciously, "but did you ever feel like the rest of the world was going mad and you were the only person still sane? Isn't that itself crazy?"

"Not crazy at all," McBride said emphatically. "I can relate perfectly. I'm there."

Stillman looked pleasantly surprised.

"Having your good friend shot, your son kidnapped, your car shot up, and your home ransacked is guaranteed to get your attention," McBride continued. "They're certainly not things that happen every day."

Stillman, incredulous, asked for the full story, and McBride obliged, recounting the last couple of days of intrigue and misadventure at The Happy Medium and University Hospital.

"So now, about all I have to go on are three cryptic phrases," he concluded, "one license plate number, and a confused college professor who shows up on my doorstep looking for answers—"

"—and who doesn't even know the right questions," Stillman concluded for him. "But listen—what were those phrases your friend used?"

McBride reached for his wallet and extracted a folded notepaper.

"I'm no cryptographer," added Stillman, "but I am a linguist. Let me take a shot at it."

"OK. First one is . . . *conceptus.*"

Stillman pursed his lips and looked distracted. "Obviously something conceived," he said tentatively.

"But what?" said McBride. "*I* can figure that much out."

"Maybe a euphemism for an unborn child, a fetus. I don't know. I know some people I could ask."

"OK," said McBride with a shrug. "Next one is . . . *Fahlgren.*"

"Fahlgren," Stillman repeated. "That rings a bell. It's a family name—a Columbus family, I think. Somebody important. Maybe."

McBride smiled patiently. He didn't know Rick Stillman well enough to razz him.

"I know," Stillman said sheepishly. "I'm a big lot of help. Give me one more chance. I'll do better, I promise."

"All right. Just one more chance. Last one is—if I'm pronouncing it right—*Chi Xi Vau.*"

Stillman had that incredulous look again. "Say that again."

"Chi Xi Vau."

Stillman shook his head. "You're not going to believe this."

"Try me."

"All right. How are you on biblical prophecy?"

"No good at all."

"Well, this would be your basic Beast of Revelation."

"What?" said McBride, dumbfounded.

"Some people call it the—uh—Antichrist."

"I see," said McBride, wondering who was the crazier—Rick Stillman or Steve Leadingham.

"Was your friend Leadingham a religious fanatic of any kind?"

"Not at all."

"The only reason I happen to know about this at all is because of the Bible translation project. Did Judith tell you anything about that?"

McBride shook his head.

"Well, she had agreed to undertake a Bible translation venture with a Chicago missions agency. It would have meant some major grant money for Cybersynchronics. That's my specialty."

Stillman briefly described the Rhema Institute and how Darnell Jones and Aaron Fitzgerald had demonstrated supposed numeric values in Scripture, using the Beast reference.

McBride had learned professionally to listen to all kinds of bizarre assertions with an open mind. This was only a little bigger stretch—and it was certainly more to go on than he had before, which was essentially nothing.

"So, what do *you* make of all this?" he asked.

Stillman furrowed his brow. "I don't know. Your friend could have been raving and delirious. Or he could have been dropping real pearls about your enemy. 'Chi Xi Vau' could be their spiritual pedigree or even their name. If so, they're obviously some kind of pagan or occult group. I'm really guessing now, but 'Fahlgren' and 'conceptus' could have something to do with their business or their location, or both."

Suddenly McBride was becoming a believer. "I like the way you think."

"Well, that's just for starters. I'd like to try some other resources—experts and data banks."

"Go on. Any other ideas?"

"No. But obviously it would be real helpful if your friend Leadingham doesn't die. And considering what happened to Peter—"

"—Steve may not be safe in that hospital bed." McBride finished the sentence for him. "I know. Peter's girlfriend, Carlotta, had tried to tell me I was being naive about that. I guess she was right."

Stillman nodded and lapsed into silence.

McBride didn't say anything, but it now occurred to him that probably the only reason he himself had not ended up on the wrong end of a trigger was because he technically was still employed as a judge. But that could end in forty-eight hours.

And then he remembered the license number. "Excuse me. I almost forgot. I have one last item—the license number of the van that spirited Peter and Carlotta off."

He called a number from memory on the kitchen console and asked for a woman named Francine. After some small talk he gave her the license number. Almost before he could say "blue-and-white Jupiter," she had the registration for him, and he thanked her.

"Any luck?" asked Stillman.

McBride shrugged negatively. "It's not going to be easy. The rascal was a rental."

"Great."

"Doctor Stillman, I'm not sure Doctor Schliesser was quite right when he suggested that I might be able to help you. But I have a fair idea that you might be able to help me, if you're willing."

Stillman smiled. "It sounds like we might be barking up different sides of the same tree. But you'd have to call me 'Rick.'"

"Yeah, well, call me 'Neal,' Rick."

They shook on it.

"Besides," said Stillman, "I've got wheels, and you don't."

"All right, partner," said McBride, laughing. "Let's saddle up. This probably isn't the healthiest place to hang out."

"Where to?"

"If you've got the time, you can give me some moral support while I pay a visit to Latchman Motors and talk to a man about a blue-and-white Jupiter van."

"I'm a vapor trail."

* * *

The auto rental was way over on the south side of town in an unlikely industrial area that apparently had been showing its age

154

for some time. Latchman Motors was just down the road, however, from a cluster of outerbelt motels and not far from a decent residential section, which probably accounted for some of its business. But there were a few flatbed, pick-up, and utility trucks for rent too. Some of the vehicles were current models. Many were not, by several years.

The real estate itself matched the immediate neighborhood—weeds popping up through the cracks in the blacktopped lot, peeling paint, and streaked plate glass on the office, which probably had been an auto showroom in an earlier incarnation. Inside was a pop machine, a TV playing out a soap opera, and a bored-looking, buzz-cut young man behind the counter, smoking a cigarette.

The kid had a dark green name tag and an attitude. The name tag said "TOBY LATCHMAN." The attitude said he was only doing this while going to college and not to get in his face because the boss was his old man.

"Yeah," Toby said unhappily, as if McBride and Stillman had just spoiled the taste of his cigarette.

"We'd like to ask you a few questions," said McBride.

"We rent cars and trucks," said the kid. "Next question."

"And vans?" said McBride.

"A few," Toby agreed.

"I'd like to rent a blue-and-white Jupiter with a wheelchair lift."

The kid blew some smoke into the air, closer to his customers' faces than Emily Post would have endorsed.

"You can have a green Jupiter—no wheelchair lift," he said suspiciously.

"Oh," said McBride, crestfallen. "It really has to have the lift. I liked that blue-and-white job. Is it rented?"

"Might be," said the kid, with the loquacity of a New England farmer.

"When's it due back?"

"Not for a while."

"The guy who's got it now—could I give him a call and see if we could work something out? Could I have his number?"

Toby ground out his cigarette impatiently. "We don't give that out. What're you trying to pull anyway? If you're not rentin' something, see ya later."

"Wait," Stillman interceded. "We'll take the green Jupiter."

McBride was startled, but he could appreciate the logic in trying to keep the ball in play. Besides, he really did need some wheels while his car was at the adjustor's and the body shop.

Initially, he had considered pulling a bluff with his expired private investigator's license and grilling the kid like a hostile witness. But he rejected the idea for fear of sending word back to the enemy about hounds on the trail.

The kid looked kind of surprised too, but he quickly got the paperwork together.

Stillman signed for everything.

McBride wondered what the professor was up to, but he was just glad not to have his own name on anything. If the kid started running his mouth, it wouldn't do to have the McBride name connected with any of it.

"Can you get the van?" Stillman said to McBride. "I really need to call the office. May I use your phone?"

This last he said to the kid, who grunted and nodded at the phone behind the counter on the desk.

Toby then grabbed his clipboard and motioned for McBride to follow him out to the lot.

Now McBride thought he had a pretty good idea what Stillman was up to.

* * *

Sure enough, Stillman all but had canary feathers sticking out of his mouth when McBride saw him next out in the lot by the green Jupiter.

"Look here," said Stillman, smiling over a scrap of computer printout. "Toby's computer just happened to be on and—"

"—you just happened to punch up the right file for blue-and-white Jupiters with wheelchair lifts?"

"Something like that."

McBride peered over his shoulder and read the rental information. Someone named Brandon Govinda was renting this vehicle by the month at a rather dear price. The charges were being picked up by something called the Institute for Pre-Life Science in a suite in the R. S. Bloom Tower in the high-rent district on East Broad

Street near the Statehouse. There was a phone number. This smelled like a front, but it was a start.

"Good work," McBride said enthusiastically, clapping Stillman on the shoulder.

"Piece of cake," said Stillman, beaming. "Computers are my business."

"Now let's go house-hunting."

Stillman looked at his watch and demurred. "I have one more class. Call me by five o'clock, wherever you are, and I'll meet you."

"It's a deal, partner."

★ ★ ★

Figuring he probably was going to have to change digs more than once, McBride opted for a Jimmy Shapiro special—the best room in the cheapest outerbelt motel. This time it was the east side Imperial Crown in Reynoldsburg, just because he remembered Jimmy frequently had found that neighborhood comfortable and anonymous.

McBride even thought he recognized the proprietor, a henpecked old guy with white stubble all over his head who seemed good at keeping his mouth shut. It probably had something to do with his ill-fitting dentures.

The old fellow almost smiled when McBride asked for the honeymoon suite. But he knew what McBride meant and tossed him the keys to 201, an efficiency that rented by the week or, if you asked politely, by the day for just a few dollars more than the other daily rooms.

McBride left a message for Stillman at Grady Hall with directions to the Imperial Crown, then took a warm, relaxing shower. He decided to lie down on the horse-blanket-pattern sofa and rest his eyes for a few minutes.

★ ★ ★

McBride was dreaming of another interview with Corrie Washington. This time he was giving her a big piece of his mind. He was actually enjoying it, at least up until the moment he realized the reporter's microphone was actually a .38-caliber police special and the cameraperson's gear was a shoulder-mounted rocket launcher.

Talk about your fireworks—the discharges were deafening.

And then he realized where he was and that the racket had to be somebody at the door, pounding as insistently as Carlotta with a bright idea. Stillman, no doubt.

He was right. It was Stillman, bearing a haul of pizza and pop. McBride's stomach leaped for joy.

At first, they chewed in silence. McBride contemplated the crime against art that had been committed on the opposite wall. By the third piece of grease, the wheels were turning once more.

"One thing still bothers me," said Stillman, chewing.

"Which is?"

"Why not just go to the police?"

McBride washed down a swallow with a slug of cream soda. He could think of a pile of cynical and uncharitable reasons that Jimmy Shapiro might give about the boys and girls in blue, but he opted instead for the rhetorical question.

"If you're Sergeant O'Malley," said McBride, "are you going to want to hear any of my story about my stepdaughter maybe abducting her brother? Or the burglary where nothing's missing? Or the red stuff on my pillow that might be blood?"

"OK," agreed Stillman. "But how about your shot-up car?"

"Random gang violence. Same as at The Happy Medium, where they did take a report. Except weaker—nobody's even hurt this time."

"Yeah," Stillman conceded sourly. "And Sergeant O'Malley would probably get a real kick out of hearing about the Beast of Revelation."

McBride startled him by snapping his fingers.

"Wait a minute. You're absolutely right. There is one cop I'd trust on this—Lieutenant Vincent Salerno."

"Who?"

McBride explained about the sheriff's detective who had specialized in occult investigations and testified in the Larrabee trial.

"Sounds like a winner to me," agreed Stillman. "Let's see if we can get him on our team. You know, I think we have a lot more cards than we realize."

"How's that?"

"Well, we've got the lead on that Pre-Life Science outfit—which, by the way, may have something to do with conceptus, at least by the sound of it."

"Yeah. Go on," said McBride, smiling. "I keep liking the way you think."

Stillman, who had been holding up one finger, now held up a second. "Now, you just came up with this Salerno fellow. And while you were doing that, it reminded me of something else—someone Doctor Schliesser had mentioned to me the same time he recommended going to you."

"Oh?"

"A man named Doctor Otto Jesperson. I don't know who he is, except that he's not in the Ohio State directory. The point is, we've not yet begun to fight. If this guy's teaching anywhere, I ought to be able to find him."

"Fine. What's he good for?"

"I don't really know. But Schliesser seemed to think that this Larrabee trial might be stepping on some big toes in the occult/pagan world. So Jesperson may hold some key to that—the Chi Xi Vau angle."

"Here's a thought. I wonder what would happen if your friends from Chicago came in here and actually started up that Bible translation project? Do they figure into this equation some way?"

"I've been as much as told to forget it."

"By whom?"

"Julian Wickner, Judith's acting successor."

McBride's eyebrows went up. "I remember *that* name. Judith despised him. Maybe you could smoke some of these characters out of the woodwork with a little provocation."

"Like starting up the translation project?"

"Maybe. You might be surprised. At this point, we just need to start rolling the dice. Unless Steve Leadingham makes a sudden and miraculous recovery . . ."

"We need to know what he knows," agreed Stillman. "Is there any way of getting him out of that hospital?"

"Not without killing him."

"It does sound like we need some miracles."

"Well, there's one more resource we're not counting."

"What's that?"

"Jimmy Shapiro."

"Who?"

"Jimmy Shapiro. Did I ever tell you I used to be a private eye?"

"No," said Stillman, fascinated. "How's that?"

"I'm glad you asked."

"Uh-oh. Let me throw another log on the fire. I feel a long story coming on."

Stillman was right.

The mood was modestly jubilant in the Pre-Life Science clinic in the bowels of Chateau Fahlgren. Angie, looking down upon the peacefully unconscious forms of her brother, Peter, and his girlfriend, Carlotta, was quite aware that she was a momentary heroine of sorts.

"Well, well," said Julian Wickner, as delighted as a squirrel in a nut shop. "A successful mission, indeed."

"*Two* successful missions," corrected Jeremy Kay, surveying their haul. "Leadingham's plug has been pulled, and we have not one but two new . . . subjects."

"And Quang will be pleased to know the emulator has been successfully field-tested," said Wickner. "There's no reason it couldn't be used with equal success on a prison security system."

"What—what do you intend to do with these two?" said Angie, trying not to sound overly concerned, because she wasn't really.

"That depends," said Kay, just as carefully. "If they're not needed, they'll be free to go. Unless they want to stick around and go through the ranks of initiation like yourself and others. But, of course, we always need subjects for OUIJA."

Kelsey Kinsey was peeling back the sterile dressing on Peter's head wound. Apparently satisfied by what she saw, she moved on to the leg injury, this time replacing some of the gauze. She then went about checking blood monitoring levels on Quang's equipment, first for Peter, then for Carlotta. There was obviously some serious sedation going on.

Kay and Wickner began moving out of the room and over to Quang's makeshift office next door.

Angie figured she should follow.

"More precisely, the answer to your question," said Kay, sitting down behind the desk, "really depends a great deal on Judge McBride."

He indicated that Angie should be seated on the other side.

Wickner remained standing.

"How's that?" asked Angie, drawing a blank.

"First of all—" Kay folded his hands before him "—it depends on your father's intentions regarding his . . . future employment."

"And secondly," said Wickner, picking up the thought, "whether he might be persuaded to have your mother declared incompetent so we can finally straighten things around, as it were, in her department."

Kay laughed. "That's Julian—always looking out for Number One. Don't you have a class or something you should be teaching, Julian?"

That's where Quang was at the moment—on campus fulfilling his university obligations.

Wickner appeared unfazed by the ribbing. "Not till this afternoon. I've managed to delegate a lot of things to Rick Stillman. Keeps him out of trouble."

Angie had some difficulty keeping up. She managed to figure out that Wickner, naturally, was interested in her mother's job. Personally, Angie wasn't too keen on that idea, and she knew her stepfather would never go for it. But she also realized this could be another test of her loyalty. She was forced to confess her ignorance, however, about her stepfather's "employment" plans.

"He's so bolluxed up the Larrabee case," Kay asserted, "that he's expected to be stepping down from the bench—to spend more time with his sick wife."

"We just want to know," said Wickner with a cloying smile, "if he's going to fish or cut bait."

"And we thought, of course, that you would be just the person to call him and find out," said Kay, nodding at the communicator at the other end of the desk.

Angie smiled. "No sweat," she said. "Why didn't you say so before?"

While she placed the call, Kay and Wickner exchanged smug glances.

Actually, it took two calls, and both were unproductive.

"His secretary says he's on vacation," said Angie, frowning. "And there's no answer at his house."

Kay swore indelicately. "Do you suppose he's playing some kind of cute game?"

Wickner shook his head uncertainly, and Angie shrugged.

"He can be—resourceful," she volunteered. "He's not stupid."

"Well, so can we," Kay said angrily. "I say we move on Larrabee right now."

Wickner nodded. "Who knows how long this mistrial business could drag on?"

"All right," said Kay, fixing Angie in his steely gaze. "Are you ready for Mission Number Two?"

"Let me at 'em."

* * *

When Jared Quang arrived, he paid scant attention to the tidings of Angie and Kinsey's successful first mission and the vindication of his brainchild, the emulator. It was almost as if he had no reaction.

Angie was learning that Quang did not wear his feelings on his sleeve—if he indeed had the full range of normal emotions and sensibilities. She assured herself that he must, just to a lesser degree.

"Of course it worked," Quang said, shrugging. "Why wouldn't it?"

Instead of celebrating, he immediately fell to work rolling out the new and improved second-generation emulator, which was somewhat larger and more complex—as befitted the magnitude of the task.

Angie had to ask him any number of times to repeat his instructions, and she was grateful in this case for his passionless demeanor. It took them much of the afternoon in repeated test runs on various pieces of equipment in the electronics shop before Quang was satisfied that she understood what she was doing well enough to improvise as the need might arise from adverse circumstances.

It was hard work. Angie realized she would have had no hope of mastering this system had she not been through the simpler first-generation version. But at last Quang was ready to pronounce her competent.

"You'll do," he said simply, coiling up some of his wires.

Just as she was preparing to unwind, relax, and do her nails, she was jolted by Quang's next utterance.

"Now you teach Elizabeth."

Angie, blinking, realized he meant *now*.

Quang, who may have been reading her reaction in her eyes, said simply, "No one really understands something until she can teach it to someone else. Besides, you might get shot or something, and Elizabeth actually would have to pick up your slack."

That was a reassuring thought, Angie reflected as Quang left to summon her partner on this assignment.

It had not taken Angie long to figure out which of her other two Chateau Fahlgren coconspirators would be picked for the mission, just as it had not taken her long to figure out which one was the doer and which the dilettante.

"Moira is simply not ready," Kay had said earlier when he informed Angie that Elizabeth Morningstar would be her accomplice. "We can't afford to have two rookies on a caper like this."

This pretty-girl Moira Stone maintained a professorial aloofness that grated on Angie. In their few and limited conversations, the Egyptologist seemed more interested in identifying the ritual traditions behind the various esoteric practices of Chi Xi Vau than in actually participating in any of these activities. Jeremy and the others, however, appeared to hold her in a good deal of esteem for whatever reasons of their own—which Angie really suspected was nothing more than a pretty face. But nobody, it appeared, was particularly expecting Moira to be doing any heavy lifting.

Elizabeth Morningstar, on the other hand, was just the kind of person to go with into the trenches. She might be a bit humorless for Angie's taste, but she was certainly a dynamic, take-charge individual who inspired confidence.

This time, when Morningstar walked into the Pre-Life electronics shop, Angie almost failed to recognize her. She looked years younger in a short skirt and without her heavy makeup and gray wig. This could have been the girl next door, if it was a neighborhood with any class. Angie could imagine some practical benefits to being able to go virtually incognito in your "normal" identity. But looking more closely, she could see the same severe yet other-worldly set to the mouth and eyes that marked the Elizabeth Morningstar of the popular "Astroscope" column.

The matronly look was just her astrologer's persona for public consumption. But in Morningstar's case, there was something more than just high regard for her in the organization; she appeared to wield some decision-making authority within Chi Xi Vau. Angie remained confused about the hierarchy, but she suspected that might be by design.

Quang appeared to busy himself with some other tasks, but Angie was aware that he was never totally out of earshot as she and Morningstar went through the same paces with the emulator that he had put Angie through earlier. She certainly hoped that this was one precaution that would prove unnecessary.

Tomorrow, Morningstar had the challenging task of creating a diversion for Angie's operation while arranging a "visit" with Roger Larrabee. This would be an acting job, more than anything else. It just might work, but Angie was making no predictions. These things involved more than one element of chance.

★ ★ ★

At the Franklin County Jail the next morning, Angie learned another piece of trivia about Elizabeth Morningstar. Her real name was Elizabeth Schmidt.

That was not, however, the name she used at the front desk. There, she identified herself as criminal defense attorney Beth Anne Perry.

And this time she looked like neither Morningstar nor the girl next door. In a smartly tailored business suit and an ash-blonde wig, this valise-toting woman was the picture of mature, professional elegance.

And when she turned on the charm, it worked wonders in the booking room with Deputy Sheriffs Terry Smith and Dan Jones. Before the two men could even think of questioning her identity, she had set them at ease with a few quick words. By the time she was done, Smith and Jones were actually laughing.

"No, these aren't aliases," Smith said, chuckling, while Jones appeared to be ogling the two women.

Angie, introduced as Morningstar's paralegal assistant, Allison Carpenter, laughed right along with them. *If they only knew.*

Her own disguise consisted of a long brunette wig, plain-glass eyeglasses, and a conservative plaid pants suit. Angie felt at once elegant and a little silly.

The deputies pointed Morningstar to one of the call directors that she could use to place her very important call, ostensibly to the Public Defender's office.

"Help yourself," said Jones, winking. "Your tax dollars at work."

Being consummate gentlemen, the two deputies even managed to busy themselves in the next room with some other matters so the ladies could make their very important call in relative privacy.

Perfect.

Angie quickly unsnapped the mouthpiece, identified the spaghetti she'd been trained to look for, and clipped the pincers from Quang's small contraption into place on the green and red wires. Once determining with a glance over her shoulder that she was not being observed, she systematically began keying in numerical sequences on the phone pad. The first combination momentarily caused every number on the line board to light up, but the next moment everything was back to normal, and she was able to continue.

Then came the reassuring chitterings of two computer modems making handshaking interface. Angie began to relax a bit. Even now, Quang and OUIJA were undoubtedly sucking the other computer dry and giving it some new programing to boot.

Suddenly there was her next cue—*beep-beep, beep-beep, beep-beep*. She depressed 0-6 three times. The beeping stopped, replaced by barely audible white noise and then finally the synthesized voice she had been conditioned to expect.

"One-oh-three A. Four-four-two-five-one," the voice droned. "One-oh-three A. Four-four-two-five-one. One-oh-three A. Four-four-two-five-one. . . ."

Angie pressed "Hold" and quickly hung up. She rose and nodded at Morningstar, who waved at Sgt. Smith through the doorway as they strode rapidly down the hall. The deputies hardly looked up as the two women whisked off toward the visitors' block. So far, so good.

Over and over Angie repeated silently to herself, *One-oh-three A. Four-four-two-five-one.*

Eyeing the black-stenciled numbers on the wall, she followed Morningstar past the visitors' block, ducking down the next corridor, rounding a corner, and coming up at the last door to an actual block of cells.

Angie watched Morningstar's fingers beat out a code on the security keypad. The door unbolted, and she braced for the inevitable catcalls as they scurried through and headed straight for cell 103-A.

By this time, she expected OUIJA to have neutralized the security cameras, not just disabling them but creating a communications failure that would appear innocent enough while presenting quite a hassle—not to mention distraction—for the jailers.

Surprisingly, there was only one puny wolf whistle from the cells, though Angie was well aware that she was the object of silent scrutiny from numerous pairs of male eyes. Maybe they were too taken aback to react quickly.

Once Morningstar located the security keypad for cell 103-A, Angie stepped up and began stabbing numbers—4-4-2-5-1. Instantly, there was a buzz and then a *kachunk*. Roger Larrabee's cell door popped forward one fateful inch and stopped.

Out of the shadows a hand grasped one of the bars, followed by an emerging face—a wispy, dark brown moustache, large, brown, doe eyes that seemed capable of sensitivity, yet undercut by a mouth in a smug grimace.

Then Larrabee was out in the hall, twisting Morningstar's arm viciously. Angie jumped back. Men began hooting, hollering, banging things in the other cells.

"Who are you?" Larrabee snarled, shoving his face next to Morningstar's.

"Your fairy godmother," she gasped. "Let go, you idiot, and let's get out of here."

Larrabee didn't exactly let go, but they did make pretty good time closing the distance to the visitors' block. Time was of the essence. The sabotaged security cameras notwithstanding, Angie knew it was only a matter of time before the jailers got wind of what was happening, or until they actually stumbled onto the crime in progress.

"Here." Morningstar offered Larrabee a small weapon that she had secreted inside her dress.

It was an illegal plastic pistol, just in case there were metal detectors. Larrabee snatched it like a cat taking a bird. Fortunately, this ruffian paid little heed to Angie, who was quietly bringing up the rear.

Then they rounded the corner and were hard upon the visitors' block. An older deputy stood outside the door, looking quite bored.

"Inside, Pops!" Larrabee ordered, waving the pistol under the man's nose.

As he spun the deputy toward the room, Larrabee extracted the fellow's service revolver from his holster. He jammed the smaller plastic pistol into his pants and kept the .38 as his visible weapon.

Inside, Angie saw another white-haired fellow sitting patiently behind the cage, where he had been apparently waiting to be returned to his cell following a visitation. That was, of course, before the jailers had been diverted by the security system malfunction.

The outlaw trio at this point certainly needed a hostage, and Angie assumed it would be the surprised deputy.

"I want *him*," Larrabee demanded, pointing at the cage.

At this, the older man nodded deferentially through the visitors' window toward Morningstar and Angie.

"Armand Schliesser," he said, as if in explanation.

Larrabee gave the deputy a violent shove toward Schliesser.

"Get the old geezer out of lockup," the inmate said. "He's coming with us."

"I c-can't." The deputy's eyes were round with fright. "I don't have that key."

"Well, you can either go find that key, Grandpa, or consider yourself our hostage."

"No, wait," Morningstar interjected. "We don't have time for that. Let me handle this."

Angie felt as incredulous as the deputy looked. She had seen Morningstar inspecting something on the doorplate to the inmates' side of the visitors' room. Serial numbers?

"OUIJA!" Morningstar called out. "Disengage VB-oh-two-six-oh-nine."

Snick.

Something perceptibly moved on the partition's door handle, and then the door itself moved slightly ajar as if by an invisible hand. Morningstar calmly pulled it open and motioned for Schliesser to join them on the other side. The deputy made no objection to being forced to take Schliesser's place in the inmates' pen.

Larrabee looked Morningstar up and down in apparent appreciation, if not admiration.

Angie kept her eyes on Morningstar. The woman scanned the room quickly, her eyes lighting on the wastebasket. She began pulling out crumpled papers and cigarette packs and stuffing them under the cushion of a chair.

"What are you doing?" Angie asked in disbelief.

"Gotta give the crew something to do." Morningstar ignited the edges of the papers with a pocket lighter. "OK, let's go."

Angie struggled to keep pace as the four of them hustled down the corridor. Larrabee already was nosing his gun into Schliesser's back.

"How're we getting out of here?" she called after Morningstar breathlessly.

"We walk." Then, pointing to the men, she added, "They crawl."

She wasn't kidding.

When they reached the end of the corridor nearest the booking room, Morningstar barked, "Crawl!"

Larrabee looked back over his shoulder in disbelief.

Morningstar kicked him squarely in the seat of the pants. "Crawl or die!" she snapped.

Obediently the two men dropped to their hands and knees. That took them beneath the eye level of the chest-high countertop that separated the work area from the walkway. It also spared them from detection by Smith and Jones and several others scurrying about in various stages of confusion.

Smith appeared to be cursing into a malfunctioning telephone, while Jones struggled vainly to raise anything but snow on the security monitors. They barely looked up as Morningstar and Angie sauntered by.

"Having trouble?" Morningstar called out politely.

The two deputies only gave her harassed glances.

"Maybe the fire's goofing up your equipment."

"Fire?" said Jones.

"What fire?" said Smith.

"Oh, the one in the visitors' block." Morningstar pointed down the hall.

Cursing loudly and knocking over chairs and telephones, the two men raced off in the direction of the conflagration.

"Shall I call nine-one-one?" Morningstar called after the retreating figures.

Angie raced behind the console and began detaching the emulator leads and winding up the wires. In another moment, she had the device safely tucked away in her shoulder bag, and they were a major step closer to a perfect mission.

Angie, her heart pounding more out of excitement than fear, was impressed with just how stimulating a good crime could be.

Meanwhile, Larrabee pushed vainly on the steel door to freedom. No dice.

"All right, Einstein," he spat at Morningstar. "What now?"

Angie hoped Morningstar's luck would hold for one more gambit.

"OUIJA!" the woman sang. "Front door, please."

Nothing. Angie's heart almost stopped beating.

"Uh—disengage, OUIJA!"

Still no response. Angie saw Morningstar drop to her knees as if examining some minute part of the interlock mechanism.

"Disengage M-oh-oh-one-oh-one, OUIJA!" Morningstar called, almost desperately this time.

Wonk.

Then Angie and the others were out the door and on the street, heading for home. Larrabee wasn't the only one who had a newfound appreciation for "spiritual adviser" Elizabeth Morningstar.

15

Detective-Lt. Vincent Salerno sat bolt upright when he got the call from Judge Wilson Neal McBride.

Instantly, he was back on The Case. To Salerno, this was the case next to which all others paled to insignificance. Every time he worked a piece of it, it was as if everything else he had been doing were just a dream.

It was the case that he just couldn't get out of his system, as much as Capt. Blasingame and the other brass expressly wished he would forget it and never speak of it again. It was the motherlode, the granddaddy of local cultism—Roger Larrabee, Sleepy Hollow, and their shadowy parent group that he'd never had the opportunity to penetrate.

And then there was the late Zona Corban, at once his greatest success and his greatest failure. It sometimes surprised him, the extent of the grief he harbored for Zona, this strange young woman whom he'd busted and turned State's evidence.

There had been no reciprocation or even acknowledgment on her part, but he had gone out of his way on countless occasions and in many small ways to see that her best interests were looked after. He forbade any of the deputies to treat her like a cheap hooker; he gave her small presents such as magazines and cigarettes. Yet, as a protected witness, she had been ultimately let down by her protectors in the worst way. And though his fellow officers would not have understood, Salerno felt responsible for her sudden and mysterious death.

He eyed the snapshot of Zona Corban taped above his terminal. Her boyfriend had snapped it at Cedar Point Amusement Park in her first moment after stepping off an authentic reproduction Demon Drop—staggering, wild-eyed, and laughing at the sky.

Salerno loved that picture. It was a unique glimpse into the ordinary side of her personality, having nothing to do with witchcraft or drugs or exotic dancing or prostitution. Giving him the photo was the closest she had come to acknowledging that she regarded him as anything more than a cop. The picture was a daily reminder that a big score remained to be settled—and that the other side played for keeps.

As a witness in the Larrabee case, Salerno had been prevented from hearing any other testimony, and he wondered what was behind the current recess in the trial, besides the slaying of Zona Corban. He had heard ugly rumors that someone had put in a fix on the case, but he hoped with all of his heart that was not true.

"Good morning, Your Honor," Salerno said, surprised by the onscreen image of Judge McBride in a sweater and open-collar shirt. "How are you?"

"Bloodied but unbowed," McBride said, smiling. "I am in need of some advice and counsel from a stand-up lawman, and I thought of you."

"You're too kind. What's on your mind?"

"Chi Xi Vau. What do you know about it?"

Salerno wished he had asked almost anything else.

"Know? Almost nothing," he confessed. "Now, suspicions—I have a lot of those. But nothing you'd probably want to discuss on the phone. Do you mind if I ask why the case is not going forward?"

"Technically, it's still in recess. There are . . . problems. That's something else we wouldn't want to discuss on the phone. I suggest we get together and do that in person."

Salerno was more than willing.

McBride said to meet him in the parking lot of the Third Federal Bank between downtown and OSU, and they'd proceed from there.

"Oh, and one more thing," said McBride. "No marked car, please."

★ ★ ★

McBride and Salerno were on their second cup of coffee in the honeymoon suite at the Imperial Crown when there came a knock at the door. It was Stillman, looking wound up and curious.

McBride performed the introductions and observed that Stillman wasn't willing to do much more than take a cup of coffee and stick himself in the corner horse-blanket chair, looking guarded and uncertain.

"It's OK," McBride said. "We can talk."

Stillman said nothing, but his eyes were going from face to face.

McBride voiced the unspoken concern. "Salerno's OK. And if he's not—"

"—you have to roll the dice sometime," Stillman finished.

Salerno smiled good-naturedly.

McBride continued. "I explained my job status to Lieutenant Salerno—"

"Vince," Salerno reminded him.

"To Vince. Basically that I may no longer be on the bench, which could well make me fair game for our friends. They wouldn't know or care about fine points such as whether the resignation is legally binding or how long I'm technically on vacation. I was just trying to delay any move to a mistrial while we got our ducks in a row. And now Lieutenant Salerno—Vince—has some news that changes everything."

Salerno minced no words. "Our pal Larrabee has been sprung from the county jail."

Stillman's eyes grew rounder and wider.

"How'd he manage that?"

"Not by himself," Salerno said. "I don't have the skinny on that yet, but it looks like he had some help from two young ladies and some kind of suspicious security system blowout. Seems like an outlaw computer could be among the suspects. Not much to go on, other than the deputies' description of the young ladies, who were probably in disguise."

Stillman looked straight at McBride. "So, what are you going to do?" McBride knew what he meant. With Larrabee on the loose and a mistrial a foregone conclusion now, was there any point to his continuing to pursue the matter? Wouldn't it be more reasonable just to give up, maybe see about getting his job back?

But he already had thought of that possibility. "No, there's still the matter of Peter and Carlotta's abduction, plus the little matter of the attacks upon my house and car—not to mention Zona Corban. Pretty hard to work within the system under such circumstances."

Salerno spoke up. "I think the judge has also managed to keep the other side guessing on just how to close the book on this case."

"I see." Stillman smiled. "Like when and how to assign it to another judge who will dispose of it."

"It's called buying time," said McBride. Then he thought of something else. "Did anybody else escape?"

"Not exactly," Salerno said slowly. "One other inmate was sprung, but he may have been a hostage. Some old man by the name of Schliesser."

Stillman's eyes nearly popped out. "Armand Schliesser?" he said, incredulous.

"That's it. You know him?"

"That's your physicist friend, isn't it?" said McBride.

Stillman nodded sadly. "I can't believe it. Why was he even still in there?"

"My guess," said Salerno, "is that Schliesser wasn't going anywhere too soon. He'd been indicted by a federal grand jury in a big civil rights case. This wasn't going to be a bond that anybody could make. This boy was in trouble with a capital 'T.'"

"Yeah, big criminal," Stillman said bitterly. "This is just what I was talking about. Good and evil have been turned upside down. Baby killers get away with murder, and good men are persecuted. Maybe the rest of the world *has* lost its mind."

McBride frowned. "You'll get no argument from me."

Stillman slumped further into his chair. "I guess I'm about ready to agree with Schliesser. He said this was an evil generation, crooked and perverse. I used to argue with him about his belief in the existence of evil as an independent force in the universe. I'm beginning to think he's absolutely right."

Salerno sighed. "You guys really have a way of lifting a guy's spirits."

"Oh!" said Stillman, startling the other two men. "I nearly forgot. I have some news of my own for you."

"Only if it's good news," said McBride.

Stillman smiled. "I think it's quite good. I talked to our friends at the Rhema Institute, and they're practically falling all over themselves for the chance to do the translation project. Without getting too specific, I indicated we might need some help with another project of our own and that we really needed to rent a facility off campus to do all of this. And, get this—they said to get whatever we need, within reason, and they'll pick up the tab."

"Super." McBride beamed. "Good work."

"The only thing is," Stillman said uncertainly, "I'm sure they'll want to work out of there too. I don't know how you feel about getting involved with a bunch of missionaries."

"No—" McBride shook his head "it's perfect. How much trouble could a couple of Bible translators be?"

Salerno was smiling too. "Talk about a great front," he said admiringly.

"Yeah," said McBride, "maybe we'll even rent an old church for the purpose. How soon can your friends get here?"

Stillman laughed. "Is tonight soon enough?"

"Yeah," said McBride. "I guess they really must be eager."

"I pick them up at the airport tonight at seven thirty." Stillman glanced at his watch. "Darnell Jones and Aaron Fitzgerald."

McBride put his hands on his knees. "Well, what are we

doing sitting here? We need to start beating the bushes for a head-quarters to rent."

"Any ideas where to start?" said Stillman.

"Well," said McBride, "when Jimmy needed a front, he generally had pretty good luck over between Lower Siddhartha and Rubicon—lots of turnover there. I wouldn't be surprised if that's still true."

"Jimmy who?" asked Salerno.

Stillman rolled his eyes. "Shapiro. And you don't want to get into that. It's a long story, believe me."

"OK. Mind if I drop by this evening? I have some ideas, and I might be able to help."

McBride nodded. "We'd be honored. If you've got help, you're in the right place because, boy, do we need it."

"Just don't give out any addresses over the phone, not even to me in the Department."

"We won't," McBride promised. "When we're settled in, I'll just call you to rendezvous somewhere like the Third Federal again. Let me have your home phone, in case it's late."

Salerno obliged.

McBride turned to Stillman with some second thoughts. "What do you think? I know I recommended going for the transla-tion project. But is that going to put you in a spot at work?"

"You mean like getting fired?"

"Yeah, like getting fired."

"I don't know." Stillman frowned. "I wouldn't think so—it was Judith's idea, and she's the division chair. But Julian Wickner is acting like he's sewing the job up for himself. And with the way everything else has been going, I hesitate to make any predictions about anything."

"Then you'd better think seriously about the worst-case sce-nario. After you're fired, it's too late to say somebody should have warned you."

Stillman shrugged. "There's not much to think about. If it's as bad as all that, something has to be done—or maybe I shouldn't be working there."

"OK, partner," said McBride. "Let's saddle up."

★ ★ ★

Kevorkian Court was one of those shopworn, cobblestone side streets off Lower Siddhartha Avenue. Its scabrous, polyglot architecture included old artifacts ranging from the majestic to the ramshackle. High upon squat Romanesque structures, ancient gargoyles glowered, gnarled wraiths of plaster, stone, and wrought iron, leering over grotesque conspiracies, brooding in regimental line atop long-deserted upper stories.

The street itself, McBride seemed to recall, had been renamed a very long time ago—from St. Something or Other, in honor of an ancient order long since departed.

It was here, with the aid of classifieds in the *Dispatch* data bank, that McBride and Stillman rather painlessly identified a facility that seemed to offer everything they had been seeking. It turned out, in fact, to be a church. To be more exact, it was the long-vacant Reformed Temple of Isis, itself originally a church of some Protestant stripe. The dingy but serviceable brick-and-stone building had been available for lease quite reasonably, especially considering the fact that the Rhema Institute was picking up the tab.

There was certainly plenty of room. Half a dozen cots and bedrolls in the fellowship hall, a few bags of groceries in the kitchen, a coffeepot in the main study, and they were reasonably well provisioned for the time being—well enough, at least, to start thinking about some serious work.

The real estate man with bushy eyebrows and bad breath who showed them the place seemed happy enough to get it rented, but he acted as though he would have been happier if they were going to use the place for selling drugs or something else he could understand.

"You guys are missionaries?" he said skeptically while Stillman signed the papers.

"Not exactly," said Stillman.

"We're just religious fanatics," said McBride.

"Oh." The man gathered up his papers and stuck his pen back into his shirt pocket. "So long's you don't make no trouble in the neighborhood."

After he was gone, McBride admonished Stillman not to go out making trouble in the neighborhood, especially among the drunks on the sidewalk.

"Well, there's one good thing," Stillman said. "If we ever

need to go into hiding, we can just go outside and lie down for a snooze. We'd be invisible."

★ ★ ★

Stillman left for Grady Hall and then for home preparatory to meeting his Chicago friends at the airport.

McBride called Salerno and arranged to meet for cheese-steak sandwiches at a fast-food place not far from Kevorkian Court.

Back at the "Temple," as McBride decided to call it, Salerno sniffed approvingly. "Has a lot of potential." He was especially impressed by the offices, work rooms, and phone lines. "Not much in the way of furniture, though."

He had a garage full of comfortable pieces they could use, he said.

McBride figured the next day he and the Rhema Institute folks would pick out some rental office furnishings and equipment as they thought appropriate. He wondered how long it had been since the place was last rented. He suspected a long time—long enough, anyway, for cobwebs to gather in many corners and dust motes to begin swirling whenever one of them walked past a window, which backlighted whatever they stirred up.

The empty rooms echoed with that hollowness that empty rooms always have, absolutely demanding furnishings to soften the acoustics. McBride found the sanctuary the spookiest place of all. There were still pews with threadbare pads and recognizable areas where an organ once resided and choirs once sang, but the platform held a flat black altar that gave him the willies. He somehow knew that the Temple of Isis folks had performed things on that table of which his Episcopal grandfather would not have approved. McBride figured he'd stick to the offices and work rooms and avoid this place.

Finally, McBride and Salerno made themselves at home on some folding chairs in what probably had been designed as the head pastor's study. He still wanted to hear the detective's thoughts—suspicions, even—on this mystery group of theirs.

"Chi Xi Vau," Salerno intoned thoughtfully. "You know, there's gotta be quite a story there. The only things I ever heard were snatches and whispers, things that you could never quite get a handle on."

"What kinds of things?"

"Oh, everybody knew that this was the kingpin outfit. But the only people who talked about it—like Zona Corban—were those who didn't really know anything. And anybody who did wasn't talking."

"The neo-pagan elite?" McBride mused aloud. "The New Age intelligentsia?"

"That's right. You don't pick this gang. They pick you. And people without college degrees or with criminal records don't get picked. Roger Larrabee and groups like the Bad Actors might be soul brothers, but they could never be part of it. If it exists. Which is all guesswork."

"You think there's a hierarchy?" McBride raised his eyebrows. "I always thought this stuff was a pretty loose assortment of unrelated space cadets, misfits, and four-flushers."

"There are about as many types of Wiccans, pagans, and Satanists as the mind can conceive. So, yeah, it is pretty loose at the street level. As you go up the ladder, it becomes more . . . there's a word . . . interdisciplinary. But the higher you try to go, the less is known about it—like the old Communist cells of the early twentieth century. That's changing, though, as they find the legal climate more user friendly."

McBride nodded. "I don't doubt that. But philosophically can you really lump them all together like that? Don't the witches claim they have nothing to do with Satan—that the devil is just stupid Christian mythology that's totally irrelevant to them?"

"Sure, they *say* that," Salerno said. "But they're dupes. Just watch their reactions to Christ or anything Christian. There's nothing neutral about their attitude there—*that's* the enemy in their minds. That's one of the reasons the so-called white male power structure is such a favorite target."

"Male authority—as symbolic of the old Judeo-Christian Jehovah God?" suggested McBride. "Maybe what they like to call Eurocentrism too?"

"Sure. Think about it. What holiday did we observe last week? Native American Day. Thirty years ago, that used to be Columbus Day. What happened? Christopher Columbus died for our Eurocentric, white male sins."

McBride was suddenly curious about his new friend. "How did you get motivated in this direction? You seem to have a . . . special sensitivity."

Salerno looked away a little self-consciously. "Well, I had a grandfather who was quite a religious person. Since my parents split when I was very young, he had a lot to do with my growing up. I guess I spent a lot of time in church, even made some kind of profession of faith. I don't remember too much about it, but I've always kind of credited that for my . . . sensitivity . . . to this stuff. It's kind of an intuitive radar for corruption."

"Speaking of corruption, what does your radar tell you about the Franklin County Sheriff's Department?"

Salerno rolled his eyes. "I like to give people the benefit of the doubt. It's probably no worse than any other law enforcement agency in this day and age—but that's not saying a lot. I just try to do my job and not worry about it too much."

There was a pensive silence, and then Salerno asked if McBride had figured out what to do about Steve Leadingham.

"Right now," said McBride, "considering that my own step-son was spirited right out of the adjacent unit, I'm as concerned about Leadingham's safety as I am about his injuries or the information that we need so badly. There's an obvious security problem there."

"Have you reported the abduction?"

McBride laughed ruefully. "Technically, there was no abduction. Peter was discharged into his sister's care."

"What does she say about all of this?"

"There's no answer at her apartment. Hasn't been for a long time. It's like she doesn't live there anymore."

"I take it you're not that close with her?"

"She divorced her mother and me seven years ago when we were practically newlyweds. She's always been very independent. I wouldn't be particularly surprised by anything she did."

"Too bad we can't just get Leadingham out of there."

McBride frowned. "No, he's still critical. He may not make it as it is."

"Does he have any relatives around here?"

"I don't think so. I remember him talking about a sister in

Florida, but I don't remember anything about his parents. Maybe they're deceased."

"It would be helpful to know if he's had any visitors."

"Yeah. I'll see if Stillman would know how to crack their medical information system."

"It might be worth a try," said Salerno, "although I feel compelled to advise you that it might also be a bit illegal."

They both had a good laugh over that one.

A little before 8:30, Stillman returned from the airport with the green Jupiter and its cargo from the Rhema Institute.

By that time, McBride and Salerno had figured out how to install the giant-screen communications console in the main conference room, as Stillman had requested. They were watching a football game and attacking a mountain of popcorn when Stillman and their guests arrived.

The Rhema Institute men were both attired in the kind of modest but serviceable business suits purchased by clergy on limited budgets.

McBride watched their reactions as Stillman performed the introductions, touching on the fact that McBride was a judge and Salerno a sheriff's detective. There were no noticeable starts, no exchange of surprised glances. Stillman apparently had clued them in already. But neither did it pass entirely without comment.

"See there, Aaron," Darnell Jones said to his companion, "you best watch your step around here, or you'll be in a heap of trouble in no time."

Fitzgerald murmured a laconic "Rather."

"I'm afraid we're the ones in trouble, if anybody," said McBride.

"It's that 'other project' that I was talking about," explained Stillman.

This time, Jones and Fitzgerald did exchange glances, expressions that McBride couldn't read clearly. But they seemed cordial enough.

He waved a hand generously. "Please look around and see if you find the facility adequate for your needs. It's close enough to campus that you could walk it if you wanted, but there's a Green

Line shuttle by here about every twenty minutes during normal business hours. If you like it well enough, we'll turn some of these rooms into bedrooms and spare the Institute the hotel bills."

With that, the tour began circulating through the old church. Stillman led the way. When they were done, he said, he would drive them to their hotel for the night.

McBride and Salerno returned to their football game.

In a few minutes, Stillman was back with the guests, smiling all around.

McBride was eager for their verdict. "I take it that it met with your approval?"

"Oh, very much so," said Jones.

Fitzgerald had found his tongue. "I am a seminary graduate, but I've never had my own church before. This will be . . . quaint."

"And I can't tell you how much we're looking forward to working with Doctor Stillman on this project," Jones said.

Fitzgerald nodded happily. "Yes, I'm pretty excited about Cybersynchronics. One day there may be entire bands of people in heaven, praising God for Doctor Richard Hanley Stillman."

It was McBride and Salerno's turn to exchange glances.

"Doctor Stillman," said Jones, "have you come to grips with those spiritual questions we discussed last time?"

Stillman was blushing. "I—I think, in a way, that's just what I've been doing."

"Well, well," said Jones, "it sounds like we have much to discuss—very much."

16

The woman's voice came softly and clearly. "Good morning, Peter."

The effect was quite like a posthypnotic suggestion. One moment he was totally oblivious; the next, he was conscious and wondering who was addressing him. He seemed to be on something much like a gurney, and at the foot of it were two unfamiliar women. The room in which he found himself was a rather amorphous construct of institutional-green track curtains approximating a large rectangle. At the opposite end, fiddling with some gadgetry, was an Oriental-looking man whom Peter could not discern clearly.

One thing, at least, was missing from this picture.

"Mr. Cathcart?" said Peter weakly.

He heard one of the women say, "He's still disoriented."

The elder of the two addressed him directly. "I'm Elizabeth, and this is Kelsey. How are you feeling, Peter?"

"Not so great," he said, trying to raise his head. It seemed as if his neck had turned to straw—or his head had turned to stone.

"Don't move," Elizabeth warned. "You need to rest."

In truth, he felt wretched. His left arm was in some kind of restraint. The light pained his eyes and aggravated his head, which already felt like something that needed drilling in a dentist's chair. Sorting out his jumbled thoughts was an effort almost beyond him. His stomach alternated between hunger and nausea.

Almost as if on cue, a bowl of chicken noodle soup appeared on a tray before him. With a little help from Kelsey, who propped up his head, Peter began imbibing the liquid comfort through a straw, and a small spot of warmth in his gut spread satisfyingly.

"Where—am I?" he blurted between slurps.

"We have a full-service operation here at the Institute," said the woman named Kelsey with a professional smile. "You're in the clinic recovery room."

"Recovery room?" Peter said with growing alarm. "Recovery from *what?*"

The women traded glances before Elizabeth spoke. "You really don't remember the shooting?"

Added to the alarm were feelings of foolishness and frustration. Try as he might, his short-term memory proved inaccessible. The effort only magnified his headache.

"No," he conceded wearily at last.

With another professional smile, Kelsey prompted gently, "Is there any history of . . . mental instability in your family?"

Peter was about to assure her that such was not the case when the awful realization overtook him that such, indeed, was *very* much the case—in the person of his own quite psychotic and institutionalized mother. And then the suspicion occurred to him: Was he next?

Peter shivered under the covers. The only thing he seemed able to recall with any clarity was a little old man named Cathcart who'd introduced him to the Savior.

"Would you like something for pain?" asked Kelsey.

"Yes." He nodded, continuing his assault on the soup.

He wondered why nobody was waving a needle at his arm, but then realized that under the restraint on his left arm was some kind of tube, possibly an IV line through which something like an analgesic could be administered easily.

Elizabeth and Kelsey watched him like a microbe on a slide as the Oriental man across the room tracked data flow from instruments on the medical cart.

At that moment the technician looked his way, and instantly Peter thought he was a man named Quang from the university. Could it be? *The* Jared Quang, the artificial intelligence wunderkind and inventor of the OUIJA system? What in the world was he doing here in a recovery room?

But wait, now. Something else wasn't squaring—like half-memories. Had he imagined or dreamed up both the Asian nurse *and* the nasty one whose name he'd memorized—Tanya Powers?

Why did he think he recognized this Kelsey? That one did seem like a dream, except that you can't dream about people you never met. Unless he was dreaming now. And why did his sister seem to be mixed up in these dream images?

Peter could feel his pulse quicken as if some part of him sensed danger. He also began to wonder if he were not feeling the effects of something like Theta Blocker, which was used in some designers for forgetfulness.

"We're getting into Delta," advised Quang quietly but pointedly.

"Well, don't let it," Kelsey said firmly, turning his direction. "Adjust the blood levels temporarily to 133 percent of maximum."

Just what were they administering to him anyway?

"Tell me—" Peter said with what he had intended to be an assertive tone, but fell far short. His head was swimming now.

"Yes?" Kelsey said helpfully.

"Uh—" It was suddenly a lot harder to put the question into actual words.

"Yes?" Kelsey said again with that synthetic smile.

"Why am I . . . " Here, he felt foolish as words manifestly failed him.

"Why are you what?" Kelsey prompted.

"I don't know," he mumbled. "Tired."

There was a very distracting buzz in his ears now. Whatever he thought he remembered was now becoming quite tangled and once again inaccessible.

"I know," Elizabeth interjected reassuringly, even suggestively. "I'll say the words, and then you say them after me. 'Phenomena manifest themselves by degrees.'"

"What?" Peter frowned.

"Isn't that profound?" Elizabeth said in a kindergarten tone. "Say it. 'Phenomena manifest themselves by degrees.'"

But Peter had his own ideas. "Broad is the way to destruction," he said with great effort. It was something he had learned from Mr. Cathcart. He liked that better than what Elizabeth had just said.

It seemed truer somehow, although Elizabeth didn't seem especially pleased.

Now Kelsey was handing him a pen.

Peter took it and examined it quizzically.

The blonde woman then placed a legal-looking document before him on a clipboard, obviously for his signature.

"It's just one of the formalities of receiving treatment here at the clinic," she said soothingly. "Universal organ donor and permission to terminate."

He just nodded, feeling foolish for being so dimwitted, and scrawled his name on the form. All he really wanted was to sleep.

"Thanks, Peter," said Elizabeth comfortingly.

"Thanks lots," said Kelsey with a mysterious smirk.

Peter slept.

Down the hall, a similar scene was being played out with different characters. Awaking groggily in this bed surrounded by green track curtains and a couple of tough customers was Carlotta Waldo.

"Just tell us where he is," Julian Wickner was insisting. "We know you know."

"I *don't* know," Carlotta kept repeating. "I don't know."

She cringed as a wild-eyed Jeremy Kay loomed over her, his nostrils flaring angrily. Carlotta feared that at any moment he might strike her.

Instead, the tall, light-haired man snapped a voice command to the intercom.

"Quang!" he said. "You need to check the medication level over here. This one's tongue isn't loose yet."

With her eyes pressed tightly shut, Carlotta was unaware when the other man entered the room. But soon she was hearing an unfamiliar voice assuring that the readings were all in their proper ranges and that all was as it should be.

"Drug effects on the human mind can be tricky," said the man, "but at the levels she's currently experiencing, ninety-nine percent of the population would be singing like meadowlarks."

"Crank it up higher," Kay ordered. "As much as she can take."

The results were almost instantaneous. Carlotta's head began to swim. She would tell them anything they wanted, if she knew it.

"All right," Kay snarled after a minute. "We'll try this just one more time. And don't play games with me, Ms. Waldo, if you value your boyfriend's health. Where is Judge McBride?"

"I . . . don't . . . know."

Carlotta opened her eyes in time to see Kay drawing back as if he finally was about to strike her.

"I wouldn't do that, Jeremy," said Wickner. "If she really doesn't know, nothing is going to drag it out of her. And if she's managed to conceal it, there's really only one thing that's going to get it out of her."

"That's right," said Quang. "Soon we'll have both of them fully integrated with OUIJA, and their minds will be an open book."

Kay spun on his heel to leave, then turned for a parting shot. "You'd better be right."

* * *

Angela Hurley guided the silver Leo carefully into the only available space in the cramped six-car lot behind the Regional Deprogramming Center and cut the engine. She sat there for a moment, scanning the rear of the old green-and-white wood-frame structure before getting out. Apparently, the basement door was the one she'd just passed on the driveway side. The one thing she was not to do was go in the front, where the regular clientele came and went.

The place was a strange fusion of brick-facade storefront, probably built on later, with a residence converted to office space in the rear. Rumor had it that this mongrelized structure on Thorley between Gehanna and Sanger streets had been a renowned crack house once upon a time, in the old days before decriminalization, long before its most recent renovation.

Angie could believe it. In any event, besides housing the Deprogramming Center for Religious Extremism upstairs, it now provided temporary haven for a couple of fugitives below decks.

She wrestled the pizza box awkwardly out of the backseat and faced the dexterity test a second time at the basement door, where it would have been much easier to turn the box on its side. But after a brief struggle, she managed to slide on through to the

186

stairs without encountering anyone who might wonder why she was taking a pizza to the basement. Elizabeth had said she'd be there too, but how many people did it take to deliver a pizza? Maybe Elizabeth had other things in mind.

At the bottom, Angie had to fish a key out of her jeans pocket and unlock another door while balancing the pizza on her other hand. It was one of those basements that had been given the do-it-yourself rec room treatment—false ceiling, fluorescent lights, cheap, fake-brick paneling, indoor-outdoor carpeting—but never quite achieved the intended effect. It was still claustrophobic, cold, and seedy.

One side of the basement, she observed, was inhabited by someone with obvious and base appetites. Cigarette butts overflowed a cereal bowl being used for an ashtray. Crumpled beer cans were strewn about the floor. Several raw centerfolds from skin magazines had been taped to the wall by a cot.

Upon that bed, stirring slowly from his slumbers, was a brown-haired young man in pants, undershirt, and stockinged feet. His bare arms bore tattoos of death's-heads, demons, and arcane symbols.

On the other side, chained to a pole, was the old physicist named Armand Schliesser, sitting on the floor and staring blankly. *Probably praying*, Angie thought disgustedly. And then he looked up at her with a faint smile.

Angie deposited the pizza on a nearby card table with undisguised contempt.

"Feeding time!" she called with a sneer.

Schliesser looked at her with what seemed a mixture of gratitude and kindly reproach. "Thank you," he said simply.

"Sure thing." She was growing more irritated by the moment. "You think praying will save your hide?"

Schliesser made no response.

Larrabee was already by the table, ripping the paper off the pizza.

"Here you go, Holy Joe!" He tossed a piece, which landed sauce down on the floor by Schliesser's left knee. "If there's any left by the time you lick that one up, you can have another piece." Larrabee laughed lustily.

Angie was startled by the sudden appearance of a fourth person at the bottom of the stairs. It was her erstwhile mission accomplice, Elizabeth Morningstar.

"I meant to be here sooner," Morningstar said, "but I got talking to Lothar."

"You got somethin' for me?" said Larrabee.

Morningstar pulled a sheet of notepaper out of her pocket. "Not for you."

Larrabee's face soured. "What do you mean?"

Morningstar handed the paper to Angie. On it was written "1412 Kensington Ave."

"Marianne King's new address," Morningstar told her.

"Yeah, we're going to give her another new address—like permanently." Larrabee chortled again.

"No rough stuff," Morningstar corrected. "The Society wants her in one piece. That's why Angie and I are going to fetch her."

"What?" said Larrabee, looking none too pleased.

"Besides, you're too hot. You're the next one who's going to have to get a new address. You can't hole up here indefinitely. There's too much risk of exposure."

Larrabee just glared. "Better not mess up."

"What's going on in Deprogramming?" Angie asked, quickly changing the subject.

"Good progress," said Morningstar. "Some of the young ladies already have agreed to terminate. Looks like Kelsey Kinsey will have some new Biota Recycling customers."

Angie saw Schliesser press his eyes tightly shut and move his lips faintly, as if in silent prayer. This had to be bad news for him.

"What about the others?" Angie asked, intrigued.

"In time," Larrabee interjected cryptically. "In time."

"He means," Morningstar interpreted, "that he and Lothar haven't had time to frighten enough of them sufficiently."

Larrabee laughed again, then upended a beer can against his lips.

"What about the deprogrammers?" Angie continued.

"What do you mean?" asked Morningstar.

"Do they—" here, she shot a glance at Larrabee "—know?"

"Do they *know?*" Larrabee repeated, incredulous. "You silly little girl! You make-believe groupie."

Angie took an involuntary step back from Larrabee's threatening advance.

Abruptly he seized her by the right forearm and jerked her roughly against him. His other hand clutched a gleaming blade with which he proceeded to tickle her throat while breathing into her ear. His breath stank of beer, and his body reeked of rancid perspiration.

His fierce words rasped. "Maybe the rest of the ladies would get with the program if they could see their fearless leader begging for mercy and cursing Christ!"

"No!" Angie heard herself cry involuntarily.

"Yes!" Larrabee snarled.

Schliesser looked up, sorrow deepening the creases of his face. "Leave her alone," the scientist protested softly but firmly.

Larrabee laughed. "This gets to you, doesn't it, old man? You ain't seen nothin' yet. Watch this!"

For an instant, Angie almost believed that she was being torn asunder. And then just as suddenly, she realized that the rending sensation was from the fabric of her blouse as buttons and material popped and shredded.

"Look at us, old man! This girl's health depends on your total obedience!"

"I don't think that's going to work, Roger," Morningstar said in a firm voice.

"You shut up!" Larrabee snapped.

Angie was crying softly. She had no idea if Schliesser was watching. Now Larrabee's forearm was around her neck, and the knifeblade was indenting a point just above her navel.

"That's better," Larrabee said, apparently to Schliesser. "Now, repeat after me: 'The name of Christ be cursed.'"

Larrabee's grip tightened about her neck, and the blade tip pricked more deeply still as an awkward silence ensued.

"Say, 'The name of Christ be cursed!'" Larrabee thundered more menacingly.

More tears spilled down Angie's face as her breath came in gasps.

"Roger—" Morningstar admonished.

The silence built.

"'The name of Christ be cursed!'" Larrabee roared.

Angie could see Schliesser, his eyes looking above her and his lips moving ever so subtly again.

And then he spoke. "Blessed be the God and Father of our Lord Jesus Christ, who has caused us to be born again to a living hope through the resurrection of Jesus Christ from the dead—"

"*Stop!*" Larrabee boomed. His arm viciously choked off Angie's breath.

"—and unto an inheritance that is imperishable and undefiled and can never fade away . . . "

Angie felt the knife blade threatening to puncture her abdomen, but that was almost incidental as she struggled for breath, clawing at Larrabee's arm encircling her throat.

". . . preserved in heaven for you, who through faith are shielded by God's power—"

This time it was Morningstar shouting, "Stop!"

Angie could hear Larrabee demanding as if far off in a dream somewhere, "Look at this, old man!"

It was herself he was thrusting roughly forward, her weak-kneed body with something warm and sticky oozing down her leg.

"—until the coming of the salvation that is ready to be revealed in the last time."

The last thing Angie remembered was the unexpected sight of Morningstar striking Larrabee's knife-wielding arm. At that moment the vise around her neck relaxed, and her breath returned. But her support was gone, and her head hit something substantial on the way down, extinguishing the lights.

17

Within ten minutes after the phoneperson had left the Temple on Kevorkian Court, Stillman managed to attach the scrambler to two of the new lines in the conference room.

McBride observed in silence over Stillman's shoulder.

Aaron Fitzgerald offered occasional encouragement while performing his own mysterious tasks at a laptop connected to the communications console.

The conference room had become their command center, where they spent most of their work time. It was the largest room, other than the sanctuary, and all the computer equipment, communications console, water cooler, and translation project paraphernalia had been installed there.

At other times McBride and his three cohorts could be found around the coffeepot and microwave in the spacious, canary yellow kitchen. At night each man had a former Sunday school classroom for a bedroom. They expected to replace the cots with real beds in the next day or two.

"There," Stillman said with some satisfaction, laying down the screwdriver and tugging several of the leads lightly. "That ought to do the trick."

"Secure enough to keep our friend Salerno out of trouble?" asked McBride. "Not to mention the rest of us?"

"I can't make a promise like that. All I can say is that it's state of the art. But, of course, it's an art with a constantly advancing frontier."

"OK," said McBride. "Once again we roll the dice."

Stillman called Salerno's number on null-video and waited while Fitzgerald made himself scarce.

McBride was reasonably comfortable with Stillman's assurances about the scrambler. He grasped just enough to know that the device multiplied the security odds by using a random-pattern scrambling sequence and splitting the signal over two lines. It would be a pretty tough case to crack and totally impossible with a conventional wiretap.

In another moment, they were hearing Salerno, sounding like a synthesized voice over a background mix of white noise. With a few minor adjustments of the controls, the lawman was coming in loud and clear.

"I want you to thank Stillman for those hot patient information records on Steve Leadingham," Salerno said.

"I'm here, Vince," Stillman called out. "You're very welcome. Once a hacker, always a hacker, I guess."

"Did you find something?" asked McBride.

"Affirmative. Of the three visiting family members, one of them was a fake."

"A fake? What do you mean? Who?"

"Rebecca Leadingham, the sister from Florida. Phony as a politician's promise."

Stillman and McBride raised eyebrows at each other.

"How do you know that?" asked McBride.

"Simple. I talked to the other two, Steve Leadingham's mother and brother—Amanda Avery and Chip Leadingham. Becky Leadingham, the sister, just got into town. She hadn't been to the hospital yet, as of an hour ago. Ms. Avery asked her to come in from Florida because her brother's just not improving."

"Do you believe them?" asked McBride.

There was almost no hesitation at Salerno's end. "I have no reason not to. What would be their motive?"

"There could be any number of things," said McBride. "Feuds, bad blood, an estate dispute, irregular toothpaste squeezing. Who knows?"

"Those things might be motives to shoot the guy, but how do they explain a phony visitor?"

McBride lowered his eyes in thought.

"Trust me," added Salerno. "They're not that kind of people. If you met them, you'd understand."

"How do you account for the phony visitor?" McBride asked.

"I don't know, but mother and brother had a funny reaction to the whole business."

"How so?"

"They said they already thought there was something kind of suspicious about things in that unit."

"What do you mean?"

"It seems Leadingham's doctor herself was confused. They said she had commented more than once that Leadingham really seemed to be failing, but all his vital signs indicated otherwise—that he was stable."

McBride wondered about the possibility of bio-tech foul play. "All right," he said slowly, deciding to trust Salerno's character judgment. "Is Becky Leadingham—the real one—going to the hospital today?"

"Yeah. Some time this afternoon, they said."

"Do one more thing for me, please."

"Name it."

"We need to send someone with her."

"Unless it's a doctor, Neal, that's not going to work. This patient is critical."

"How about a clergyperson?"

There was momentary silence on the other end. "A what?"

"A minister," said McBride. "They still let them in, don't they?"

"I guess so. What are you up to?"

"We happen to have a man of the cloth here who's also a man of the computer. Let's have Reverend Aaron Fitzgerald go in with her for moral support—and to see what he thinks."

"I don't know . . . " Salerno said slowly.

"You have a better candidate?"

"No. But what if he does find . . . funny business?"

"That's why I think we need a lawman such as yourself also at the scene."

"I don't have any problem being there, but if it's for anything more than moral support, I'm going to have to get the city boys involved. The Leadingham shooting is their case, you know."

"You think that's . . . practical?"

"You mean do I think I can find one honest city cop?" said

Salerno. "Yeah. Things may be bad, but not that bad. I've got one or two decent friends over there. Besides, we need to talk about some other reasons for getting them involved."

"Give me a hint."

"Well, at this point I have to be a little concerned about Marianne King. She may not be totally what she appears to be, but we can discuss that later. Right now, she could be in some danger with Larrabee on the loose."

"I see," said McBride. "See if you can get us an update on the jailbreak while you're at it. Some of us are a little concerned about Doctor Schliesser too. We need to know if we should keep worrying."

"That's easy enough."

"Meanwhile," said McBride, "I'll see if I can get Fitzgerald on the case. Can you make the arrangements with the family?"

"Be glad to."

★ ★ ★

It was about 12:30 when Stillman, Jones, and Fitzgerald arrived at the front door of the Temple, lugging bags with little metal-handled goldfish cartons full of Chinese food.

"Who had the moo goo gai pan?" Stillman called as they began laying out the goodies on the conference room table.

"That's me," said Fitzgerald. "With the hot and sour soup."

The rest of them sorted through the lo mein, subgum, won ton, fried rice, egg rolls, and various sweet and sour delicacies and then fell to ingesting it all with dispatch.

It had been a lively morning. After strategizing with Salerno, there had been a class for Stillman to teach and some orientation and introductions to be performed in the Linguistics Division on behalf of Jones and Fitzgerald, while back at the Temple McBride ordered some additional office furnishings and did some heavy navel-contemplating.

After lunch, Fitzgerald was to meet with Salerno and volunteer for duty in the Leadingham affair. McBride planned to pursue some research of his own with the help of ALEX. It was time to get to the bottom of those clues. Conceptus . . . Fahlgren . . . Chi Xi Vau. They were never out of his mind for long. And very soon he needed to pay a visit to the Institute for Pre-Life Science on Broad Street.

"Listen," said Stillman importantly, waving a chopstick. "Fitzgerald helped me figure out who this Otto Jesperson was."

"Aaron earns his keep every once in a while," Jones said.

Fitzgerald was unfazed. "It's just a matter of finding the right database. Fortunately there are even databases now to help you do that."

"Jesperson?" said McBride, then thought he remembered. "Was that the guy Schliesser recommended you contact, in addition to myself?"

"Correct." Stillman pincered a piece of egg roll. "Turns out he's the late Otto Jesperson."

"That's a lot of help." McBride heaped another pile of fried rice onto his plate.

"It's a lot more help than you'd think. Otto Jesperson was a professor of religious studies at old Whitehall College, which you might know was merged into OSU twenty years ago as a satellite campus—primarily for continuing education. That generally means night school for adults. Jesperson retired about the time the merger occurred. He's been dead a few years, but Schliesser may have known him personally."

"How does that help us?" asked McBride.

"Well, he was apparently such a wonderful teacher that they conferred a measure of immortality upon him. They turned him into a computerized instruction image—called the Interactive Professor. If you have questions in areas like cultural anthropology, mythology, and comparative religion, the Interactive Professor has your answers. It must have involved some major grant money at the time, but I don't know if the program is even used for anything today."

McBride still didn't get it. "Why did Schliesser think that would be helpful?"

"I guess that's for us to figure out," said Stillman. "It's intriguing. I haven't had a chance to do more than scratch the surface with this. Want to see him?"

McBride shrugged. "Why not?"

"ALEX," Stillman called, "access database Whitehall/Interactive Professor—Jesperson."

In another moment, the close-cropped, white-haired image of a grandfatherly gentleman with metal-rimmed glasses in a book-lined study took shape on the wallscreen.

Interactive computer simulations were not totally alien experiences for McBride, but he always marveled at their realism. This fellow, for example, looked as if he had just answered the phone and was eager for a rousing discussion of religion and politics—or, at least, religion.

"Good afternoon," said the old fellow. "I am Dr. Otto Jesperson. How may I be of assistance?"

Stillman aimed a chopstick at McBride. "Go ahead and stump the professor."

McBride had no trouble coming up with something. Questions were something he had in generous supply.

"Conceptus. What can you tell me about that?"

Jesperson explained that bioethicists had devised the clinical term *conceptus* to replace earlier terms that had implied the existence of a soul in the unborn human and inhibited the free use of fetal tissue in medical research. He also traced the political sequence from the US Supreme Court decision in *Roe vs. Wade* to the passage of the Freedom of Choice Act by Congress, establishing abortion as a constitutional right, and finally to the upsurge in ritual child sacrifice in the early twenty-first century.

"This type of activity is not without historic precedent, particularly in seventeenth-century Europe," Jesperson said. "For further information, you may want to select topics related to the Black Mass, midwife-abortionists, and the court of King Louis XIV."

"Thank you," said McBride. "May I ask you another question?"

"Certainly." Dr. Jesperson nodded slightly.

"Do you have any information regarding the term *Fahlgren?*"

"I am sorry, I do not. You might want to try an alternative data bank."

"OK." McBride was warming to this game. "Chi Xi Vau."

"Hchee Xee Vau," said Jesperson, giving it the technically correct pronunciation.

From there, the scholar launched into a discourse on the Greek symbols and the various interpretations of Revelation 13:18, most of which McBride already had heard.

Stillman leaned toward him. "You can interrupt and make him narrow it down to something more specific."

"OK. Excuse me, Dr. Jesperson, but I would be more interested in learning the possible significance of a group's calling itself by that name."

"This calls for wisdom," said Jesperson. "While no one can discern the motive of another with certainty, there are observable trends and patterns. Essentially, anyone who accepts this mark, according to the prophet of the Apocalypse, is aligning himself or herself with the Beast and thus against God in the ultimate contest between Good and Evil.

"Contemporary cult groups, then, have adopted this symbol as a mark of defiance, proclaiming their preference for eternal damnation over submission to Christ. Thus, some interpreters believe this symbol is applicable both to a multitude of individuals and to a single individual who will lead this rebellion—hence, the Antichrist."

"What would be the attitude of such individuals toward civil authority?" McBride wondered aloud.

"One must assume it would be equally defiant. Another name for this Antichrist is the Man of Lawlessness."

"Thank you, Doctor Jesperson. I believe that will be all."

"You're very welcome," said Jesperson, whose image froze and then winked off.

"Sorry," said Stillman. "I guess it wasn't all that helpful."

McBride scratched his chin with the fat end of his chopstick. "Don't be so sure about that."

"Oh? Why do you say that?"

"I think these pieces will all make a lot more sense when we're able to put a few more of them together," McBride replied. "Besides, look at this."

Eyes twinkling, he shoved toward Stillman a saucer containing the crumbs of a fortune cookie and its little cellulose insert.

Stillman picked up the tiny slip and read the red-lettered fortune aloud. "In time, all things will be revealed."

"Yeah," said Jones, laughing, "but it didn't say to whom."

"'In time,'" said Fitzgerald. "Does that meant this generation or the next?"

"You guys," McBride said disapprovingly. "What a bunch of wet blankets!"

* * *

Aaron Fitzgerald, feeling a little out of his element, rode silently to the third floor in the hospital elevator with a tight-lipped woman in her late twenties on one side and a deliberately nondescript plainclothes police detective on the other. And silently he prayed, watching the numbers change up above the double doors.

To a careful observer, an involuntary clenching and unclenching of the woman's left hand at her side might have betrayed some anxiety. And to anyone who knew Steve Leadingham, there could be little doubt that this trim young brunette with the Florida tan was close kin. There were the same easy smile, mischievous eyes, and generous mouth.

Rebecca Leadingham—the real one—impressed Fitzgerald as a young woman who could handle herself, not someone who wasted a lot of time worrying about things she couldn't change. But now, this junior advertising executive also gave the clear impression of being someone who feared this situation might be one of those things. Fitzgerald had noticed that at the mention of her brother's precarious condition, the easy smile and mischievous eyes would harden into something tighter and more guarded.

The detective was an unobtrusive-looking fellow named Ray Overholtzer. He had a receding hairline and a firm physique. He looked as if he would have rather been bowling, which could have been a studied pose. Sgt. Overholtzer was, in fact, off duty. But he and Vince Salerno went back a long way together, and Vince would do the same for him anytime.

The head nurse at the CCU nursing station seemed about as pleased to see the three of them as to find a case of drug-resistant TB. Steely gray eyes moved distrustfully beneath short black bangs. The gray-and-red name tag on her white uniform said "TANYA POWERS, RN."

"Rebecca Leadingham," said the young woman, as if wanting to get this over with. "I'd like to see my brother, Steven Leadingham."

Suspicion danced across the nurse's face as her eyes moved from Ms. Leadingham to Fitzgerald to Overholtzer and back again. It was clear that she wasn't about to roll out any red carpets.

"Immediate family only," Powers said with an intense stare.

Becky Leadingham was not about to be intimidated. She touched Fitzgerald's elbow. "This is a pastor, Reverend Aaron Fitzgerald," she said. "He's going with me."

The nurse looked surprised, and not pleasantly so. But before she could say anything, Fitzgerald was proffering his ID.

"I assume your institution has no rules prohibiting prayer for its patients," he said with a slight edge.

Powers, now looking a little desperate, pointed a pen at Overholtzer. "And I suppose he's your fairy godfather?"

"Watch your mouth, lady," said Overholtzer, flipping his badge. "I'm just making sure there's no trouble. Funny things been happening. I'll stay out here with you."

Powers blinked in disbelief, evidently realizing they had her. Her eyes darted again from face to face before capitulating.

"Ten minutes," she growled grudgingly, as if the time were being deducted from her own lifespan.

* * *

Fitzgerald, not knowing quite what to expect, had prayed for discernment for whatever he found inside that critical care room. Now, beside the unconscious form on the bed amid a profusion of lines, sensors, wires, and various intravenous attachments, Fitzgerald's first thought was that the man was already dead. The skin on the face and hands had an ancient look, pallid and actually wrinkled.

Yet he could see quite clearly that the bedside monitoring console was tracking quite active vital signs on the data readouts. With the growing sense that something didn't add up here—that something was very wrong besides the obvious—Fitzgerald resumed praying for discernment. He felt directed to pray for deliverance from deception.

"Oh, Steve, Steve," Becky Leadingham was saying as she took in the sight.

In an instant, Fitzgerald thought he had the answer. At least, he believed he knew the reason the man looked like something from Death Valley. But, looking at his watch, he also knew he didn't have much time.

He began pushing the bed a little to one side so that he could pull the monitoring cart farther out from the wall for closer inspection.

"What are you doing?" Becky Leadingham asked tremulously.

"Your brother needs water," Fitzgerald said urgently. "Find a cup and get him some as quickly as you can—preferably without drawing attention."

"I think there's a water fountain around the corner," said Becky.

"Go for it." Fitzgerald quickly got his hands into the apparatus.

"Eh?" he said to nobody a moment later. "What's this?"

He had located the monitoring system's diagnostics, but none of it was functional, as if something was overriding. That fit. He just had to find out what was doing it.

Becky Leadingham returned. "What should I do with this?" she said, holding out a paper cup of water.

"See if you can get him to take some of it."

"Wake him up?" the young woman said uncertainly.

"That's usually best for drinking," Fitzgerald agreed. "If you don't, he may never awake again. Crank up the bed, for starters."

While Becky Leadingham wrestled with the bed, the patient, and the water, Fitzgerald wrestled with the biometric gear, unplugging one lead after another. He had suspected as much, but it was still amazing to see the disconnected wires lying there on the cart while all the same numbers, curves, and spikes continued to be displayed on half a dozen monitors and printouts.

"It's all a total fraud," he declared. "If we had been any later . . . "

He let the thought trail off and turned his attention to an unidentified little black box plugged into the back of the switcher unit. Fitzgerald unplugged it and watched as instantly all data flow died. *Voila!* He systematically unhorsed every remaining connection to the switcher to eliminate any possible signal input and then reconnected the mystery box.

Instantly, the displays returned to their old tracking patterns as if receiving a real patient's respirations, pulse, and electrocardio and other measurable activity.

He unplugged the device once again and held it up for inspection, like a poisonous snake. "It would appear that somebody didn't want your brother to recover from his injuries," he said thoughtfully, turning the gizmo around in the light to get a better angle.

When Ms. Leadingham failed to respond, Fitzgerald glanced over to see her stroking her brother's forehead and trying to coax him to accept the cup's contents. The patient looked to be at least semiconscious.

Fitzgerald set the contraption down atop the console, reached for the nurses' call-light, and pushed the button.

"Yes?" a woman's voice said after a moment.

"We need a doctor in here, quick."

"Is there a problem?"

"No, but there's going to be if there's not a doctor here lickety-split."

"Ms. Powers is on her way."

"In that case," said Fitzgerald, "please see that Sergeant Overholtzer comes back here too."

Fitzgerald turned back to the bed and noticed that Leadingham's lips and the fingers of one hand appeared to be moving. If he wasn't mistaken, some water actually was going down the pipe.

Suddenly the door flew open, and Tanya Powers burst into their midst, eyes wide as they fastened on the spectacle of Becky Leadingham ministering to her brother. The nurse's mouth worked soundlessly for a moment before words came.

"Stop!" she commanded. "What do you think you're doing?"

"Trying to save my brother's life," said Becky Leadingham, "which seems to be more than you were doing for him."

Powers' eyes fastened next on Fitzgerald amid the disassembled monitoring equipment. Something appeared to snap. She marched straight to the apparatus, grasped the little black box, and spun around.

"Get out! Get out!" she hollered hysterically, looking from one to another.

Fitzgerald was starting to wonder what had become of Overholtzer when the door was flung open yet again. In came an official-looking man with moustache, white coat, and stethoscope. Overholtzer followed not far behind.

"Oh, Doctor Bondurant," Powers said, flustered and looking for all the world as if she wanted to ditch the gizmo in the nearest dumpster.

"Yes. Well, what is really going on here?" the man said quite pointedly.

"They—these people are endangering this patient."

Becky Leadingham turned around with fire in her eyes.

"The only danger to my brother is from this hospital! I want him out of here!"

Fitzgerald began to explain. "I think you'll find, Doctor—uh—"

"Bondurant," the man supplied.

"Doctor Bondurant—that the real endangering came from the fact that this patient's feeding lines have been tampered with and some blasted device implanted to create a bogus data readout."

Bondurant was already inspecting the nutritional lines and the serpentine monitoring system.

"What the—" he said just a moment later, wiggling some empty tubing and tracing back along it to the source. "Who would do something like this?" Who indeed? All eyes turned toward Tanya Powers—except that Powers was there no longer. In fact, she was nowhere to be seen. The very spot where she had stood only moments ago with the strange device was quite vacant now.

This time, Sgt. Overholtzer spoke up. "Doctor Bondurant," he said, "let's get Mr. Leadingham out of here."

The doctor looked up with a hesitant, quizzical expression.

"I'll take responsibility for the transfer," said Overholtzer, "until the family doctor signs all the right papers."

"Riverside," said Becky Leadingham. "We want him transferred to Riverside Hospital."

"Certainly," said Bondurant, looking quite disturbed. "I'll see to it right away."

After Bondurant left the room, Fitzgerald moved to Leadingham's bedside. He was mildly surprised to see that Leadingham's eyes were half open and displaying a small spark of life.

Fitzgerald placed a hand atop one of Leadingham's. It was cold and dry.

"I'm a friend of Neal McBride," he explained. "If you can speak at all, we need to know why you were shot. Can you tell me what they were trying to stop you from saying?"

Leadingham's eyes opened even wider. He licked his parched lips and appeared to be trying to speak, but nothing would come out. Faintly, he moved his head to one side and then the other, as if signaling his failure.

"Can you give him some more water?" Fitzgerald asked.

Becky was able to get him to finish the cup.

"Who else knows?" Fitzgerald persisted. "If you can't tell us, is there somebody else who can?"

Leadingham appeared to be rallying himself for a last-ditch effort to communicate.

"M-Moira," he croaked, barely audibly. "Moira . . ."

But the effort was too much. He closed his eyes and lapsed once more into unconsciousness.

18

There was a conspicuous twinkle in Julian Wickner's aqueous blue eyes, a hint of some lurking mischief, as he scooted a mug of ginseng paua across the mahogany desk toward Moira Stone.

With his white goatee, gold earring, and indigo velour jacket, Wickner looked as much like an underworld conspirator or dealer in stolen art as a classical scholar or university administrator.

Moira, businesslike in a light cream sweater and green pantsuit that picked up the color of her eyes, sniffed at the aromatic cup before presenting it to her lips. If Wickner liked it, she was suspicious. Her oversize hoop earrings danced among her auburn locks as she tossed her head and made a face. The stuff was nasty.

She made no attempt to conceal her disdain for old fools such as he, and Wickner made no attempt to conceal his disregard for the opinion of others such as she. As her superior, Wickner had prevailed upon her to dig up some information for him, and Moira had found it awkward to decline. But she didn't have to like it.

"So, where are these two dirtballs from?" Wickner inquired casually.

"Chicago. That's the headquarters for their outfit, the Rhema Institute."

"What is that?"

"Some kind of fledgling missionary organization. They plan to translate the Bible into other languages, destroy native cultures, things like that, I suppose."

"Why would Richard Stillman want to get involved with that kind of thing?"

Moira wondered what Wickner was up to. She reminded herself that none of this—even Rick—should mean anything to her.

"My contacts say it was originally Judith's idea, out of professional curiosity because of the language groups involved," she said evenly. "And, of course, Rick saw it as a chance to demonstrate the wonders of Cybersynchronics."

"How reliable is your information?"

"Excellent."

Wickner nodded and paced across to the window. His Grady Hall office overlooked a good piece of Fraternity Row, including the lavender-tiled roof of the gay/lesbian fraternity/sorority.

"How do you—ah—feel about Stillman and his friends?"

Moira frowned. This was getting a little personal.

"I have no feelings for Rick," she asserted. "I haven't even seen him for . . . a long time. Maybe he's getting a little flaky in the religion area. And about these Bible translation geeks, I care even less."

Wickner affected a look of concern. "Well, perhaps Rick needs a little intervention for his own good."

No reply was specifically sought, and Moira offered none.

He let the thought hang for the moment as he meandered back to the desk. "Do you know," he resumed, "if Rick actually has engaged yet in any joint professional activities with these individuals on university time?"

Moira was somewhat startled. "I have no idea. Why do you ask?"

"Rick already has some . . . potential liability . . . in the Armand Schliesser scandal. He can't afford to get himself mixed up any further in questionable political activities. As his friends, we have a responsibility to save him from himself. Don't you think?"

"I would have no idea."

Wickner's eyes narrowed.

"Don't you have an overseas research sabbatical proposal pending before the Senior Faculty Committee?"

"Yes," Moira said, her eyes widening. "My dig on Crete next spring. What about it?"

"Oh, just wondering," he murmured. "Having any difficulty getting approval?"

"Well, they're not setting any speed records with my request. It's a little touch-and-go because I have to commit one way or another pretty soon or lose the opportunity. Why? Aren't you on the committee?"

"Yes. I'd just hate to see you lose out needlessly. That's all. Maybe I could be helpful on your behalf."

Moira got the picture. "What is it you want now?" she said dourly.

Wickner licked his lips. "More of the same. Just find out whatever you can about the status of this Bible translation project and anything else that might be hazardous to Stillman's health."

"Only one problem . . . ." Moira said, corrugating her brow.

"What's that, my dear?"

"'My dear'?" Moira repeated, now corrugating her upper lip. "A little chauvinist today, are we?"

"Save the rhetoric for the chumps, sister," Wickner said coldly. "What's your one problem?"

"Getting further information may require . . . personal contact."

Wickner smirked. "Unlike . . . marriage?"

"You really don't know when to stop, do you?" she flashed. "You can still respect the feelings of others, even if you don't have any of your own."

"I have feelings," said Wickner, stroking his goatee and smiling. "I just don't pay attention to the ones that get in the way. Right now, for example, I have a strong desire to see you make the grade with the Society. I'd also love to see you get that dig on Crete. But I could get over it."

Moira just glared.

Wickner's smile faded. "And I certainly would hate to see anything . . . unfortunate . . . happen to Stillman. But I could get over that too."

Moira got up and gave him one final glare before moving toward the door.

"I know you'll do the right thing," he called after her. "Just do it before you exhaust all the other alternatives."

"I'll think about it," Moira said over her shoulder as she marched out the door.

* * *

This is it, Angie told herself as she stood on the doorstep of 1412 South Kensington Avenue. She rang the bell and listened to the autumn wind scatter the October leaves all around her.

Nobody had said it in so many words, but there was every indication that if she successfully completed this mission, her Society membership would be in the bag. No longer would she be on the outside looking in or suffering continued indignities from the likes of Roger Larrabee.

She almost hoped initiation wouldn't mean the end of cloak-and-dagger assignments. She was developing a degree of confidence at them. Like this caper. She was hiding behind no disguises this time. This was the real Angie Hurley—with her red-and-blue plaid flannel shirt, jeans, boots, ski jacket, and all.

It also didn't hurt that she had a snootful of the designer "Dare." This evening the world was her oyster, triple cherries on the one-armed bandit. In her meditations and incantations, Ashtoreth, her spirit guide, had been promising greater things to come, urging her to soar to new heights.

Marianne King didn't stand a chance.

"Who is it?" came a voice over the speaker by the door.

Angie supposed that it was Marianne King. It was female, at least.

"Angela Hurley. You don't know me, but I'm Judge McBride's stepdaughter."

"Oh," said the disembodied woman after the slightest hesitation.

"I'm sorry if this is an inconvenient time to talk, but I'm just . . . so worried about Dad."

"Hold on."

Angie was aware of a front window curtain being drawn a few centimeters to the side as if someone was checking her out. In another moment the door began to open. It was early evening, and the lingering aroma of a recently completed dinner—something Italian, maybe—wafted out toward Angie's nostrils.

"How did you find me?" the woman said hesitantly through the outer door, open only six inches.

"Through the police," Angie fibbed. "Sergeant Detwiler suggested that I talk to you."

"Oh." Marianne King opened the door the rest of the way.

Angie smiled her way through the door, through a tiny foyer, and into a living room tastefully but modestly furnished with twentieth-century antiques—sofa, love seat, rocker, recliner.

Ms. King, a slender woman in a black turtleneck and blue jeans and with a weariness about the eyes, perched on the edge of the rocker and indicated that Angie should have a seat anywhere.

"I don't believe I know Sergeant . . . Detwiler." A measure of uncertainty clouded her face.

"That's because I made it up," said Angie, still standing.

"What?" Ms. King's eyes became saucerlike.

Angie was emboldened further by a soft door noise in the foyer.

"We track down all traitors to the Society," she said, smiling. "I'm going to have to take you in for questioning."

Panic erupted in the woman's face.

"Are you crazy?" she said in a high pitch. "I'm not going anywhere."

Marianne King stood up from the rocker, a little late.

At that moment Angie saw the woman's eyes leap to the foyer, where Elizabeth Morningstar was entering the living room with a nasty-looking pistol aimed in her direction.

"Good evening, Ms. King," said Morningstar. "We meet again. Don't worry about the gun. I don't plan to use it, except as a last resort. Angie here is a martial arts aficionada. So I wouldn't try anything."

"What do you want?" Her eyes darted back and forth.

"We'll ask the questions," said Angie. "Just come with us peacably, and you won't get hurt."

The gun disappeared into Morningstar's trench coat, but it was clearly still in her hand. "March!"

"Get a coat or jacket," Angie advised. "It's a little nippy out."

"But no funny moves," said Morningstar.

In the foyer, Ms. King's trembling hands removed her own trench coat from a hook and put it on. Then all three were out the door, Marianne King in the middle.

They got into a blue-and-white Jupiter van that was parked out front. Angie situated Ms. King in a second-tier bench seat and secured her hands with plastic cuffs while Morningstar started the engine and answered a message on the carphone.

When Angie got into the front seat, Morningstar's face bore an expression of concern approaching alarm, rather atypical of Morningstar even under moderate stress. This must be something significant.

"What's up?"

Morningstar was silent until they had inserted themselves into the flow of traffic. Then she announced, "The heat showed up on the doorstep. A couple of plainclothes detectives began asking the deprogrammers questions about us and Roger, whether they had seen us, whether they could look around the place, and so forth."

"Did they let the men in?" asked Angie, quite alarmed.

"Yeah, eventually. They apparently didn't have a warrant, so the deprogrammers stalled them long enough to get Roger and Schliesser out the basement door."

"Where are they now?"

"We're supposed to look for them at Hayes and Wolman."

Angie bit her lip. The obvious, unspoken thought was that the authorities might well be doing the same thing, especially if the basement-door caper had been witnessed by surveillance of the deprogramming center.

But she was certain the same thought had occurred to Morningstar. This strange but resourceful woman undoubtedly would be clever enough to avoid such an obvious trap. Wouldn't she?

Their rendezvous at Hayes and Wolman was by necessity within walking distance of the Deprogramming Center. As they approached the vicinity, Angie began looking about for police. She quickly realized that any nosy authorities were not likely to be in a marked car. Any parked car with an occupant suddenly appeared a potential threat. And there were too many of those to track. She was forced to give up the exercise and trust to fate.

Abruptly, Angie spied two figures, not far from the corner. They stood in a loop bus shelter, in the shadow of an ancient tavern's fluorescent beer sign. One man appeared to be supporting the other by a hand upon the forearm, although it could just as easily have been the hand of restraint.

Morningstar pulled over.

Angie popped open the curbside door. "Doctor Schliesser?" she called timidly.

"Shut up and drive!" Larrabee rasped. He shoved Schliesser onto the second bench seat beside the other frightened captive and took the seat immediately behind the driver .

"Well, well, well!" Larrabee said a moment later to the woman beside Schliesser. "Marianne, my love!"

The woman stared straight ahead without comment, although Angie noticed in the half light that her chin seemed to be quivering.

"Where to?" Morningstar asked.

"Headquarters," Larrabee snapped.

"'Headquarters'?"

"The castle, stupid!"

"Roger," Morningstar said patiently but firmly, "you know that's the one place we must avoid at all costs."

"I guess you don't learn real quick, do you?" Larrabee said threateningly. "I said shut up and drive. The Society is going to have to give me a little more help than two bimbos who can't keep their mouths shut—and one who isn't even a member. Maybe I'll get some action if I just show up at the big boys' doorstep."

Morningstar, obviously upset, tapped the brakes as if to stop, seemed to think better of it, and gunned the engine. A moment later, they slowed again to follow an access ramp out onto the outerbelt freeway. As they eased their way into the slow lane, Morningstar punched redial on the carphone out of sight of the backseat.

Larrabee bristled at the first electronic ring. "What's this?"

At the second ring, an indeterminate male voice answered. "Hello?"

"Brandon, let me talk to Kay," Morningstar said quickly.

"Shut that off!" Larrabee demanded.

"Jeremy's not here," Brandon said. "Who's with you?"

There was a deafening roar as the carphone blew to pieces. Angie, her ears ringing, realized that Larrabee had just fired a pistol pointblank into the device. She also felt a fierce burning at several points in her left leg, apparently from some shrapnel from the carphone or dashboard.

This man, Angie marveled, seemed capable of just about anything, rational or not. And she certainly seemed injury-prone around him. Her abdomen was still tender from the stab wound and the half dozen stitches that Kinsey had put there to close it.

She next noticed Morningstar's right arm, which appeared to have suffered a similar shrapnel misfortune in two or three places.

"Now, look what you've done!" Morningstar was saying with unusual stridence.

Angie thought at first that she was referring to their flesh wounds. But then Morningstar directed the van off onto the berm as it began losing power and decelerating.

"What's going on?" Larrabee demanded.

"Obviously, you've screwed up something with the engine or the electronics with that move."

Angie noted, however, that Morningstar's foot had left the accelerator and shifted to the brake before they started slowing. What was she up to?

Larrabee began swearing.

And then Angie, too, spotted what Larrabee was seeing through the back window. At a distance, an inconspicuous automobile several car lengths behind was following them slowly off the road.

"We'll have to split up," Morningstar announced. "This is where I check out, Roger."

"Not so fast!" Larrabee protested, as the van bumped to a halt. "You're staying with me."

The sound of Morningstar's door popping open was answered immediately by the impact of a pistol butt striking the back of her head on her way out. But it was a glancing blow, just causing her to stagger for a step before colliding with the open driver's door and reeling again.

Angie saw the woman reflexively feel for blood. Then she twisted about in her seat for a better view through the rear window. Two men were approaching on foot from the car parked a hundred meters or so behind them.

Larrabee thrust Schliesser out the door into the bright October moonlight and gave him a tremendous shove toward the weedy offroad shadows. The older man went stumbling, nearly falling. Larrabee plunged down the embankment after him toward the cover of trees.

"No!" yelled Morningstar. She broke toward the men, then raced back and opened the front passenger door.

"Here!" She extracted a pair of objects from the glove compartment and dropped one into Angie's lap. It had the shape and weight of a pistol. And then Morningstar was vanishing into the underbrush.

Angie was jarred from her semiparalysis by the beating tongues of light from an oncoming police car. Without further reflection, she ordered the last occupant, Marianne King, out of the van. Together, they stumbled and skidded down the slope. Once

Angie tripped, whacking limbs wickedly against stony objects and scraping her left ear and cheek before regaining her footing, all in seconds. Marianne, still beside her, appeared to stumble and go down but quickly recovered, even with her pinioned hands.

At first Angie didn't even notice that the gun was no longer in her hand. When she did, she was almost relieved. As little as she knew about pistols, she was probably lucky that she hadn't shot herself when she fell.

At the bottom, she looked skyward as a swimming patch of stars through the trees overhead assembled itself into constellations. Back atop the hill, the revolving light was punctuated occasionally by some form or another passing in front of it. The only sounds coming to her were those of running water and two or three voices in the distance, one male sounding utterly out of control with rage.

"This way!" she commanded, before Marianne could get any ideas.

The woman would have no reason to know that Angie had lost her gun. Besides, Ms. King probably knew it would be a tough chore to climb back up that hill manacled, in any event.

Angie and the woman followed the voices toward their origin. The moon and fortune lighted their way, and after a short while they were out of the thickest woods and into a clearing by a small creek. On the twisted bank stood two figures, a third—Schliesser—calf-deep in the stream. The frantic voice, naturally, was Larrabee's.

"Curse Christ!"

"Roger!" Morningstar was calling, less frantically, but her voice sounded ominous and eerie nonetheless. "There's no time for this. The police will be here any minute."

Angie stopped in her tracks. She could hear Schliesser murmuring as he stood, eyes uplifted, in the stream. "Yea, though I walk through the valley of the shadow of death . . ."

Larrabee broke off his commands to the old man and began chanting ugly-sounding phrases in a strange tongue.

For reasons unknown, Angie's body hair began to stand up. Knees trembling, she stumbled behind a tree too small to hide her. Where was her chemically induced valor now?

"*Roger!*" Morningstar shrieked, now at the edge of frenzy. Something in what Larrabee was ululating had triggered the woman's full alarms.

From somewhere behind them in the thicket came distant crashing sounds.

"No, not the sacrifice!" Morningstar yelled. "That won't help you now."

Larrabee continued only louder, aiming his pistol at Schliesser.

"Thy rod and thy staff, they comfort me . . ."

Behind the tree, Angie felt as if she had been transported fully conscious into one of her strangest nightmares. She was seeing things she had trouble crediting, although her vision was quite distinct in the brilliant moonlight.

There was Elizabeth, glancing over her shoulder nervously, dashing off farther into the woods, where she disappeared. Then Marianne King, silhouetted, was pointing something heavenward with both hands. And now the object unleashed a flash of white and an echoing concussion.

"Stop!" the woman shouted at Larrabee.

Was that what had become of the gun? Had it found its way into Marianne King's hands?

Larrabee wheeled and unleashed a volley of his own.

Marianne sank halfway to her knees, possibly wounded.

Immediately Larrabee returned his attention to Schliesser. Angie could barely hear what he said next.

"Prince of the Air, receive my sacrifice."

Yet, Schliesser's words continued softly. ". . . and I shall dwell in the house of the Lord . . ."

Shots rang out one by one, five in all.

" . . . forever."

Amazingly, Schliesser was still standing. Had Larrabee missed? Was the man supernaturally invulnerable?

The old man coughed a very small cough, but something dark glistened at the corners of his mouth. One knee sagged and then the other, until he was kneeling in the stream. Then Schliesser was on his side in the water, a dark stain spreading in the eddies around him. His left hand bobbed slowly in the current, as if reaching for the gibbous moon reflected on the surface.

Through her horror, Angie realized she had stopped breathing. All of her boldness was gone. And then yet another improbable development occurred—another gunshot, with a different acoustic signature.

Angie peered around the tree to see Marianne standing with her arms fully extended before her, wrists still pinned together with plastic cuffs.

At the water's edge, Larrabee wobbled and clutched his side. Angie was close enough to read his expression and guess his thoughts. She saw him raise his gun hand, his lips flaring in rage. And then he froze with the immediate recognition that his rounds were spent. Animal terror added to the rage, and he dropped the pistol to begin stalking Marianne with his bare hands.

And Angie was close enough to hear what the woman said next, though without any way to interpret the meaning.

"This is for you, Joshua!" Marianne King sobbed.

The shot sounded. Larrabee shuddered and halted in mid-stride, his face frozen in hatred as his heartsblood soaked his shirt from the inside. Just as quickly, he was on his back in the water, bobbing beside the now quiescent Schliesser. The image etching itself into Angie's mind was of a four-fingered left hand with liquid slivers of distorted moon slipping through its grasp.

"Satan, receive his spirit," Marianne King said bitterly, her arms limp before her. The gun slipped carelessly from her grasp to the ground.

Somehow, Angie missed the sounds of men crashing through the brush into the clearing. In a daze, she realized that several of them were approaching. Then one of them in a smart uniform was addressing her as "Miss" and fastening something cold to her wrists.

"You have the right to remain silent . . ." he began.

19

McBride pretended to read a magazine, one of those rich-and-famous-lifestyles publications, while the secretary-receptionist pretended to ignore him. Yet every time he lifted his eyes from the page, ostensibly to check the clock on the wall above her head, he found her eyes just darting away from him. He would smile or wink and go back to reading.

This Sharon Fortney, as her nameplate identified her, would frown and continue babbling into the phone. It sounded as if she were interrupting an ongoing conversation with a friend to take occasional business calls, which she quickly handed off to the appropriate person.

If a receptionist was supposed to project the company image, this had to be an unusual company. There was just too much of everything—too much lipstick, too much eye makeup, too much perfume, too much jangling jewelry, too much frosted hair, too much her.

McBride could tell that Sharon Fortney didn't like him. He was probably a curve ball she could do without. Maybe they didn't receive many visitors this way at Diversified Communication Services, 36 East Broad Street, Suite 1815.

McBride's investigative instincts were shifting into high gear over this intriguing lair on the eighteenth floor of the R. S. Bloom Tower. This was where the Institute for Pre-Life Science officially called home—along with a dozen other organizations with names such as the Forum for Separation of Church and State, the Pagan Awareness Coalition, Deprogrammers United, and Ohioans for Decriminalization.

That last one caused him some pause. Decriminalization of what? Were there any "victimless crimes" left to champion?

All were one cozy family under the roof of Diversified Communication Services, according to public records. McBride had found that each one was incorporated as a tax-exempt charitable organization. A check of elections records turned up non–tax-exempt political action committees with similar names plus Diversified's address and phone number.

But the most interesting revelation of all came when he checked the Secretary of State's corporate records for the Institute for Pre-Life Science. The incorporators all appeared to be obscure names, but the statutory agent was one he recognized immediately: Nina Bonito—a partner in the former law firm of Judge Charles Gamble.

McBride also knew they had been close friends, very close. Their closeness was allegedly the reason that Nina was no longer married to the same gentleman. It had not been particularly scandalous, just common knowledge. But now it was a connection that made McBride feel most uncomfortable.

He hadn't been too surprised when Sharon Fortney responded with a blank stare to his inquiry about the Institute for Pre-Life Science. No, he didn't have a delivery. He wanted some information about the organization for a possible contribution.

She hadn't looked convinced, but she let him have a seat while she asked a Mr. Donleavy if he would speak to him.

And now it appeared that he would. Sharon Fortney finally bade adieu to her phone friend and stood up.

"Mr. Donleavy will see you now," she said coldly, indicating that he should follow her through the door behind her desk and down the hall.

He did so, finding himself enveloped in a cloud of cloying perfume in her wake. At the end of the short hall, they entered a high-ceilinged, intensely lit room where an orgy of fine art occupied every reasonable square centimeter of wall space. There were antique chairs and sofas—and the smell of money. On the far side was an office with its door slightly ajar, and on the door was the name "D. L. Donleavy."

Ms. Fortney opened it the rest of the way and let McBride take it from there. No introduction, no by your leave.

Behind the desk were a half dozen picture windows with an even more breathtaking view of the city than McBride had enjoyed in his old office. It was a roomy, magnificent workplace with an honest-to-goodness chandelier, glassed-in bookcases, liquor cabinet, and CEO-style monster desk with virtually nothing upon its surface but a pair of Brazilian gentleman's leather loafers belonging to a self-confident man with an expensive cigar, bald-head with scraggly side hair down to his shoulders, salt-and-pepper beard, a semipermanent sneer, and the redness of dissolution about his smallish eyes.

"I'm Neal McBride," he said after each had sized up the other long enough.

"Devin Donleavy," said the man without rising, let alone extending a hand.

Donleavy continued smoking, obviously content to let McBride explain his presence, if he could. He left the definite impression that giving any sign of interest was entirely beneath him. McBride wondered how long this character would keep it up.

"Nice office," McBride said, sweeping his eyes about the room.

Donleavy blew more smoke straight up.

"You mind statin' your business?" he said at last. "I'm a busy man."

Somehow, McBride doubted it, but he let the statement pass.

"I'm looking for information about an organization that seems to have a profile about as low as the Winter Holiday temperature in Duluth."

"A name would be helpful," the man suggested.

"The Institute for Pre-Life Science."

"Never heard of it," Donleavy said too quickly, his eyes narrowing. "What kind of information?"

McBride extracted a checkbook from his breastpocket. "Anything. I've got a check here for ten thousand dollars, but I need more information about this organization before we decide to contribute. But I guess if you never heard of it . . ." He tucked the checkbook back into his pocket.

"Just a second." Donleavy removed his feet from the desk and sat up straighter. "Did you say the Institute for Pre-Life Science?"

"That's right."

"Well," the man said, X-raying McBride's face with his eyes, "who is this 'we' you mentioned?"

"We don't give that out. Just anonymous benefactors. What's it matter, if you never heard of this Institute?"

"My memory just improved. What is it you're after?"

"We'd like to know what they do, for starters. Then, maybe some names of the leadership. Do you have some literature, anything in black and white you can give me?"

"*Literature?*" said the man, almost amused. "I don't think so. It's just a group of fetal farmers that want to keep their livelihood safe and legal. They're growin' all sorts of things to benefit medical science these days. You'd be amazed. They might even be able to grow you a brain. How about that? Do I get the money now?"

"How about leadership?" McBride persisted. "Does the name 'Fahlgren' mean anything to you?"

Donleavy's eyes became heavy-lidded, and the cigar went back into a corner of his mouth for a couple of puffs while he considered McBride's question. Then he extracted the cigar and addressed the intercom.

"Sharon. Get Bryan and Ed for a Number Five. Have 'em wait in the outer office."

McBride was not fooled for a minute. He recognized a call for muscle when he heard one.

"Let me ask you a question," Donleavy said, patiently tapping off the excess ash. "You can make out your check to Diversified or Pre-Life. Makes no difference. We'll make sure you get the right thing if you want the tax deduction. What do you need names for?"

McBride wanted to pull the plug on this pretty quickly.

"We just need to know more about the organization."

"Why?"

"I don't really consider that your business." McBride extracted his checkbook again. "Are you telling me you don't want our money?"

"Not at all," the man said, grinning humorlessly. "Maybe you could just leave your address and phone, and I could have somebody get back to you."

"No, thanks." McBride ripped off the top check, crumpling it in his fist, and replaced the checkbook in his breastpocket. "Don't call us; we'll call you."

As he began to make his retreat, Donleavy called after him. "What did you say your name was?"

"Neal Armstrong," McBride said from the door. "One small step for man—a flying leap for you."

He definitely wasn't going to wait around and find out exactly what a Number 5 was.

* * *

"There have been some more developments," Salerno said on full video—unscrambled—from the conference room wall-screen.

Just from the grim look on the big lawman's face, McBride knew something was up, something major.

"Larrabee and Schliesser are both dead—shot to death." Salerno paused for that nasty reality to sink in.

There was silence all around the table as eyes flicked back and forth among the four men, whose labors had just been interrupted.

Stillman had been brainstorming elements of the translation project with Fitzgerald and Jones, while McBride had been compiling a list of names, from Fahlgren through Institute incorporators, that he wanted searched through all available data banks. And now all that was forgotten.

The only sounds in this dreadful interim were an errant burp of the water cooler in the corner and Fitzgerald's muttering something under his breath. Stillman looked pale and stricken.

McBride at last spoke up. "Give us some details, Vince."

"There have been two arrests. Marianne King—and Angela Hurley."

It was McBride's turn to feel the invisible kick in the gut.

"Charges?" he said, barely able to get the word out.

"Both held for investigation of agg-murder," said Salerno, "but I'm told the evidence—powder traces and ballistics, mainly—all points to Larrabee pulling the trigger on Schliesser and Ms. King pulling the trigger on Larrabee."

"And Angie—" began McBride.

"—was an apparent accomplice," Salerno concluded. "Arrested at the scene. Whole thing happened off Route 315, just this side of Worthington, down an embankment through a little woods by the Olentangy."

"Any idea what started it?" McBride asked.

Salerno shook his head. "Makes no sense. Without the gunplay, Larrabee might have gotten away, maybe. But it would have been a real long shot—and it could be he knew that. Anyway, Ms. King's statement indicated Schliesser was quoting Bible verses, which drove the guy nuts."

Fitzgerald, who had confessed to being something of a mystery novel fan, jumped in. "So then, Ms. King slew her son's slayer?"

Salerno nodded. "Looks that way."

McBride smacked the table with the flat of his hand in frustration. "We're always a day late and a dollar short," he exclaimed. "We need to get ahead of the curve. Hadn't you mentioned, Vince, that Ms. King might be in some danger with Larrabee on the loose?"

Salerno nodded again.

"Why was that?" Darnell Jones asked.

"Didn't you say something about her not being quite what she appeared?" McBride prompted.

"Right," said Salerno. "Maybe if the trial had proceeded, we might have had a surprise or two. Larrabee's lawyer might have tried to establish the fact that Ms. King wasn't totally blameless in her son's death."

McBride's eyebrows went up. "How so?"

"All I know is that Ms. King had had some prior cult involvement herself. And she may have been a fetal donor to a legit recycling center. At least, I know the defense was trying to establish that fact. My guess? She also might have been a fetal donor for an outfit like Larrabee's for blood sacrifice. Maybe they pay more than the legitimate fetal farms do. So—"

"So, maybe full-term Joshua was a . . . breach of contract with somebody?" McBride suggested.

"Somethin' like that. Maybe she just couldn't bring herself to terminate him."

"Mothers can be mawkishly sentimental that way," said Fitzgerald.

"Now, as for Angie—" McBride began.

"Ms. King says she was grabbed by two women, including Angie," Salerno interjected. "So, maybe one did get away. But Angie appears to be a player—had something to do with Peter's disappearance. Then she turns up again with Larrabee and another kidnap victim. Wouldn't be surprised if she was even involved in the Larrabee jailbreak."

"Maybe I'll get a chance to ask her some of those questions," McBride thought aloud. "If she'll talk to me. Her normal policy has been not to."

Salerno looked concerned. "You going to try to see her?"

"Sure. First thing in the morning."

"You think that's wise?"

"You mean from a security standpoint? Don't you think the jail is a safe place to talk?"

"I'm more worried about coming and going," said Salerno. "Your enemies might be expecting you to make just such a move."

"On the other hand, Angie's too great an opportunity to miss," said McBride. "There's no telling how much she knows about all of this. She might escape indictment in the shootings, and then those questions may never be asked. Besides, she's—my girl."

While they finished discussing security precautions, Jones turned to Stillman, who had been sitting the whole time in dejected silence.

"Look, my man, I know you were close to Schliesser, but it's only for yourself that you grieve."

Stillman looked up, a measure of surprise in his haunted eyes. "What do you mean?"

"Simply, that from everything you've told me," said Jones, "I'm sure that Schliesser was a believer. That means he's home now with his Father. Absent from the body, present with the Lord."

"Which is much to be preferred," said Fitzgerald.

It seemed all too much for Stillman, who continued to stare woodenly.

"We've got to get our act together," Salerno was saying. "First, Zona. And now this, with Marianne King. I even said something like this could happen. They must be laughing at us."

An uncomfortable silence ensued in which McBride imagined he almost could hear enemy laughter somewhere in the wings. Maybe demons in the Temple narthex. He stood up to walk around and shake it off. His imagination was giving him a case of the willies.

"Thanks, Vince," he said. "You've really brightened our day."

Salerno looked like he was about to sign off, then changed his mind. "One more thing. We have something else to check out—a clue from Leadingham. Does the name 'Moira' mean anything to anyone?"

Stillman rose slowly to his feet, looking pale and stricken all over again.

"Did—did you say 'Moira'?"

"That's right," said Salerno. "Leadingham could only get out the one word, 'Moira,' as if this was somebody who knew something. Do you know somebody by that name?"

"Yeah," said Stillman. "I was married to one."

"If it's the same one," said Salerno, "then you have a job to do with her. But it might not be the same person. There was no last name."

"Oh, it's probably her," said Stillman, shaking his head slowly. "This is just the kind of crazy thing she'd get messed up in."

"There's one sure way of finding out," prompted Fitzgerald.

"Yeah," said Stillman wearily. "And when I'm done with her, I'll go have tea with the Queen of England."

★ ★ ★

After Salerno hung up, McBride listened with half an ear as the two men from Chicago offered up some prayers for encouragement and discernment. Stillman began asking Jones some religious questions that McBride didn't bother to try to follow. His own thoughts kept returning to a room in the mental health center and a cell in the county jail.

He was puzzled finally to hear Stillman telling Jones in a heavy voice, "I think I'm about ready to . . . do business, Jonesy."

Jones, exchanging glances with Fitzgerald, told Stillman they'd get together in a while to discuss this "business" further.

McBride hoped Rick wasn't going softheaded. But then, he was forced to admit that neither Jones nor Fitzgerald seemed particularly flaky in any other regard. In fact, he held both of them in growing esteem.

Before McBride quite knew it, these two men had Stillman almost back to normal, kicking around the current status of the translation project. McBride gathered that it wasn't going much faster than anything else just now. Since he never involved himself in these discussions, he was surprised to hear Stillman asking for his input.

"Did Judith ever talk about her work at home?"

"Not much. And if she had, I wouldn't have understood much of it."

"There were things she wouldn't discuss with me, either," said Stillman. "I always suspected she was working on something that could have a real bearing on this project. In fact, I think it's why she was interested in the Rhema project in the first place."

"I doubt that I'll be much help, but you can try me."

"All right, Your Honor. I'd like to direct your attention to one particular subject. Did Judith ever mention anything about monogenesis—the idea of a common origin for all language?"

"Monogenesis," repeated McBride. It wasn't the first time he had heard that word—and where else could he have heard it but from Judith? "It rings a bell. Oh, it seems she also talked about a cognate-something regression system."

"What was that?" interjected Fitzgerald, his eyes brightening.

"I don't know. I just remember her talking about working backward toward some common roots among Indo-European and other language groups. You see you're quickly exhausting my knowledge of the subject."

"Would the names mean anything to you?" asked Stillman.

"They might. She had me read some of her papers occasionally—just to make sure none of it made sense to ignoramuses, I think."

"How about Nostratic?" asked Stillman.

"Yeah, that sounds like one of them."

"Amerind? Sino-Caucasian? Indo-Pacific?"

"All of those. I remember her complaining that it was nearly impossible to go back past a certain point in time because the prototypes were mostly guesswork. She complained about working with faulty data."

"I bet," Stillman said knowingly. "I probably could have given her some technical assistance if she'd asked, but it would be just like her to keep me in the dark and then spring something like this on me without warning."

"Wait," said Fitzgerald. "Did your wife maintain any files on this work? It could be helpful to us."

McBride shrugged. "No idea."

"ALEX," Fitzgerald called.

Botticelli's Venus obediently appeared on the wallscreen, indicating that ALEX awaited instruction.

"Search for any subject files on linguistic monogenesis, author Hurley-McBride, J."

It took only a moment for ALEX to respond. "Negative."

"It was worth a try," said Fitzgerald.

"Hold on," said Stillman. "ALEX, next-of-kin security override; access all note files on previous subject/author or anything related to cognate regression."

There was the slightest pause before ALEX responded. "Author deceased?"

"Author . . . incapacitated under—" Here, Stillman faltered.

"Competence," McBride suggested.

"Thanks," Stillman murmured. "Competence."

ALEX haggled again. "Kin relationship to author?"

"Husband," McBride answered. "Wilson Neal McBride."

"Security override code?" ALEX asked.

Stillman's eyes darted around the room, seeming quite at a loss. "Time to play a good hunch," he told McBride.

McBride uttered the first thing that popped into his mind. "Maxie."

"Uh, override code 'Maxie,'" Stillman said dubiously.

"Maxie?" Jones whispered.

McBride shrugged. "I don't know. Just a name she liked."

Suddenly the screen lit up with columns of entries, indicating a multiplicity of files.

"Bingo!" Stillman said excitedly.

"Smashing!" said Fitzgerald.

"Shazam!" said Jones.

McBride just smiled.

20

McBride was almost surprised when they said Angie would see him. He had half expected her to refuse his visitation request. And now, waiting for her, he marveled at feeling a hundred times more nervous than he had felt in the lair of D. L. Donleavy and his goons. He supposed it had something to do with his guilt and frustration over never being able to establish a relationship with this stepdaughter who remained a veritable stranger.

Then he saw her approaching, escorted by a jailer and looking small and withdrawn inside a standard-issue green prison outfit. There was a decided droop to her boyish black hair, which lacked its normal luster, and a certain insolence to her mouth and in her dark brown eyes as she took a seat behind the window in the visitors' block.

Then McBride noted an expression almost of surprise and realized she probably was reacting to his half-grown beard and the casual sweatshirt and jeans, all somewhat out of character.

"You look almost—normal," Angie said, changing her expression to an approving smile. "I almost didn't recognize you."

"That's probably the nicest thing you ever said to me," McBride said lightly.

"Nothing personal. I guess you really can't help it you're a reactionary white male member of the privileged class. Or should I say 'former member'? How's unemployment?"

"Such a kidder you are." McBride smiled, determined not to let her ruffle him.

"No, really. I heard that you'd quit."

"I'm on vacation. Now that Mr. Larrabee has bought the farm, I can take some more time off."

In truth, he was most likely an ex-employee. The only question was whether he had left the door open wide enough to sue his way back—if he so desired. At this point, that was doubtful.

"So—uh—where are you spending this vacation?"

He knew very well that she was trying to turn the tables and pump *him*. He didn't like it, but he didn't have to let that show.

"Oh, just puttering around. Visiting accused murderers—things like that."

Angie smiled, but he could tell by her eyes that he was getting to her.

"How come you're never home?" she asked. "There's never an answer. Have you moved out?"

"That's funny. I was going to ask you the same thing." When it became clear she wasn't going to respond, he continued. "How did you become acquainted with Mr. Larrabee? And how exactly did Mr. Larrabee . . . get dead?"

"Lay off the judge bit," she said quietly. "I'm not on trial, and you don't scare me."

"I hope not. That's the farthest thing from my mind. But you are in a very serious spot."

"I—didn't kill anybody." She looked down at her hands.

"Just hanging around with friends who do?"

Angie continued staring downward.

"Where have you been living the past few weeks?" McBride ventured.

Still no answer.

McBride figured he had nothing to lose at this point. "Where's Peter?"

"I—I don't know," she said unconvincingly. "But I'm sure he's OK."

"Or Carlotta," McBride continued. "Your name was on Peter's hospital discharge papers."

Angie shrugged. "Maybe somebody forged it."

"What do 'Fahlgren' and 'Chi Xi Vau' mean?"

Angie looked up, quite startled. Her eyes became a window through which he could almost read the answers to all of his questions, if he only knew the language. But after a long moment it became clear that she was not going to translate for him.

"Why should I tell you, even if I knew?" she said with feigned disregard.

"Angela," McBride said, taking a deep breath and reaching down into some buried pain. "I have to tell *you* something, in case you're not aware of it."

Angie rolled her eyes wearily and sighed without comment.

"From the first day I knew you, when you still had braids in your hair and braces on your teeth, I have—loved you," he continued with some difficulty. "I consider you my daughter, my only daughter. For whatever reason, you have never allowed me to love you, to touch you. But if I could do it now, I would reach in there and put my arms around you and hold you and tell you I still love you."

"Oh, stop," said Angie with an unsteady voice. "You're breakin' my heart."

Despite her hard words and lowered head, McBride could see that her chin was quivering. In another moment there were a couple of faint sniffles. Very quickly and unobtrusively, she swabbed at her nose with something.

The she looked up with anxious eyes that belied her tough tone. "You don't expect me to believe that . . . chauvinist garbage, do you?"

"Knowing you, maybe not," McBride said softly. "But it's true, Dimples."

Angie bit her lower lip and looked away, but not before McBride spotted the tears welling up. "Dimples" was the pet name he had called her during those special times as a young teenager when she still looked to him for occasional advice, guidance, help with her homework, and something resembling fatherly warmth and affection.

That was before it became politically incorrect for her to submit to male authority, those three short years before she decided to take the legal step of separating herself from the authority of both parents. For McBride, it had hurt more than he would have imagined.

Invoking that nickname now cost him the pain of being plunged back into that misery. *Funny,* he thought, *how those things have a way of resuming full strength, unabated, as if no time has passed.* He also wondered what it was now costing Angie.

"What right do you have to come in here and get me all upset?" she said, anguish in her voice.

She made no attempt to hide her tears now, wiping them with her piece of tissue and the heel of her right hand.

"All right, Angie," said McBride tiredly. "Maybe I can't make you believe me, or even listen to me. Shall I just go, then?"

She nodded woodenly.

"All right. I'll leave. But before I go, there is one question I'd really appreciate having answered."

"What?" she said sullenly.

"Why did you divorce your mother and me? We had no intention of denying you anything, virtually any freedom you wanted."

"Close doesn't get it," she said. "But I wouldn't expect you to understand that."

"Angie—" he started, but he couldn't go on. His own voice faltered somewhere in his throat and his chest tightened. He stood up.

Then finding his voice again, he continued. "I still love you, no matter what. And I will help you in any way I can. I guess you have to decide whether it's worth setting aside your pride to ask. This is real life, Angie, with real consequences. I would not want to be in your shoes right now with what's facing you."

Something seemed to get through that time. Maybe she did understand the seriousness of her situation. Maybe she was having second thoughts about the hardness of her heart.

"Neal," she began slowly, "it's not that I don't appreciate what you're doing. Look—Peter and Carlotta are OK. Don't worry about them."

"I thought you didn't know where they were."

She bit her lip again. "Maybe I do know something, a little

bit. Jeremy says we're on the verge of the greatest breakthrough in human intelligence in history."

"Jeremy who?"

Already, Angie looked as if she might be having second thoughts.

"Can I—confide some things in you?" she asked.

"Sure," said McBride, his heart quickening. "I can't make any promises about how I'll use the information, but I need to know."

"I'll tell you . . . everything," she said, starting to cry again. "Just get me out of here."

"What?"

"You'll bail me out, won't you? I'll tell you anything you want to know."

McBride's hopes fell again. He was tempted to pump her first, but he couldn't honestly do that.

"Sweetheart, there's no bail for aggravated murder," he said somberly.

Angie looked as if he had slapped her.

"Get out of here," she breathed. "Get out of here!"

Then she began swearing. She called him vile names, unleashing a torrent of venom. In a gesture of total futility, she hammered the plastic window between them with her fist and thought of some more names to spew. A jailer tapped her on the shoulder and indicated her visit was over.

Over her shoulder as she left, she hollered to McBride, "Don't bother me anymore. Just get out of my life. I don't know you. You're . . . nothing!"

★ ★ ★

On his way out of the jail, McBride was surprised by a two-man reception committee outside the booking room—Sherm Dygert and a newspaper reporter whom McBride thought he recognized. Salerno had been right—his enemies would be waiting for him to make this move, and somebody at the jail had been designated to tip them off.

"Neal!" Dygert called out.

"Judge McBride!" said the reporter, vying for his attention too.

McBride shoved past them, having no intention of breaking stride or stopping to speak.

"I need to talk to you about your resignation," Dygert said, trying to place a hand on McBride's forearm.

McBride shook it off.

Dygert tried to step in front of him, but not quickly enough.

"I have nothing to say." He broke the tackle and headed for the goal line.

At the door, a photographer zeroed in on McBride's grim visage and began snapping a shutter at him repeatedly.

"Judge McBride!" another voice called after him. Things were starting to become quite confused.

McBride stuck out his chin and headed for the steps, spotting an unmarked sheriff's car with its engine running. He broke into a jog as several voices began calling him back.

In another moment, McBride was sliding into the seat beside Lt. Salerno and slamming the door.

"Get me out of here, Vince," McBride murmured. "Just get me out of here."

★ ★ ★

It was the middle of a riptide night for Angela Hurley in Cellblock E of the Franklin County Jail. Sleep was nowhere in sight, and unwelcome thoughts chased one another like tomcats in a dark alley. Sounds were few—the occasional muted strain of a radio down the hall, a dreamer's muffled cry—and all the more distracting because of their randomness and unpredictability.

She was feeling recriminations about her callous treatment of her stepfather, new doubts about her involvement with the Society and her role in seizing Peter and Carlotta.

There were rumors about her newest abductee, Marianne King. Angie had heard through the jailhouse grapevine that Marianne was not at all herself. They said she wept for hours, often uncontrollably, sometimes crying out for forgiveness.

And most of all, there were new questions about Angie's own fate at the hands of the legal system—and about the very people who were expecting her to stick her neck out for them. Would Jeremy and the others just let her rot in here? If the Three J's were willing to go to such great lengths to spring Larrabee from jail, why not herself and Marianne?

These and a dozen other troubling matters were dancing in Angie's head when suddenly a shadow fell across her cell door. It was a human-size shadow, but it took a few moments for her pupils even to register the outline of the form. A woman's figure, garbed all in black, appeared to be keying something into the corridor security pad nearest Angie's cell. What was this all about? She momentarily experienced a disorienting rush of deja vu as the ghost of an incarceration past collided with the present. Shades of Elizabeth Morningstar, springing Larrabee from the slam. No sooner had that subsided, than there came an auditory jolt.

Kachunk!

A thin shaft of soft light ran the height of her cell door where it had inched forward from the frame.

"Who—who's there?" Angie called softly and tentatively into the dark.

"Angela Hurley! Get a move on!" the shadow-shrouded woman rasped, pulling the door farther open.

A hand closed on her wrist, and almost before she knew what was happening, she was stumbling down the corridor in the tow of the mystery woman. She began to wonder if it were possible that she was dreaming. As they descended in the brighter light of a staircase, suddenly Angie recognized the person.

"Elizabeth!"

It was hardly logical, but this was the last person Angie would have expected to see. Maybe it was the way Elizabeth had vanished into the woods that night without a trace as the bodies began falling into the moonlit stream. Her reincarnation here was just one more wild card in a game gone berserk.

The woman made no reply, but swung her sharply around a corner, where they stopped outside another cell. Elizabeth Morningstar breathed several quick words too low for Angie to hear into a device too small for her to make out in the dark. The woman then repeated the process of tapping out a security code on the keypad, and that cell door, in turn, popped open.

"Help me get her out. *Quickly!*" Morningstar commanded.

As Angie might have guessed, the occupant was Marianne King—a very subdued Marianne King. In fact, it took some maneuvering to get her onto her feet and moving, zombielike, out the door. Even in the dark, Angie had the impression that Morningstar was being none too gentle about it. But soon they were cruising down the corridor, headed for freedom, presumably.

Angie could feel her own panic beginning to rise, the nearer they approached the booking room that flanked the front entrance. Shouldn't Elizabeth be starting a fire or creating some other kind of distraction to cover their escape? Wouldn't they need to drop down and crawl past the deputy jailers? None of that was happening, and it was unnerving.

Had Elizabeth lost her senses? Would they all be shot?

And then they were at the strait, preparing to attempt passage. In sight was the steel security door to freedom. But at the two front desks sat Deputies Smith and Jones, like the Argonauts' monstrous ship-eaters, Scylla and Charybdis of old. In this case, the guardian monsters appeared remarkably placid. In fact, their eyes appeared to be closed, though they were sitting upright. *Certainly curious,* thought Angie, her apprehension turning to wonder.

Morningstar, leading the way, walked up to the men and stopped. "When you awake, you will remember nothing of this," she said.

There was an obedient silence. Morningstar glanced at Angie and Marianne, then strode quickly behind the counter.

"Disengage M-oh-oh-one-oh-one, OUIJA!" she cried, working something with her hands.

The steel door chunked open. Morningstar's hands came out from behind the security console with something resembling a Quang emulator newly detached.

Angie hurried Marianne to the door. She paused just long enough to look back and hear Morningstar bid the deputies adieu.

"Hail, Ashtoreth!" the woman said, moving out from behind the counter and heading to the door herself.

Just before shutting the big steel door, Morningstar called back to the men. "Hail, Molech!"

And then they were free. Angie stood blinking under a streetlight on a late-night downtown avenue that appeared all but deserted. No sooner had she begun to get her bearings, than the dark shadow of a car appeared out of nowhere at curbside. A door popped open.

"Get in!" Morningstar ordered.

Angie climbed into the back with Marianne, while Morning-star got in front beside the driver. Before the interior lights winked out, Angie caught a momentary glimpse of their chauffeur—Kelsey Kinsey. Angie also got a mental snapshot of Marianne, huddled in the corner, head bowed and tightly clutching a small white book. Probably still weeping.

In the uneasy silence of the getaway, Angie was surprised to hear herself become the first to speak. It must have been nerves.

"What was the . . . deal . . . with Smith and Jones?"

"Who?" Kinsey replied, half turning to Morningstar.

"The jailers," Morningstar said. "That ol' black magic got 'em in a spin."

"Down and down they go." Kinsey laughed. "Round and round they go."

"Hypnosis?" asked Angie.

"Something like that," Morningstar agreed, as if addressing a child who could not be expected to understand.

Stillness returned as the car edged stealthily through the night. Angie realized she had not noticed the make of the auto, but it clearly was not the Jupiter van. That vehicle probably now resided in an impound lot somewhere.

"Angela Hurley," said Morningstar, "you did tolerably well in the freeing of Roger Larrabee, employing the tricks of techno-logy. But technology needs augmenting. Technology harnesses the forces of the material world; sorcery, the forces of the spiritual. I had hoped to enhance your education in that regard."

The passengers lapsed into a momentary silence. Angie won-dered why Elizabeth had phrased her statement about furthering Angie's education in the past tense. Sorcery was a subject of great appeal to her.

"Where are we going?" she asked, changing the subject.

Morningstar waited a long moment before responding.

"The two of you must answer for Larrabee's death," she said at last. "One of you pulled the trigger. We will have the truth as to which one."

Panic rose anew in Angie's breast. "I didn't do it!"

"Of course not," Kinsey said sneeringly. "They don't have a merit badge for manslaughter in Campfire Girls."

Angie was startled to hear Marianne breaking her silence.

"Leave her alone. She's telling the truth."

"I see," Morningstar said, apparently surprised. "She's going to make it easy for us. Well, there will be a price to pay, Ms. King. In the meantime, my dear Angela, we have to decide exactly what to do with you once and for all."

"What—what do you mean?" said Angie, truly puzzled.

Kelsey Kinsey chuckled. "Let's just say that in the contest for Society membership, there are no second prizes."

Angie wasn't exactly sure what that meant, but she certainly didn't like the way Kinsey began laughing all over again at her expense.

It was at that point that Angie noticed there were no handles on the inside of the backseat doors.

21

2300 Hell Avenue.

Among all the other verbiage on the wallscreen, those words glared like a toxic warning label. McBride shook his head. He had come across some colorful names in the course of his investigations, but this was one of the more unusual.

"Cute," he said aloud.

"Eh?" said Aaron Fitzgerald, who had wandered into the conference room with a mid-morning cup of tea and a plate of scones. "What gives here?"

Darnell Jones had flown back to Chicago to tend to some Rhema Institute business, while Stillman and Fitzgerald plunged into the technical portion of the translation project. Before long the place again would be writhing with data, printouts, and Cybersynchronic programming.

McBride needed to get a jump on things with his own agenda before that happened. "Just reviewing my notes." He gestured toward the wallscreen. "Moira Stone's address. How would you like to live on Hell Avenue? Would you buy a house in Hell?"

McBride couldn't recall Fitzgerald's laughing before, but he was doing it now.

"Maybe it's part of a subdivision. Hades Estates or something."

Stillman looked up from his programming at the main console at the far end of the conference room. "I've never been to Moira's place, but I think it's a townhouse in the Columbus View area. ALEX, access street guide, correlate twenty-three hundred Hell Avenue with twelve closest cross streets, twelve closest parallel streets. Display corresponding map."

Instantly, names and lines representing streets and avenues criss-crossed in a grid on the big screen. There were some ordinary names, but a liberal portion of the picturesque as well.

"Yes, see?" said Fitzgerald. "Look at those—River Styx Road, Inferno Avenue, Purgatory Street, Torment Court, Incubus Way."

"I don't get it," McBride said. "How does something like that happen?"

"Aaron's right," said Stillman. "Look. It *is* a subdivision—Lost Souls Acres. There's been some renaming of older city streets, but you only see things of this magnitude in the newer developments. It's very chic to mock the old sensibilities, you know."

"Well—" Fitzgerald turned serious "—in a sense, we all live on Hell Street."

"What?" said McBride, sensing a diversion coming on. Still, in Fitzgerald's case his digressions were more interesting than most people's main themes.

"A fellow countryman," said Fitzgerald, "once described America as the first nation to go from barbarism to decadence without ever having known the intermediate state of civilization."

McBride and Stillman both chuckled.

"But that's not just America," Fitzgerald continued. "The old Judeo-Christian ethic that previously undergirded all law, morality, and codes of conduct in the West is moving from endangered species to extinction. Scratch a modern man today, and out will come pagan blood. 'Do unto others' has been replaced by 'Do what thou wilt.' As a judge, you probably saw that more acutely than most of us."

McBride nodded. He couldn't disagree. The Larrabee case had not been his first inkling that crime today was something more than a surface problem.

"But it was ever thus," said Fitzgerald. "We've probably never been far from relapse into blood sacrifice, fertility rites, and worship of the heavenly bodies. Even the names of our days of the week continue to give honor to the pagan gods and goddesses."

"Hey, throw another log on the fire," said Stillman. "As a linguist, I'd like to hear about that."

"Well, you know where Sunday and Monday come from," said Fitzgerald. "The sun and moon. And then—"

McBride was intrigued by the change in Stillman. Something had happened, he knew, probably last night before Jones left for Chicago. Richard Hanley Stillman was definitely not the same person that McBride had met even a few days ago. There was some subtle, undefinable alteration in his mood or spirit—a new single-mindedness. It was almost as if some kind of internal dilemma had been resolved, purpose restored.

He also knew it had to be more than just the translation project, though that had suddenly turned golden as well. A major breakthrough, they were calling it.

"What's with him?" McBride had asked Fitzgerald. "Did he win the lottery or something?"

Fitzgerald gave him a funny look and said it was far better than that—he had laid up treasure in heaven. Under the mixed-up circumstances, McBride decided to drop it. It was probably something personal—something "spiritual"—that he wouldn't understand.

There was more pressing business to take care of now. Before the translation project took over Stillman and Fitzgerald's agenda for the rest of the day, McBride wanted the undivided attention of their fresh minds. Reluctantly, they agreed to continue their diversion with the Interactive Professor some other time.

"We have other data banks to pursue," McBride told them. "Just now I'm more concerned about Fahlgren. Rick, before you get ALEX tied up all day in Cybersymphonics, how about launching one of your magic searches on the name 'Fahlgren'?"

"That's 'Cybersynchronics.' Yeah, I've been planning to do a local genealogical search."

"Great."

"What about Angie?" asked Stillman. "Did you get anything useful?"

"Very little. She started to open up, until I told her I couldn't bail her out. Then we had a bit of a scene. But before she clammed up, she did let slip one thing. She referred to a 'Jeremy' as a major player in some aspect of this."

"Jeremy?" said Stillman. "Jeremy Kay?"

McBride shrugged. "Was that the screwball who gave that lecture at Gunnison Auditorium?"

"Yes. Judith said Angie was dating him. What did Angie say about him?"

McBride searched for the right words. "It was some crazy statement, that he was on the verge of . . . the greatest breakthrough in human intelligence in history. Something like that. It didn't make a lot of sense."

"That sounds more like Jared Quang—although in Jared's case, it could almost be true."

"Maybe they're working together," said McBride. "It might be something, might be nothing. Let's add Kay and Quang to your list while you're running the check on Fahlgren. We make a few more pieces fit together, we might see a picture."

"What do you want to know?"

"Anything. Everything. Start some dossiers. I'll show you some of the standard public record sources we used in the Organized Crime Division. Meanwhile, I may start pounding the pavement again and try working some people sources."

"You don't think that's dangerous?"

McBride shrugged. "In this case, doing nothing is dangerous. Before anything else, though, I want you to get hold of Moira.

That's key. If Aaron understood Leadingham correctly, we need to know what she knows."

"Is Leadingham still unable to talk?" Fitzgerald asked.

"His sister says he's talking a little," said McBride. "Right now, the immediate problem is—mental."

"Amnesia?" Stillman asked.

McBride nodded. "Seems like it, and there's no guarantee it will be temporary. Meanwhile, we have to try Moira."

"How soon?"

"Now."

"I was afraid you were going to say that," Stillman said with a sigh.

* * *

Waiting for the phone to ring at the other end, Stillman realized his palms were sweating. This was silly. He wasn't a teenager, calling his first girlfriend, for crying out loud. This was Moira Stone, his ex-wife. She probably wouldn't be in her office, anyway. And she never seemed to be home—on Hell Avenue—unless she was doing call screening.

To his surprise, the phone rang only twice. Then someone picked it up.

"Hello," said the all too familiar voice. "Ancient Studies. Moira Stone."

Stillman swallowed hard. He hoped he could fast-talk her into staying on the line and hearing him out. Considering the fact that she'd been failing to return his calls, he doubted it.

"Hello," she was saying again, raising her voice slightly.

"Uh, hello," blurted Stillman. "This is Rick, Moira."

Again he was surprised, as the video sprang unexpectedly to life on the conference room wallscreen. Stillman forgot to breathe for a moment as he took in the sight of his beloved Moira, smiling serenely back at him and looking, if anything, even more beautiful than his tortured mind cared to remember.

"Hello, Rick," she said quite pleasantly. "What a coincidence this is."

"Uh, how's that?" he managed to say.

"I was just thinking about you."

238

Stillman had expected anything but this. "You were?"

"Yes, Rick. Don't you remember? You called me. I was going to return your call."

"Oh. Yeah. That was a good two weeks ago."

"Well," she said, smiling, "better late than never, right? What's on your mind?"

Stillman was amazed. This was far too easy.

"I wanted to—see how you were getting along."

"Is that all?" She sounded unconvinced.

"Well, since then there's been something else too," he groped. "Do you know a fellow by the name of Steve Leadingham?"

The smile went off her face for just a second. "What if I do?"

Stillman did not want to get sidetracked. "Does, uh—do you know anything about something called 'Chi Xi Vau'?"

There was the slightest pause, while Moira reapplied her smile. "You're not in the office?"

"No."

"Can I come over? When do you have classes?"

"Not till this afternoon. But why don't I go to your office? I don't want you to make a long trip."

"This really isn't a good place to talk about something like that. Where are you?"

This was getting out of control.

"Hold on a second," said Stillman.

Her picture on the screen froze as he put her on hold to consult with his colleagues.

"Shall I arrange to meet her someplace safe? We can't have her see this place, can we?"

McBride spoke up. "I think that's exactly what she should do."

"What?" said Stillman, taken aback.

"Does she keep secrets well?" asked McBride.

"Not at all."

"Good," said McBride, to Stillman's continued bewilderment. "Then she's perfect. Remember, we want word to get around, and we want to draw the other side out."

Stillman nodded slowly. "But what about you? We don't want your whereabouts getting around."

"Now's the time for me to start hitting the streets anyway. Maybe I'll even do the outerbelt motel routine for a while."

Aware of time ticking away, Stillman quickly took the call off hold. "Sorry for the interruption," he said.

"Somebody at the door?" Moira asked, a bit skeptically.

"Something like that. Actually, we've got a pretty exciting translation project going on here. Wait till you see it."

"Great. I look forward to it," she said, then asked directions.

Moira looked up after she'd written down the address. "That's not far at all," she said with slight reproach.

"Yeah, I guess you're right," Stillman conceded. "See you soon."

* * *

By all rights, Stillman should have been beside himself, in a dither, waiting for the only woman he had ever really loved to come waltzing through the front door and back into his life within the hour. On top of the conflicting emotions engendered by that prospect, he was expected somehow to finesse her into spilling information that she might not be particularly interested in disclosing. And right afterward, he and Fitzgerald would finish translating the Bible into all the tongues of the unreached peoples of the world—and then, he mused, they might as well proceed to the problems of poverty, disease, and crime.

But Stillman surprised himself. Once McBride had vacated the premises and ALEX resumed the Cybersynchronic process, he found himself forgetting all else. In fact, by the time Moira did arrive at the Temple a while later, he was no longer troubled by butterflies. Creative juices were flowing. Anticipation and discovery were in the air. He was reminded of that Sphinx on his Grady Hall office wall—as if its riddle were about to be cracked for once and for all.

ALEX was retrieving files, searching databases for cross-references, and making two printers work overtime while he and Fitzgerald vied for turns calling the shots as if they were Wall Street brokers on the floor of the Exchange in the final hour before the close. Stillman found it surprisingly difficult to tear himself away as progress toward a substantive working language model appeared to be taking shape. For once, he dared to think that they were onto something that actually would work.

And then suddenly the door chime sounded, and there stood before him in the half-lit narthex the living, breathing embodiment of his unfulfilled dreams and failed hopes—this brilliant, auburn-haired beauty who emphatically didn't need him. Gazing upon her familiar face and into the abyss of her green eyes risked the fatal spell all over again, but it couldn't be helped.

How much of this enchantment was intentional could only be guessed. Surely she must know that importing that fragrance—lilies of the valley—into his presence again would have a devastating effect upon him.

Stillman escorted her into the full light of the main hall and on to the threshold of the conference room nerve center, where Fitzgerald and Jones appeared to be as frenetically occupied with their business as air traffic controllers in a snowstorm.

"I can come back later, if this is a bad time," Moira said, looking a bit taken aback by the frenzied scene.

"No, no." Stillman led her farther down the hall to the pastoral study, where there was more quiet and more comfortable furniture. "I wouldn't dream of it. It's so—good to see you. Coffee?"

"No, thanks. Uh, Rick, what are you doing, living in a . . . church?"

He chuckled over the irony of the question. "Should I interpret that as an expression of concern for your ex?"

"Not at all," she replied, somewhat sharply. "It's just a bit . . . out of character, don't you think?"

"Not anymore," he said, warming to the game. "This is a Bible translation project here, after all. And besides, do you think it's possible that some of your assumptions about me might be out of date by now?"

"I . . . ," Moira started, then faltered, obviously not knowing quite how to take him.

"I don't really live here, anyway," he continued. "I've been wearing out the office couch at Grady Hall. Some nights I stay here. But sometimes I even sleep in my own bed in that old Dublin Road bungalow—right across the hall from our room."

Stillman knew her well enough to tell that Moira was a shade pinker in her cheeks and ears, trying valiantly not to betray an emotional response.

"You always were a sentimental fool," she said coolly.

"Yes, but now," he said on impulse, "I'm also an entirely new creation."

"What?"

"A follower of Christ."

"Oh yeah, sure," Moira said, rolling her eyes in disbelief. "And I'm Madame Butterfly. Tell me what you really want from me."

"I want to know," he plunged in, "why a dying man had your name on his lips."

Moira smiled. "It's the effect I have. Dying men everywhere do that."

"Steve Leadingham," Stillman said, suppressing irritation. "Do you know him?"

"Not really," she said mysteriously, as if enjoying tantalizing him.

"What's that mean?"

"He and I just a have a mutual friend."

"Who?" he asked, half expecting her not to answer.

Moira smiled as if reading his thoughts.

"Gretchen LeMieux. Steve's one-time inamorata. Why?"

"There are some mysteries for which Leadingham supposedly knew some answers."

"Such as?"

"Such as the disappearance of Peter McBride and Carlotta Waldo. Such as this mysterious Chi Xi Vau. If you don't know anything about these things, just tell me and we can stop playing games."

Moira's eyes became distant as she considered the request.

"You know," Stillman persisted, "Leadingham very well may have been shot because of something you told him."

"No," she said quickly. "That's not true."

"Or something you told Gretchen LeMieux?"

Her eyes resumed their furtiveness.

"This is getting nowhere," she asserted. "We're talking about violating a confidence for a thimbleful of questionable information. I'd have to think about that."

"I'll wait."

"For what?"

"For you to think about it."

"Oh," she said, smiling again. "Just like that?"

"Take as much time as you want—five, even six minutes."

"Sorry," said Moira with some finality. "Betraying confidences is a matter of hours and days, not minutes. Besides, you haven't told me exactly what you're doing here."

"Would you like the tour?" asked Stillman, rising to his feet.

"Sure."

★ ★ ★

Fitzgerald was somewhat loath to interrupt the work at this point, but he graciously squeezed Moira's hand and charmed her with his accent and good manners.

"Are you at all familiar with Cybersynchronics?" he asked diplomatically.

"Painfully."

"Well, it seems that without knowing it, Doctor Hurley-McBride had advanced to within a hair's breadth of identifying the prototype tongue from which all modern language families derived," he explained, beginning to warm to the discussion. "That's what ALEX, we believe, is beginning to generate up there right now, right before our eyes—the missing ancestor of all Indo-European and Afro-Asian tongues."

"Really?" Moira said. "How so?"

"It's a little like computer-enhanced photo-mapping. You have enough of the picture that the computer can project patterns, factor out junk, and reconstruct the remainder within a tolerable margin of error. With the right key, it's actually turning out to be a lot easier than anyone would have suspected. If Doctor Hurley-McBride had confided in Rick, he might have helped her clear the whole thing up a long time ago."

"What was the key?"

Fitzgerald's eyes began to shine. "Time. Too much of it."

"What?"

"It seems that Doctor Hurley-McBride, as well as most other scholars, had been assuming processes that took hundreds of thousands, if not millions of years through multiple sources and inter-actions. We simply shortened the time frame and did single-source regression analysis over just a few thousand years."

"That was Rick's idea?"

"Well—" Fitzgerald hedged slightly "—I had something to do with it too."

"I'm not sure I follow the significance of all of this," she said, turning more serious.

"Monumentally significant," Fitzgerald said quietly, eyes twinkling. "Doctor Hurley-McBride's methodology also made it possible for ALEX to get a geographical fix on the genesis of Proto-Speak, as well. Just the concept alone of a single origin is disastrous to conventional evolutionary models."

"I don't get it."

"Oh, Rick could make your eyes water with all of the reasons evolutionary gradualism dictates that there should be no ultimate common denominator among tongues—spontaneous speech generation as the byproduct of larynx and brain development over extended time periods among isolated people groups in various and sundry locations, et cetera."

"Trust me," said Moira. "He already has."

"But what we actually found," Fitzgerald continued, ignoring the editorial comment, "was hard at first even for catastrophists like us to believe."

"Yes?" she said with an edge of impatience.

"It was like sending a time machine back in history to take pictures. ALEX's regression analysis with anthropological factors placed us between the Tigris and Euphrates rivers, squarely in the middle of ancient Sumer and Akkad, around the year 4800 B.C., where the trail ended."

"So?" she challenged. Now they were in her field.

Fitzgerald looked mildly surprised at her blankness. "Doctor Stone, have you ever heard of the Tower of Babel?"

"*What?*" she said, somewhat flustered, if not irritated.

"The confusion of tongues. Contrary to modern convention, different peoples did not develop different tongues because they were isolated from each other. Rather, they were driven apart by virtue of their language differences."

"But—the *Tower of Babel?* Aren't we a little old for fairy tales?"

"Clearly, *something* monumental occurred in the vicinity of the city of Babylon that affected subsequent generations. Our evidence circumstantially supports the biblical account, involving the ziggurat, or tower. This stairway to heaven represented man's attempt to elevate himself to Godhood then and there rather than obeying God's command to spread out and inhabit the earth. So, God scattered them by confusing their speech."

"That has to be absolutely the most ridiculous thing I've ever heard!"

Fitzgerald gestured toward the screen. "You can see for yourself if you like."

"No, thanks," Moira snapped. "Next thing, you'll be trying to tell me that all of this information was brought ashore by a guy named Noah who had a big ark."

"Not at all," Fitzgerald said, unfazed. "The Flood was well in advance of the confusion of tongues."

Moira shot both men a toxic look. She obviously thought she had just been fed a bunch of malarkey.

"Rick," she said wearily, softening a bit, "just what are you trying to accomplish with all of this . . . nonsense . . . besides getting yourself into a whole lot of professional trouble?"

"I'm glad you asked that, Moira," he said, looking pleased. "It's a little like your search for the 'unified field theory' in the ancient mythologies. This proto-tongue will be our Rosetta Stone. Our next big project is digitizing the scriptural text. Then we'll have the ability to translate it into any modern language. It's only a matter of letting ALEX crunch the numbers for the current languages."

"But to what end?" she persisted. "Is this 'scriptural text' a euphemism for Bibles?"

"God's Word." Fitzgerald nodded. "To every creature. Now."

Moira, obviously disturbed, excused herself. She had heard quite enough.

22

Stillman figured something was up when he found the wall-screen in his Grady Hall office lit up with a message to see Julian Wickner as soon as possible. He also had a pretty good idea what it might be about. After all, McBride had been hoping to draw out the opposition with the translation project. It was just that Stillman would have preferred to draw attention to the work in its completed state, with no further chance of failure or interruption.

As acting division chair, Wickner now occupied Judith's administrative office. Entering the genteel outer office with its elaborately potted ferns and tasteful mahogany-toned seats for cooling one's heels, Stillman was quite unprepared for the sight of the tall, young woman who was now working as secretary-receptionist. What, he wondered, had become of Judith's Lillian? Surely Wickner, in his acting role, wouldn't have let her go?

More disturbing, he realized he knew this stony-faced woman from some other context. He just could not make the connection no matter how he tried.

"Doctor Stillman is here," she told her communications console, which apparently responded in some inaudible fashion. Then the woman looked up blankly at him.

"Doctor Wickner is expecting you," she said, unsmiling. "He'll be with you in another minute or two. You may have a seat."

Her voice suddenly made the connection in Stillman's memory.

"Ella!" he blurted with a flash of recognition.

He recalled with some pain their final conversation that frightful night when Schliesser and the young women had been led away. But a larger surprise was yet to come.

"I don't believe we've met," the woman said coolly. "You must have me confused with someone else."

It would be an understatement to say he found that assertion difficult to accept. Staggering would be more like it. He *knew* this woman. This was Ella, from Schliesser's place. It was a little surprising that he remembered her name, but he did. He came a step closer and studied her face more closely for reassurance.

Superficially, her appearance had been rendered more fashionable in a plum-colored dress with gold necklace, earrings, and bracelet. The cut of her light brown hair was shorter and more carefully layered, but these were definitely the same deep brown eyes and the same smooth complexion that made her appear even younger than she probably was. And yet, there was some subtle thing, an expressiveness, missing.

"Your name is Ella, isn't it?" he said, more for effect than for information.

"Yes," she said with a so-what tone.

"Did you know a Doctor Schliesser?" he ventured. "Armand Schliesser, physics chair?"

"Who?" she said convincingly. "Never heard of him. Sorry."

"No matter." He took a seat near her desk. "Just a friend of mine, a close friend—who was killed recently. Murdered, that is to say."

"Oh," Ella said, as if told it might rain that afternoon. Most peculiar. In the medical realm, they would call it a flat affect.

"Doctor Wickner knew Doctor Schliesser too," said Stillman calculatingly. "Though I wouldn't have called them exactly . . . friends."

"I'm sure I wouldn't know about that," she stated, turning her attention to some business on her desk.

"In fact," he continued anyway, "Doctor Wickner had been trying rather successfully to ruin Schliesser professionally before he turned up dead. I'd like to hear what Doctor Wickner knows about all of this."

None of his efforts had any apparent effect. The woman made no comment. He was forced to ruminate silently about Schliesser and his tragic demise. That train of thought threatened to turn ugly, as he found himself working up to some serious animosity toward Wickner.

Fortunately, some signal on the console apparently indicated that Wickner was ready for Stillman before he reached full burn. Ella escorted him around the corner to Wickner's door, gestured for him to enter, then abruptly vanished without another word.

The first thing Stillman noticed was that the furniture was not just rearranged—it was all new pieces. This was not something that squared with the idea of an interim directorship. The second thing he noticed was the nostalgic, tempting aroma of—what? Roasting chestnuts!

"Greetings, Rick!"

The high-backed swivel chair revolved 180 degrees behind the oversize desk, bringing a smirking Julian Wickner into view.

"Hello, Julian."

"It's so good of you to stop by."

"My pleasure," Stillman fibbed.

"Have a seat." Wickner indicated one of the sumptuous chairs in the same mold as those in the outer office. "What can I offer you to drink? The recreational beverage of your choice."

Stillman believed it. A set of glass cases behind Wickner's desk appeared to hold a variety of bottles and decanters. Wickner already had a cup of something at his elbow, probably Irish coffee.

"Nothing, thanks," Stillman said quietly.

"Have some chestnuts, my man," said Wickner, placing a copper bowl on the butler table beside Stillman. "They're microwaved, but you can pretend they're roasted."

"Thanks," he said, not liking the implication if it wasn't a coincidence. "Why did you want to see me?"

Wickner's smirk faded just a bit as Stillman ignored the offering. "Actually, I was wondering if there was anything you might want to talk to me about," he said mildly.

"I don't think so," Stillman replied firmly. "Such as?"

The last hint of a smile left Wickner's face as he lifted the cup to his lips and kept his eyes on Stillman while he sipped. "Oh," he said as if plucking at an idea at random, "any . . . conflict of interest you might have with your university responsibilities."

"No," Stillman asserted. "Have you heard anything to the contrary?"

"Just—rumors."

"What kind of rumors?"

"Oh, hardly worth repeating," Wickner said offhandedly with a dismissing wave.

"But you will, anyway," Stillman suggested.

"Are you sure you wouldn't like something to drink, Rick? There are children going to bed sober tonight in Bangladesh."

Stillman, shaking his head, sat silent and unmoving.

Wickner refilled his cup from a dispenser behind his desk. "Let's just say," he continued, without looking up, "that I'm confident that you wouldn't *intentionally* violate a directive that could jeopardize your position."

"Are you threatening me, Julian?"

"Of course not."

"What is this—directive—you're referring to?"

Wickner appraised him with half-lidded eyes while swirling the contents of his cup. Then he chuckled humorlessly, as one who was used to suffering fools.

"If you think back to when Judith went into the . . . institution," he began patiently, "you will recall that I sought your cooperation as I strove to assume the duties of interim division chair. You also will recall that you gave me your pledge that you would not be launching any new independent projects during this interim period. Certainly not without prior approval, at least."

Stillman nodded faintly while Wickner paused.

"Since then, I have received reports that Judith's condition is not improving. In fact, it's deteriorating. Rick, it's even more imperative now that I have your cooperation—and that you keep yourself free for other . . . eventualities."

"What kind of eventualities?"

Wickner laughed and drained some more of his beverage. "This interim chair business is looking more and more permanent. However, unless some kind of severance is worked out for Judith, I may have no authorization to hire an additional body for the teaching load."

Stillman was beginning to smell trouble.

"The implications, of course," Wickner said, "are that you could be in for a serious increase in your own teaching load next quarter."

As ominous as that sounded, Stillman realized that a more sinister issue loomed. "Of course, you have my cooperation, Julian."

"Do I?" Wickner said with that half-lidded look again. "Then how do you explain *this?*"

With that, he held up a computer printout that promptly unfolded itself down to the floor segmentally.

Stillman rose from his chair and bent over to inspect the document more closely. It was a list of files from Judith's research into linguistic monogenesis, clearly showing that they had come from university memory banks via ALEX. The printout itself contained no proof that the files had been accessed by his own system at the Temple, but he himself knew only too well that they had.

Wickner had fully anticipated such angles. "I suppose you could say that this printout could have come from anywhere."

Stillman shook his head.

Wickner continued as if oblivious.

"To which, I guess I could produce a witness, if necessary. And, I suppose you could claim that these exercises were conducted at home on your own time. You and Sturgis, after all, were the developers of the ALEX system, and you have all of those rights, of course. And you might even claim that you have enjoyed carte blanche in the past to do work at home, accessing university files. And that might wash—might, that is, were it not for the fact that you had been expressly directed not to engage in such independent projects, especially ones involving nonuniversity people who in this case are outright religious—"

Stillman interrupted while Wickner searched for the appropriate epithet. "Julian, if this is a disciplinary hearing—"

"—religious nuts! No, this is *not* a disciplinary hearing!"

Wickner stopped, appearing almost surprised by his own vehemence. He forced a smile, which to Stillman appeared more as a malignant leer. He drained the remainder of his drink in one chug and set the cup down on its saucer with a clank.

Wickner leaned back, stuck a small, black cigar between his teeth, and fished in his pockets for a light. His eyes remained fixed upon Stillman down the length of the stogie as he touched its tip with flame. A wreath of smoke enveloped his head.

"I have a question, Julian," said Stillman abruptly.

"Eh?"

"Just how are you planning to work out this 'severance' with Judith?"

"You mean as regards competency, power of attorney—that sort of thing?"

"Exactly."

"Well, I'm glad you asked that." He blew a long, lazy plume of smoke toward the ceiling. "That's something I had wanted to discuss. In fact, I had hoped that you might have some ideas on that matter."

Stillman's eyes narrowed, pondering where Wickner might be driving.

"I have to tell you that I don't want to see her severed from the university," Stillman said. "I would do everything in my power to see that that never happened."

Wickner chuckled, rose from his chair, and began pacing.

"Your loyalty is admirable, Rick, quite admirable. I could only hope that under . . . different circumstances . . . you might have even half that much loyalty for myself."

Stillman, feeling increasingly uncomfortable about the direction of the conversation, said nothing.

"Your problem, Rick, is that you're too virtuous for your own good. Where has all this virtue gotten you? If you would only see things my way, I could arrange for . . . professional opportunities that now you could only dream of."

"See things your way? Like forsake the translation project?"

Wickner laughed. "If you want to put it that way. Your negotiating position is rather weak."

"Then what about Judith?"

Wickner sobered. "Just support me."

"I don't believe in blank checks."

"Of course not," Wickner agreed. "I'm talking about a contract buyout proposal to the family—on generous terms, of course."

"They'll never agree to something like that, Julian."

"Oh, you think not?" Wickner chuckled under his breath. "This is a family with lots of legal and medical bills piling up. I'm sure they could be made to see it our way."

Stillman shuddered at the thought of "our" anything.

"Besides," Wickner said in a slightly conspiratorial tone, "we could use you on our team, Rick."

"*We?*"

"That's right. Kay and Quang and I. There are . . . developments . . . in the offing regarding OUIJA that will have major ramifications for the field of artificial intelligence—and beyond."

"Kay?" Stillman asked, trying not to sound too interested. "Jeremy Kay?"

Wickner said nothing but gave a dismissive wave with his cigar.

"Julian, have you discussed this with Quang? I think he'd have a different opinion on the matter."

"Leave that to me. Just knock off the translation project."

"That's a whole lot easier said than done," Stillman asserted, "since Judith executed an agreement with the Rhema Institute and the work is already commenced. In fact, it's well under way."

"Well, then," said Wickner with an air of finality, "you'll just have to decide whether you choose to follow Judith—or myself. I sincerely hope for your sake that you choose well."

* * *

Peter, unable to crank out one more erg, let his weight fall forward onto his forearms on the handlebars while his feet coasted to a stop on the stationary bike pedals. He was whipped. This physical rehabilitation was brutal. In his weakened condition, he tired quickly, but not as quickly as he had the day before.

"How does that feel?" asked Kelsey Kinsey, moving toward him.

"Nasty," he said, panting.

"Poor baby!" Kinsey said, extending her lower lip in a miniature pout.

Peter had the impression that she thought the expression was cute. He thought it was grotesque.

Kinsey pointed the fat end of Peter's crutch toward his face.

He grasped it with his left hand, stuck it under his left armpit, gripped the rear of the bike seat with his right, gave himself a little boost, and slid neatly off onto the floor. For a second, it felt as if his knees would buckle, but he simply clung more firmly to the crutch until his legs found the strength to hold him upright. At least it didn't hurt much anymore. He mopped his forehead with a towel.

"When can we get out of here?" Peter hobbled slowly to the examining table on the other side of the room.

"Shouldn't be much longer, "although your little friend is still mightily confused. She's going to force us to do a full-blown psych workup. You kids complain about restraints, and then we find her wandering around down the hall among all the breakables and the expensive stuff. You can't have it both ways."

"You people give us a lot to be confused about," he said, allowing Kinsey to take his crutch and help him onto the table. "I don't understand why we can't get a clear explanation about this place."

Kinsey commenced with his pulse and blood pressure.

"Not much to explain. Outpatient physical rehab under hospital contract—as you've been told repeatedly. Try not to give in to frustration. You may have some lingering effects of the concussion for a while yet—confusion and so forth."

Sure. Just as repeatedly, he'd been given no very good reason for Carlotta's presence here or why he couldn't make phone calls. It didn't add up. "Trauma," they'd called Carlotta's condition. What that had to do with physical rehab he couldn't guess. And "Rules" was the only thing they'd say about the phone. The concussion routine was wearing thin. There was nothing wrong with his thinking, so long as they kept the needle out of his arm and the dope out of his veins.

The woman bent down to appraise the pinkish, nicely healing wound on his left thigh. She had to push the leg of his athletic shorts up a bit to do so. Her fingers felt like indecent things upon his flesh. He shook them off impatiently after a moment.

Kinsey laughed. "What's the matter, hot stuff?"

Peter glared as she shone a penlight into his eyes and peered into his pupils. Then she tousled his hair and let the soft back of her hand slide across his cheek.

"Will you quit that?" Peter said irritably, jerking his head.

"You need a shave," she said casually. "Would you like me to do it for you?"

"Lady," he said with what he hoped was an insulting tone, "if you think I'd let you get anywhere near my throat with a razor, you're out of your mind."

Kinsey didn't laugh that time. "What's wrong with you this evening?" she said with apparent exasperation. "Maybe we need to keep you under closer observation."

"Why don't you explain to me one more time why I can't make phone calls?" Peter said sourly.

Now she was laughing again, a little tinkling laugh that sounded as if it was largely at his expense.

"Why make phone calls when you can have the real thing?" she teased.

Peter frowned. "What do you mean?"

"Do you feel up to having visitors?"

"Are you kidding me? Who?" He sat up quickly enough to feel a little dizzy again.

"Your sister," Kinsey said with a little smirk. "If, that is, you feel like making the trip upstairs according to the rule book. I know how you hate the wheelchair."

"I changed my mind," he said. "I *love* the wheelchair. It's the only way to fly."

"OK," said Kinsey. "Jeremy wants to talk to you too. Let's roll 'em, then."

★ ★ ★

The elevator ride was the first time Peter had been out of the basement. He noticed that the numbers inside the elevator went up to four. He and Kinsey stopped on three.

"Pretty freaky outpatient rehabilitation facility," he observed as Kinsey wheeled him out of the elevator. The corridor reminded him of Medieval Europe when gilded griffins rampaged on banners and escutcheons of red and green.

"Welcome to Chateau Fahlgren. There's more that goes on here than just medical science."

"Is this a . . . castle?" asked Peter incredulously as he began trundling away from the elevator.

"Your powers of observation are keen beyond the telling."

There must be some law against making fun of guys in wheelchairs, Peter thought as they proceeded down the eerie corridor. The gloom, the massive stonework, the flickering ersatz oil lamps, the high ceilings, and the ancient martial tapestries conspired to raise the hairs on his arms and the back of his neck. His stomach was taking to this ride about the same as it would take to an airliner's abrupt loss of altitude.

Behind him, this Kelsey Kinsey was growing horns in his mind's eye. He could just about picture his companion attired in a caped robe and peaked hat, consulting a leather-bound formulary and producing some hideous potion from an ancient amphora. Surely, at any moment there would be a raven flapping about.

Abruptly, she stopped, rapped twice on a nondescript, darkly varnished door, and barged through without further ado.

A large-shouldered, dark-haired man with craggy brow pulled wide the door to reveal a set out of Central Casting. Flaming logs in a stone fireplace. French Provincial furnishings. Period antiques. High, coved ceiling with a crystal chandelier. Parquet floor. Grand piano in one corner. Dumbwaiter in another. Rows of gilt-edged books on mahogany shelves. Bottles of fine wine on a credenza. Subdued, piped-in baroque harpsichord and flute.

On a gold-and-red brocade couch angled toward the shimmering shadows emanating from the fireplace were Jeremy Kay and Angie, his hand atop hers between them. They looked for all the world like a melancholy royal couple burdened down by the various petitions of their vassals and countrypersons, though without any doubting of their own ability to execute the requisite judgments and decrees.

"Angie!" cried Peter, his heart leaping.

Except for a tired little smile, it was almost as if she hadn't heard.

And then, as if on some cue, a white-haired man with a Greek sailor's cap and gold earring entered through a different door and joined the gathering by the fireplace. Peter recognized him as a man named Wickner who had worked with Peter's mother. He appeared to have important papers in his hand.

Peter didn't know what to say, so he said nothing and watched as the door swung open again, this time for a second wheelchair, pushed by Elizabeth Morningstar. And again Peter's heart leaped.

"Carlotta!"

Just as quickly, his joy turned to concern as he observed her vacant stare and near-catatonic expression. Some kind of small cable ran from a device on her chair to another attachment at the back of her neck.

Then the door opened one last time, and in came the man they called Quang. He seemed to have some concern about Carlotta's paraphernalia.

"What's wrong with her?" Peter cried. "What *is* this?"

It looked like Quang was about to answer, when Wickner interrupted.

"Routine monitoring," he said unconvincingly, moving to Peter's side.

"Of what?"

"It's a type of biofeedback, to restore a little hypothalamic equilibrium," Wickner asserted. "Another innovation of our good friend Doctor Quang."

Peter shivered, from the implication of the words as well as from the older man's piercing gaze. The eyes inexplicably repulsed him, and Wickner's breath hung in the air like stale cigars and alcohol.

He looked at Angie. He wanted to talk to her, but she seemed disengaged, as if this whole scene were an unwelcome distraction. What was with these people?

Then Angie spoke up. "There's something you need to read, Peter."

Wickner extended the papers slowly.

Peter accepted them cautiously. He unfolded the pages and began scanning them for a central theme. After a minute, he believed he had found it—in the person of Judith Hurley-McBride. The document seemed to involve some kind of financial terms for a settlement with the university in return for his mother's agreement to take retirement at an age that otherwise would involve little or no financial remuneration.

He scowled. "Has anybody asked Mother how she feels about this?"

"No, of course not," said Angie as if it were of little or no consequence.

Wickner interjected, "In her unfortunate state, your mother needs us, those closest to her, to look out for her interests."

Peter smelled a Wickner-sized rodent. "And I suppose you know *just* the right person to take her place."

"I have been in regular contact with the mental health professionals, Peter," Wickner said patiently but reddening slightly. "They can do a lot of things today with modern techniques, but they all assure me that there is no chance your mother will ever work again."

Peter swallowed hard. Was it just his natural unwillingness to accept a harsh reality—or was there something more here, something really not credible? But then he thought of something, a very obvious thing. "What's this got to do with me? Why don't you take this up with my dad—my stepfather?"

This time Jeremy Kay spoke up. "Neal McBride—ex-Judge McBride—seems to have become a . . . missing person. If you think you can find him, that would be fine too. We would be very much in your debt."

Peter stared speechlessly. This was going all wrong. Ex-judge? Missing person?

"What do we want from you?" asked Wickner rhetorically. "Very simple. We want you to sign this instrument and present it to your mother for her signature."

"What? If she's so incompetent as you say, what's the value of her signature?"

Actually, a darker question arose about the value of his own signature so long as Neal McBride was alive and well. But he wasn't about to voice it.

"Good question, my boy," said Wickner. "It may yet prove unnecessary to have it, but let's just say it would be . . . nicer that way. Isn't that right, Angie?"

Angie merely nodded and exchanged glances with Jeremy.

Then Peter was startled to hear Carlotta's voice for the first time.

"Please don't be difficult, Peter," she said, with a peculiar absence of the proper inflections.

"Why don't you tell her to bark like a dog?" Peter snapped angrily. "Or cluck like a chicken? And why not ask Angie to take on this little mission of yours, if it's such a wonderful thing?"

"Peter, through a combination of circumstances that your sister can explain to you," Wickner said evenly, "she has technically become a fugitive from justice."

"That's right, Peter," she said with an edge. "I can't leave this place."

"Otherwise, you would do it?" he said incredulously.

"Yes," she declared.

Peter, ignoring the twinge in his left leg, rose unsteadily to his feet. "What's the matter with you? Sell out your own mother? I don't understand anything that goes on here—or any of you people."

With that, he pursed his lips and tore the document from top to bottom, then side to side and over again. Using surprise to his advantage, he limped over to the fireplace and hurled the pieces into the flames, where they began to dance and curl.

"You shouldn't have done that, Peter," Angie said to his back.

"No, you shouldn't," said a nearby voice, apparently that of Jeremy Kay. "Brandon, secure the prisoner."

Turning, Peter was confronted by the hulking figure of the bruiser who had originally opened the door on this nasty fireside scene. This time, he looked intent on doing bodily harm. Peter raised an arm in self-defense and took a step back. The actual blow came in the stomach. Peter crumpled to his hands and knees, smelling wood smoke and trying to breathe despite a caved-in feeling.

The bruiser named Brandon picked him up under the armpits like so much cordwood and tossed him back into the wheelchair, which skidded backward a good meter on its locked wheels. While Peter's head spun, two pairs of hands secured his arms and legs with tight restraining bands.

"Prepare subject for integration," said Kay with a wave of his hand.

Beside him on the couch, Angie was smiling knowingly.

23

When this is all over, McBride thought, *I'll have to consider buying some stock in the Imperial Crown company.*

This time, his Jimmy Shapiro special was a west side Imperial Crown off the outerbelt at New Rome. He hadn't exactly planned it that way, but it was near the exit, and when he saw the sign, it was irresistible. He guessed he was just a sentimental sucker.

The proprietor, a heavy-set, middle-aged woman with thick glasses and dark, dyed hair, was not so amused by his request for the honeymoon suite as the old gentleman across town in Reynoldsburg had been. In fact, her expression told him she didn't much care for his general demeanor or perhaps even his haircut. Actually, the feeling was becoming mutual. It was something about her carnivorous fish eyes and the way she slapped the key down on the counter.

Whatever, it was still Room 201 with the same horse-blanket decor and a similar artistic travesty on the wall, an orgy of cuteness involving a young lad, one puppy, and a squirrel. Otherwise, it had all the same amenities—in all the same places even.

McBride found the total effect oddly comforting in its own predictable way. The first thing he took out of his bag was a plug-in screen for the communications console, knowing the standard equipment would be null-video here. Besides, even more than that, he needed the scrambler for security.

The next thing was to fetch ice from the machine down the hall and a couple of cans of pop across the way. Back in the room, he poured himself an icy cream soda and called up the Temple. Within moments, he and Stillman were blinking back at each other.

"Can you try Salerno and make it a three-way?" asked McBride.

Stillman shrugged. "If he's available. I can certainly try."

"He's expecting our call."

Sure enough, in another minute McBride was able to eyeball both Stillman and Salerno on split-screen.

"We need to hear about Moira," McBride prompted. "How did it go?"

Stillman grimaced. "Passably." He sounded as if that might be stretching a point. "But before I forget, I have some other updates both of you need to hear."

"Shoot," said McBride.

"The translation project has succeeded in attracting attention." Stillman watched as two pairs of eyebrows went up. "Julian Wickner called me into his office and insisted that I stop the project immediately."

"Are you going to?" asked Salerno.

"I don't know. It's so near success, I don't know what difference it could make."

Salerno looked concerned. "How did he know about the project?"

"From little things Julian said, it sounds as if Moira was the source of his information. Nothing I could prove, of course." Stillman put on his concerned look. "The more disturbing thing was an ultimatum he gave regarding Judith."

"Regarding Judith?" McBride echoed. "What kind of ultimatum?"

"A kind of loyalty test requiring me to choose between Judith and Julian. It started out in regard to her authorizing the translation project, but it quickly turned to the fact that Julian is angling to have her severed through a contract buyout or whatever. I get the feeling that others might be involved in this somehow and there might not be a lot they would stop at. Again, nothing I can prove."

McBride felt the color drain from his face and something sick crawl into his belly.

"'Others'?" said Salerno. "Like who?"

"That's another point. There were echoes of Angie's words about a big breakthrough—although Julian called it 'artificial' intelligence rather than 'human' intelligence. And he specifically named Jeremy Kay and Jared Quang as partners in this affair. So we were on the right track there. Julian spoke as though he was inviting me to join their cause, but it felt more like trying to co-opt or neutralize me."

"Gentlemen," said McBride, "we've been pretty slow on the uptake on some previous threats. What are our chances of not making the same mistake again? I have a real vested interest in this one."

"Are you suggesting," asked Salerno, "that Judith could be in some physical danger?"

"You heard what Rick said. The kind of people who might stop at nothing. Can we put a watch on the Riverside Mental Health Unit?"

"I don't know." Salerno frowned. "Let me work on that."

"What's the problem?" asked McBride apprehensively.

"Overholtzer tells me he's still taking heat over that little caper with Becky Leadingham at University Hospital."

"What kind of heat?"

Salerno shrugged. "Static. Questions. Minor harassment. He wasn't so much complaining as letting me know that some of the toes we're stepping on have departmental connections."

"I was afraid of that," said McBride.

"Goes with the turf." Salerno shrugged again.

"It's about time for me to check in with Judith over there again," McBride commented. "It's been a few days."

"I'm not sure I'd do that just yet," Salerno said. "Until I've worked something out security-wise. Rick may be right about these characters we're up against."

"OK. Anything else?"

"Yeah. Fahlgren," said Stillman. "I've got a reasonable start on that one, but just a start."

"Good," said McBride. "Let's hear it."

"Turns out there was a Claude Fahlgren at the turn of the century, a computer software magnate in the area of telecommunication databases, some of which are still in use. He was a Columbus boy who became fabulously wealthy for a season before falling prey to a familiar occupational hazard. It seems he started his own company at the height of his technological success, but he proved to lack the same acumen as a businessman. Eventually the financial landscape became littered with the carcasses of his corporate creatures.

"He was found penniless and dead one day in a corner of the basement of his palatial chateau, a needle in his arm and liquid death in his veins. Supposedly the mansion stood vacant for many years after a succession of tenants moved out, claiming it was haunted."

"That's an interesting story," said McBride. "I think I even heard some of it myself years ago. But what's the connection for us?"

Stillman looked a bit sheepish. "I was hoping you'd tell *me*."

McBride sucked his lip. "It has to fit somewhere. Maybe there's a connection with Donleavy's ilk—the fetal farmers and the rest of that crowd. Remember those organized crime public record checkpoints? Civil litigation filings, US Tax Court records, Board of Zoning, Secretary of State Corporate Division—all of that. Run the checks for any correspondences between the Donleavy types, particularly the Institute for Pre-Life Science and Claude Fahlgren—or any of his 'corporate creatures'—and see what you get."

"All right," Stillman agreed. "Maybe we'll put the translation project on hold for a few days, anyway, and buy ourselves some time."

"I'll do some checking too," said Salerno. "That story kind of rings a bell. It might be worth a routine check on the current status of the old Fahlgren estate. Do you have a location?"

"Not yet," said Stillman. "Several candidates come to mind, under different names. But names change. I'll pursue it."

"Great." Then McBride changed the subject. "Are you going to tell us about Moira?"

"Sure. What there is to tell. We were half right about her."

"How's that?" asked McBride.

"Well, she apparently was the source of Leadingham's information, but she didn't talk to Leadingham himself."

"No?" McBride was quite surprised.

"Moira emphatically would not tell me what she knew, but she did téll me how the information got to Leadingham. Does the name 'Gretchen LeMieux' mean anything to you?"

"Sure," agreed McBride. "Steve's domestic partner for quite a while, off and on. More off than on toward the end, I think. Is that who Moira was talking to?"

"That's right. For what that's worth. She wouldn't say beans about the nature of the information."

"That's OK. It's a lead. Did Moira say where to find Gretchen?"

"No. That was the extent of it."

Salerno jumped in. "You're lucky she told you that much. Why do you think she did?"

"It was like . . . swapping information. She seemed to be a lot more interested in Cybersynchronics than she ever had been when we were married."

"Which fits with the idea that she's conduiting information on the translation project to somewhere," said Salerno.

"Right," said McBride.

"But I also had the feeling," Stillman said, "that she had some ambivalence about what she was doing, as if she was having some kind of conscience struggle—which for her would be a novel idea."

"What you have to do is develop this relationship and try to keep the exchange going," Salerno added.

"I don't know what else to tell her that we can afford to let get out."

"We'll think of something," said McBride.

Salerno thought of something. "I wouldn't be surprised if her friends would be interested in the whereabouts of Neal McBride."

Stillman was incredulous. "I wouldn't actually tell her, would I?"

"If you did," Salerno said, "we could just change his location, but leave a confirming trail."

"The important thing," said McBride, "would be establishing whether there is such an interest. If so, maybe you could convey a similar strong interest in the whereabouts of Peter and Carlotta."

"Yeah." Stillman agreed, but sounded a bit reluctant.

"Is there a problem?" asked McBride.

"Just a . . . little personal thing. Developing this 'relationship' with Moira is not going to be a lot of fun. I think I'd rather go back and repeat junior high school."

McBride shuddered. "Hate her guts?"

"Not at all." Stillman shook his head. "And therein lies the problem. It would be a lot easier if I did."

"Good luck," said McBride, then changed the subject. "Vince, how soon can you get me a current address for Gretchen LeMieux?"

"Twenty minutes, if you have the previous address or her Social Security number. Twenty hours to twenty days if you don't."

"No problem. We can probably do both. She moved out a few weeks ago from Steve Leadingham's address in German Village. Nineteen-oh-something on Sumner Street. Rick may be able to get you her Social Security."

"I can?"

"Maybe," McBride said. "Stands to reason Moira knew Gretchen through the university. I think Steve even said she worked in some business office there, in which case you can probably pull some strings, electronically speaking."

"Sure thing."

"Gotcha," said Salerno. "Call you back in twenty."

"Minutes, I hope," said McBride before hanging up.

★ ★ ★

McBride pulled into the front parking lot of the Ambassador Arms, found a spot with a good view, and cut the engine. His eyes became radar sweeps for Gretchen LeMieux. He turned on the classical music station and killed time listening to a Vivaldi oboe concerto and worrying about her using a different entrance.

As he suspected, Gretchen LeMieux hadn't moved far—just a few blocks over in the Village. Jimmy Shapiro had taught him that alienated lovers tended to go either very far away or stay pretty close by, with very little in between. If there's ambiguity in the split, the one moving out tends to hedge the bet by making potential reconciliation as painless as possible—no furnishings and baggage having to be carted back and forth clear across town and so forth.

McBride was also correct about the university job. Gretchen LeMieux was a graphics designer in the OSU Office Services Department, which produced the majority of university internal publications. Ascertaining that her quitting time was 4:30 P.M., he had gathered up some reading material, jumped into the green Jupiter, and headed for the high-rise apartment building on Emory Road, a major thoroughfare a half dozen blocks east of Leadingham's place on Sumner.

When it got closer to 5:00, McBride grabbed a book, got out of the van, and walked into the lobby. Its only occupants were a young girl with pigtails being taught *"Sur le Pont d'Avignon"* by a grandmother on an old piano that could use a bit of tuning.

He felt reasonably inconspicuous as he settled into an overstuffed chair with a good view of the front and rear entrances. The only disappointment was in discovering that he had not picked up the Griffith novel about nineteenth-century Wyoming, but a commentary on the book of Habakkuk that belonged to Aaron Fitzgerald.

The name sounded like a foot disease, but he figured Habakkuk must be one of the Minor Prophets. What he didn't know about the Bible would fill volumes. And, he figured, this must be one of those. On impulse, he looked in the index under "justice," a subject close to his heart, and found an intriguing reference in the first chapter.

"Therefore, the law is ignored and justice is never upheld. For the wicked surround the righteous; therefore, justice comes out perverted."

"Justice." There was a word laden with meaning for a judge. Wasn't there supposed to be a Day of Judgment? For the first time, he found that thought oddly reassuring. Considering the vast injustices and massive miscarriages of justice in the world, that would be a very busy day, he thought. Yet, he wasn't so sure how he himself would come out in that kind of reckoning. When this was all over, maybe he would sit down and have a nice, long talk with Messrs. Jones and Fitzgerald.

Just then a blonde woman wearing a smart, teal blue trench coat and gathering no moss rolled across his field of view on a beeline to the elevators. Bingo.

McBride kept his eyes perfunctorily on the words of the Habakkuk commentary until he heard the elevator doors open and close, swallowing its passenger. After a moment he strolled over to the water fountain and took a token sip, letting his eyes roam across the elevator numbers to note that it was stopping on the seventh floor to unburden itself.

He sat back down with Mr. Habakkuk and moved his eyes around on the page for another minute or two to give the woman time to get settled. Then he casually went looking for the Up button.

At Apartment 716 he had only to ring once before there was a familiar, dubious voice over the door speaker.

"Who is it?"

"Crimefighter," he confided quietly to the door mike, not wanting to broadcast anything in the hallway, least of all his name.

The door was unlocked in two stages by the same blonde who had worn the teal blue coat. Her hair was now hanging down to her shoulders, and she was wearing a simple blouse, denim skirt, and no shoes.

"Come in," Gretchen LeMieux said. "I almost didn't recognize you with that beard."

They passed silently through a small, darkened living room into a spacious, cheery kitchen.

Gretchen was a little older than Leadingham and McBride, probably in her early forties, as was Judith. She had always impressed him as the cheerleader type—freckles, dancing blue eyes, small turned-up nose, and a healthy ego.

"Can I buy you a drink?" she said as he took a seat at the breakfast bar.

"I don't think so."

"I'm having one," Gretchen said, opening the refrigerator. "Are you going to be unsociable?"

"Oh, all right," he said, capitulating. "Got any cream soda?"

"Yeah," she said disgustedly. "You always were such a Boy Scout."

266

Almost before he could say "carbonated red pop," Gretchen poured him a cream soda on the rocks and herself a white wine in a tall pilsner glass. She took a healthy swallow and then spoke first.

"So, who shot Steve?" she asked quietly.

"As far as the police are concerned, nobody. Probable random gang violence. Or maybe a couple of lead meteorite fragments."

"My, aren't we cynical today," Gretchen observed.

"Have you talked to him?"

She gave him a funny look. "Nobody talks to him."

"What do you mean? I thought he was improving since he got out of University."

"Physically, yes." She tapped the side of her head with a finger.

"Amnesia still?"

She nodded. "The doctor says it's the responsive kind, but it may involve long-term therapy."

"Gretchen, I need to ask a personal question," he said, steeling himself with a slug of cream soda.

"Permission granted, I think," she said, taking another drink.

"Were you on speaking terms with Steve after your—split?"

Her eyes narrowed, and she did look somewhat put off by the question.

"Yes—and I didn't shoot him, Neal."

McBride held up a cautionary hand. "I wasn't suggesting for a moment that you had. I think he was shot by someone who was trying to prevent some information from coming my way. It's that information that I'm trying to get at."

Her eyebrows went up.

He continued. "And Steve himself seemed to indicate Moira Stone was the source of the information—except that he never spoke to Moira, according to her."

"I see," she said carefully. "I'll tell you what I can, if it won't get me shot. But you have to give me a clue."

"I'll give you three," said McBride. "Conceptus, Fahlgren, and Chi Xi Vau. And they all tie in somehow with Roger Larrabee. Did you follow the trial?"

Gretchen nodded, took a healthy swallow, and closed her eyes while it went down. "Why don't you ask Moira?"

"We did."

" 'We'?"

"My friends tell me she doesn't want to talk. Do you have any idea why that might be?"

"Not at all. But I think I can help you a little with your clues."

"Anything you can tell me."

She poured herself some more white wine and offered McBride a refill on the cream soda, which he declined.

"I have to drive," he said.

"You ever do any meditation, centering, reaching the higher self—anything like that?"

McBride shook his head.

"Ever read anything about it?"

He continued shaking his head.

"OK," she said with the sigh of one forced to build the clock before she can tell you the time. "There's this guy named Jeremy Kay, a major figure in the Metapersonal Psychology movement, who's written this great book *Hologram: Appropriating Divinity.* I've read it twice. Moira and I attended his lecture recently at Gunnison Auditorium, and he was *great.* She got into an argument with somebody who claimed that Jeremy Kay was connected somehow to the Devil's Night case. At the heart of the dispute was that organization you named."

"Chi Xi Vau?"

"Yeah."

"Do you know the other party in this discussion?"

"No, never laid eyes on her before or since. Anyway, Moira got sort of indignant, insisting that this Chi Xi Vau outfit was more —you know, white magic. They apparently support a 'conceptus' research thing—a biota recycling facility where serious science goes on. This other woman was arguing that these people were really occultists and involved in the dark side of artificial intelligence, as she put it."

"The 'dark side of artificial intelligence'? What does that mean?"

Gretchen shrugged. "No idea. The only other thing I can tell you is that Jeremy Kay and his friends operate out of a place called Chateau Fahlgren. I still don't know of any connection with Roger Larrabee. But it would break my heart to think ill of Jeremy Kay. He's such a babe."

"Where's this Chateau Fahlgren?"

"I got the idea it might be out in the Millersfield/Jefferson Woods area, maybe. Sorry I can't be more helpful."

"No," said McBride. "That's a lot of help."

"Don't count on it."

McBride gave her a curious look. "Eh?"

"I don't even think 'Fahlgren' is this place's proper name. And you know how many old mansions are out there?"

"Oh, well. That might not be too hard to run down. Who are these other 'friends' of Jeremy Kay?"

Now he was getting all shrugs.

"Do you recall anything else from this—argument—that might be helpful?"

"Not a thing," she said without hesitation. "More cream soda?"

"No, I must be going," he said, rising. "Any idea how we could get Moira to open up about all of this?"

"Get her mad," Gretchen said, smiling mischievously. "Other than that, she's kind of defensive, like she's maybe a little involved with these people somehow."

"Thanks a lot, Gretchen." He moved toward the door. "I can't tell you how much I appreciate your help."

"I know it wasn't much." She escorted him through the living room again. "Just—watch your step. OK?" She gave him a worried look out the door.

He said he'd watch it.

* * *

Somebody else was watching it too.

McBride was aware almost instantly that he was being followed as he rolled out of the parking lot and approached the first light on Emory Road. It was that feeling of knowing that another vehicle was precisely mirroring his moves. By the second light he went into evasive mode, darting in and out of lanes and irritating every other driver on the road. The tail car did the same. He figured, being that obvious, that they couldn't be too swift. At the third light, he floored it and sailed through amber turning red. The tail car crashed through anyhow.

McBride kept it floored, but the Jupiter van was not exactly a high-performance machine, and soon his friends were closing the gap on an open stretch. At the last reckless second, he hit the brakes, swerved right, fishtailed onto a narrow industrial parkway road, and floored it again. So did the tail car.

It was at this point that McBride began to suspect that this guy was an undercover cop. Most drivers would have missed the last turn or wiped out trying. His suspicion was confirmed in another moment as the van's emergency radio channel crackled to life.

"Pull it over, Mac," said a tough-guy voice. "County sheriff."

He pulled it over and got out. Rarely had he had such bad vibes even from a criminal defendant standing before his bench as he got from these two bruisers piling out of the unmarked car and lumbering his way. Even their gait was the same, with the wide, rangy way weightlifters—or guys with big illusions—carry their arms out from the body.

McBride smelled big trouble as he surveyed the terrain and concluded that he was too far from Emory Road and not close enough to any parkway establishments for the restraining influence of any witnesses.

"Afternoon, officers," he said as the plainclothes pair intercepted him.

"Let's see some ID," said the older of the two, an ugly cuss with a toothpick.

McBride handed over his driver's license, which was snatched from his fingers as if it weren't rightfully his.

The younger officer, a gap-toothed kid with what appeared to be a permanent sneer, handed his cohort another paper for comparison.

"Well, Judge," said the cop after a moment, "or maybe I ought to say Mr. McBride—does the owner of this vehicle know you're out joyridin' in it, runnin' red lights, and speedin'?"

"It's a rental, from Latchman Motors."

"Well, let me rephrase that," said the cop with exaggerated politeness. "Does the rentee, Mr. Stillman, know what you're doin' with this vehicle?"

It was one of those questions that has no right answer, like not beating your wife anymore. The only defense in such a case is another question.

"You know about entrapment, officer?" McBride said with his best balance of respectful firmness.

"I'll ask the questions, pal." Toothpick's glare was deadly.

"Without a light or siren or even markings, I could hardly be expected to know you were police, could I?"

"That might help you out of a fleeing rap if you were in lawful possession of the roadway otherwise," said Toothpick with an evil grin.

McBride could only shut up or argue. He shut up. This was not going well. Cops in the normal performance of their duty do not grin.

This time Sneer spoke. "And just what were you up to, casing the Ambassador Arms?"

"Do I have the right to remain silent?"

"You ain't under arrest—yet," said Toothpick.

"For that matter, I haven't seen any police ID on your part."

Sneer came a step closer. "This is my ID, pal."

Suddenly McBride's left ear was ringing, and he was seeing spots. He was sure there had to be a red handprint on the side of his face and head. Sneer had closed the same hand into a fist, in case McBride was thinking of responding. He only hoped somebody somewhere was praying for him.

Sneer picked up his license from the top of Toothpick's clipboard and deliberately released it, letting it flutter to the ground.

"Oh my," said Sneer. "Look what I did, silly me. Would you mind picking it up, Your Honor?"

McBride stood still, wondering if he ought to start praying himself.

"A wise guy, huh?" Sneer said. "I said pick it up."

When McBride still failed to move, Sneer hammered a fist deep into his gut, doubling him halfway over. A vicious chop to the neck put him on all fours. Bells were ringing, and the crowd was cheering for him to get off the canvas.

"Pick it up!" Sneer commanded. "With your teeth!"

When McBride could breathe again, it hurt fiercely. He envisioned himself rising to his feet and taking this young punk apart piece by piece with his bare hands. Except that if he did lose control and laid a hand on either of these gentlemen, he knew they'd have him locked up on a felony charge within the hour. And that would be the end of everything else he was trying to accomplish. His only hope was to ride this out and take whatever they chose to mete out. But the galling frustration was almost worse than the physical pain.

The next thing McBride knew, he was tasting shoe leather. He hoped this wasn't going to send him to the dentist. And then came a wracking pain in his side, as several ribs absorbed a punishing blow. They were kicking him like a dog now. A swift one in the seat of the pants sent him sprawling forward on his face, eating dirt.

He was losing track of the blows. One of the men rolled him over to work on the other side. There was no further question of his retaliating now, even if he wanted to. He was finished.

And then, oddly, it stopped.

McBride, on the threshold of unconsciousness, thought he heard another vehicle in the distance and imagined he saw some flickering lights.

"Uh-oh!" said a voice like Toothpick's.

"Let's beat it," said a voice like Sneer's.

McBride may have fainted. When his eyes next opened, he thought for a second he was with Jimmy Shapiro, flying down the highway. And then he thought it was Vince Salerno in the driver's seat. A siren was sounding and lights were flashing.

And then he was out again.

24

Moira pushed back her plate with its remnants of quail and decided to invoke her rights as a guest.

"Can we talk about something other than Tanit and Kali and all these . . . Jezebel goddesses?"

"Of course, my dear," said Julian Wickner, wiping his lips with a large linen napkin. "What would you like to discuss?"

"How about 'integrating'?"

Jeremy Kay answered, smiling graciously. "By all means."

It had been a sumptuous lunch in this stately, sunlit dining hall overlooking the wooded hills of Fahlgren. But her two hosts seemed to harbor a rather morbid and ulterior curiosity about these ancient goddesses of human sacrifice. They only laughed when she asked if they intended to revive the ancient pagan practices. She could only interpret their failure to deny it as some kind of posturing. Surely, they jested.

She hoped that they would be a bit more forthcoming about this integrating business. So far, she had gathered only that it involved some kind of consciousness-expanding computer/human interface.

"The best explanations are often illustrations," said Kay as the young woman named Ella began pouring the espresso. "Observe.

"Ella," Kay said with authority.

The pallid young woman stopped what she was doing and turned toward him.

"Yes?" she said softly.

"Moira would like to ask you a question." Turning to Moira, he directed, "Ask her to comment on some subject in the field of fine art or aesthetics or cultural anthropology."

"Anything?"

"Anything."

"All right," she said without hesitation. "Tell me about Botticelli's Venus."

A distant look in her eyes, Ella began reciting precisely after a moment: "'Of the Greeks as they really were, of their difference from ourselves, of the aspects of their outward life, we know far more than Botticelli, or his most learned contemporaries; but for us, long familiarity has taken off the edge of the lesson, and we are hardly conscious of what we owe to the Hellenic spirit. But in pictures like this of Botticelli's you have a record of the first impression made by it on minds turned back toward it, in almost painful aspiration, from a world in which it had been ignored so long; and in the passion, the energy, the industry of realization, with which Botticelli carries out his intention, is the exact measure of the legitimate influence over the human mind of the imaginative system of which this is the central myth.'"

Moira hung on every word as Ella proceeded to catalog the artist's cold light, the blowing wind, the foaming sea, the falling roses, the goddess's "dainty-lipped" shell, concluding, "'And what is unmistakable is the sadness with which he has conceived the goddess of pleasure, as the depository of a great power over the lives of men.'"

Moira was impressed. "Bravo! What—whose words were those?"

"Walter Pater. 'The Renaissance.'"

"Pater," Moira said reminiscently. "I seem to recall that he had a rather sublime statement on the appreciation of beauty."

Ella nodded. "'What is important, then, is not that the critic should possess a correct abstract definition of beauty for the intellect, but a certain kind of temperament, the power of being deeply moved by the presence of beautiful objects.'"

Turning to Kay, Moira asked, "Is she doing graduate work in art criticism?"

He shook his head.

"Don't tell me that you have the entire book committed to memory?" she asked Ella. Moira, who had been mostly jesting, was flabbergasted when Ella nodded, again matter-of-factly.

"Is this one of those cases of eidetic memory that you read about?" Moira asked Wickner and Kay.

Wickner only smiled. Kay shook his head.

She turned back to Ella. "Just how many books do you have committed to memory, in their entirety?"

Ella shrugged as if the question were inconsequential. "Lots."

Something did not add up here. Anyone with this kind of cerebral capacity certainly should be able to count that high.

"Thank you, Ella," Kay said with a certain finality. "I should point out that there is really nothing exceptional about this young woman's faculties—she is of quite ordinary intelligence. IQ of one fifteen, I believe. Now, Moira, if we could adjourn to the basement research wing, our good friend Quang would be more than happy to show you how this is done."

"Just a minute," said Moira. "You mean this young woman's brain has become essentially one big—computer download?"

Wickner grinned again.

"More or less," Kay conceded.

"How do you feel about this, Ella?" Moira interjected, not ready to end this colloquy quite yet.

"Feel?" the woman repeated blankly.

"For the sake of science," said Moira, playing a hunch, "let me ask you another memory question. What presents did you receive on your sixth birthday?"

Ella blinked and furrowed her brow, but said nothing.

"Can't you recall?" Moira pressed. She noticed that Wickner and Kay were fidgeting a bit in their seats.

Ella shook her head, looking straight ahead.

"Well, then, what presents did you receive on your *last* birthday?"

Again, the blank stare.

"How *old* were you on your last birthday?"

Nothing.

"What was your mother's name?"

Instantly, Ella burst into tears. The goblet that she had been holding shattered on the floor. In another moment she had fled halfway to the door, sobbing.

"Such questions are irrelevant," Kay pronounced with a hint of pique. "Ella has a whole new life now with a brilliant future ahead of her."

"Is this just an updated version of what they used to call 'brainwashing'?" Moira challenged.

"Moira," said Wickner with a warning edge to his voice. "You must learn to withhold judgment until you have all of the facts. The fact is that this young woman was one of the unfortunate captives of that deviate Schliesser and his forced pregnancy center. It's only natural that she would have some emotional scars from that trauma."

Moira was certain that Wickner was lying through his teeth.

"Quang awaits," Kay urged.

★ ★ ★

As Quang looked on beatifically, Kelsey Kinsey and Elizabeth Morningstar were attempting an odd dialogue with a young man in a patient bed. Moira edged closer to hear what Morningstar was saying.

"Phenomena manifest themselves by degrees," she seemed to be saying. Morningstar would then pause expectantly as if awaiting a response, which never came.

The young man actually looked quite unconscious. There was something familiar about his features. Moira noticed that a wire proceeded from the back of his neck as though a part of it.

Quang, with a bit of a flourish, drew back the track curtain to an adjoining area to reveal a young woman seated in lotus-position on a workout mat. An identical cable was attached to her occipital region. Moira recognized after a moment that the woman was Angela Hurley, staring through half-lidded eyes as if in some kind of trance state.

"Phenomena manifest themselves by degrees," Angie was intoning softly in apparent response to the words spoken to the young man.

Moving down one more space, Quang drew another curtain to reveal a third person, a sad-faced brunette seated in a high-backed chair with the same cable connection, uttering the same formula in time with Angie.

"Phenomena manifest themselves by degrees."

And then Moira thought she recognized this person too—the mother of the victim in the Devil's Night trial—without recalling her name. But how was it that these two individuals were responding to words spoken not to them, but to a third, mute person? It did not appear that they were audibly receiving Morningstar's spoken words.

And though the young man remained silent, the chain reaction continued with a new message.

"Dualities are the phenomena of illusion," said Morningstar.

"'Dualities are the phenomena of illusion,'" said Angie.

"'Dualities are the phenomena of illusion,'" said the other woman.

"So," Moira directed to Quang, "are these three wired in series or in parallel?"

"Quite humorous," Quang asserted, unsmiling. "Disregard the cables; they're transitional. As we move from working model to final implementation, it will, of course, become a wireless system."

"Do you have a model that's downloaded the Yellow Pages? I need a good carpet cleaner."

Quang ignored the remark.

Now, Kelsey Kinsey was plying the young man with yet more words to live by. "Ontogeny recapitulates philogeny." While the statement was echoed down the line, Moira searched her own memory for a meaning she once knew, but it was in vain.

"What you observe is a step beyond artificial intelligence," Quang continued. "Why just create computers that merely think like humans? That's stuff for dilettantes like Richard Stillman and that Cybersynchronic claptrap. What we're developing here is something incomparably superior—humans with the intellectual capabilities of modern mainframes! Imagine that, if you can."

"To what end?" asked Moira impulsively.

Quang, far from put off, appeared to embrace the question. "Evolution, for one thing. Omniscience, for another. With these new capabilities, we will be able to accomplish anything. Virtually nothing will be impossible for us. Godhood, at last."

"Hail, the new master race!" Moira knew she was pushing the limits even for her own well-known impertinence. "If that poor zombie Ella was any indication, it would appear that these new capabilities come at great personal expense. What did your computer do to her? Did you fill her up with *War and Peace* and Plutarch's *Lives* and who knows what until her personal, read-only memories were obliterated?"

"Moira—" Kay took a step toward her.

Quang waved him off. "That's all right. That's why you're here—to see what humans and computer can do together. Ella was simply an experiment—to test the capacity of the human brain in isolation. But in practice there will be no need to use adult humans routinely for data storage."

Now Moira was beginning to steam. "So. Ella is no more significant to you than a . . . silicon chip?"

Quang gestured across the room and out toward the Pre-Life lab complex across the hall. "Those minor memory artifacts no doubt exist somewhere within the system. They perhaps could be reprogrammed."

"And what do you mean by 'adult humans'? Do you mean children are fair game?"

"Not precisely," said Quang, his eyes narrowing. "Tell me. Prior to this demonstration, I believe Elizabeth and Kelsey gave you the tour over there in Biota Recycling. How did you find it?"

"Crowded." Moira maintained her bravado. "Dozens and dozens of—pre-lives. A veritable multitude of junior organ benefactories."

Quang's face creased into a facsimile of a smile. "Organs and tissue, yes. But much more. Think of them as dozens and dozens of Ellas—on a smaller and simpler scale, of course. Each one linked cerebrally and functioning almost as a single neuron in a developing meta-consciousness."

Moira was momentarily speechless, until she remembered something else that had bothered her in Pre-Life. "Some of those —biota—looked pretty mature to me. How long can you keep them in the tank before they start demanding solid food and the keys to the car?"

"That's one of those things that remains to be seen," said Quang. "But you must understand that any awareness they have is defined and ordered through OUIJA central processing. Therefore, independent thought is highly unlikely. Also, the vast majority of them surrender their ophthalmic organs at some point, which further reduces their independent perceptions. And every one is necessarily terminated, anyway, after so long in the harvesting process. We are continually pushing the frontier, however, in reducing the number of other organ systems required to support brain vitality. Who knows where this will end?"

"So, these biota and OUIJA are in a . . . symbiotic relationship?"

"You might say. Eventually, you should be able to get Peter here to give you the insider's view of the process."

Peter? So that was why the young fellow looked so familiar. Judith's son. The possible implications were disturbing.

Recovering, she continued to press the cynic's conceit. "Are you starting a collection of neurotics named McBride and Hurley? Where's the batty grand dame herself?"

When Wickner spoke, he reminded Moira of several sleazy, old movie rogues played by Peter Lorre.

"That's something we wanted to talk to you about, Moira."

★ ★ ★

A vast sea welcomed Peter with a benign swell and a warm caress of a breeze as he left safe harbor well behind. It proved an unimposing expanse, demanding no particular exertion to negotiate across its surface or to plumb its depths. Gradually, he became aware of a substratum, an effervescence, that was less than sound but more than thought—like the subliminal murmur of an invisible audience. Once he recognized it, the phenomenon was impossible to dismiss. In fact, this audience was becoming increasingly restive, its undertones differentiating into separate expressions.

Like porpoise song . . . or the cooing of doves . . . or a symphony of crickets . . . the Little Ones composed a sublime chorus of preconsciousness, form minus content, thought without identity, body absent location.

Peter imagined galaxies of fireflies . . . submarine fields of jellyfish . . . sentient reefs of coral . . . swarming bees . . . the purgatorium of a multitude of tiny souls.

Clearer and nearer now, he began to tune into the frequency of the Little Ones. Though he did not know them, he began to understand that they were ones whose eyes had not yet shed their first tear, whose lungs had not drawn their first breath. Yet bits of them, separate and removed, lived in other bodies, hearts beating in other breasts, kidneys filtering blood in other excretory systems, cerebral cortex patching ruined pathways inside other crania. Their collective subconsciousness had been allowed—channeled, even—to lap over their normal borders to overflow and commingle freely with one another.

Peter had another image—a Byzantine network of neurons, electrons, capacitors, synapses, silicon chips, ionic media of sodium and potassium, fiberoptic spaghetti, hemoglobin, and glucose. Together they manufactured fevered fancies, processed obscure data, and communed surreally with entities unknown.

Before he knew it, Peter had been sucked into the thick of it, flooded with information a thousand times too rapidly for his own limited brain to grasp. Somehow this communal Mind had been programmed to perform in ways his feeble intellect could only begin to imagine. The blur included a maddening jumble of faces and voices that defied identification, though he realized only too well that he knew some of them. Surely they could be resolved if only he tried hard enough.

Just beneath the surface of wakefulness, he roused his will to assert itself upon this cascade of data to bring something—anything—into focus. And then, with Herculean struggle, came the familiar shock of recognition—in multiples. These were voices that more resembled thoughts than sounds, but out of the melange could be discerned the distinctive vocal patterns of Jeremy Kay, Jared Quang, and Julian Wickner. These were the voices that seemed to be calling the shots and directing the data flow. They were also the dominant psyche, a luxuriating presence—oddly singular—that seemed to draw its vitality and buoyancy from the captive sea of Little Ones.

Was it audible thought? Or was it silent speech? It was impossible to tell. At the moment Peter seemed to be one link in a chain of gibberish from Elizabeth to Angie, who in turn was connected to the one named Marianne King. After that, he could only guess.

Absent from this network was the one for whom his heart longed—Carlotta.

But it was still possible to pray, and so he did. If there was a way to get to her, he would find it.

* * *

Angie saw the fright in Carlotta's deep, sultry eyes as she inserted the hypodermic needle into the young woman's arm. Deftly, just as Kelsey had taught her, Angie injected the sedative, removed the needle, and daubed twice at the tiny, welling red spot. She then tossed both syringe and cotton ball into the trash.

"You should thank me," said Angie. "This allows me to release you from any IV hookup for a while."

Carlotta wasn't breaking any speed records with gratitude. She glared from the bed, where she was held fast by various restraints.

"I know you," Angie said darkly. "You're just like me. Wait till you see what integrating is like. You'll want it all the time."

With that, she plugged Carlotta and herself in, to begin their slow descent through what Jeremy called discrete consciousness.

Angie relaxed and reflected on how quickly things had changed. It was difficult to believe that not so long ago she had been on the outside looking in, frustrated over her seeming inability to merit admittance to the Society. And now she had virtually instant access to its inner sanctum.

Her relationship with Jeremy had been brought back on track, better, in fact, than ever before. Jeremy seemed genuinely pleased to have her loyal service as a rookie member of the team. What's more, she had entrée to OUIJA, which was superior to sex or designers, anyway. And so utterly—addicting!

Angie also reflected on the increasing frequency of her integrations and their lengthening duration. There was little else that she would rather do. So what if she wanted to do it all day or all night? What harm could there be? It had not escaped her attention that Jeremy and Quang appeared to ration their own communings with OUIJA carefully, as if concerned by some potentially deleterious effects. Oddly, Kinsey seemed to eschew this integrating business altogether. To each her own, Angie observed.

As for herself, she was unaware of any hazards, mental or otherwise. To the contrary, she imagined that she was absorbing additional megawattage of psychic energy each time she integrated and that her entire spiritual being was expanding far beyond the bounds of her flesh and bones. She felt like a transcendental Leviathan, feeding off the Little Ones as if they were spiritual plankton, there for the sole purpose of supplying metaphysical nourishment. And then the power they released when their wretched little bodies were offered in ritual sacrifice!

Sitting cross-legged before the enormous wall projection of Shiva the Destroyer, Angie muttered a private mantra. As she did so, the image of Shiva began to dance, slowly at first, to its deadly drumbeat. Carlotta should have been receiving the same image.

Like a willing drowning victim, Angie watched her life replay before her mind's eye, starting with the recent past and hopscotching backward.

Once again, she was present at her own initiation, skyclad and carrying a premature infant boy up the steps to an Aztec-style altar. This was not just any child; it was the offspring of a woman from Armand Schliesser's forced pregnancy center. And it was not just any woman, but a woman whom Angie personally had persuaded to give up her child. The mother, of course, was told only that the late-term pregnancy was being terminated and the products of conception—the biota—would be used for "scientific" purposes. And by this worthy blood sacrifice, Angie was rendered acceptable to the Goddess, to the Horned One—and to the elite of Chi Xi Vau.

Then the scenes began to change at an accelerating pace. Channeling with Jeremy in Gunnison Auditorium. Communing in meditation with her new spirit guide, Ashtoreth. Doing the Lower Siddhartha Avenue scene loaded on designers. Imbibing goddess-consciousness "thealogy" at the feet of elder sisters and professors of Womyn Studies. Several personal visits to termination centers. Short-term relationships with various boyfriends and girlfriends. Volleyball games in the school gym. Various stuffed animals. One very special doll baby.

And then came the rush of personal obliteration as her conscious awareness descended through sleep with dreams to dreamless sleep to creature instinct to primal tropism to insensate. And in shrinking to nothing, she expanded to the All.

282

She was one with the Goddess. She was Kali, with a blood-stained knife in her hand and a string of human heads about her neck.

* * *

Across town at the Riverside Community Mental Health Facility, Angie's mother was dreaming once again.

At first, Judith seemed to be back in counseling with ALEX, except this time it was not in Grady Hall. She was in a pre-term clinic, and ALEX was lecturing to her on reproductive freedom. Judith was arguing. That was not his role! He was supposed to be objective, nondirective. What did he mean, telling her it was murder? He couldn't tell her what to do!

Then she was strapped to a hospital gurney, exhausted and very frightened. Somewhere out of sight behind her, a newborn infant wailed.

"My baby!" she cried out. But the crying continued, and she could not move.

At last, a green-gowned doctor appeared, his face obscured by a surgical mask.

"My baby!"

The man ignored her and strode in the direction of the crying. In his hand was a long knife.

The sounds she heard next, barely human, propelled her to the outer reaches of terror. "My baby!" she shrieked one last time as the walls seemed to close in. Her soul was tearing asunder from the torment, the unspeakable grief, as she choked on hot, bitter tears. The room swam. Her ears were ringing.

And then, the surgeon reappeared, his knife dripping. With his other hand, he slowly removed the mask.

Judith was riveted. She knew that face from somewhere. Or did she? There was a dark brown moustache, wispy like a first growth. And those eyes—large, brown, doe eyes that seemed capable of sensitivity.

The man smiled, a smug grimace, decidedly unpleasant.

Judith screamed. Again and again and again.

25

Stepping just right, as if he were stiltwalking on banana peels, McBride found that the pain of his injuries could be tolerated—just. Even his middle initial hurt this morning.

The man in the kitchen mirror had a face only a doctor could love, especially if the doctor was a plastic surgeon. This was a day when McBride would have preferred being someone else, almost anyone else. He was just grateful that Salerno had been shadowing him when he had his unfortunate encounter on Emory Road. Things could have turned out much differently.

"My, don't you look like something the cat drug in," said Darnell Jones, coming into the kitchen, like McBride, for a cup of coffee.

Jones was back from Chicago and trying to get caught up on developments in his absence. Having been briefed by his colleagues, he wasn't totally unprepared for this pathetic sight.

McBride was in temporary retirement from the outerbelt motel circuit while he nursed his wounds. Salerno had brought him here the night before, after some X-rays and minor emergency room treatment. The detective-lieutenant and Overholtzer had arranged for some stepped-up surveillance of the Temple for a while, as unobtrusively as possible. McBride was in no hurry for further dealings with unfamiliar officers of the law.

"If you love me, you won't make me laugh." He pulled up his shirt to reveal an elastic chest binder.

"Cracked ribs?" asked Jones.

McBride nodded, showing a little surprise at the instant diagnosis.

"I have some experience in that department," Jones explained, raising a pair of fists. "Ex-Golden Gloves."

"Yeah? So where were you when I needed you?"

"Seriously," said Jones, putting down his dukes, "your willingness to submit to injustice was a victory of sorts. Do you realize what you would have lost if you had responded in kind?"

"I thought about that," said McBride, "and it was about the only thing that kept me from rearranging the guy's face."

"Can you think of a historic parallel?"

"Christ before His accusers?" said McBride without hesitation.

"My, you *have* been thinking," said Jones, impressed. "Want to talk about it?"

"No, I'm still thinking," said McBride. "Rick had been saying his problem was the reality of evil. For me, it may be the reality of good. You know, where is God in all of this—especially in terms of justice and authority."

"Hmm," said Jones, showing an intent look. "That's a good question. Let's talk about you. Were you fired from the judiciary?"

"No, I voluntarily and temporarily relinquished my position on the bench for a specific purpose and until such time as I might be able to reclaim it. It was the same idea as not punching that crooked cop in the nose, even though I wanted to and he deserved it."

"You had a higher purpose that you set above even your own welfare?"

"That's about it," McBride agreed, beginning to sense where this was headed.

"Then, Your Honor, I submit that you, of all people, should understand the principle. There is no contradiction between Christ's laying down His life and His claim that 'all authority has been given to Me in heaven and on earth.' Incidentally, His followers are looking for His return to reclaim His rightful authority—"

"Which He voluntarily and temporarily relinquished," put in McBride quietly.

"—and to establish justice," Jones concluded.

Now McBride was really thinking. He fell silent, hobbling out the door and down the hall with Jones, trying not to spill his coffee. Either some of these things were starting to make sense, or he'd had one too many kicks in the head.

"Ho," he said, startled by what he found in the conference room. "What is this?"

Stillman spoke a command, and ALEX ceased whatever linguistic gymnastics it had been creating on the wallscreen.

Aaron Fitzgerald looked up, momentarily befuddled. It all looked suspiciously like the translation project—the *defunct* translation project.

Stillman looked a little sheepish. "It's the translation project," he admitted.

"I thought we'd mothballed that for now," said McBride, gingerly depositing his coffee mug on the conference table and easing his bones into a seat.

"I . . . unmothballed it. After what happened to you last night, I changed my mind. Here you are, laying your life on the line—and I'm trying to protect my *job?* I had to decide what was important to me, and I guess I've decided."

"Do you fully understand the potential consequences?"

Stillman nodded. "And I'm fully willing to accept them. We're too close to stop now."

"Besides, Your Honor," said Fitzgerald with a gleam in his eyes, "it's the Rhema Institute what's paying for most of this, and it's Bible translation we're paying for—not to underwrite a home for the rehabilitation of decrepit, invalid American jurists."

Fitzgerald ducked as McBride, chuckling, sent a balled-up paper sailing past his ear.

"Boys! Now, boys!" Jones chided.

McBride squinted in pain. The impulsive movement had cost him physically, but it was a good hurt nonetheless.

"If you love him," said Jones, "you won't make him laugh."

"OK." Stillman changed the subject. "You should be encouraged to hear that we may have solved the Fahlgren puzzle."

"Oh?" At least it didn't hurt, much, to raise his eyebrows.

"Your record checks worked," said Stillman. "I believe what we have is the location for the Institute for Pre-Life Science. It's the old Halsey Estate in Jefferson Woods near Millersfield, situated in a massive eighteenth-century-reproduction French chateau."

"So, where does 'Fahlgren' come in?" asked McBride.

"I'm coming to that. William Halsey was a partner with Herman Bond in Halsey-Bond commercial real estate developers.

They went bust a few years ago for lack of new shopping malls to build, or something. Now, remember Claude Fahlgren? It was Fahlgren's castle that Halsey acquired after that revolving door of tenants who were afraid of spooks."

"Mr. Halsey didn't believe in ghosts?" McBride suggested.

"He did believe in the esoteric—apparently—in his later years. After his death several years ago—under some mysterious circumstances, but that's another story—the estate passed into the hands of an organization called the Institute for Metapersonal Research. Original incorporators included William Halsey—and Jeremy Kay."

McBride's eyebrows went up again, and stayed there.

"This Institute," Stillman continued, "shows up as one of Donleavy's groups, along with the Institute for Pre-Life Science. Another link is the same statutory agent for both institutes—a Nina Bonito. After the Institute for Metapersonal Research took title to Halsey's property, it seems they began to call it Chateau Fahlgren again, although to most people it's still the old Halsey Estate."

"And so," said McBride, "this castle in Jefferson Woods appears to be our location for the Institute, the fetal farm—"

"Yes. Forty-four sixty Lindbergh Road."

"And the most likely place to begin looking for Peter and Angie and Carlotta," McBride said.

"It's all circumstantial, but it adds up," Stillman told him.

"Is Salerno on top of this?"

"He's going to watch the place. He says it's not like calling in an air strike. We have to find some evidence of criminal activity. And even then . . ." Stillman left the rest unsaid.

No one had an overabundance of confidence in the legal system just now, least of all McBride.

"Good work," he said. "I think we're finally getting somewhere. But now you get the crack investigator's reward."

Stillman's eyes searched McBride's face. "What's that?"

"Another assignment. Something of pressing urgency. I would do it myself, but it needs to be addressed immediately—by somebody a little more ambulatory who isn't on a police hit list. In fact, Jonesy, I would like you to assist Rick on this one, if you wouldn't mind. Aaron can stay with the translation work."

"Anything," said Jones. "Name it."

"What is it?" Stillman asked.

"Judith. Maybe I'm getting paranoid, but I'm worried about her, especially with this talk about a buy-out and all of the strange things that have been happening. I'd like an assessment of her situation."

"Are you thinking about trying to arrange some protection?" Stillman asked. "We're getting Salerno and Overholtzer spread as thin as hoarfrost on a pumpkin."

McBride shook his head.

"Or moving her?" Jones asked. "Even if we could do it, I'm not sure one place is any safer than another."

McBride was still shaking his head. "Information. Just get me information. We may have to let the other side make the first move."

"'Evidence of criminal activity'?" asked Stillman.

This time McBride nodded.

* * *

"May I help you, gentlemen?" asked Selena Goren, the whiskey-voiced therapist, as Stillman and Jones took seats before her desk on the business side of the airy office.

"It's about a colleague of mine, Judith Hurley-McBride," Stillman began.

Goren's eyes instantly narrowed, then shifted from one man to the other.

Stillman sensed that this slender, middle-aged woman with the penetrating gaze was not someone to be trifled with.

"In that case, I doubt that we can have much of a discussion," she said curtly. "Patient confidentiality, you understand."

"Then, just listen to us," Jones insisted.

Goren's eyes registered faint surprise as they fastened on Jones.

"Some powerfully nasty things have been happening to members of Doctor Hurley-McBride's immediate family," he began, "and we have reason to believe that she herself could be in additional danger. Doctor Stillman here is prepared to lay out the particulars."

Stillman began relating the general story of the McBride family's misadventures, from Judith's odd behavior during the Larrabee murder trial to son Peter's mysterious shooting and disappearance. And then there was the matter of daughter Angie's alleged involvement in several criminal matters, including jailbreak, kidnapping, and murder.

"And now Judith's huband, Judge McBride, has been driven from the bench, and just last night he was assaulted by a couple of plainclothes policemen," he concluded.

"You might say we're beginning to sense a pattern here," Jones quipped, although the humor appeared lost on his audience.

At several points in the account, Goren appeared to be on the verge of an utterance and then to think better of it. Stillman wondered if she were an ex-smoker; he seemed to picture her somehow with a cigarette. She had that kind of squinting concentration.

Finally, she spoke. "Why are we having this conversation?"

Stillman sensed that he and Jones were about one step from finding themselves out on their ears if they didn't come up with a pretty good answer.

Jones, however, was equal to the occasion.

"We'd like to know why Doctor Hurley-McBride has not been mainstreamed, why she has been kept confined for so long" —he held up one finger after another— "and whether you will help us in our effort to have her released. We'll go ahead with or without your help, but we'd prefer to have it. And the first thing we'd like to do is to see her."

There was that squint again. "Just a minute." Goren abruptly rose and walked from the office.

Stillman looked at Jones, then used the brief interlude to pray silently for Judith and the McBride family.

"Well," Goren said more assertively when she returned. "Let me give you the straight scoop here. Judith is . . ."

Here, she paused, looked down, interlaced her fingers before her, and leaned forward before continuing, as if grasping for the right words. "Judith is a real . . . piece of work. She is completely, perhaps permanently, delusional, and none of the normal treatment modalities—other than antidepressant drug therapy—

has any significant effect. Do you know what form her primary delusion takes?"

"No," said Stillman. He glanced at Jones, who looked just as blank.

"That she's *pregnant*," Goren said with a hint of disdain. "She's even given this mythical child a name—'Maxie.' Now, do you have any idea why she might be engaging in this particular form of delusion?"

Stillman, shaking his head this time, was quite surprised to hear Jones speak up.

"Let me guess. She had an abortion, and this is a pathological form of compensation resulting from the denial of overwhelming guilt."

Goren, obviously taken aback, began to redden.

Stillman was uncertain whether that was the reaction of one hearing the very words of anathema or of one whose thunder has been stolen.

"You *do* know her, then," the woman said almost accusingly.

"Nope," said Jones. "Just a . . . sanctified hunch. Years ago, they used to have a thing called postabortion stress syndrome. I'd guess you wouldn't have a diagnosis like that anymore."

Goren eyed Jones with a mixture of curiosity and apparent distaste. "No, and thank goodness thinking people have outgrown that kind of superstitious nonsense. Objectively, abortion should be no more traumatic than having some minor elective surgery—like, say, breast implants or liposuction."

"But my colleague is correct that Judith did have an abortion?"

"I didn't say that," said Goren a bit defensively.

"The real question, though," said Jones, "is why you're suddenly sharing this much information after telling us you couldn't discuss the case at all because of patient confidentiality."

Jones was absolutely correct again, Stillman realized.

Goren sighed. "That's somewhat academic now. When I left the room a few minutes ago, it was to call the Community Mental Health Center for an update on her condition. I hadn't checked for some time, although I've had a—feeling about it. And, as of now, she's downgraded to terminal."

"What?" Stillman said, alarmed. "What does that mean?"

"Just what it sounds like. Your information is obviously a bit outdated. The mental health profession hasn't been 'mainstreaming,' as you put it, for years. That's where most of the unfortunate street people used to come from. Can you imagine anything so insensitive? Now, they're just—terminated when their cases are incurable. It's so much better that way."

"For whom?" said Stillman, a sense of outrage stirring.

Goren apparently chose not to hear the remark.

"So in this case 'terminal' doesn't really mean 'not expected to live,'" said Jones, "but rather 'scheduled to die.'"

Goren squinted again. "You have a somewhat perverse way of putting things. But you've got the general idea."

"When—is there a date set for this . . . termination?" Stillman asked, his alarm growing.

"No," said Goren in a patronizing tone. "These things take a little time. First, official notification of terminality has to be sent to the next of kin and to the admitting physician."

"Would that be you?" asked Stillman.

Goren nodded. "And I haven't even received that notification yet."

"What's next after notification?" asked Jones.

"There's a mandatory thirty-day moratorium to allow time for the physician or family to dissent. In that case, there would be a hearing relative to the impaired prospects for recovery before the medical academy, which would rule in the matter. Absent such objections, it would simply be up to the health care custodian to schedule termination at the provider's convenience after the thirty days."

Stillman shuddered. "By what means? Lethal injection?"

Goren appeared weary of the discussion. "No, by means of gangland-style drive-by shootings. What do *you* think?"

Stillman couldn't believe his ears.

"Do you plan to register a 'dissent' in this case?" Jones said pointedly.

An android smile insinuated itself onto Goren's face as she quietly rose to her feet, signaling end-of-interview.

"I'm sorry I am unable to answer any further questions at this time." Her freeze-dried expression veiled any true feeling behind her steely gray-blue eyes. "Should you later desire to make any further inquiry regarding this case, please feel free to contact my attorney, Ms. Stephanie Hudson."

★ ★ ★

Back at the Temple, the unsettling news would have to wait. McBride was asleep, and they figured he needed it. But in the conference room, Stillman and Jones found Fitzgerald atwitter with anticipation.

"Right good progress we've had here in your absence," he announced with a glimmering eye. "The royal moment of truth is what we've got now."

"Backwards is what your royal sentences have become," said Stillman.

"Eh?"

"Nothing. Any reason we shouldn't go for it right now?"

Fitzgerald shook his head. "Let 'er rip!" he called out.

With that, Stillman looked up, swallowed hard, and addressed the blank wallscreen.

"ALEX, run Genesis chapter 1 in Proto-Alpha language base, display one column Proto-Alpha, one column Hebrew text, and correlate with Cybersynchronic matrix for language sets, all."

By the time the screen sprang to life, it had cleared itself to blank turquoise. "New set created," ALEX responded.

"Clear new," Stillman directed.

A moment later, ALEX answered, "New set cleared."

Stillman knew in his heart that this had to work, but he couldn't help a case of sweaty palms and shallow respiration anyway.

"Reprogram subset," he directed.

"Ignore all previous?" ALEX said with mild-alarm vocal inflection.

"Ignore all previous," Stillman confirmed.

"Define reprogram subset limits," ALEX reminded patiently.

"Simplest common denominators, redefine all," Stillman said, respecting ALEX's inbuilt cautions.

ALEX said in his rare doublecheck tone, "Mainframe time cost approved?"

"That too."

After the longest pause Stillman could recall ALEX ever making, a rush of characters began tracking across and down the screen in two columns, Hebrew on the right and a modified Roman script on the left for a phonetic rendering of the Proto language. His eyes raced to track the flow, but it was impossible to keep up.

Fitzgerald appeared pensive, disquieted.

"Something's definitely amok here," he murmured after a moment.

"Like what?" said Stillman, almost defensively.

"This is not Genesis. I can tell from the Hebrew."

"What is it?"

"I'm getting individual words, but no meaningful phrases."

Stillman decided to address ALEX directly.

"Stop, ALEX. Return to oh-one-oh-one and give English, audible."

In another moment he found himself well nigh unable to believe his own ears as ALEX intoned: "Phenomena manifest themselves by degrees."

"What?" said Stillman, bewildered.

"Phenomena manifest themselves by degrees."

"Next verse," Fitzgerald instructed hopefully.

"Dualities are the phenomena of illusion."

"What?" Stillman said again, dumbfounded.

"Next," said Fitzgerald.

"Ontogeny recapitulates philogeny."

"What is this?" said Stillman, unhappily.

Only some of the sounds Stillman heard next made any sense. He could make out the bleat of an occasional third-level diagnostic attempting to assert itself and then failing, apparently being overridden by some other programming. Other sounds could only be some form of serious malfunction.

And then the screen erupted in a pixel shower of high-density snow before resolving to the familiar turquoise. But in place of Botticelli's Venus rose the Hindu hag goddess Kali, leering with utter malevolence. In her right hand was her gruesome, dripping dagger.

26

Marianne King's small, white book turned out to be exactly what Moira had suspected—an honest-to-pete Bible. Not just *a* Bible but, as it proclaimed in gold lettering on the cover, *The Holy Bible*.

Moira picked up the volume from the coffee table and turned it over. In the back were the obligatory maps of the Israelites' wanderings through the desert, the territories of the twelve tribes in Canaan, and the colored-line routes of Paul's missionary journeys. In the front and middle were pages crinkled as if someone had left the book out in the rain or done a great deal of crying over the open leaves.

Marianne looked up with haunted eyes from the lone chair in her Spartan room as Moira thumbed through the little volume. It fell open as if from habit to Psalm 69, where the pages were especially crinkly and these words were underlined: "Save me, O God, for the waters have threatened my life. I have sunk in deep mire, and there is no foothold; I have come into deep waters, and a flood overflows me. I am weary with my crying; my throat is parched; my eyes fail while I wait for my God."

Just for a moment, something deep within Moira resonated in harmony with the spirit of this cry. And then, catching herself, she dismissed it with the contemptuous snort especially reserved for members of the Flat Earth Society, Luddites, Christian fundamentalists, and other fire-breathing oddballs. Still, what possible justification could Wickner and the rest have for keeping this pathetic woman locked in this meager room?

"You read this a lot?" she held up the Bible to see if she could draw the woman out.

Marianne nodded almost imperceptibly. OK, so she wasn't dying to talk. Try another subject.

"Do you see Angie around here much?"

This time Marianne shook her head, answering softly. "She's one of them now. Aren't you one of them too?"

"'Them'? The Society?"

Marianne nodded. "Chi Xi Vau."

Moira realized that Marianne had asked her a very good question indeed. *Was* she one of them?

"Wickner and his friends take a lot for granted," she said slowly. "Like my being one of them. They assume I'm just dying to learn the secret handshake, work my way through the merit badges, and become part of their little esoteric inner sanctum. They never assume they could be wrong."

"What *are* you doing, then?" the woman asked as if genuinely interested.

"Seeking. I'm a seeker after truth, wherever it may be found. But I'm no joiner."

Marianne King looked skeptical. "That sounds real dangerous. They told Angie there are no second-place finishes in this business."

"What does that mean?"

Marianne seemed unsure. "What does it sound like?"

"Like they think they can intimidate Angie."

"Unlike yourself?" the woman said this time with skepticism in her voice.

"I can take care of myself. I'm still waiting for some answers."

"To what?"

"Lots of things. I've never had a straight answer, for example, even to what Chi Xi Vau stands for."

"You don't know?"

"No. It sounds like a fraternity. You know something about it, I take it?"

Marianne rolled her weary eyes. "The number of the Beast and his New World Order."

Moira was at a loss. "Come again?"

"It's all in Revelation chapter 13—the Antichrist and six-six-six."

"You don't believe *that* stuff, do you?"

"It's immaterial what I believe. It's their name. Only they can explain why they do what they do."

Moira thought aloud. "Kay, Wickner, Quang, Morningstar, Kinsey, Eckart, now Angie—how many others are in this thing?"

"Lots."

"What's your connection in all of this?"

Marianne smiled ruefully. "I'm a dropout."

"You were a member of the Society?"

"Not a member—more an associate. I was useful to them for a while in the circles that Larrabee and Eckart traveled. But I was out before I was really in. They thought I had a familiar—a spirit— but I was just a multiple-personality sicko—your classic victim of satanic ritual abuse and multiple personality disorder." Here she actually smiled. "They thought I was a *terrific* channeler."

Moira laughed, despite herself. Relaxing, she sat down on the floor opposite Marianne and leaned against the coffee table, where she felt herself to be much less imposing, looking slightly up to the red-eyed woman rather than down upon her.

"How do you get over something like that?" she asked.

After honking her nose in a tissue, the other woman asked abruptly, "You really want to hear my sad story?"

"Indeed," Moira agreed readily.

"It's not just my story. It's the story of—" Marianne's voice began pinching, then choked off entirely. The tears started flowing all over again. It was another minute before her breathing resumed enough regularity to croak out the remainder of the sentence.

"—of a little boy named . . . Joshua."

★ ★ ★

There they were again, anomalous propagations in the field.

Peter could tell that there was another presence, one like himself, not completely compatible for some reason with the program, which required total submission.

Maybe he could establish contact, but he would have to be cautious. He had learned the hard way that if he strayed too far from the program into unauthorized activities, whoever or whatever was in charge of things invariably increased his sedative blood levels to near catatonia, something to be avoided at all costs. The only thing that seemed to work was doublethink, but how wonderfully it worked—and how ironic!

"Phenomena manifest themselves by degrees."

So long as he regularly interspersed the correct mantras, he could send other short bits through the interface and sometimes even receive a response. It had worked with Marianne. They'd even managed to pray, briefly.

But this was someone different, someone else female. It had to be Carlotta!

"Phenomena manifest themselves by degrees. Carlotta!"

After a long moment an answer came softly but distinctly. "Peter?"

"Dualities are the phenomena of illusion. Yes, this is Peter. Is that you, Carlotta?"

"Yeah. Why are you talking so . . . strange?"

"Ontogeny recapitulates philogeny. As long as one of us says 'Simon says,' we can talk—until I figure out a better way. I'm slowly learning my way around this queer system. Are you OK?"

"Yeah. I'm just in the next room over. Marianne's on your other side. Why do they keep you hooked up to this . . . system . . . all the time? They only put me on for brief periods."

"All is one. I don't know. I think it's supposed to be punishment for refusing to play ball with them. What they don't know is that I'm learning to use the system for my own purposes. These are sick puppies, Carlotta. Quang even has some kind of emergency self-destruct built in. But whether it destroys just OUIJA, the whole castle, or all of central Ohio, I don't know. And I don't want to find out. There may be a way to communicate with the outside, if I can figure out how to bypass the security protocols."

"So, why doesn't their mind control work on you?"

"We are one. They can sedate me, but they can't control my thoughts. 'Greater is He who is in me than He who is in the world.' That's what the Bible says."

"What?"

"Do what thou wilt. We have a greater power than our enemies could ever dream of. Don't be afraid. I want you to pretend that you enjoy 'integrating.' Convince our handlers to let you do it all the time. That way, we can keep talking. I can teach you how to resist control. OK?"

"All right."

"As above, so below. Next, I want you to listen to me now with an open heart."

"You mean an open mind, don't you?"

"As the universe, so the soul. No, I mean an open heart. For now, just listen. Will you do that?"

"I guess. Whatever you say, Peter."

"Atman is Brahman. Let me start by telling you about a man named Cathcart—although, for all I know, he might have been an angel—"

★ ★ ★

No one was more surprised than Stillman to find that Moira was not only returning his phone calls now, but she was even willing to go to lunch with him.

They met at Cleopatra's, a cozy establishment featuring Mediterranean cuisine, subdued lighting, and some measure of privacy. Moira's only ground rule, which she established over the phone, was that he not grill her about anything, especially in regard to castles or biota recycling or secret societies. She indicated that she didn't want to be difficult, but she had a lot to think about just now without being pressured.

Her protestations may have been unnecessary. By the time they had ordered, Stillman had all but forgotten why they were there in the first place. He had fallen under the Moira spell all over again. He found himself getting lost in her emerald eyes and paying more attention to her countenance and expressions than to her actual words.

"Rick," she said at last, slightly exasperated. "What's wrong with you today? Aren't you listening to a thing I say?"

"Uh—are you wearing a new perfume?" he said lamely.

"I'm not wearing perfume."

"Oh. Well . . . " Here he just let his heart speak. "When we were . . . married . . . I did tell you that you were . . . beautiful, didn't I?"

She looked genuinely taken aback, more so, in fact, than he would have guessed. He felt his face reddening and immediately regretted speaking so impulsively.

But before the moment became too awkward, Moira recovered. "Marriage was the other subject I should have asked you not to bring up," she said pointedly. "Anyway, it was more the institution than the person that I was rejecting."

"Why," said Stillman with exaggerated delight, "that's probably the sweetest thing you ever said to me."

Then they both laughed. Was it possible that they could enjoy one another's company again, for just a little while? He thought it would be more difficult than this, trying to talk around so many forbidden subjects.

And then the waiter arrived with the spread—generous platters of baba ghannuj, tabbouleh, hummus, falafel, and stuffed grape leaves.

"So," he said as they filled their plates, "you think Julian is pretty upset with me?"

"That's exactly what I've been trying to tell you. I don't know exactly why, but I've never seen him so upset with someone. Have you been a good boy and pulled the plug on that translation project like you were supposed to?"

"Sure. Sort of."

"Uh-oh. What does that mean?"

"It was more like it crashed."

"Oh?" she said suspiciously. "Otherwise, you'd still be going forward with it, you mean?"

"Well," he hedged, "maybe we ought to put that subject in the same place with the castle and the fetal farm."

"Rick," she began with a hint of exasperation. "I—let me be blunt. What is this . . *religious* thing with you?"

"Religious thing?"

"I mean *you*—and this fundamentalist stuff that seems to be going around like a virus."

"A virus?"

"You know. Schliesser was bad enough, but he was an old man. Then you and the Chicago Bible thumpers—and now this Marianne King person. All rather intelligent people to be involved in this kind of thing."

Stillman's heart leaped. "Marianne King! The mother of the baby in the Roger Larrabee trial?"

"Yes."

"She's a believer?"

"If that's what you want to call it."

"How do you know this?"

Moira started to say something, then apparently thought better of it.

Stillman shook his head, half teasingly. "And you talk about my being in hot water with the Senior Faculty Committee!"

"What do you mean?"

"Marianne King is an escapee, wanted for murder. If you even know her whereabouts and don't report it, you're making yourself an accessory."

"Is that part of the Boy Scout oath?" she said with acid tones.

"It's part of the laws of this land, for which some of us still have some regard."

"So, does this conversation make you an accessory to an accessory?" said Moira, softening a degree.

"If I don't turn you in." Stillman suppressed a smile. "Come to think of it, I may just have to make a citizen's arrest. Or run away with you—"

"Rick!"

"Sorry."

"Besides," said Moira, "I meant it when I said I was making up my mind about some things. Right now, I'm still gathering information."

"So what do you know about Marianne King now? Or shouldn't I ask?"

He was a bit surprised when Moira decided to talk about it, albeit somewhat obliquely. It obviously was weighing on her mind at the moment. Without saying where the conversation occurred, she related how Marianne King had wept over her sins and the blood she had spilled.

"Rick—" she looked down in deep reflection "—I began by thinking that this woman was unhinged—and finished by questioning the rightness of my own heart. I've not done half of the things she has done, but I certainly have approved of most of them."

"Yes?" Stillman said after a long moment of silence. "What did Marianne have to do with her son's death?"

300

"I'm getting to that." Moira looked up with troubled eyes. "Earlier, she had been involved with a garden-variety Wicca coven, where she had known this Zona Corban—Leah Andrews, the prosecution witness who turned up dead during the Joshua King murder trial. Marianne feels responsible for her blood too. You see, Marianne eventually graduated from this little Wicca group to a more sinister enterprise that dealt in human embryos."

"What outfit was this?"

Moira just stared at him.

"Oh, yeah. I'm not supposed to ask."

She hesitated and glanced around before continuing in a lower voice, "After Marianne had provided—sold—several concepti, she was approached for a full-term child for . . . ritual sacrifice."

"Joshua?" Stillman ventured.

Moira nodded. "She was promised rewards and advancement, but once she had the baby, she changed her mind. Maternal instincts took over, and she couldn't go through with it."

"And so, the child was kidnapped?"

"And sacrificed anyway. Yes."

They left the thought hanging in silence for a time.

"That must have been awful for her," he remarked at last.

Moira only nodded again.

Stillman was as interested in her reaction to these events as he was in the circumstances themselves, knowing her political leanings. Was it a slip for her to use the term "maternal instincts"? That wasn't the old liberationist Moira. Had something changed in her outlook? If it had, it didn't appear that she was about to volunteer the information.

"So, why are you telling me all of this?"

"I don't know," she said carefully. "Partly out of guilt, maybe, that I was letting Julian manipulate me to get to you."

He took that as a tacit admission that she had been Julian's conduit on the Bible translation project. She had to know that he could figure it out, anyway, but saying so gave everything else she said greater credibility in his eyes.

"I sense that Marianne's story had moved you," he prompted.

"I don't know quite how to put it, but hearing that story really caused me to consider—" Here, words seemed to fail her.

"The reality of evil?" Stillman suggested.

"Let me just say there are . . . other things, in the area of mind control, that need looking into."

"'The greatest breakthrough in human intelligence in history'?"

Moira's eyes widened, but she shut her mouth.

"You're not thinking of doing anything foolish, like play the hero, are you?" he asked. "These people will do more than revoke your library privileges."

"Heroine," she corrected. "I'm accepted. Right now, I'm Julian's heroine."

He was insistent. "Moira, take it from me—you don't know what you're going up against. As Schliesser used to say, 'We wrestle not against flesh and blood . . . '"

"Spare me the Sunday school lesson, please."

"Moira, I speak from experience, because you're about where I was several months ago, wondering about the reality of evil and needing to discover the reality of God."

"Oh, please."

"I want to present the facts to you about the way of faith. You owe me one good hearing. You can do that much for me—and for you. Consider it atonement for betraying me to Wickner. All right?"

When Moira opened her mouth to object, he cut her off. "You asked me a question that I never got around to answering."

Her face framed a question mark.

"What is this 'religion thing' with me?" he answered.

She smiled as the waiter began to collect the dishes and he reached for the check.

"We'll see." She rose from her seat. "Maybe next time."

He paid the bill, then caught up to her at the door.

"One more thing," he said. "Do you have a Bible?"

Moira gave him a strange look. "Of course. I am thoroughly grounded in all of the great mythologies."

"Look up Acts 2:21. Memorize it. It might . . . save your life."

On the street, Moira gave him an even stranger look.

As he watched her disappear in the opposite direction, Stillman hoped with all of his heart that it wouldn't come to that.

27

McBride scanned the conference room table. With the five of them all seated silent and poker-faced, including Vince Salerno in the flesh this time, the group resembled a council of war. Perhaps in a way it was.

"Gentlemen," McBride began, "I believe we all realize that we're at the point where we're going to have to make some serious decisions. As much as anybody here at this table, I have lost nearly all confidence in the integrity of our legal system, and I've been reluctant to take our concerns to the authorities out of fear that we'd be blowing our own case, if not risking our lives."

He looked around the table and saw a couple of nods.

"However, we are reaching the point in our investigations where we will need to act on the evidence we have. We now know something about the nature of the criminal acts being committed, and we think we know the headquarters location of this ongoing criminal activity. The question is whether to take these matters to the appropriate authorities and give them the opportunity to do something about it. If the legal system refuses to act on the basis of the information presented to it, then we've eliminated one option and we proceed to the next—whatever that might be."

He paused to allow some shots at his trial balloon.

"I'm more concerned about how the legal system will react," Salerno interjected. "One misstep, and they could shut us down—or worse. You know that from personal experience."

"Recent personal experience," McBride agreed, massaging a sore rib. At least his black eyes were now just faint yellow with faded purple.

"Hold on," said Fitzgerald. "You two chaps were just involved in a case against Roger Larrabee. The state was willing to prosecute that one. Aren't you writing off the legal establishment a little blithely?"

"Small fry," Salerno said with a dismissive wave. "Every step of the way I had the brass breathing down my neck to make sure the investigation didn't get out of hand. Larrabee was a scapegoat—a guilty one, but a scapegoat still."

"And you see where it got us," said McBride. "A mistrial, three dead people, three missing in action, and the rest of us jumping at shadows."

Jones spoke up next. "Maybe I'm missing something, but aren't we talking kidnapping here? If our local officials are all corrupt, which may be debatable, why don't we just go to the feds? Or are you going to tell me they're all on the take too?"

"Jury's out on that one," said Salerno, then looked at McBride. "You want to get into Frank?"

McBride nodded. It was time.

"As Neal knows," said Salerno, "my brother, Frank, is with the Justice Department in Washington. I've been feeding him information in this case."

Stillman, Jones, and Fitzgerald exchanged looks of surprise.

"Yeah," Salerno continued, noticing the reaction. "Frank is the bigshot of the family—former FBI agent, now attorney for 'Special Investigations' slash 'Communications,' whatever that's supposed to mean. There's a misnomer for you. Highly classified stuff, maybe national security. You can't talk about it. But he said he'd nose around on this a little."

"Can we get him now?" asked McBride.

Salerno glanced at his watch. "He's expecting my call. Whether he'll tell us anything, I don't know."

Salerno began punching in numbers for a bigscreen hookup.

"Will he talk to you while we're in the room?" asked Jones.

"Are you kidding? He tells me so little, it couldn't possibly make a difference. D.C.'s got him a little jaded. Half the time even I don't know exactly how to read him, and he's my own brother. But you'll see what I mean."

Once connected, it took Salerno a minute of fast-talking and name-dropping to circumvent the bureaucratic brush-off, and then they were put on hold for another minute.

"Hey, Vinnie!" chimed brother Frank at last. "How you doing? Who're your friends?"

As the introductions were performed, Salerno's four friends gazed at a younger and somewhat more urbane-looking version of Vincent Salerno, larger than life upon the bigscreen.

"Have you had a chance to check into those things we discussed?"

"Yeah," said Frank almost tiredly. "The Institute for Pre-Life Science you'll find by various names in all sorts of places, most major cities. Same game—different names, different faces. They're your basic fetal farmers, biota recycling whatchmacallits. It's not just a local phenomenon. It's a major industry. Did you know that the health care business as a whole is America's largest industry?"

"I didn't," said Vince.

"And fetal tissue—the canned baby racket—is big business too. Medical science has saved people from all of the cheap diseases, so now we can get sick with the expensive ones, the ones that require entire organ transplants, implants, and all kinds of cannibalization. People want to live, Vinnie."

"Yeah, OK. I get the picture. But what about these other groups?"

Frank looked at a sheet of paper in front of him.

"The Institute for Metapersonal Research and all the rest with the funny names, Greek stuff—I'm sorry, I'm not coming up with anything on them. But you'll probably find them tied together in various ways, lobbying, political action committees, et cetera. You may find them personally distasteful, but it's perfectly logical and mostly legal.

"Look, once we decided to protect abortion as a fundamental right in this country, it was inescapable that we'd have all kinds of people trying to make a buck at it and some crazies even making a sacrament out of it. You think you're going to turn back the clock, you try arguing with the blind people's lobby or the diabetic people's lobby. It used to be shameful, and women used to have to pay big bucks to have an abortion. Now they're free at the government clinics, and some of the private places are paying the women for their business—concepti, as they call it in the trade."

"I had no intention of debating abortion—" began Vince.

"I'm sorry, you got me started. You want my advice? Stay away from this stuff like the plague. You can only lose bigtime."

"Why?"

"Why? This fetal farm stuff is a no-win battle. That war was fought years ago, and nobody wants to reopen that can of worms. You might as well try to start Prohibition up again. The fact is, these people have got the law on their side, and they've become quite powerful. Nobody wants to cross them, and that's all I'm going to say on the subject."

"I'm sorry to hear you say that, Frank. I told you how these people here are suspected of major criminal activity. Last time I heard, the FBI still considered kidnapping to be a federal offense. Not to mention local law enforcement corruption."

"Come on, Vinnie," said Frank, sounding a bit impatient. "You make allegations like that, you better have some good, hard evidence to back you up. Even then, who's going to listen to you? Does your county prosecutor care about stuff like that?"

"No, but I'm asking you—what about you big, smart guys in Washington?"

Frank laughed humorlessly. "I'm sorry to burst you bubble, bro, but maybe you haven't heard. The war against crime is over—and we lost."

"I can't accept that."

"Where you been? Surely Columbus, Ohio, can't be that far behind the times. You hear the same news I do. Our society has collapsed, and we're living in the ruins, just fighting holding actions."

"Come on, Frank. Don't you think that's a little cynical, even for you?"

"Hey, I'm not the one who blew up the Statue of Liberty or started the California redwood fires or decriminalized all the so-called victimless crimes. In some places now it's become a sport to lynch white males. All you gotta do is listen to the carnage in a few news reports to figure out that nobody's gonna get very worked up about a few more counterculture crackpots in Columbus, Ohio, who are accused of consorting with the devil. Come to think of it, at this stage of things, *we* probably would be considered the counterculture now."

"I certainly don't read the same crime reports you do—"

"OK. Let me give you a hot tip. The smart money's on lawlessness; crime pays. It's up in every category, and not just in the United States but in virtually every Western nation. Especially now.

"In a few days it'll be October Holiday again, and already the dams are bursting everywhere you turn. Major bank heists daily. Violent sex crimes in broad daylight. Muggings right on Main Street. Highway robbery. Arson epidemics. Random terrorism. Even human sacrifice, blood rituals, and cannibalism. You name it. Even some things you probably never heard of. Each new October is worse than the last one. I predict we're really going to have an October Holiday this year to remember for a long time."

Frank appeared to be punching some keys at desktop level. "I'm sending you some hard data right now—unclassified stuff. You'll see what I mean."

Vincent looked crestfallen. "So, if you were me—"

"If I were you, Vinnie, I'd walk away from that department so fast, buy me a nice fetal farm somewhere, and start rakin' in the retirement dough."

"Nice talkin' to you, Frank," Vincent Salerno said morosely.

"Ciao."

* * *

"My recommendation," McBride said in the quiet room after the bigscreen picture faded, "is that we hold off filing any actual complaint until we ourselves have such good, hard evidence of criminal activity at   what is that address?—forty-four sixty Lindbergh Road, that it can't be ignored."

Silence prevailed. There were no dissenters.

"How's that surveillance coming, Vince?"

"Well . . . " Salerno extracted some photos from an envelope. "Rick's information was obviously accurate. We've placed some of the players at the scene."

Stillman slipped the photos into the scanner one at a time so they could be displayed on the bigscreen. They weren't the sharpest photos in the world, obviously taken at a distance through car windows with a telephoto lens, but the subjects were clearly identifiable.

First onscreen was the image of an intent-looking Oriental man with thick-lensed eyeglasses.

"Jared Quang," said Stillman.

Then appeared a handsome blond man wearing a smug expression, followed by a white-haired male with a gold earring and a cockeyed smile.

"Jeremy Kay and Julian Wickner," said Stillman.

"The only problem is," Salerno said, "this could just as well be your friendly poker game or an Audubon Society meeting. The auto tags trace back to the Institute for Pre-Life Science. That says nothing about their activities, but it's a start. We keep it up long enough, maybe we get lucky."

"That could take forever, Vince," said McBride. "What's Plan B?"

"There isn't one yet. Unless we can get somebody inside under some pretense, like the gas company looking for a leak or something—"

"Which could be real dangerous," said McBride. "We may yet have to do that, but only as a last resort."

Salerno agreed. "Any volunteers? The only other possibility is recruiting an informer from within, somebody who has access to the inner sanctum."

"Rick," McBride asked, "how's it going with Moira?"

Stillman took a deep breath. "You just described her," he said quietly.

"What?"

"Somebody who has access to the inner sanctum. I hate to blow the whistle on her like this, but I'm afraid she's going to get hurt playing heroine."

"What does she know?" McBride asked.

"Enough. She won't tell me, of course. But she told me enough to convince me she knows whereof she speaks. She's been talking with Marianne King, for example, but she won't say where. It's obviously the castle. She also won't talk about Judith, which means she knows something."

Salerno's eyebrows went up. "I could hazard a wild guess."

"Hazard away," said McBride. "That's why we're here."

"It stands to reason that they're planning to grab Judith, and Moira is having some qualms."

"That's what she's having, all right," said Stillman. "This

would be a good time to lean on her, Vince."

"Sounds like a good idea," said McBride.

Salerno nodded thoughtfully. "I'll get right on it. I can lean with the best of them. Any idea which way I should lean?"

"Don't let her have any room to maneuver," Stillman advised. "She'll hate me for this, but tell her you know she's been talking to Marianne King, and that technically makes her an accessory to murder."

"She'll hate you, all right. Neal, Overholtzer is trying to keep an eye on Judith, but I'm not sure I can ask him to do much more than that."

Everything within McBride cried out to send in the cavalry, storm the beaches, free the lady in the tower. He was seeing Judith's face, beautiful and tragic, and a new wave of longing and regret swept over him. But he quickly suppressed it. He must not sacrifice the ultimate goal to his personal needs, or Judith's.

"No, Vince," he said slowly. "I don't think we should try to stop a grab. It may be the only way to get the goods on them. I'm not overly confident about getting action from the authorities solely on the basis of one informer like Moira."

"Man," said Salerno, "you guys are hard core. It's great police logic, but pretty tough for the women. I hope they appreciate it later."

"Let's hope so." McBride looked from face to face. "Anything else to discuss?"

Fitzgerald spoke up. "Yes, Your Honor. Rick and I have some important information from our post mortem of the ALEX crash. It's not pretty."

"All right."

"You first, Rick," said Fitzgerald.

"Well— Stillman cleared his throat "—I was able to do some strategic downloads," Stillman began. "Not only is ALEX dead in the water, but virtually everything in regard to the Proto language base has been wiped out. That actually made the search fairly simple, considering the fact that the whole system was dead and had to be networked with another university mainframe to do anything."

Jones interrupted impatiently. "Stop talking like Fitzgerald and just tell us what you found."

"It appears from responses to routine diagnostics that the operating system was simply overwhelmed by self-replicating program errata."

"That means a virus ate it," Fitzgerald translated.

"Well, yes," said Stillman, "but it would have to be a more diabolical virus from a more powerful artificial intelligence than man has yet created. Simply put, with today's fail-safe systems, what happened to ALEX is not supposed to be technologically possible."

"But it happened," Salerno observed.

Fitzgerald's mouth formed an ironic smile. "Impossible, that is, with one possible exception."

"OUIJA," said Stillman. "Quang, being the actual creator of several modern security system protocols, is the one person who well might know ways to circumvent them."

"But it was not totally without fingerprints," Fitzgerald commented.

"Right." Stillman nodded. "All of ALEX's security programming was either wiped out or turned to garbage, apparently random junk. On a hunch, I had some cryptosynchronic analysis run on it and found that it may be junk, but it certainly wasn't random."

Jones was now on his feet and pacing. "OK, what was it?"

"We still don't know what most of it is," Stillman said, "but Aaron and I were able to identify its morphogenesis."

Jones wrinkled his nose. "Its what?"

"Its functional origin," Fitzgerald interjected. "Computer analysis shows it to be—believe it or not—some form of ritual incantation."

"Like a magic spell?" McBride asked.

"That's correct," said Stillman. "Unfortunately, it all resides now in that other university computer, and I'm afraid to push my luck. I'm sure I've already attracted enough unwanted attention just doing the crash post mortem."

"But I have a hard copy of the full text," Fitzgerald said, to Stillman's obvious surprise. He pulled some papers out of his valise and peered at the last page. "The interesting thing to me is the very last two words before ALEX died—'Ashtoreth' and 'Molech.'"

"Ashtoreth and Molech," Jones repeated. "The pagan gods."

"Correct." Fitzgerald nodded. "And wherever they appear, it's generally in the context of child sacrifice."

Jones stopped pacing. "Child sacrifice? That's pretty heavy."

"Is there a connection here?" asked McBride.

"Our instincts say yes," said Stillman, "but we've only begun to ask some of the right questions. We need more information."

McBride for once was intrigued. "Have you asked the Interactive Professor?"

Stillman and Fitzgerald looked at each other and smiled.

"Righto," said Fitzgerald. "We were just getting ready to do that, weren't we, sport?"

★ ★ ★

Dr. Otto Jesperson smiled his usual grandfatherly smile on the bigscreen, as if he had been asked a question regarding the Good Ship Lollipop rather than about demons, abortion, child sacrifice, and occult practices.

"First of all," said the old gentleman, "the question often arises as to what, if anything, is ultimately behind pagan idolatry. Aren't all of those idols of wood and stone and the gods and goddesses of ancient mythology just so much stuff and nonsense, having their origin solely in the imagination and with zero basis in reality?

"Not so, from the biblical perspective. Scripture is quite clear that these forces have real existence and are, in fact, demons—*shedim* in the Hebrew, *daimonion* in the Greek. When the Israelites made the golden calf in Horeb and worshiped the molten image, for example, the Old Testament says, 'They even sacrificed their sons and their daughters to the demons . . . to the idols of Canaan.' Similarly, in the New Testament Paul said that 'the things which the Gentiles sacrifice, they sacrifice to demons.'"

"Thank you, Doctor Jesperson," said McBride. "So, are Molech and Ashtoreth demons such as you describing?"

"Most assuredly." Jesperson smiled politely once again.

"All right, old boy!" Fitzgerald cried. "Don't stand on ceremony. Give us the whole *megilla*."

"He means give us the references," Stillman said patiently.

"Leviticus contains curses against consulting mediums and spiritists and sacrificing offspring to Molech. Throughout Scripture we find references to child sacrifice, sexual immorality, perversion, and various pagan/occult practices intertwined, almost as if they were part and parcel of each other.

"First Kings says Solomon's thousand wives and concubines caused him to turn from Jehovah and follow pagan gods, including 'Ashtoreth, the goddess of the Sidonians, and Milcom, the detestable idol of the Ammonites.' It says Solomon also worshiped 'Chemosh, the detestable idol of Moab,' and 'Molech, the detestable idol of the sons of Ammon.'

"Genesis explains the origins of Ammon and Moab. Lot's two daughters, reared in Sodom, got their father drunk and committed incest."

"So," said Fitzgerald, "these pagan deities trace back to the depravity of Sodom."

"Correct," said Jesperson.

"What about the Sidonians? Who, then, were they?"

"Phoenicians—as were the people of Carthage, which abounded in child sacrifice. Wicked Queen Jezebel was a Sidonian. Ashtoreth was the wife or consort of Baal. To the Canaanites, she was Asherah, consort of El. Other regional variations included Ishtar, Ashtart, and Astarte. The Hebrew 'Esther' may be related. It means 'star.' The Greek root 'aster/astron' gives us words like 'asteroid' and 'astrology.'

"The same goddess was identified in the Greek pantheon as Aphrodite—that's how we get the word *aphrodisiac*. And to the Romans she was Venus, the goddess of love, especially physical love. Hence terms from 'veneration' to 'venereal.'"

"OK," said McBride. "I get the picture with child sacrifice. But how do you connect the killing of unborn children?"

"The prophet Amos condemned the Ammonites for ripping open pregnant women 'to enlarge their borders.' That means to be victorious in war. A twentieth-century American Christian named Eric Holmberg observed that 'since a distinction between fetus and infant relative to their humanity is, in fact, meaningless, the sacrifice of a fetal child serves the same purpose from a spiritual perspective as the sacrifice of a postnatal child or an adult.'

312

"So, we today in the twenty-first century should say that it is no less barbaric to slay a prenatal child for personal convenience or for occult ritual or for vital organs than it is to sacrifice a postnatal child for military conquest or a successful harvest."

McBride stood up. "Thank you, Doctor Jesperson. You've given us much to think about."

"Yes," said Salerno, "beginning with why these demon names should be found in a computer crash in the first place."

"I guess that's for us to figure out," said Stillman.

McBride shivered. Had somebody turned down the heat?

28

Moira wiped the palms of her hands against her slacks once again to expunge the clammy perspiration. She supposed it was only natural that she be a little nervous. Technically, what she was about to do was just a bit illegal, after all. What if it didn't work? She could think of several potential charges, beginning with kidnapping and impersonation.

She glanced at her companion. Normally, she respected assertive women. But instinctively she had disliked this Kelsey Kinsey from the start. There was just something about her. Come to think of it, there were several things. She found Kinsey's patronizing, overbearing attitude grating. She even objected to the woman's appearance, her glasses with their red plastic rims, and her obnoxious pseudointellectual hipness.

Most of all, she resented Kinsey's self-confident composure while Moira herself was dying inside as they stood waiting at the front counter. The Edna R. Jarvis Rehabilitation Center and Hospice didn't appear to be exactly overstaffed this morning.

It took Moira a moment to realize that Kinsey was addressing her, and she asked her to repeat.

"I said, are you going to the ball Thursday night?" Kinsey asked again, louder than Moira would have liked.

"I—I don't know," she stammered. By Thursday, she might be dead or in jail—or integrated into OUIJA.

She realized that Kinsey was talking about the Chateau Fahlgren Halloween costume ball. Under different circumstances, it might be something to think about. But how could this woman make idle chit-chat at a time like this?

Finally, a flighty and rather unkempt young man appeared at the reception desk.

"May I help you?" he asked as if he'd rather be someplace else too.

As soon as Kinsey had identified herself and Moira and insisted on speaking to the person in charge, the diminutive fellow quickly disappeared into some inner chamber. He reappeared less than a minute later with a more authentic-looking gentleman.

"Doctor Kravitz," said the older, bearded man with half-glasses sticking out of the pocket of his white smock. "How may I help you?"

Moira noticed that Kinsey looked exceptionally pleased. That was curious.

"I'm Kelsey Kinsey from the Regional Deprogramming Center for Religious Extremism, and this is Doctor Moira Stone from Ohio State University. She's a colleague of one of your patients here, Doctor Judith Hurley-McBride. We've come to transfer her to our facility."

Dr. Kravitz's eyebrows rose to impressive heights. "That's odd. I don't have any workup on Doctor Hurley-McBride for release, and I'm the medical director. Let me check."

Before Kinsey could respond, Kravitz had moved to the nearest work station and begun typing commands on a terminal keyboard. Considering the fact that most residents here were just making their last stop before the cemetery, it probably seemed unusual that a patient actually would be leaving vertically. And in

Judith's case, it would have been only a few days since being transferred in from the Riverside Community Mental Health Facility in the first place.

A moment later Kravitz looked up with the smug expression of a true bureaucrat. "I'm sorry, but there's no authorization in her medical records for transferring this patient anywhere. In fact, there's not even a record of any request for a transfer. Who did you say you represented?"

"The Regional Deprogramming Center for Religious Extremism," Kinsey said with a cold edge. "Doctor Hurley-McBride was an unfortunate victim of fundamentalist indoctrination. Isn't that right, Doctor Stone?"

"Yes. Yes, that's right," Moira blurted, feeling a bit foolish, not to mention dishonest.

"Well, then," Dr. Kravitz said officiously, "why has none of that come to light in her case history? Do you think you might have the wrong patient?"

"Oh, no, Doctor Kravitz. We've got the right patient. And we are taking her with us. Doctor Stone has the discharge papers."

"What?" Kravitz said incredulously.

Moira extracted a manila envelope from her valise and handed it to the doctor, who put on his half-glasses to examine the document inside.

Moira had no idea what it was, but from Kravitz's reaction it must have been a corker. The man looked as if he had just suffered major physical trauma with blood loss. Speechless, he started to hand the papers back.

"That's all right, Doctor," Kinsey said with apparent satisfaction. "You can keep that. We have the originals."

"I bet you do," the doctor muttered, finding his voice at last. "I'll—uh—I'll see what I can—uh—do."

It couldn't have been more than three minutes before Kravitz returned with some forms for them to sign. Somehow, any sign of smugness or assertiveness had departed.

Kinsey was about done with the forms when she suddenly stopped and held up the last sheet. "What does all this mean?" She pointed to a particular section.

Kravitz gave her a peculiar look. "Doctor Hurley-McBride was terminal, you know."

This time it was Kinsey's turn to be taken aback.

Moira, too, was shocked by that disclosure, but she got the distinct impression that if Kinsey had it to do over, she would have been just as happy to stop right there and let the poor woman go to an early grave.

But it was too late. At that very moment, Judith Hurley-McBride herself slowly rounded the corner, a nurse at her elbow.

Moira's first impression was that Judith looked rather older than she remembered her. The half-circles under her eyes were certainly darker and her eyes themselves perhaps more sunken. She also appeared to be moving somewhat purposelessly and looking almost disoriented.

In another minute the peculiar young man reappeared, this time lugging a couple of suitcases, obviously Judith's.

"I'll go get the car," Moira said, suddenly wanting to be out of there quickly and sincerely wishing that she had never come in the first place. She tried to comfort herself with the knowledge that this harebrained scheme may well have saved Judith's life, albeit inadvertently.

They loaded Judith uncomplaining into the backseat. Kinsey climbed in the front passenger side, and Moira drove.

"So, what were those papers I gave Doctor Kravitz that seemed to curl his beard?" Moira asked as they headed out of town.

Kinsey opened another manila envelope and dumped its contents out onto the seat between them.

Moira looked down—and almost drove off the road. There in living color were unexpurgated photographs of Dr. Kravitz in most compromising positions with a variety of individuals of both sexes, at least some of them apparently patients.

"Where—uh—did those come from?"

Kinsey only smiled and continued looking straight ahead. Apparently, she had no intention of entertaining such questions.

"Oh!" Moira blurted, suddenly remembering something very important. She punched several buttons and then picked up her carphone.

"Gotta get my messages," she said by way of explanation.

What she was really doing, however, was activating the radio beacon so that Lt. Salerno would know to begin shadowing their flight to the Chateau. Witnessing this latest abduction of one Judith Hurley-McBride should come in most handy when it came to providing evidence to obtain a search warrant for the premises.

Moira just hoped this monkey business didn't end up very badly for all of them. Rick would never forgive her if she got herself killed despite his admonitions. On the other hand, it might be a while before she forgave Rick for putting Salerno on her case.

As they reached the outskirts where suburbia blended almost imperceptibly into genuine countryside, Kinsey at last broke her silence. Half turning to the back, she inquired of Judith, "How are we doing back there?"

"Fine," came the dull reply. And then, after a moment, "Kicking."

"What?"

"Kicking," Judith repeated.

"Who's kicking?"

"Maxie."

"Who?"

"Maxie—my baby."

"Oh, for—" Abruptly, Kinsey began laughing shrilly.

Moira realized it was the first time she had heard Kinsey laugh. It was not a pretty sound, more akin to obscene glee.

"How precious!" Kinsey said. "I'm really good with babies, you know. Can't get enough of 'em." She began snickering all over again.

★ ★ ★

"There they go," the captain said to the sergeant on a back channel.

At that moment a late-model green Gemini four-door cruised by their off-road vantage point behind a convenient huddle of shrubs on a curve where traffic had to slow considerably.

"You get that?" Capt. George Blasingame radioed.

"Ten-four," responded Sgt. Ron Mendez from the other vehicle. "I got a visual on three white female subjects."

"No replay yet. Here comes Suspect Number Two."

At that moment, a royal blue Astral, clearly one of the department's unmarked cruisers, sped by, following the first vehicle along State Route 105 toward Millersfield.

"Got it," Mendez chimed. "Instant replay coming up."

After only a few seconds of radio silence, Mendez resumed his analysis.

"Vehicle Number One registered to the Institute for Pre-Life Science. Positive photo ID made with occupants—Kelsey K. Kinsey, Moira R. Stone, Judith E. Hurley-McBride."

"Bingo." Blasingame was enthusiastic.

"Vehicle Number Two registered to Franklin County Sheriff's Department—occupants Vincent B. Salerno, Wilson N. McBride."

"OK, let's roll 'em."

With that, the motorcade of two became a convoy of four. Blasingame, confident that he knew the itinerary, allowed the first two cars the maximum leeway up ahead.

The last thing he wanted was to tip Salerno that he was being followed while he himself was tailing Hurley-McBride's abductors. Instructions on this one came from the highest levels. Nor did the captain wish to create a spectacle with a caravan of suspicious vehicles bursting simultaneously upon tiny Millersfield.

It was not long before Route 105 became Main Street in the village of tidy lawns, aluminum-sided bungalows, post office, two gasoline stations, one convenience store, one Presbyterian church, and four stop lights.

In no more time than it took for two of those four lights to turn from red to green, Blasingame and Mendez were heading out the other end of Millersfield onto Sleepy Hollow Drive and on past larger suburban tracts. Here were split-rail fences and more elaborate split-level homes with recreational vehicles parked out back. Soon the terrain began to roll once again. Weeping willows appeared in greater abundance, and the homes spread even farther apart. Behind these dwellings were children's swingsets, doghouses, and big red barns.

At Grimes Road, Blasingame followed Mendez turning right. "Are we still locked in?" he radioed.

"Ten-four." The green Gemini, he reported, had made the

same turn ahead of them and proceeded toward the mansions and lakes and golf greens of Jefferson Woods.

These were the lavish acres devoted to the polo and hunt clubs, the chateaus, and the stone-walled estates of the leisure class and the captains of industry. Needless to say, this was alien turf for the likes of Blasingame and Mendez.

Out of curiosity, Blasingame had checked the computer archives. There had been remarkably few calls for service recorded in this district in all of the decades since such records began to be kept. In most cases, it would have been just like this operation—totally off the books. These were folks who generally didn't allow problems to occur or, if they did, took care of them themselves.

Blasingame figured he was the highest-ranking officer in the department with no personal relationships with any of these esteemed residents. He was quite happy to remain in the dark for security's sake.

And Mendez knew even less than Blasingame. He didn't know, for example, that if this fool Salerno went too far, it would become their job to take him out. Blasingame preferred that that not happen. Fool that he was, Salerno wasn't all that bad a guy. But if he had to, Blasingame was ready to do whatever duty demanded.

For that matter, he wouldn't at all mind getting a crack or two at this rascal McBride.

* * *

When he saw the green Gemini signal for a left turn from Grimes onto Lindbergh Road, McBride knew there was no mistaking it now. Judith and her two abductors without doubt were headed for Chateau Fahlgren.

"Easy does it, Vince," he told Salerno, fearing their eagerness would lead them into temptation.

If their blue Astral was spotted in the Gemini's rearview mirror turning onto Lindbergh too, it might be all over. Vince had to lay off the gas.

"Don't worry, Your Honor," said Salerno. "I'm not about to blow it now."

This would be their first view of the lions' den, the haunted mansion, McBride thought. They rounded the same corner onto

Lindbergh, and he wondered if it would match the Gothic, fog-shrouded, moonlit image that resided in his brain. Probably not. He was prepared to be disappointed, knowing what kinds of things got called castles today.

And then he caught the first whiff of trouble, a suspicious presence in the bottom corner of their own rearview mirror. He had been keeping an eye on a vehicle pretty far back on Grimes Road, but now it was turning with them. This might not mean anything, he told himself. But somehow, he doubted it. His gut instincts were rarely wrong, and his gut was sounding an alarm.

"Vince, there's a possibility we might have company on our tail," McBride said quietly. "It might be a resident, but, just in case, let's not stop at the Chateau. Just drive by very slowly, and I'll do the best I can with the video."

"Whatever you say."

Around a bend they came at last within sight of an enormous high-walled estate. McBride was not disappointed after all. Nestled within its own grove of magnificent oaks, pines, and cedars was an elaborate, multi-story, eithteenth-century-reproduction French chateau complete with dark slate mansard roof, fake battlements, parapets, mullioned dormer windows, and sculpted pilasters.

But he wasn't going to have time to take even a windshield tour. His attention was drawn to the brake lights of the green Gemini as it paused at a guard station for permission to pass through the narrow iron gate and traverse the winding access road to the chateau itself.

McBride rolled down his window. He aimed his video recorder at the car's rear plate and then trained it on various car windows as they came into direct range. Through the viewer he could make out three women inside, but he was not at all sure they would be recognizable without computer enhancement. He stopped shooting as Salerno glided on past.

"We can double back," McBride told him, "and maybe snap some of them while they're out of the car, if we hurry."

"And we'll find out if our company behind us is friend or foe." Salerno floored it.

A moment later, they found out. Despite their top acceleration, the maroon car behind them was closing the distance. The gap was narrowing slowly, but there was no question that it was closing. Fortunately, Salerno and McBride were coming up quickly upon another road, which they would reach just before the other party caught up.

"Hang on," said Salerno, tramping on the brake.

McBride didn't know how Salerno did it, but somehow they managed to pull out of it without rolling the car. Now they began tearing down this new road. Out a side window he saw a sign that said "Connell Road." Out the back, he saw the maroon car grind past with its brake lights on, then throw it into reverse to make the same turn and rejoin the chase down Connell.

"I think we can make it to Gebhardt Road," said Salerno, pushing the pedal to the floor. "My goal is to get back to Grimes and get you headed toward Millersfield. Hope your legs are good. You may have to hoof it."

"Wait a minute. How do you know who's tailing us? It might be nothing but kids."

"Trust me. It's the law."

Someday McBride would have to ask Salerno how he knew that. Right now, things were a little too hectic.

Sure enough, the maroon car was closing on them again. Only this time, the Astral's security channel crackled to life with a flash of deja vu for McBride.

"Pull it over, pal," said a familiar voice. "County sheriff."

But now they were at Gebhardt, and Salerno wasn't going to pull it over. He executed another of his gut-wrenching turns, but this time the maroon car was ready for him and stayed right on their tail.

"Don't force me to shoot," the radio voice said again.

"Problem is," said Salerno, "we're not quite close enough to Grimes yet. He's gonna have to be patient."

But their pursuer had run out of patience. McBride ducked as small particles of glass bounced off the back of his head. He glanced back and saw the rear window looking like a spider web.

"I'll try not to hit your gas tank," the man radioed.

"OK," said Salerno, easing off the accelerator. "Grimes Road is straight ahead. I'll try to create a diversion long enough for you to beat it in that direction. If you're real lucky, you might hitch a ride into Millersfield or some place where you can call Rick or somebody for help. If you're not, you'll have to hoof it to a pay phone or a friendly neighbor. Just don't do anything foolish. We can't afford to lose you."

"But—"

"Don't argue with me, Neal," Salerno ordered. "There's no time to cook up a better plan. The fat's in the fire."

With that, he pulled the Astral to a stop on the berm and got out.

McBride did the same, tucking the video recorder into his jacket, where it created a pretty obvious bulge.

"Hi, Sarge," said Salerno as a sour looking, dark-complexioned plainclothes cop in his late twenties approached with gun in hand. "Neal, meet Sergeant Ron Mendez."

McBride got a sinking feeling—and a sudden desire to break a jaw. "Sneer," he said under his breath.

"What?" The man didn't wait for a response. "I believe we've met. So, Lieutenant, this is the kind of thing you're doing when you log in as 'on the road,' eh?"

"Yeah," said Salerno. "I generally try to halt crimes I find out about—even abductions in Jefferson Woods."

"Oh," Mendez said unhappily. "Going to be difficult, are you?"

Just then McBride realized another car was fast approaching from behind and decelerating. There was the sound of brakes, tires on gravel, and then a car door slamming.

A beefy man with a varicose nose and an attitude lumbered toward them.

"Hi, Captain," Salerno said cheerfully. "Neal, meet Captain George Blasingame. Remember his face well."

"Oh, I do," said McBride. "Toothpick."

As before, the man ignored the remark. Instead, his eyes fastened on the bulge in McBride's jacket.

"What you got there, son? Don't make a move while Sarge here checks you out."

Mendez holstered his gun and yanked open McBride's jacket front. McBride caught the video recorder before it hit the ground, but Mendez grabbed the camera before he had a good purchase on it.

"Nice machine." Mendez gave it a once over. "Too bad it's broken."

With that, he swung the recorder about by its long strap a full revolution and then brought it swiftly down full force on the pavement. There was a sickening sound of metal and plastic destruction as parts and pieces flew, some rolling across the road.

But something else was in the making just as quickly.

"Now," Salerno breathed to McBride, then stepped forward to confront Mendez.

Presumably feeling his space violated, Mendez gave Salerno a shove, inadvertently in the face.

Salerno spun around with a haymaker to the jaw that nearly lifted Mendez off his feet. If he'd had dentures, they would have been in Pennsylvania.

In the confusion, McBride took off like a shot.

Blasingame had pulled a gun, but it would do him no good in trying to separate Salerno and Mendez, who were putting each other in various holds.

Before anybody noticed what was happening, McBride had slid behind the wheel of the maroon Scorpio. He peeled out toward Grimes Road, thinking how much more efficient this was than trying to hoof it. And how much more illegal.

No doubt they'd put a radio alert out for him in no time. But McBride figured he'd have plenty of time to get to Millersfield, ditch the car, and make that phone call. It was waiting for a rescue lift that would be the killer. By that time, they could have his picture up in all of the post offices between here and Borneo.

Abruptly he decided not to drive into Millersfield. It was too obvious. Besides, there was no guarantee how far Sneer and Toothpick might be behind him—although Sneer was probably in urgent need of getting that jaw wired. It was probably best to ditch the car now before anything unfriendly appeared in his rearview mirror.

Just outside Millersfield, he turned left onto a residential road, found a cul de sac, drove to the end, and cut the engine. He walked briskly, but not fast enough to attract undue attention, half way down the street and then picked a house that looked as if somebody might be home.

Before he could ring the bell, the door popped open, and a startled teenage couple stared back at him.

"Hey, look at this, Sherry," said the guy, laughing and showing a lack of dental care. "Maybe a fugitive from justice, huh? Think he's runnin' from the law?"

Sherry, an equally frowzy young woman, began laughing too, as the door swung open and they tumbled out onto the front porch.

"Uh—" said McBride, "I'm out of gas, and I'd just like to make a phone call if I could."

"Sure, Mister." The guy laughed some more. "Just dial nine-one-one."

Sherry was laughing like a hyena now. They both smelled boozy.

McBride was afraid he'd made a big mistake.

"Nah," said the guy, sobering a little but still smiling. "Come on. Forget the phone call. I'll take you wherever you wanna go, so long's it's not out of state."

Indeed, the young man stepped off the porch, led his girlfriend to the driveway, and popped open the rear door of his jalopy. He indicated with a grand gesture that McBride should get in. So he did. Now they both looked a bit older than he'd first pegged them. Maybe this wasn't a mistake at all.

"Where to, buddy?" said his chauffeur, sliding behind the wheel.

McBride hesitated. "I don't want to inconvenience you. Where you headed?"

"First off, I got to take Sherry to work at the airport," the young man said as he backed out of the driveway. "After that, wherever."

"It just so happens," McBride improvised, "that I'm staying at the Imperial Crown at the Reynoldsburg exit off 270."

"Oh, sure," said the guy. "Piece of cake. That's so close, I'll take you there first."

Breathing the booze fumes, McBride hoped Sherry's job didn't involve anything like flying airplanes.

"Hey, buddy," said the young man again. "You really runnin' from the cops?"

"Something like that," McBride agreed, smiling.

"Cool," said the guy.

"Ultra," said Sherry, giggling.

29

The summons to appear immediately before the Senior Faculty Committee arrived by courier in Rick Stillman's Grady Hall office at precisely 8:01 A.M. The notice gave him no time to reconnoiter, not even any time to fret. It requested his presence As Soon As Possible. That meant Now.

Though he had considered the possibility of come-uppance for some time, this development caught Stillman very much off guard. For that reason he assumed it couldn't be the worst-case scenario—full-blown disciplinary action such as suspension. Things like that, he figured, took a bit more planning.

Therefore, he was all the more surprised when he ambled into the Polo Room at Grady Hall—not the usual venue for the Senior Faculty—and found a somber-faced klatch of professors around the oaken conference table. All looked more like mourners at a wake. The proceeding, led by Dr. Cynthia Qualls-Keach, had all the ambience of a necktie party.

Qualls-Keach was best known as founder and director of the Womyn's Law Project. The respected feminist sociologist and lawyer had made a name for herself and the Law Project twenty years ago by successfully arguing before the Supreme Court for US reparations to descendants of the victims of the Salem witchcraft trials in the seventeenth century, using Mormon genealogical records to identify beneficiaries. She had cleverly defused a potential scandal over her own entitlement as a descendant by turning over her portion to AIDS Awareness/Safe Sex programs in the public schools.

Stillman recalled one other salient characteristic. In all of his years at the university, she had never once spoken to him, not even to return a greeting. But now she was making an exception.

"Good morning, Doctor Stillman," said Qualls-Keach, indicating that he should take the empty seat at the opposite end of the long table. "Before we get started with the matter at hand, I'd like to ask you a question just out of . . . curiosity."

"Certainly," said Stillman, moving to his seat.

Not one head turned, not one pair of eyes looked his way, as he slid into the chair. Among them he noticed Julian Wickner and a few other of his fans. All dozen and a half faces were trained either on the tall, strapping middle-aged woman standing at the far end of the board, or on a single sheet of paper on the table before each of them. There was one at Stillman's place too.

It was headed "The matter of the separation from The University of Dr. Richard Hanley Stillman." Below that was the time —"8:00 to 8:45 A.M." After all, there were classes to teach and so forth. The rest of the sheet contained fill-in-the-blank lines under the heading "Causes for Dismissal." Stillman wondered why there shouldn't be a similar list headed "Reasons for Retention." In the free marketplace of ideas, this smelled like a rotten cantaloupe.

"It has come to our attention," said Qualls-Keach, "that you allegedly have told more than one person about a desire to change your name."

Stillman felt as if half his brain had been anesthetized. He was drawing a blank.

"Change my name?" he said dully.

"Yes, that's what I said," said Qualls-Keach, as if this were ninth-grade health class. "Perhaps I can refresh your memory. Do you recall ever saying you wanted to change your name from 'Stillman' to 'Stillperson'?"

There was an ugly silence. Despite himself, Stillman began to redden. "Oh, sure," he said lightly, hoping to break the tension. "I used to say something like that on occasion. Just a dumb joke. You know."

The tension didn't break. Three dozen eyes didn't blink. Stillman could feel his stock plummeting by the second.

"Can you explain the point of the . . . joke . . . for us, Doctor Stillman?" asked Qualls-Keach with a granite expression.

"Uh—" He faltered, feeling as if he'd been caught parking in a handicapped spot. "No. I guess you would've had to be there."

He became aware of several professors exchanging rolling-eyeball glances with one another.

"I see," said Qualls-Keach without expression. "All right. Now for the matter at hand. Doctor Wickner, will you give your report."

"Colleagues," Julian Wickner said gravely, "no report is really necessary, as such. Not only has Doctor Stillman admitted to the unauthorized use of university facilities in promotion of a reactionary, fundamentalist cause—a *Bible* translation scheme—but I have been gathering evidence as well that he was also involved with the late Doctor Schliesser et al. in other crimes against women, including but not limited to a fundamentalist indoctrination and forced pregnancy center. Depending upon your good pleasure, I intend to refer this evidence to the sheriff and prosecutor for further investigation and potential criminal prosecution."

An unpleasant murmur began percolating among the assemblage at the long table. Was it suddenly colder in here?

"Yes, Doctor Honeycutt," said Qualls-Keach, recognizing a raised hand at the middle of the table.

Dr. Randolph Honeycutt was a melodramatic, flamboyant thespian with a riot of reddish blond hair and a bow tie. He also was, appropriately, chair of the Performing Arts Department and a supporter of various political causes, all of them chic.

"Since we are here," said Honeycutt, "I would be interested in knowing the answers to a couple of other things. (A) Is it true that Doctor Stillman is a confirmed monogamist? And (B) has there been any investigation into these allegations we hear about Doctor Stillman's sexual harassment of female graduate students?"

Qualls-Keach turned back to him. "Would you care to respond, Doctor Stillman?"

He shook his head and prayed silently as the murmur volume built again.

"Then let me attempt to address those points, if I may," Wickner interjected. "I do not believe Doctor Stillman would challenge your description of him on that first point. Unfortunately, he is not the only one. His own division head, Doctor Hurley-McBride, is also a confirmed monogamist. It's an unpleasant fact of life that these things still exist in an imperfect world. In Doctor

Hurley-McBride's case, this problem may resolve itself in a little while as we negotiate a severance arrangement.

"Insofar as Doctor Stillman is concerned, it is my opinion that we already have sufficient evidence at this point to warrant suspending him from the university at once, pending formal dismissal for cause. Some of these other matters that you allude to—I would suggest that you simply bring them to me, and I will include them among the other matters for referral to the authorities for criminal prosecution."

"Is that acceptable to everybody?" asked Qualls-Keach.

"So move," said Dr. Honeycutt.

"Second?" prompted Qualls-Keach.

"Second," two or three more voices said in unison.

"All in favor, 'Aye.'"

The chorus was resoundingly in the affirmative.

"All opposed, 'Nay.'"

Deafening silence. And it wasn't even 8:30 yet. No one would be late for his or her duties.

"Doctor Stillman," Qualls-Keach announced, "you are hereby suspended from the university indefinitely, in contemplation of ultimate severance. Do you understand the action being brought in your regard?"

"All too well."

"Do you have anything further to say in the matter?"

"Only one thing. May God forgive you."

Then he began working his way toward the door before someone decided to start throwing chairs.

★ ★ ★

McBride and Salerno sat in the horse-blanket chairs in the Imperial Crown honeymoon suite and commiserated with each other over their respective conditions of unemployment. Salerno sipped black coffee, and McBride nursed cream soda on the rocks.

"So," said McBride with a thin smile, "welcome to civilian life."

Whenever McBride was tempted to feel discouraged, he remembered back not that many days ago when he had sat behind the wheel of a gray Capricorn with a shattered windshield and two blowouts and realized the size of the mountain he had to climb. At least now he was into the ascent. He had precious little to show for it yet but some hope—and that wasn't so bad. Sometimes you have to be all the way down to appreciate up.

It seemed that Salerno, however, was still bottoming out.

"It was a pretty . . . empty feeling, handing over my badge."

"At least you're not behind bars, which slugging Mendez could have bought you. Assaulting an officer and then obstruction of justice would be a logical place to start."

"It could still happen. They might save that for after the departmental hearing, but I don't really think so."

"Why do you say that?"

"Right now, I think they already have me where they want me. They probably want me to sweat the possibility of charges so maybe I'd keep my big mouth shut. In their eyes it gives them a better handle on me—greater leverage."

"Yeah," McBride mused. "If they prosecuted you and you didn't cop a plea, there could be all kinds of embarrassing stuff coming out about castles and abductions and secret societies. Except for one thing."

"What's that?"

"Theoretically, they could accomplish the same thing preferring charges against you, if they really believed you'd cop. Their leverage in this case would be the carrot of dropping the charges against you. I think the prosecutor would tend to go along with that."

Salerno shook his head. "No, I think they'd see that as too risky from the standpoint of running my mouth. Keeping this under wraps has to be their top priority. Besides, Neal, you're supposed to be helping me see the bright side of things."

"Sorry. I believe in hoping for the best and planning for the worst. Anyway, have you decided how high a price you're willing to pay to continue exercising your vocal cords?"

Before Salerno could answer, the phone rang. McBride jumped, expecting Stillman on the other end. He was.

"I wonder if the Rhema Institute has any openings," said Stillman.

"Oh?" said McBride with a sense of foreboding.

"I've been suspended from the university preparatory to discharge."

"Welcome to the club," said McBride, getting Stillman's picture to appear on the portable scrambler screen. "I promise not to say I told you so."

"What happened?" asked Salerno.

The night before, McBride already had given Stillman the basic story of Judith's abduction, their aborted surveillance attempt at Chateau Fahlgren, the fisticuffs that led to Salerno's suspension, and his own creative getaway. Now it was Stillman's turn to give an account.

"It was your basic kangaroo court," he told them. "Julian Wickner, of course, pretty much led the charge. Some of my friends, such as Cynthia Qualls-Keach and Randolph Honeycutt, fired off all kinds of trumped-up stuff, and there was a unanimous vote of the Senior Faculty Committee to suspend me preparatory to termination.

"Obviously, Wickner had had all this waiting on tap and decided to go for it when we proceeded with the translation project. Obvious, too, is the fact that he—or Quang—must have been monitoring ALEX in some fashion, which lends credence to the notion that the crash was engineered by the same characters."

McBride pursed his lips. "I'd certainly like to hear what Wickner, Quang, and Kay know about this Ashtoreth/Molech business."

"Wouldn't you, though?" agreed Salerno.

Stillman signed heavily. "Even though I was half-expecting this, it still hurts to think that there's not a single person on this faculty I could call a friend."

"Well," observed McBride, "aren't we a happy lot—an ex-judge, an ex-cop, and now an ex-prof. How about Aaron and Jonesy? What are they up to?"

"Ex-Bible translators?" Salerno suggested.

"They're still seeing what can be salvaged from the project, but it's a real mess." Stillman rubbed his chin. "They've been talking about returning to Chicago while they sort this out. Obviously, I'm not going to have further access to university computers, and I still don't know if ALEX can be brought back up, even on the same system."

"Aaron and Jonesy would probably be wise to clear out," McBride said. "If you think things are grim now, you haven't seen anything yet."

Stillman blinked. "What do you mean?"

"So much for gathering good, hard evidence to present to the authorities. Until the events of yesterday, I was reasonably hopeful of getting Vince enough information to obtain a search warrant for Chateau Fahlgren. Now we've undoubtedly blown our insider's cover—and Vince is out the door."

"And Moira," Stillman lamented. "They said she called in sick today, but there's no answer on Hell Avenue. Do you think they're holding her at the castle?"

"No question about it," said Salerno. "They're not stupid. They have to know how we managed to tail them with Judith—that Moira tipped us. She could be in trouble, Rick."

"Won't her department get concerned," asked McBride, "when she keeps missing classes?"

"No, not with Wickner and the senior faculty calling shots. Just like I'm sure she didn't actually call in sick today."

"Well—" McBride scowled "—it looks like Plan B is all that's left."

"'Plan B?'" Stillman looked baffled.

"Yeah, you remember," said Salerno. "'Hi, I'm from the gas company. Just checking to see if your castle leaks.'"

"A commando action?" asked Stillman. "I'll volunteer. It's my fault Moira's in there. I should have stopped her."

McBride raised a hand. "If you're looking for whipping boys, how about me? I've got a wife and two kids in there, and I allowed Judith to be used for bait."

"Whipping boys we can do without," said Salerno. "Volunteers we can use. I still have friends in law enforcement. If we can just get inside the castle, I think we can arrange some backup—off the books. It would be pretty much a one-shot deal, but that's life. The biggest trick would be getting inside without a warrant."

"But not impossible." McBride's eyes were twinkling.

Stillman instantly picked up the nuance. "What are you driving at? You have something up your sleeve?"

"Maybe. Vince hasn't heard about this yet, either." He punched some buttons on his portable console and got some null-video white noise. "Listen to this. I called my number at home for messages and got this—I've already erased the original, just in case."

The next sound was clearly a synthesized voice—and yet not that of a total stranger.

"Hi, this is Peter," the voice asserted somewhat mechanically. "I don't even know if this will work, but maybe you can hear me. Neal, I'm here at Chateau Fahlgren with Angie and Carlotta and Marianne King. We're all being absorbed into this Quang system called 'OUIJA.' It's some kind of crazy experiment in artificial intelligence. They're all excited about some great breakthrough that involves 'higher powers' and human sacrifice.

"I swear I'm not making this up. You've got to stop them, Neal. Somebody has to do something. Carlotta and I are holding out pretty well with a little help from above, but Angie is really absorbed in this thing. Whatever these people plan to do is going to happen pretty soon. I'll try to get back to you with more information. You might try to communicate with me by voice modem. OUIJA's external number is two-seven-three-five-six-six-six. Thanks. 'Bye."

McBride felt his heart racing all over again.

Salerno looked astonished.

Stillman perked up. "He didn't mention Moira and Judith. How old is this?"

"Hold on. There's more. This one was dated day before yesterday, the twenty-seventh."

"There's another one?" Stillman asked.

McBride reached for the console. "Yes. A brand new one—this morning."

"Play it, Sam," said Salerno.

In another moment the same null-video white noise and the familiar synthesized voice was heard again, but with better clarity.

"Neal. This is Peter again. Can you hear me? I need to know. We may be running out of time. If they ever figure out what

I'm up to, I could be in big trouble. Marianne says Mother is here. She and Moira Stone were brought here yesterday. If I don't hear from you today, I'm going to have to do something—maybe call nine-one-one. I'm afraid that could backfire, but I've go to do something.

"I've also learned about a Halloween ball they're planning here. I guess that's where they plan to have a sacrifice and call on their higher powers. I know this all sounds crazy, but believe me, Neal, they're capable of anything. Somebody is going to die if we don't do something. Please contact me. You can try voice modem. OUIJA's external number is two-seven-three-five-six-six-six. Please."

"What are we waiting for?" said Stillman. "Let's do it."

"You know how?" asked McBride.

Stillman grinned. "Sure thing."

Salerno had another thought. "I wouldn't do it from here. We don't know that OUIJA doesn't have call-tracing capability on incoming. The fact that Peter can get out undetected may be just a fluke."

"No sweat," said Stillman. "I'll record it here at my end and transmit it from a pay phone."

"One other possibility," said Salerno. "Could this be a trick?"

"Anything's possible," said McBride. "It's not Peter's actual voice. I happen to think it's the real thing, but who's to say? We'll just be very careful what we say."

Stillman, who had been working at something below screen level, looked up. "Do you know what you want to say?"

"I think so," said McBride.

"I'll give you a countdown—five-four-three-two-one, re-cording."

McBride cleared his throat quickly.

"Peter. This is Neal. I understand your situation and fully appreciate the urgency involved. Whatever you do, please do not call the police. That probably would backfire. We'll take care of that from our end. Just relax and sit tight. It will be just like Turkeyfoot Canyon. Try to learn everything you can about the security system there. Just remember old Turkeyfoot. See you real soon. Oh, and see if you can smuggle out an invitation to the ball. We'll send you a separate message with a data line number. Good-bye."

"Got it." Stillman touched something. "I'll get it to Peter as soon as we hang up."

"Turkeyfoot Canyon?" Salerno gave McBride a funny look.

McBride smiled. "Peter will know exactly what it means. Two years ago we were vacationing in Montana at a place called Turkeyfoot Ridge. Peter went rappelling in the canyon while Judith and I were trail riding. His line came loose from its anchor, and he almost plunged to his death. He was, however, able to hang onto the face of the rock and yell his head off, which we eventually heard on our return loop. When I located the problem, I was able to drop another line beside his and rappel right down to where he was. Then I just took him down to the bottom piggyback. Since then, we've been . . . closer."

"So," said Stillman, "'Turkeyfoot' kind of means emergency rescue mission."

"Yeah. As in 'going into the jaws of hell after you.'"

"Almost literally," observed Salerno.

McBride added, "It also means to hang on real tight. I just hope I can pull it off one more time. This time, though, I'm not real sure where the bottom is."

"What about the invitation to the ball?" asked Stillman.

"Just a longshot. Peter's pretty clever. If he can figure out how to talk to us through that . . . Frankenstein contraption, he just might be able to hook us a copy of the right boilerplate to get in the front door."

"Are you thinking of playing party crasher?" asked Salerno.

"You guys catch on fast. Of course, anybody with a better idea is welcome to offer it up right now."

There was a moment of silence as stray ideas and thoughts and fears chased their tails.

Stillman broke the tension at last. "We'll need some costumes."

"Oh, that'll be great," said Salerno. "Can I go as an armored personnel carrier?"

"No," said McBride, "but this will be the time to lean on your law-enforcement friends for some one-shot backup. Think you can arrange that?"

"Yes, sir. I'll get right on it. At least we know what the place looks like now."

"I wonder . . . " McBride's voice trailed off.

"Wonder what?" asked Stillman.

"Do you suppose Ashtoreth and Molech are the 'higher powers' Peter keeps referring to?"

Nobody hazarded a guess on that one.

30

The lady from Hell Avenue shivered as she was led into the ornate chamber with its vaulted ceiling and glimmering fireplace. Her knees were unsubstantial, her hands felt like something out of a meat locker, and her shivers threatened to turn into shakes.

As much as Moira Stone hated this kind of reaction, it was inescapable. The burly attendant named Brandon, who had escorted her here, had handled her roughly once already. She didn't want any repeat of that business.

Seated on a brocade couch before the fire was Julian Wickner, frowning coldly. Jared Quang sat nearby in a wingback, fiddling with some laptop device. Piped in from somewhere came the subdued bedlam of "Night on Bald Mountain." Even the flames in the fireplace seemed more like an orange arctic aurora.

"So," Wickner pronounced icily as Moira stopped in front of him and shook Brandon's frigid fingers off her elbow. The statement seemed to reverberate.

Such a word—"so." It was just a syllable, and one that meant very little when followed by other words. But when it was left alone, to hang in the air, it implied everything and nothing.

Like an abstract painting, it conveyed whatever the hearer chose to find in it.

At this moment, Moira was finding the crack of a gavel, the slap of a backhand, the pronouncement of sentence, the slam of a dungeon door. She began to wish for the silence to be broken, for some gentler reality of other words to dispel her own cruel imaginings.

At last, Wickner looked her full in the face and spoke. "Shall I go through the tedious exercise of trying to trip you up with some trick question, or will you spare us both the trouble and make a clean breast of it?"

Moira wished she could think of something to say, but there was nothing.

"Shall I take your silence as a confession?" His voice rose a bit.

"To what?" She spoke a bit sharply herself.

"To what?" Wickner repeated incredulously, his face showing a weariness. "I had hoped you would spare us this tedium, but perhaps I gave you too much credit. Do you expect us to believe that Lieutenant Salerno and Judge McBride just happened to be driving by and spotted you and Kelsey transporting Judith here?"

"Maybe they had the hospice staked out," Moira said flatly. "McBride is Judith's husband, you know."

"So then, your position is denial on the basis of coincidence. Is that right?"

Moira said nothing.

"Let's have some audio, Jared," said Wickner, glancing over at Quang.

Quang hit a button on the laptop.

"Gotta get my messages," she heard herself say, apparently over a carphone.

There followed a succession of tones, which triggered a regular beeping. After another moment, the beeping stopped and was replaced by a steady tone. It also triggered a clear and indicting recollection in Moira's brain.

"Our friend here," said Quang, switching off the recording, "was calling eight-seven-four-nine-nine-five-one, which turns out to be a surveillance monitor for the Franklin County Sheriff's Department. This particular monitor is assigned to car seventy-seven, operated by Lieutenant Vincent Salerno."

"There you have it, my dear." Wickner grinned at a glass of amber fluid that had appeared in his hand. "Hoisted on your own sweet little petard."

Moira began to think she would prefer to take whatever they planned to hang on her, rather than submit to a marathon of Wickner's inebriated clevernesses, as appeared about to occur.

"Sit down, sister," he said throatily, the smile fading. "I have a theory, and I would like you to sit down and hear me out."

Moira continued standing as a matter of principle, though her knees would take a long time forgiving her. Wickner chose to ignore her unresponsiveness.

"My theory," he said, swirling the contents of the glass as close to the rim as he could without spilling over, "is that you're not the Benedictress Arnold—ha ha!—that you might appear to be."

"What am I, Julian?"

"I've always had the highest regard for you, Moira, in every sense of the word. My theory is that you are playing along with these . . . Boy Scouts . . . as a way of avoiding legal difficulties— and perhaps securing your position with Chi Xi Vau."

"Interesting theory," Moira noted.

"You like it so far?"

"How would that 'secure my position,' assuming there was one I wanted?"

"In other words," said Wickner, still swirling away, "you might lead Stillman, for example, to believe that you still . . . cared for him, as a way to extract vital information that might be useful to us."

"Oh. Then I'm a double agent?"

"Exactly," he said gleefully, letting the contents of his glass settle. "With quite satisfactory results, I might add, even now."

Now Moira was getting suspicious. "What do you mean?"

"Well, that little farce with the caravan through Millersfield and Jefferson Woods had a happy ending. Our law enforcement friends were doing their own monitoring, and they caught Lieutenant Salerno in the very act. He's now ex-Lieutenant Salerno."

He laughed again, stopping only to drain the glass. As he did so, he watched Moira's expression.

"How about McBride?" she asked.

"Wilson McBride," said Wickner, frowning. "That thief. He got away by stealing a sheriff's cruiser. And he calls himself a judge."

Moira grinned, at risk of irritating Wickner all the more.

He poured himself another drink. "But that's precisely where you come in—as a double agent. That's exactly the kind of invaluable information you can provide. You find out where your pal the judge is holed up, and you tell us. You help solve a crime—and you retain your freedom. Very simple."

"Right," said Moira brightly, looking around. "OK. I guess that means I'll be popping off. I'll call you when I find out something, Julian."

Before she even turned fully around, Moira sensed Brandon's dark shadow looming toward her. She froze.

"Nice try, sweetheart," Wickner said, grinning. "But I'm afraid it's not quite that simple."

"Don't call me sweetheart," Moira said, wanting to smack him.

"OK, Moira. You want to hear the deal?"

She nodded tersely. This was becoming quite wearisome.

"You sit right here by Quang and me and his machine while I ask you a few who, what, when, where, and whys, phone numbers, and addresses. And then we'll talk about the terms of your freedom and double agency and so forth."

"You mean ratting on people—like Rick and McBride," Moira said, her voice rising.

Wickner's eyes narrowed. "It doesn't matter so much to me what you choose to call it—"

"I call it detestable," she spat. "And just what do you plan to do with such information? Kidnap some more people? Perform some more mind control experiments? Have you been watching too many horror videos, Julian?"

"Don't take that tone with me, Moira," he warned. "We're about to bring the power of a higher intelligence to all humankind. You'll see."

"I'm going to take more than that with you, Julian Wickner," she shouted, snatching the laptop from a very surprised Jared Quang. In three swift steps she crossed to the fireplace and flung the machine into the flames.

338

"Why do people insist on doing that?" Wickner asked rhetorically.

Quang jumped to his feet and grabbed a poker to rescue the
device from the fire.

"The last person who did such a thing in this room paid a
steep price," said Wickner, rising to his feet and fixing Moira with
a murderous gaze. "You, my dear, are about to discover the full
price of foolishness."

Their eyes connected in an interlock of rage and fear. Moira
believed it was the most dangerous expression she had ever seen in
a man's eyes.

"Take her away, Brandon," Wickner said, straightening
himself. "You know what to do."

★ ★ ★

"Good morning, Mother," Angie said.

Judith blinked awake at the sound of a familiar voice. And
then a well-known figure moved into her line of sight.

"Angie," Judith said dully.

Two other pairs of hands helped her from bed into her
wheelchair. She now realized that something was wrong with her
biochemically. It was as if they had withdrawn her antidepressant
medication and replaced it with sedatives. She sensed the tightening grip of a new round of anxieties but felt too wrung out even to
voice a complaint. There had been a time when she resisted the
medication; now she lived for it.

"I want you to meet someone," said Angie, pivoting Judith's
wheelchair toward the door and rolling out into the hall. "You'll
like it here, Mother." Angie backed her through a pair of hospital-
style crash doors into another area.

"Pre-Life Science" said the sign at the entrance.

"What is this?"

"Jeremy thought you'd like to see the Little Ones. And I
thought you'd like to see Peter."

"Peter," Judith repeated, as if pronouncing the name of an
elusive memory.

They stopped outside a green-draped cubicle. Angie drew
aside a track curtain to reveal the recumbent form of an apparently

unconscious young man wearing a cervical collar and various attached restraints. The collar appeared to contain a type of electrical hookup to some bedside high-tech equipment of mysterious design.

"Is he—is he sick?" Judith asked softly.

"No, Mother," Angie said with a little laugh. "Far from it. He's integrated with OUIJA now. And that means he's better than well—he's experiencing meta-consciousness."

"What?"

"Don't worry. Jeremy will explain everything to you very soon."

Angie pushed Judith farther down the hall and through more crash doors. And then they were perambulating an area consisting of rows and rows of objects like bassinets with bubble-tops and a profusion of wires and hoses. "Biota Recycling" was the sign here.

Ella and Kelsey were there too. Maxie seemed to be kicking again.

Kinsey popped open one unit and began pulling on a rubber glove.

"What is she doing?" Judith asked with some apprehension.

"Just watch."

Then Kinsey was lifting the lid and reaching into the tank.

"Hail, Ashtoreth! Hail, Asmedai!" intoned Angie.

"Hail, Anath! Hail, Molech!" chanted Ella.

Out of the tank came a fetal child, gray and wrinkly, trailing several kinds of umbilici. Kinsey held it up proudly.

Ella continued reciting. "What formerly was disdained by hypocritical moralists as a selfish act on the mother's part is now ennobled. She is no longer ridding herself of an unwanted child but making a humanitarian contribution for the benefit of her fellow beings—and, in fact, a sacred offering. For to the woman in feminist spirituality, our craft has an even more fundamental meaning. It is a womyn's religion, a religion of the earth, vilified by patriarchal Christianity, and now, finally reclaimed."

Angie added, "And in the end for us, a sacrifice pleasing to the gods. May the Goddess pour out her power upon us. May her curse be poured out upon those who are opposing us."

Judith at first thought the child was deceased, until she noticed finger and hand movement. And then the head twisted about on its short neck. Its eyes were open and staring right through her.

All eyes, in fact, were upon her.

"All is one," said Angie.

"All is one," said Ella.

"All is one," said Kelsey.

All those eyes became a boring into her soul, a breaching of all of her desperate defenses. As the room spun about her, Judith felt barriers in her heart and mind crashing together, locked doors bursting asunder. Her final panicked thought was that she might pass out.

★ ★ ★

The hands on her arms were like bands of steel.

Moira, struggling and crying, had never known fear of this proportion. Not to mention the utter humiliation of being practically stripped before a half dozen pairs of eyes and being dragged kicking and screaming to what appeared to be an operating table. And now, she was virtually out of control of her body and her emotions.

Dear God, what were they going to do to her? Turn her into a biochemical zombie and feed her to this artificial intelligence? Erase all of her personal memories, like Ella? Something even more diabolical?

"Prepare subject for integration," Jeremy Kay intoned evenly, disregarding her cries.

Moira watched in horror as a robot arm descended over her, tipped with a dripping hypodermic needle. Now her greatest fear was for her own sanity. Her last coherent thought was that it would serve them right if she flipped out and ruined their experiment. And then she began screaming anew.

"God, have mercy!"

"Which god?" Kay spat.

And then it came to her, verbatim, the verse that Rick had insisted she memorize. "And it shall be, that everyone who calls on the name of the Lord shall be saved."

And so she called out, "Jesus Christ!"

Abruptly the robot arm halted, inches away.

Kay swore fiercely. "Tape her!" he snapped.

Someone gagged her tightly. Moira closed her eyes and braced for the needle stick. There. She barely felt it. Then there was a slight searing. What was happening? She refused to open her eyes. Everything was becoming confused. It was almost as if she were praying, though she didn't think she knew how. And then she was reminded of someone who loved her—Rick. Would he say, "I told you so"? She didn't think he would. Why had she thrown his love into the dirt and walked on it? For some reason, for the first time, it grieved her. Julian was right—she had been foolish, but not in the way he had meant. And so heartless.

But then another thought struck her from out of a twilight nowhere. Wasn't that what she had done with God? What a mess she had made of things!

Now she was incapable of opening her eyes if she tried. All of her strongholds were crumbling. Oblivion loomed.

Before she went under, Moira became aware of a still, small voice echoing, "Everyone who calls on the name of the Lord shall be saved."

Could that be true, even for the likes of Moira Stone?

★ ★ ★

"Next!" Kay cried, wiping the blood from his gloved hands onto his surgical apron.

Dr. Greer and Kelsey Kinsey always did the actual implantation of the Quang integrator, but they were allowing him an increasing role. Generally, Kay made the initial incision and then, when the bone-drilling and implantation were complete, he closed up. Initially, he had merely assisted with the final procedure, but over time he had become proficient enough at suturing to do it himself.

His goal was to master the bone-drill, too, so that he and Quang eventually could do these procedures unassisted. This would become particularly useful by the time Quang perfected the more permanent, wireless integrator and they were doing these implantations on a volume basis. With OUIJA's inimitable assistance, Quang already had become an adept self-taught cyberanesthesiologist.

As Greer and Kinsey wheeled out the pallid, intubated form of Moira Stone, an attendant ushered in one blinking, confused Judith Hurley-McBride in a wheelchair.

Kay set down his cutters. "Greetings, Doctor Hurley-McBride."

"Do—do I know you?" Judith looked up uncertainly.

"Jeremy Kay," he said benignly.

Something definitely connected in Judith's jumbled store of memories. She didn't know quite what it was—but she knew that it was nothing good. In fact, she was experiencing an inexplicable rush of panic. Why was she put in mind of auditorium lights and ambulances? Maxie began kicking.

"Something wrong?" Kay inquired.

"My baby," she said, as if in explanation.

"Let's get something straight," Kay said sternly. "You have no baby. You are not even pregnant."

His face loomed threateningly over her as two strong pairs of hands guided her onto the padded table. A chill seized her bones. Now she was certain that she knew this face, this voice, but she could not quite put the pieces together. Who was he, and why was he saying these terrible things? What were they planning to do to her? She began to weep, as she tended to do so easily these days.

"Don't . . . hurt my baby," she pleaded.

Kay laughed derisively. "This *baby* is a creature of your sick imagination only."

"No!"

Kay ignored her. "Your mind is impaired. Prepare to be repaired."

Then he began laughing all over again.

That laughter, that voice—random pieces were beginning to fit together in the recesses of her memory. The first image that came to her was that of a younger man with a moustache, wispy almost like a first growth, and large, brown, doe eyes that seemed capable of sensitivity. Maxie was kicking again. She had no idea why she associated this other strange man with Kay, but something was telling her that great danger lurked here.

"Prepare subject for integration," Kay directed.

Judith gasped involuntarily as various restraints tightened about her limbs. The blonde woman with red-rimmed glasses named Kelsey was instructing her to hold her tongue if she did not want to be gagged. Looking up past this woman, she saw a robot arm slowly descending, tipped with a hypodermic needle, oozing some vile secretion.

She screamed anyway.

Roughly, the blonde woman began stifling her cries with gauze.

The arm resumed its descent. And then she remembered. She remembered the dreams, recurrent nightmares in which her baby . . . terminated. She remembered Gunnison Auditorium, the place where Angie had demonstrated channeling with this Jeremy Kay and where Kay had led her hypnotically back to her own birth—and into the land of madness. And she remembered another time, long suppressed, in a pre-term clinic when she had presented herself and her baby for . . . the unspeakable.

She remembered. Dear God, the horror of it all . . . Could there ever be forgiveness?

Yes, came the whisper of a suggestion from somewhere.

And then the arm was upon her, delivering its poison sting.

31

Superstition was rising in the east as Neal McBride made his way on foot at dusk down Lower Siddhartha Avenue. He looked occasionally over his shoulder and from time to time patted the police .38 riding snugly in his shoulder clip.

Up and down the Avenue, between Odin Circle and Kali Street, gargoyles glowered in the twilight world of cold stone and deepening shadow. Structures sank gable by gable, cornice by cornice, silently, almost imperceptibly, into the gathering gloom, like drowning men in the sea. To the east, a pale silver moon emerged gradually from fading twilight, ascendant between Leo and Libra.

And then Virgo herself began to assume astral shape as Spica and thirty-eight winking sisters assembled her sequin-robed form: First Lady of the Zodiac, Sister to the Queen of the Underworld, Virgin Mother. She whom the Hindus called Kauni, the Maiden;

whom the Persians called Khosha, Ear of Wheat; whom the Hebrews knew as Bethulah, Abundant Harvest; to the Egyptians, Isis, Goddess of Fertility; to the Babylonians, Ishtar, Goddess of Love.

Behind windows on the Avenue, minor constellations of candles guttered and leaped about, casting hideous silhouettes of strangers' faces and windowshade cords into the neon storefront jumble. A carnival spirit animated a pulsing tide of radical bikers, rowdy lesbians, furtive antique dealers, upscale pushers, boozy yuppies, pseudointellectual iron workers, and other Siddhartha Avenue regulars. The night air was thick with unspoken promises and unimagined intrigue.

And then came the clarion call of an enthusiastic female voice: "Free needles! Come'n get 'em!"

The cheerful soprano belonged to a well-scrubbed young woman who could have been an Ohio State University freshperson but was actually a social worker from the Choice Task Force. Several pairs of hands fumbled for the paraphernalia kits, anxious to dispense with the preliminaries and get directly about their business. No idle talk; just spikes, veins, and junk, in that order, with trembling fingers.

Did this always go on in broad daylight? McBride wondered if he was just slow on the uptake and if he had lived too long in wood-paneled studies lined with lawbooks. Or were things, in fact, going from bad to worse before his very eyes? There had always been a few cities—Amsterdam, Munich, San Francisco—where anything went, but Columbus, Ohio?

And now what was that furtive struggling he spied in the alley he was passing?

McBride shivered and turned up his collar against the frigid fingers of October that were disheveling his hair. He was making his way back from the Maglev station to Kevorkian Court and the former Reformed Temple of Isis. To cover all bets, he had paid for another night at the Imperial Crown, armed himself with a pistol, and hopped on public transit. He hoped the others were equally cautious. He was well aware that it could only be a matter of time before the enemy discovered the Temple lair.

That was why he and Salerno and Overholtzer were coming to the Avenue armed. And that was why Overholtzer and a friend named Carney were being posted at the second-floor window of a building across the street.

Just two blocks from Kevorkian Court, McBride was daydreaming, taking encouragement from a new report about Steve Leadingham's improving condition. He blinked as a wind gust touched his face, and the next moment he was taking an involuntary half-step backward from oblivion. With the resounding impact on the pavement inches before McBride, time itself seemed to stop.

Then he saw, staring up at him from the fractured sidewalk, an angry demon face, contorted in wrath and frozen in malice. Down the middle, between the piercing eyes and neatly bisecting the nose, was a clean vertical crack. Abruptly, the two halves fell apart like a cut apple. It had been a gargoyle from a fallen chunk of cornice.

McBride shook his head to clear his jumbled mind. A murmuring crowd had begun to gather. It was then that he realized that there was blood on his face, the result of some errant shard's creasing his forehead.

"Take it easy, fella," someone was saying.

And then McBride felt very foolish. He realized he was standing there with his gun drawn. He put it back to bed and walked quickly away from the spectacle. If he wasn't very careful tonight, he might just shoot somebody.

★ ★ ★

McBride was most surprised to discover that Aaron and Jonesy, far from packing it in and flying back to Chicago, were still at the Temple, acting every bit as if they were still working on a major project. They and Salerno and Stillman were gathered around the conference room table, talking and drinking coffee. Someone had set a cream soda at the head.

In response to all of the funny looks, he explained how a close encounter with a gargoyle had resulted in the plastic bandage strip on his forehead. Then he opened up Operation Turkeyfoot by offering Jones and Fitzgerald their walking papers.

"Jonesy, we truly appreciate all that you and Aaron and the Rhema Institute have done, but I am not asking you to stick around for this operation tomorrow. We're talking pretty rough stuff."

"That's why you need us all the more," said Jones. "You need a secret weapon. Besides, it looks to me like you can't afford to be turning down Golden Gloves help on your team."

"Yes, Your Honor," said Fitzgerald. "You chaps had best count us in, if you know what's good for you."

McBride smiled. "We're not talking a few punches and jabs here, Jonesy. We're talking the possibility of real casualties."

Jones shrugged. "I made up my mind a long time ago in the spiritual battle not to love my life so as to shrink from death."

"To be absent from the body is to be at home with the Lord," Fitzgerald said, "which is much to be preferred."

"Also," said Jones, "you're going to need a couple of warriors who know something about pulling down strongholds by prayer. What's that verse, Aaron?"

"'For the weapons of our warfare,'" quoted Fitzgerald, "'are not of the flesh, but divinely powerful for the destruction of fortresses.'"

McBride suddenly was seeing a mental image of a haunted castle. "Chateau Fahlgren."

"Precisely," said Fitzgerald.

"Yeah," said Salerno. "I vote we count these gentlemen in."

McBride nodded. They were big boys, and they knew the risks. Besides, something told him he really could use their help.

"Rick," he said next, "have we heard from Peter?"

"Yes, sir. And wait till you hear this. Oh—I forgot—there was another message first."

"Hey, Crimefighter!" said a creaky voice on null-video. "This is Steve. Give me a call when you get a chance. The rumors of my brain death are greatly exaggerated. Maybe you can cheer me up with your rubberface routine. G'bye."

McBride smiled. It was great to hear Leadingham's voice again. He was clearly weakened, but the old spark was still there. McBride promised himself to get hold of his old friend as soon as this was all over—one way or the other.

Moments later, Stillman had a second null-video playback going, and they were hearing Peter's synthesized voice once again.

"Neal. This is Peter. Got your message loud and clear. There's nobody I'd rather have with me, going down Turkeyfoot

Canyon. I've made super progress with the security system. But I'm starting to worry about getting myself free from OUIJA. Am I chasing the bear, or is the bear chasing me? Mother and Moira are being integrated into the system now. I'm afraid for them, being unbelievers. I'm especially worried about Mother.

"I think this big event scheduled for midnight tomorrow at the Halloween ball has something to do with raising demons. I think that's what these higher powers are all about. This big-deal breakthrough could be a pretty nasty thing. Luckily, I'm able to access OUIJA system files at will now, and I have made six phony entries in the Samhain Ball guest list. You will find invitations under six phony names in a transmission on the data line. Neal, whatever you do needs to be done before midnight tomorrow. After that . . . I just don't know. Good-bye. Peter."

"I didn't know your son was a believer, Your Honor," said Fitzgerald.

McBride shrugged his shoulders, as if to say neither did he.

"What did he mean about the bear chasing him?" asked Salerno.

"It sounds to me," said Fitzgerald, "a bit like what they call 'ego diffusion.'"

"'Ego diffusion'?" said McBride.

"That's where the person, especially an adolescent, begins to take on the characteristics of some other significant person in his life."

"Even a computer?" McBride asked. "Then he *is* in serious danger being hooked up to that thing?"

"Probably not directly, but I'm only guessing," said Fitzgerald. "As a believer, he should be somewhat immune to most types of mind control and even demonic influence."

"That's a real plus for us—and Operation Turkeyfoot, as you call it," said Jones, "to have a believer in the position that Peter is in."

"The greater worry may be the unhooking." Fitzgerald frowned. "It's only natural that after a prolonged time of having his own mind bundled with an artificial intelligence that Peter would begin to grow accustomed to—even dependent upon—this accelerated functioning. There could be a serious withdrawal reaction, not to mention some physical debilitation if he's been incapacitated for too many days."

McBride thought uneasily of astronauts who returned to earth after prolonged space flights and were unable to walk under their own power, even suffering calcium loss from their bones.

"The good news," said Stillman, "is that I don't believe Peter has been integrated into this thing so long that the effects will be irreversible."

"But the bad news," said McBride, "is that we won't have the luxury of weaning him off the system. Even if we can get to him, it's going to be a matter of yanking a plug in a split second."

"And praying," said Jones.

"OK," said McBride. "Rick, did we, in fact, receive anything on the data line?"

"Yeah, something. I'm not sure just what, yet. Fortunately, even with ALEX down, we still have some computer functions, including data lines and imaging capabilities. Just let me punch this thing up."

Stillman manually entered some keyboard commands, and on the wallscreen appeared a flowing, simulated handwritten text in ornate calligraphy. Its borders were adorned with various astrological, alchemical, and occult symbols that the individuals around the conference room table could hardly begin to decipher.

This particular invitation, directed to a Howard R. Perliss, offered Mr. Perliss the enticement of a "Samhain Gala, an October Holiday to remember, a full-costume Halloween ball extraordinaire" at Chateau Fahlgren, 4460 Lindbergh Road, Jefferson Woods, beginning at 8:00 P.M. October 31st. In chic hyperbole, Mr. Perliss was promised "mind-expanding experiences, electrifying scientific demonstrations, and even celestial visitations from worlds beyond."

There were five other images just like it, but with different invitees named, just waiting to be printed out on good card stock.

"Who's Howard R. Perliss?" asked Salerno.

McBride was laughing now. "Peter's high school gym teacher. Rick, is there a Harry Anders in there?"

"Yeah," said Stillman, looking into a monitor. "There sure is. Is there a pattern here?"

"Anders was Peter's track coach. "There's a pattern there, all right."

"Uh-oh." Stillman was still looking into the monitor.

"What's the matter?" asked Salerno.

"Who's June Arbogast?"

"His Spanish teacher, I believe," said McBride. Then the light went on. "It looks like one of us is going to have to go to the ball in drag."

"No." Stillman laughed. "She's the sixth one. Fortunately, there are only five of us."

"Righto," said Fitzgerald. "That'll be a powerful incentive for all of us not to misplace our invitations."

"Well," Salerno began significantly, "if this is show-and-tell, I've got something too."

"Please share," McBride said.

"It's the stuff that Frank downloaded to me—the crime stats. Rick, if you'd be so kind as to run that file up on the display. You know, if the average person really knew what was going on, I don't think anybody would go out of their house any time of year. You'd think October Holiday was becoming a three-hundred sixty-five-day-a-year affair. There was one report here that I found particularly disturbing. I think Frank may have been putting up a callous front for appearances. Look at this."

An official-looking document appeared on the wallscreen. McBride, recalling Frank Salerno's apparent condescension, was surprised by what it contained. Despite brother Frank's disclaimer, this appeared to be a classified internal report concerning "influences" of certain elements on state and federal government.

The executive summary seemed to be a compilation of various "choice" organizations that had lobbying privileges before the Ohio General Assembly and the US Congress. These were outfits that advocated the right to choose "alternative behaviors" in areas currently deemed illegal. Prominent in this list were the Institute for Pre-Life Science and Chi Xi Vau.

Appended was a smaller report on the activities of one Elizabeth Morningstar, an astrologer and registered lobbyist for those two organizations and a dozen others. McBride was astounded to read how Morningstar had insinuated herself into the counsels of government, including as "spiritual adviser" to Ohio Governor Lillian Kerr and even to President Walker's chief human services adviser, Barbara Tate-Hirsch. Most intriguing—and part of what could have inspired the report—was the fact that Morningstar appeared to have no personal history—no date of birth, no Social Security number, no fingerprints, and no voice-pattern ID.

McBride let out a mute whistle. Life would be easier, he believed, not knowing some things.

"Well," he said at last in the silence. "At least, I can now appreciate a little better your brother's cynicism."

"Let's not let ourselves get discouraged by trusting in horses and chariots," said Jones. "Remember we have weapons that are divinely powerful. Lord, open our eyes that we may see your mountain full of horses and chariots of fire."

"May I ask you a personal question, Judge?" said Jones.

"Anybody who joins me in battle may ask me personal questions."

"Have you ever read the Bible?"

"Some. But it always seemed like it was written to somebody else—like I was on the outside looking in."

"You know what you have to do," said Jones.

"Yeah. I've got to get started on my costume. The ball's tomorrow night."

"No, you know what I mean."

"I know," said McBride. "I'm thinking, Jonesy. I'm thinking."

★ ★ ★

Healed.

When Judith Hurley-McBride next awoke, it was with a sense of assurance that all of the cobwebs had been swept out and the confusion was gone. And she remembered *everything*.

It was a bittersweet sensation, knowing that the broken pieces were back in the right places and being able to think rationally again—but also knowing the full, painful import of the things she had wanted to put out of her mind and forget.

Maxie.

Had she really been obsessed with the belief that she was

pregnant? It was hard to believe that she had been so fully deluded and deceived. And yet, even now there was a pang of regret over her flat belly and empty womb. It was almost as bad as having a . . . termination . . . all over again.

Despair threatened to choke her breathing. Ironically, it had been almost easier for her to be crazy. And now she could not even move. Restraints of some kind kept her immobile in this place like a sensory-deprivation environment. She could not tell whether it was very dark here or she was simply blindfolded. And now panic began to take hold. This was no time to become claustrophobic, she told herself.

Easier said than done. Now she began writhing and pressing against the restraints. She tried to cry out, but there was something blocking her mouth. And then came a surge and a tingle, as if she were receiving the initial rush of a sedative.

Please, no more drugs, she begged silently. Wouldn't it be better just to die? And then she began wishing fervently for her own demise.

Judith was most startled by the firm command of a voice out of nowhere—a strong, familiar male voice.

"Desist, OUIJA! In the name of Christ."

And then this young voice was addressing her.

"Mother?" It was a communication that was more than thought, less than speech.

"Peter?" she responded reflexively, without thinking.

"Yes. And someone else too."

"Who?"

"Marianne King," said a woman. "You might know who I am. My son was Roger Larrabee's victim—Joshua."

Judith was reminded of a certain face with a wispy moustache and brown doe eyes. There were fear and pain in the remembrance. And then she was reminded of her own little one. She knew this woman's pain.

"And I know your pain too," said Marianne King.

"Is there any . . . hope for it?"

"Only one. Would you like to hear about it?"

"Well, yes," Judith said, incredulous that anyone could claim to have a real answer. "Just don't talk to me about religion."

"All right," said Marianne. "I'll talk to you about a relationship with Someone who understands . . . ."

Marianne spoke on—about the Good Shepherd who laid down His life for the flock, the Jewish carpenter who was nailed to a tree and lifted up to draw all people to Himself across the centuries—to this very point in time. One perfect sacrifice for all people, for all time.

Each word fell like rain on parched soil. Judith was past convincing. Now the pump was primed, and she wanted more. She wanted it all, now.

And she said so.

Very quickly and very simply, Marianne laid out the way of surrender and salvation. They prayed. And then they wept together for a long time—one mother's heart to another.

32

October Holiday.

Dia de los Muertos. Samhain. Devil's Night. Halloween. Trick or treat. A day of sacrifice coast-to-coast to unleash the powers and principalities of darkness. A night for haunting.

In Seattle, San Francisco, and New Orleans, bands of intoxicated revelers ransacked and pillaged retail stores and shopping malls, raping people of both sexes and all ages. Erotic spectacles were depicted on elaborate floats to cheering, liquored-up crowds along main thoroughfares.

In Detroit, St. Louis, New York, and Chicago, howling mobs set fire to everything that had not been torched the year before. For added entertainment, occasional bystanders were hogtied and tossed into the flames. Small boys with stolen recorders taped the screams for posterity and late-night parties.

Wichita, for no other apparent reason than a play on its name, hosted a major assemblage of witches, warlocks, and druids, who performed no overt mischief of their own other than offering copious sacrifices of man and beast to invoke the presence of the powers and spirits in all of the other locales.

In Dallas, Pittsburgh, and Buffalo, private gatherings of Christians opposed to the deeds of Devil's Night were disrupted by gangs chanting profanities and blasphemies, who proceeded to defile the altars with acts that would have caused the men of Sodom to blush.

In Baltimore, Los Angeles, Nashville, and a few other places, some who eschewed sterile euthanasia in state-run thanatorium clinics celebrated their final hours with elaborate eulogies before committing public *selbstmord* by sundry means, ranging from lethal ingestion to self-immolation. This, while loved ones videotaped the events and drank themselves into oblivion.

Ohio had its share of revelry and merrymaking as well.

In Cincinnati, exotic dancers from across the river in Newport, Kentucky, led exuberant throngs of young people in various stages of undress—despite the October chill—on a rampage through downtown, smashing windows, overturning cars, and bellowing obscenities over bullhorns. There were also occasional outbursts of "Go, Bengals!"

In Cleveland, a festive parade of pagans culminated in a magic circle on Public Square with ritual incantations and a powerful demonstration of drawing down the moon.

And in Columbus . . . it was a very special October Holiday.

Urged on by a ringing denunciation of white male patriarchists in general and a stinging rebuke of the chauvinist-imperialist-colonialist Christopher Columbus in particular, a swarm of right-thinkers and misandrists focused their wrath upon a huge statue of the explorer near the Statehouse.

"Not only is it a disgrace that this city is named after such a symbol of oppression," shrieked a young woman with a bullhorn, "but this very name is an outrage and an offense. 'Christopher'

354

means 'Christ-bearer.' So, in remembrance of all of the innocent, exploited natives of America and the wretched of the earth every-where—bear this, Christ-bearer!"

With that, dozens of pairs of hands began yanking on the thick orange nylon braid coiled about Columbus's neck far above the crowd. The initial efforts proved to be of little avail. The mighty sculpted white male stayed put, continuing to gaze implacably out over the heads of the Lilliputians below.

A frustrated, unpleasant murmuring arose. It was gradually superseded by a louder, rhythmic incantation and the invocation of an unseen force. Renewed power flowed through the arms and hands attached to the cords.

Almost imperceptibly at first, the giant figure began to wobble upon its footing and then to rock more distinctly to and fro as expectations of success built. The opposing teams of rope-pullers, as in a variant tug-of-war, capitalized on the yawing movement, alternating their efforts to enhance the sway in hopes of reaching the point of no return.

At last, Columbus's center of gravity swung out a centimeter past that very point, and, after a momentous pause, the colossus toppled, smiting the ground with the stupendous impact of mighty oaks felled by lightning.

The celebrants raised a lusty victory cry despite the fact that one of their number, an unidentified young woman, lay crushed beneath one of the now dozen or so fractured pieces of sculpture. The explorer lay disjointedly on his back, the eyes in his severed head continuing to stare heavenward as if the whole affair really were of no moment. After briefly savoring their triumph, the assailants resumed milling about, circling the stone corpse and taking up implements of destruction.

"Yes, Dana," TV reporter Joe Fortunato was telling a live camera while lights blazed upon the fading-twilight scene, "as Governor Kerr had predicted earlier in her term, another hated symbol of male oppression has been erased from the landscape. Perhaps the City Council backers of the movement to rename the city will receive a big boost as a result of this.

"But now, as you can see, Dana, this crowd celebrating October Holiday has received a big boost from what just happened here. With the help of a few sledgehammers, they're making quick work of what's left of Christopher Columbus. Big chunks are being turned into little chunks."

The camera followed as Fortunato turned to accost a passer-by lugging a sledgehammer. "Say, would you mind if I borrowed that for a minute and took a few swings myself? Thanks. Dana, as you can see, I'm getting a once-in-a-lifetime opportunity here to strike a blow for freedom. So, I'm going to try my hand at demolition and see if I can get into the swing of things, so to speak. For Number One News, this is Joe Fortunato, reporting live from the Statehouse lawn."

And with that, stone chips began flying as Mr. Fortunato commenced whaling the remains of Christopher Columbus with abandon.

★ ★ ★

Along Lower Siddhartha Avenue and its tributaries, the sky was black with the smoke of a half dozen blazing structures. One of these flaming buildings was the former Reformed Temple of Isis on Kevorkian Court. But its current tenants, unaware of this conflagration, were off site, anxiously preparing to present their printed invitations for admittance at the guard station of an eighteenth-century-reproduction French castle in Jefferson Woods.

McBride eyed the high-walled estate from just outside the massive iron gate. Chateau Fahlgren seemed incomparably more imposing by night. The first time, it had looked regal and expansive; tonight, it appeared to his heightened imagination as the diabolical capitol of an evil empire.

A gaunt, atavistic guard with heavy-lidded, deep-set eyes checked his invitation and murmured monosyllabically to someone over a portable phone. The only thing this brute lacked was a hunch to make the cliché complete.

The grounds themselves presented no moat, burning fagots, or army of trolls chanting "Yo-he-ho!" But otherwise, the place gave every appearance of being designed to unnerve.

Perhaps it was the way light from the moon and a mercury vapor floodlight collided in the same giant, fractured reflection upon a Versailles-like array of leaded window panes. The effect was a bizarre mosaic that overwhelmed McBride's pupils in the dark and tempted his disoriented imagination to fill in numerous grotesque lines in the pattern.

The chill breeze that set the flag fluttering and snapping and sucked the warmth from his bones had something to do with it, not to mention the weird, possibly alchemical symbols upon the cryptic banner itself. The ancient stones of the chateau walls, chiseled in moonlit high-relief, seemed to suggest the furtive intelligence of a race of builders only nominally human.

He shivered and reminded himself to forget Neal McBride and to practice being Howard Perliss. A mistake such as forgetting one's name at a critical moment could be fatal. Overholtzer and Carney would be working remote backup, but once inside the lions' den, McBride and his commandos would be pretty much on their own. At that point, anybody on the outside could be little more helpful than General Custer's brass band at the Little Bighorn.

At last, he and Salerno were waved through to find a parking spot near the south end of the castle. The second car, with Stillman, Jones, and Fitzgerald, was right behind—three make-believe teachers of geometry, health, and physics masquerading as divine creatures. Their arrival was timed deliberately late into the festivities, when chaos and revelry—including chemically induced stupefaction—should be at its peak, affording maximum cover for some trick or treat of their own.

The Turkeyfoot Five filed into the opulent foyer, five magnificent ersatz archangels in electric, white flowing garments, gleaming bronze faces, and golden eagles' wings.

McBride led the way down the marble-floored corridor. Ahead lay an arched doorway lighted by an enormous crystal chandelier and marked off by velvet ropes on brass couplings and a stylized pointing finger mounted on a sandwich-board placard.

Inside the cavernous grand ballroom, he observed a bizarre, milling throng resembling the cast of a classical Roman orgy, but melded with the phantasmagoria of a bad dream from the Dark Ages and all the sinister mythologies of dark ages past. It was an Underworld motif, complete with the suggestion of a subterranean River Styx flowing through otherworldly mists. Strolling about with cups of mystic potions were men and women from the neck down. Above were the heads of goats, jackals, crocodiles, falcons, cobras, lions, boars, and other beasts. Around any corner one might expect Charon the boatman.

Here and there a head turned momentarily, but in their own way the five angels of light were not completely out of keeping with the unearthly ambience of the occasion.

"Don't put much credence in anything you might see here this evening," Stillman whispered to his fellow cherubim. "Other than the costumes, much of it is doubtless an illusion."

"Holograms?" McBride said.

Both Fitzgerald and Stillman nodded.

He sincerely hoped that statement was true, as he spied a large arabesque decanter oozing a silvery mist in which several grotesque and malignant genii floated about.

"The most important thing," he warned, "is not to speak with anyone unless absolutely necessary. Don't give anyone too easy a time identifying you."

"Especially you, Rick," said Salerno. "There's bound to be some people here from the university who might be able to recognize your voice."

"I will speak only with the tongues of angels and not of men."

"Saying 'No Englais' will do just fine, Rick," McBride advised. "Preferably with an accent."

"Hello! What's this?" Jones was intent upon a figure moving in their direction on a deliberate intercept course.

From the neck down, it had the powerful physique of a male bodybuilder or nightclub bouncer. From the neck up, it was a tri-headed canine with gleaming fangs set in three independently moving mouths.

"Greetings, Cerberus!" Fitzgerald called out when the creature reached hailing distance.

"You know this guy?" asked McBride.

Fitzgerald motioned the others forward. "Just follow me. If I'm correct, we'll be better off joining the crowd. We'd be causing him greater alarm by not mixing."

Sure enough, the canine character began to back off and turn his attention elsewhere as soon as the five spirits moved away from the doorway and entered further into the flow of things.

Salerno's eyes widened. "How'd you do that?"

"Elementary," Fitzgerald told him. "Cerberus is the ancient watchdog of Hades. So he doesn't care who comes in. He just has to make sure nobody gets out."

Salerno rolled his eyes. "Oh, great. I wouldn't think of leaving. The night is young."

"Abandon all hope—" Stillman muttered.

McBride turned to Fitzgerald. "Since you did such a great job with that character, let's have you and Jonesy and Rick circulate up here in the ballroom while Vince and I slip out and do a recon mission downstairs. We need to fan out quickly and see if we can locate the captives."

"—all ye who enter here," Stillman finished.

"You OK?" McBride inquired pointedly, then glanced at his watch. "I don't know how much time we'll have to try to pull this off."

"No good," Stillman said gloomily. "How are you going to get around that watchdog with the six eyes?"

"Yes," said Fitzgerald, "with three-hundred-sixty-degree, twenty-twenty peripheral vision."

"Come on." McBride snorted in disbelief. "That can't be for real. You yourself said most of these things are illusion anyway."

"Who knows?" said Fitzgerald. "We have to assume that he's got at least one good pair peeled for troublemakers—and others we don't know about may be doing likewise."

"All right," McBride said. "Then our only option is to create a diversion right here."

"Yes," said Stillman, "and Aaron and I should be able to locate a data line somewhere on this floor to tie into. If we can tap in and make contact with Peter, he should be able to pull some strings in the security system."

Fitzgerald's eyes swept the room. "In the meantime, we ought to be able to create a brief power blackout."

"*Real* brief." Jones turned to McBride and Salerno. "You boys be ready to steal for second the moment the lights go out. You won't have more than a few seconds."

Fitzgerald and Stillman parted their robes to reveal a quick, comforting glimpse of portables with plenty of connecting cable.

McBride nodded. He and Salerno migrated gradually toward separate exits.

* * *

It was only then that Stillman became aware of the heady atmosphere that had been building among the celebrants. Was there something in the air? Truly, so many new and bizarre stimuli were assailing each sense by the moment that it was quite disorienting. Unidentifiable scents and incense were alternately tickling his nostrils. Dialogue from some dramatic spectacle in the center of the ballroom was tangling itself in his ears and reaching his brain in a verbal jumble.

Already, he noticed, Fitzgerald was standing next to a fixture on the far side of the room, staring in Stillman's direction as if trying to catch his eye. As he and Jones moved to join his comrade, Stillman became more clearly aware of the meaning of the thespian dialogue that occupied the center of most attention.

"Go and make a careful search for the child," thundered a bearded actor in purple robes. "As soon as you find him, report to me, so that I, too, may go and worship him."

Stillman forced himself to disengage his eyes from the scene, although the temptation was great to speculate as to why the player seemed so familiar—probably somebody from the university he had met once or twice.

Instead, he began picking his way toward Fitzgerald through the crowd, being careful not to move too hastily or be overly conspicuous. He made a special effort to keep mental track of that Cerberus chap and maintain a healthy distance.

It turned out that Fitzgerald indeed had located something, apparently a small utility box underneath a fixture with the correct receptacle configuration. Stillman and Jones turned their backs to him to provide cover. Fitzgerald began running a connection to his gear.

The crowd was tittering, covering the sound of Fitzgerald's tapping out commands on his miniature keyboard.

"Crucify him!" shouted a loutish voice.

"That's later, thou flaming lout!" rejoined another, to the audience's amusement.

Through a gap in the crowd, Stillman now could see a good portion of the dramatic scene. A raven-tressed damsel struggled in the clutches of a brute whose hand covered her mouth. They apparently were in a barn with various head of cattle and goats and sheep and several exotically turbaned Zoroastrian magicians. One of the Persian sorcerers was holding aloft a squirming newborn infant whom he had plucked from a feeding trough. If an illusion, this was exceedingly realistic.

From behind, Stillman could hear Fitzgerald saying something into his lapel mike. It sounded like "Peter!" Stillman resisted the impulse to shush him.

Now, the purple-robed figure advanced on the magus with infant, drawing a long-bladed sword.

"Is this indeed the one prophesied to come?"

The two other magi nodded in agreement.

"The king of the Jews?" the man asked with undisguised contempt.

"Yes, Your Majesty," they said in unison.

The babe began to wail, quite convincingly. The robed one lifted his sword to a smiting angle. Somewhere, a drum began to throb.

Stillman's heart leaped into his throat.

And then the ballroom was abruptly plunged into darkness. Utter gloom penetrated the sudden silence and spread a cloak of morbid imaginings. There ensued a muttering and a shuffling of feet.

About the time that Stillman thought his eyes must have adjusted, for he believed he really was able to see some shadowy movement, the lights sprang back to life. Instantly, he craned his neck in an effort to spy McBride and Salerno across the ballroom. He was relieved to see that they were nowhere in sight. He hoped that even now they were streaking down some corridor below, in pursuit of Peter and Judith and the other captives.

Now the scene before him had changed drastically. The previous characters were clearing out; the babe was nowhere to be seen.

A fellow resembling unholy Neptune or Poseidon now occupied the limelight. Dominating by his presence, the trident-brandishing deity surveyed the audience, waiting for his subjects to quiet themselves. At last they seemed to get the message, and the restlessness abated.

"Joyous October Holiday!" Poseidon declared. "Now we come to the highlight of the evening."

As the character paused for effect, his voice and words suddenly clicked in Stillman's memory. *Quang.*

"Skeptics have said that artificial intelligence was an idea whose time would never come. They may have been right," Poseidon-Quang said dramatically. "However, we have managed to achieve something far better—hyperintelligence. With the marriage of the intuitive yet finite human mind to the astounding capabilities of modern computers, we have arrived at the dream of the centuries. Behold, the superman/superwoman."

Instantly, without even a dimming of house lights, another figure appeared in their midst, accompanied by a loud murmuring and intermittent crashing of sea waves. There, just several meters from Quang, stood perhaps the loveliest creature Stillman had ever seen. In all her fair-skinned glory, she appeared a living, breathing Renaissance painting. In fact, was this not his own familiar Venus— foam-born Aphrodite? Was this real, or was it another hologram?

Remembering himself, he averted his gaze to her face—and received the greatest shock of all.

"Angie!" he mouthed.

* * *

In the bowels of the castle, McBride and Salerno raced down one gloomy corridor after another. McBride's skin tingled with the expectation of unnamed terrors lurking around each corner. It had been an immense relief when he first heard Peter's real voice in his own ear, but this was no time for pleasantries.

"Keep going," Peter murmured into his earpiece. "You're getting closer."

And then, suddenly, they were there. Above a double set of swinging doors they could discern in the half-light a sign bearing the words "Pre-Life Science."

Unfortunately, something else was there as well. Up from its sinewy coils rose the hideous head of the fattest python since Apollo drew his blade on Mount Parnassus. Its eyes fastened on McBride like laser beams, its tongue flicking nervously. Instinctively, he pulled his police revolver and drew a bead on the swaying head with a trembling hand.

"Don't shoot!" Peter pleaded in his ears. "It won't hurt you."

"Are you sure?" McBride's heart was trying to hammer its way out of his ribcage.

"Yes!"

McBride held his fire. He braced himself and closed his eyes as the serpent pounced.

Sure enough, he was able to draw another breath unmolested.

"I don't know how to make it go away," Peter was saying, "but I can change it."

The python melted into a snarling Doberman pinscher with lips quivering over gleaming fangs.

"Just ignore it," said Peter.

"Holograms?" asked Salerno, leading the way through the swinging doors.

"Of course," said Peter.

"How did you know that Neal was about to shoot?"

"I'm watching you through the hallway security cameras," replied Peter. "Please hurry. I have no idea how much time we have."

Around the next corner and down the hall was another sign: "Biota Recycling."

"You're almost there," said Peter.

* * *

In the ballroom, Stillman was perspiring nervously. Time was running out. Something very much to be avoided appeared in the offing. Whatever Fitzgerald was doing behind him, he hoped it was working. Like Jones, he had no choice but to stand and watch the gruesome spectacle before them.

Angie/Venus was chanting in an alien tongue in a voice not quite her own. What was this language? Something Semitic, it seemed.

Various costumed revelers were dropping to bended knees in

obedient response to suggestions that their conscious minds could not fathom.

"It is time to seek the privilege of visitation from the God and Goddess," said a mature female voice.

"Elizabeth Morningstar," Stillman overheard one stranger say to another.

"Prepare the sacrifice," proclaimed a male voice, also familiar. Jeremy Kay?

He stole a glance backward. Fitzgerald knelt with a slender cable attaching from the wall to something inside his robe. His finger held an object to his ear. His head was cocked to one side, listening.

Turning back, Stillman saw an infant being handed down a line of hooded celebrants like an occult bucket brigade.

The "Aphrodite" Angie image increased in brilliance as she continued uttering her eerie stream of glossolalia.

Stillman's skin was really beginning to crawl now. He watched the babe being handed up the three steps to a platform where crouched an altar of metal and stone. He prayed that what he saw was just another hologram.

But now Morningstar, garbed in the weird raiment of a Celtic priestess wearing horned diadem, was presiding over the infant with a drawn blade. An ugly tattoo built from an unseen drum. Morningstar joined Angie's incantation, creating a dissonant stereo effect.

"Cut the power!" Stillman said, turning to Fitzgerald.

The knife was raised into the air above the altar.

Behind him, Stillman could hear the faint clicking of key-panel keys. Fitzgerald was talking, again apparently to Peter. The lights flickered—once, twice, then returned to normal. "Aphrodite" appeared caught in a momentary freeze-frame, but that, too, passed.

"No good," Fitzgerald said in frustration. "There are too many feeders."

A mortal sentence was pronounced.

A wave of sick dread engulfed Stillman. He shot a glance at the upraised knife and heard the quickening tempo of the drums, climaxing in a double-time tattoo.

And then abrupt silence. The *athame* plunged home.

Stillman was too stunned to look away or even to close his eyes as the blade did its grisly work. A great cry of exultation went up from the invisible, many-throated beast. The drums resumed their hammering, this time a slower, more powerful syncopation, hypnotically suggestive of the spirit realm.

His knees were wobbling. He feared for a moment that he might pass out. Nor was his stomach very pleased.

And then cried a voice, which he clearly recognized as that of Julian Wickner: "Hail, Ashtoreth! Hail, Molech!"

33

Something was among them. Stillman sensed a prowling something, a devouring something—maybe two somethings. They were a pair of uncaged beasts, unleashed lions whose passage could be detected only by the ripples in the grass.

Stillman's nostrils were assailed by a foul odor, a stench of death. And then he saw them. Or rather, he saw where they were not. They were walking black holes vaguely in the shape of men, sucking in light, yet giving nothing off but vibrations of corruption and dread. Breathing had suddenly become a struggle.

He sensed that Fitzgerald was beside him.

"D-d-do something!" Stillman stammered.

"Rick, this is *not* a hologram," Fitzgerald breathed.

Stillman imagined his partner's breath billowing out as a frozen plume in an unearthly chill. Reality and illusion were losing their distinction here.

Then he saw the one thing he most feared. *They*—the very

source of evil—were approaching. And it seemed that every evil eye in the massive ballroom was being fastened upon the angelic trio. Now it was changing from intolerably cold to uncomfortably warm.

Two other figures approached as well. By her horned crown, the one had to be Elizabeth Morningstar, and the other apparently Jeremy Kay. Morningstar lifted her right arm and pointed squarely at Stillman and Jones.

He could hear Jones praying quietly, though not his exact words.

"Interlopers!" Morningstar bellowed hoarsely.

"Charlatans!" Kay cried in a much deeper voice, one that reminded Stillman of Warka Izdubar in the temple of Baal.

An ugly undertone was building. Stillman felt like raw meat on a vulture's platter.

With a finger to one ear, Fitzgerald dropped to his knees again in the corner, muttering something urgently to Peter.

" . . . .demons!" he was saying. " . . . shut it down!"

And then the evil entities were upon them.

Stillman was bowled aside as if the ground had given way. He saw Jones go down.

Once again, the lights flickered. Something crackled around Fitzgerald's portable hookup. In a flash, the linguist was on the floor. It appeared that his ear and finger were both gone. Vacant eyes stared at the ceiling.

★ ★ ★

Downstairs, the commandos found a cubicle that ought to be Peter's. McBride tore aside the green track curtain. There lay a figure on a bed cloaked in shadow. And then he was hearing in stereo.

"Dad!" came Peter's voice, simultaneously in McBride's earpiece and from the bed.

McBride and Salerno rushed to the bedside and feverishly began undoing all of Peter's restraints and fasteners. There was no time for tearful reunions.

"Aaron!" Peter cried. "Something terrible has happened. And something worse is about to, if I can't figure a way to pull the plug on OUIJA."

"Peter," said McBride, "we've got to get to your mother and the others before anything else. You don't even know that Rick and Jones are still alive up there."

"I'm sorry," said Peter, close to despair, "but if we don't stop OUIJA now, none of us may get out of here. But how?"

"Wait a second." McBride turned to Salerno. "How did OUIJA knock out ALEX?"

"We don't know for sure that OUIJA did it."

"Yes, we do," said Peter. "In fact, I think I know how to access the—*that's it!* Let me internalize for a minute."

They stared down at him, unstrapped from the bed but still connected with his headgear, as he searched OUIJA systems. Judith, Carlotta, Marianne, and Moira were somewhere down the hall, but at this point they may just as well have been on another planet.

"Vince, see if you can find the women."

"Right."

Suddenly, Peter quite visibly ceased breathing. His entire body went rigid, and his face reddened from the effort of some intense internal struggle.

"Peter!" said McBride. "What's wrong?"

When Peter at last opened his eyes, they were filled with terror and panic.

"Run!" he screamed.

"Did you do it?" McBride asked. "Did it work?"

"Run!" Peter screamed again. "Get out of this place while you can!"

This time, McBride paid attention. He began viciously ripping wires from Peter's headgear to free him.

"Just unplug the cable in back." McBride did so and then boosted the boy out of the bed. Peter's knees immediately caved, and McBride picked him up in the fireman's carry.

"Hang on," said McBride. "Think Turkeyfoot Canyon."

In the hall, he was met by a very unhappy and frightened looking blonde woman with red-rimmed glasses. Behind her hurried two more women, plus a third being carried by Salerno.

"Judith!" said McBride, his heart leaping.

"Hurry!" Peter shouted.

Something was happening above them. Unrecognizable sounds. Strange vibrations.

Down the corridor, McBride was greeted again by the snarling Doberman. This time, he ignored it and began running recklessly.

He had a nagging feeling that someone was missing, one of the women. He did a mental inventory—Judith, Carlotta, the red-haired one named Moira. *Marianne!*

"Marianne King!" he shouted. "Back the other way!"

"She wouldn't come," the blonde said. "The fool."

"It's too late!" cried Peter. "Get out of here!"

He was right. It *was* too late. The unrecognizable sounds had reached down into the castle basement, and suddenly the corridor behind them collapsed, disappearing in an angry cloud of swirling debris. Multiple explosions ripped through the chateau infrastructure. All light failed.

The only way was straight ahead, no looking back.

In a netherland of semiconsciousness, McBride stumbled down a darkened corridor with a punishing weight on his shoulders and various unintelligible shouts all around. He was losing all track of time and space, the whereabouts of his comrades, and even whether his eyes were open or closed. He climbed an endless flight of stairs, legs and lungs straining from the extra burden. He thought he wouldn't make it, then repeatedly found just enough strength for another step.

And then came the deep rumble of a granddaddy discharge that removed the very ground from under his feet and turned out his lights.

★ ★ ★

Now, it was raining a cold rain where he had been slam-dunked into unconsciousness. Smoke was everywhere. It was in his eyes. McBride began coughing. Something told him to get moving. But something else—a vicious pain in the back of his head and a knee that hurt like fire—told him not too fast.

Peter! Where was Peter—and Judith—and the rest of them?

Another small explosion sounded. McBride began clawing his way over stone and rubble in no particular direction, except upward away from the smoke. Only adrenaline and a half-delirious prayer gave him the strength to push on.

"Hold it!" shouted somebody with authority. "There *is* one more. I can't believe it. He must be an asbestos zombie."

In another moment, several pairs of hands were helping McBride up onto higher ground. It was a tremendous relief to be able to breathe good air again, but it was physically impossible to remain standing. He was far too weak, and his knee would not stand the strain. The hands eased him to the ground—into a cold puddle. But even that was better than standing. He was spent.

"Judith!" he cried. "Peter!"

None answered but the rain.

Then he saw that he was bleeding—not badly but in numerous places. His white angelic robes were now filthy tatters. It was as if he had gone through a window without opening it. Maybe he had. He also wondered if he had suffered a concussion.

Then the helping hands were guiding him onto a stretcher and hoisting him precariously off the ground. A patch on the man's jacket said, "Jefferson Twp. Volunteer Fire Dept." Just as he was summoning the strength to ask again about other survivors, McBride heard a familiar voice.

"Neal!" called Darnell Jones with obvious delight.

Jones, walking unsteadily under his own power, looked a little banged up too, but not quite so badly as McBride. He and Jones seemed about to share an ambulance ride.

"Where are Judith and Peter?" asked McBride anxiously. "Do you know?"

"They're all right," Jones assured him. "They look better than you do, but they've gone to the hospital already."

The paramedics scooted him onto one of the ambulance beds.

Jones climbed in mostly unassisted. "You and Marianne King were the last of our people unaccounted for," said Jones, sitting on the other bed. "Rick is all right. Aaron is . . . gone. He was apparently electrocuted somehow."

"*Dead?*" said McBride. It didn't seem real.

"That's right," Jones said quietly.

McBride's head ached. A paramedic was wrapping his arm with a blood pressure cuff.

"I don't know about Salerno," said McBride, remembering. "But Marianne King is a casualty. She didn't come with us. For that matter, how did *we* get out?"

"The grace of God." Jones shook his head. "The sheer grace of God. One of the firemen told me it appeared that everybody who survived was on a basement staircase, protected from the main force of the blast—and near an outside wall, which buckled out."

And then the terrible thought. "Angie?"

"Rick and I were the only ones who made it out of the ballroom, Neal. We ran like demons were after us—which they were—when the power flickered the last time. I think we were going down the same staircase you were going up. Then—the explosion. I'm sorry."

"You mean—" the full implication began to sink in "—there were no other survivors? All of those people—"

"Judge," said Jones deliberately, "take a look at the castle—and then you tell me the answer to that."

McBride took a last look before the ambulance doors shut. It had not even occurred to him that the heap of rubble he was seeing was Chateau Fahlgren—what was left of it. The notion was staggering.

But for the still-standing flagpole with the Chi Xi Vau banner snapping in the wind, he might not have believed it. The rest was detritus and wreckage, smoldering and sputtering in the light October rain beneath roiling clouds of smoke.

★ ★ ★

Mercy Hospital had its own October Holiday problems. Its emergency room was overflowing into the corridors with victims of Devil's Night mayhem. Any but the dying would have a long wait to see a medical professional this night.

McBride's group was large enough that the ER workers set them up in a separate waiting room. The place was a dismal affair, with torn vinyl seats, overflowing ashtrays that reeked, and stark lighting. Salerno, limping, impatiently confronted an obnoxious TV with the color out of whack and shut it off.

Overholtzer and Carney ran interference, giving statements

to other lawpersons. A TV reporter named Joe Fortunato stuck his head in and asked if anybody wanted to talk.

"Yeah," said Overholtzer, backing him out into the hall. "Here's a quote: Beat it!"

Jones took a brief hike down the hall. When he returned, he was carrying cans of pop.

"Anybody want a cream soda?"

"Over here, Jonesy." McBride pointed to the table in front of him.

Judith's head was resting on his shoulder, and he didn't want to move. She had fallen asleep.

Stillman sat next to Moira. He took her hand and told her she was still as lovely with a skinned nose and much of her beautiful red hair burned off.

"Thanks," Moira said wearily. "You really know how to make a girl feel good."

McBride noted that they did make a lovely couple.

Carlotta was sitting very close to Peter, crying silently. Peter just looked dazed.

When heads were clearer, there would be tears for Aaron and Angie and Marianne, he knew. The same could hardly be said for the Three J's or Elizabeth Morningstar or any of their subordinate lackeys, weasels, and toads. One could only hope that they were gone forever to the abode of Ashtoreth and Molech, never to return.

Peter was the one to worry about. He had survived the sudden unplugging from OUIJA, but now he had to cope with the death of his sister. Now was the time for agonizing second thoughts and recriminations. But releasing the fatal virus into OUIJA's operating systems—and inadvertently triggering the self-destruct sequence—had seemed at the time the only way of saving any lives.

"I don't believe Aaron's death had anything to do with what you did or didn't do, Peter," Jones told him. "And to be absent from the body is to be at home with the Lord. As Aaron used to say, 'which is far to be preferred.' Believe me, Peter, God knows what He's doing."

Peter nodded resignedly. "Oh," he said then, apparently remembering something. "Guess who I saw running off into the woods away from the ruins?"

When no one responded, he answered himself. "Elizabeth Morningstar."

McBride shivered. He saw Stillman and Moira trade glances.

"Trick or treat," Moira said through puffy lips and then smiled weakly.

★ ★ ★

A mere half hour later, the ER staff started getting around to their party. Judith was nominated to go first, considering her weakened condition.

McBride's head still hurt. Jones was still sitting on his left, ruminating over a diet cola. Stillman was to his right.

"So, is the Bible translation project dead forever?" McBride asked.

"I don't know," said Jones. "Even with the big crash, we still learned many valuable things. But with Aaron gone . . . " He looked around McBride at Stillman. "You know any good linguists?"

Stillman looked startled and then smiled. "I know a tolerable linguist who's going to be needing work."

"Maybe we can work something out."

Jones looked at McBride curiously. "How about you, Judge? You think you might go back on the bench?"

"Honestly, it's too soon to begin even thinking about anything like that. I really don't think it would work. With a smart lawyer and a good lawsuit, it's possible I could win my job back—maybe. But there'd be a lot of messy details and awkward questions—like that stolen sheriff's cruiser."

"I see what you mean."

"Maybe I'll go back into the private eye business. I certainly don't think I could practice law in this perverted, corrupted system."

"Yes," Jones said, "but the problem's deeper than just shortcomings in the system. The fundamental problem is in the hearts of men, far beyond questions of cops and courts and guns and judges. It's a heart problem. And I think you know the answer to that."

"Yeah," said McBride slowly, a kind of bitterness tinging his voice.

Jones looked puzzled. "Anything you want to talk about?"

McBride shook his head, then changed his mind. "It's Angie," he said in a voice deep and full of pain. "At the jail, just for a moment, I thought I was reaching her. I told her how much I wanted to help her, to hold her—how much I loved her. I know I was starting to get through to her, but I couldn't pull the trigger. All at once she . . . hardened, and it was all over. She got away. I lost her. And now all hope of reconciliation—gone forever."

"You didn't lose her," Jones corrected quietly. "Angie had every opportunity to turn back, and she refused. That's the same for all of us, Neal. We get more than ample opportunity to lay down arms and throw ourselves on the mercy of the God of grace, the merciful Judge. But too many of us just throw those opportunities away."

Judith was coming back through the double doors into their waiting area, looking drained. Her right arm was in a sling, and they were pushing her in a wheelchair, but she looked reasonably intact otherwise.

A nurse followed her with some papers. She called the next patient. "Wilson McBride!"

Jones's words suddenly made a lot of things click for McBride, like a chain reaction: The mothers who had given up their children to slaughter, one born, one unborn. The daughter who had spurned the hand of mercy. The son who had responded and been saved. And McBride himself, who had been the object lesson—the judge laying aside his privileges to search out and rescue the lost. How could it be any clearer?

He did know what he had to do.

"Wilson McBride!" the nurse called, a little louder.

Jones was speaking again. "Think about it—the fact that we're sitting here alive. We've seen an amazing deliverance, an incredible demonstration of God's grace."

McBride nodded. "You're right, Jonesy."

People were pointing at him now.

"Wilson McBride!" the nurse called, much louder.

"Yes!" responded McBride, snapping out of it. "Coming."

He was coming. He wouldn't wait to be called again.